MW01120882

On the Wings of the Wind

FRANK PANCAKE

WestBow
PRESS
A DIVISION OF THOMAS NELSON

WestBow Press books may be ordered through booksellers or by contacting:

WestBow Press
A Division of Thomas Nelson
1663 Liberty Drive
Bloomington, IN 47403
www.westbowpress.com
1-(866) 928-1240

Because of the dynamic nature of the Internet, any Web addresses or links contained in this book may have changed since publication and may no longer be valid. The views expressed in this work are solely those of the author and do not necessarily reflect the views of the publisher, and the publisher hereby disclaims any responsibility for them.

Any people depicted in stock imagery provided by Thinkstock are models, and such images are being used for illustrative purposes only.

Certain stock imagery © Thinkstock.

ISBN: 978-1-4497-0729-3 (sc)
ISBN: 978-1-4497-0730-9 (dj)
ISBN: 978-1-4497-0728-6 (e)

Library of Congress Control Number: 2010940010

Printed in the United States of America

WestBow Press rev. date: 12/29/2010

Dedication

This book is dedicated to the memories of relatives and friends that have inspired my life in many wonderful and positive ways.

Frank Cody Pancake Sr.
Robbie Dellinger Pancake
Richard E. Pancake
Shirley Lewis Pancake
Louis S. Pancake
Marlyon Pancake Lyon

Harry F. Smith
Ruth Bishop Smith
R. Ivan Payne
Faith (Faye) Payne
Joe Ford

Barbara Aylor Carpenter
Margaret Trimmer Smith
Hobart W. Hesse
Merriette (Mert) Moore
M. M. Bean

Acknowledgments

Lisa Mayo Miller -- she 'computerized' my illegible handwriting over and over - multiple times - with patience and candor. There would not have been a book without her assistance.

Julie Melampy -- the savoir faire on computer glitches, a great hand and a great help!

Kristin Lindgren Henningsen, a very dear and good friend who encouraged and inspired my efforts in writing the book from day one when it first became an idea, a vague notion or blot in my imagination.

Brianna Finnegan -- she edited the flaws, misspellings and general shortcomings - word by word, chapter by chapter; every and all other errors are committed by the author.

Thomas A. Stargell -- who read, advised, counseled, corrected, encouraged and wrote the foreword. He kept the ship on course.

Bobby Smith Pancake, my wife, who assisted with all of the peripheral matters and happenings that came up during the long time -- from the beginning to the end -- of the writing of the manuscript.

Frank Cody Pancake III, our son, who awakened within me an interest in the Civil War, accompanied me to battlegrounds, provided books on that war and otherwise whetted my interest and appetite in such matters.

I also thank Frank Smith, Betsy Kingsbury, Glenn Lankford, Mike Colley, Ann Maynard and Ty Bauer for their input and guidance in reviewing the manuscript and offering suggestions.

Last, but by no means least, I thank Sherri Haines Pancake, daughter-in-law, who assisted in my search for the publisher.

I would be remiss not to mention my three grandchildren -- F. Cody IV, Cole and Cassidy.

Foreword

For thirty-eight years I was privileged to work with students on the middle, secondary, and adult level in the study of History and Social Studies. My role ran the gamut from classroom teacher, Social Studies Department Head, Clinical Instructor of Teacher Associates from the University of Virginia and Longwood University, Instructor of Adult Education, and Secondary Education Social Studies Representative to the University of Virginia Curry School of Education. Most years, these roles were assumed all at the same time. Obviously, I constantly search for better methods and more useful tools to teach or learn about the era before and during the American Civil War.

Frank Pancake's first novel, "On the Wings of the Wind", presented the opportunity for even the most ardent history buff to become a learner or to reacquaint with the time and events leading to, and including, most of the war years. There was also a wealth of instruction for those wishing to learn this section of American History for the first time. Pancake was meticulous with his historical descriptions of events, social, political and military. He took great pains to explain in full the history leading to the war. He methodically carried the reader through the major events of the war until July 1, 1862, and the battle of Malvern Hill. He described in detail the interaction of military and political leaders from both North and South with their subordinates and peers. The reader became knowledgeable of their unique personalities, idiosyncrasies, and reasoning for their actions. Not forgotten, and most interesting, the novel included the military life and training of the regular army enlisted man. We saw him in leisurely camp life and went with him into battle. Pancake does justice to what was behind the making of a fighting unit. Simply put, the author did his job to account for historical accuracy and attention to social, political and military detail.

Impressive was this work's ability to capture the flavor of the language and writing skills of the era. Many readers will be surprised to read sections where characters refer to the classics in speech and writing. Education of this time period certainly did include the understanding of the great thinkers and achievers of the past. We are treated to quotations from Bacon, Carlyle, Franklin, Newton, Herrick, Locke, Dickinson, Cicero, Burns, Tennyson, and Longfellow. It was quite normal to use the words of the masters and perhaps there will be readers who will discover how truly beautiful words can be.

"On the Wings of the Wind" did not shrink from the hard issues of the day. The book incorporated enormous amounts of Northern and Southern social history into the story. One staggering impact to moral consciousness was Pancake's analogy: "The white man has a Bill of Rights while the black man has a Bill of Sale." We read throughout of slavery and states' rights, the rights of women, and Sectionalism which works in such strange ways.

Lastly, and so importantly, this book is a love story. It is about a boy so greatly loved by his family. This boy became a young man and chose to leave the safe haven of this home to pursue an education. The new environment to which he entered was far different from his native North. At the prestigious University of Virginia he was challenged to study both sides of moral and cultural issues. He was further encouraged to decide his own personal beliefs and defend them. He found new loves as genuine and intense as his old loves. He shouldered grave responsibilities and carried out the necessary decision process of a man of his time. He accepted the ultimate challenge to defend his principles and he went to war.

I sincerely wish this novel had been written when I taught. I would have read, studied, and recommended it as a text; an historical chronicle; a description of social history; a study of geographical and political differences; and a fascinating account of an array of fictional and factural humans. Perhaps I would have read it as it may be best enjoyed by most readers, a beautiful story with an ending that is guaranteed to be remembered.

Thomas A. Stargell
Scottsville, Virginia

Chapter One

How Firm a Foundation

Good fortune always seems to smile on young Robert Holcomb, or "Robbie" as he is known to his friends and family. Good luck just seems to embrace him. He is one of those fortunate few who always seem to be in the right place at the right time. Every day seems to be his lucky day. Everything just seems to go his way, to fall precisely into place. It isn't that he is lucky or fortunate some of the time; it seems that he is lucky all of the time. He is aware of this seemingly good fortune at an early age, yet he more or less takes these things in stride. He seems to be neither impressed nor distressed by these happenings.

Nor is he alone in recognizing the presence of good fortune that always embraces him. His parents notice it, their friends notice it, his friends notice it, and the townspeople notice it. He just seems to have been born under the right sign, under the right star; it is as if some magical or mysterious force is constantly hovering over him, constantly protecting and providing for him. Occurrences seem to be predestined. Even more astounding than his apparent good luck is the fact that no one seems to resent it. Contrary to logic, he is extremely well-liked throughout Bedford Springs, New York, a town of some two thousand people on the banks of the Hudson River.

He was born on July 4, 1842, the son of Robert Livingston Holcomb and Mary Hancock Holcomb. His parents are third-generation descendants of men who had signed the Declaration of Independence. Patriotism is highly regarded in their families. God and country always come first over all other matters. Robbie will learn about patriotism and its importance as he matures, what it means, and why the constitutional freedoms of America must always be protected against intruders, and that these freedoms must be respected at all costs. By birthright and birthplace, Robbie is a genuine Yankee, an all-American boy in an all-American family, living an all-American dream. He is in truth and in spirit a dyed-in-the-wool Yankee Doodle Dandy.

Although sharing the same first name with his father, he was not given a second name. He is not a junior, nor is he ever so addressed. However, having two Roberts in the same family can be confusing, so early in life he is referred to simply as Robbie. Seldom is he ever addressed by his given name. To those who know him or meet him, he is always Robbie Holcomb.

The family, although not extremely wealthy, is nonetheless well-to-do. They live in a large white twelve-room house on one of the hills overlooking the town of Bedford Springs and the nearby Hudson River. The house is not a mansion, nevertheless it is an imposing structure; a far cry from the usual working-class homes found in Bedford Springs and in other towns and villages along the river. The architecture is distinctively Federalist, with a quaint New England twist. Robbie's father is the third-generation owner.

The Holcomb place, as it is called, is a well-recognized and established landmark, visible from every point in Bedford Springs and for many miles in either direction up and down the Hudson River. The view from the house naturally has many advantages by overlooking the town and the river. It is a spacious house with a grand view. From nearly every window on the front of the house, the Holcombs enjoy a panoramic, picture-perfect scene. They can identify every home, every business, and every public establishment in the town below. They are privy to observing the commerce on the river, what is shipped in and what is shipped out, what goes up river and what goes down. They have a perfect view of the Holcomb Mill, a family-owned textile manufacturing business operated by Robbie's father. Anything and everything that happens in Bedford Springs is in full view of the Holcomb place.

The view from the rooms to the rear of the house is an exact opposite of the frontal view. They overlook a private, secluded garden and vast acreage of wooded land. The garden is the Holcomb's place of solitude: their place to meditate and relax; a place to dream. The garden is a different world, an earlier time in history, a place for a young boy to dream.

The Holcomb house is more than a family residence. It is the centerpiece of the Bedford Springs community. The interior is elaborate and stately. Every room is picture-perfect, magnificently detailed and furnished, as intriguing as it is beautiful. A spiral staircase leading from the spacious entry hall to the second story is breathtaking. Hand-crafted mantels, doors, and window facings complement the furniture and the decorations. Everything is precisely in place, as if the rooms and the furnishings had all been designed as a single unit.

In spite of its exquisite and stately interior, the house has a down-home warmth. The Holcombs always convey an atmosphere of cordiality and friendliness. They make certain that visitors and guests feel welcome and comfortable. This is their nature. They are elegant hosts, always with a sincere warmth about them.

It is in this house, in these surroundings, that young Robbie Holcomb will live and learn and grow through the first seventeen years of his life. It is an environment of love, and of sharing, and of caring and respecting, and most of all, of mastering responsibility and compassion for others. These are the influences and the values that prevail in charting the course of his lifestyle, his life commitment, as he grows and as he matures, as he changes from a carefree youth into a young man eager to accept the responsibilities and challenges of manhood.

The Holcomb textile mill is the primary source of employment for residents of Bedford Springs. The town exists because of the Holcomb Mill. Like the Holcomb house on the hill, the mill had been built by Robbie's great-grandfather just after the Revolutionary War. Although it has weathered hard times over the course of its existence, it has never closed, except for Sundays and special holidays. Great-grandfather Holcomb, affectionately referred to by the townspeople as the "old man," had been deeply religious. He believed that man should avoid work on the Sabbath. That policy, established by him, has never been violated. It will always be the policy at the mill.

Millwork is laborious and exhausting, but it is nonetheless considered the premier place of employment in Bedford Springs. Whites, free blacks, and women are employed at the mill under its open door employment policy. Discrimination of any sort is never tolerated in the workplace, and it has seldom been an issue or a problem anywhere in Bedford Springs. Wages at the mill average nearly a dollar a week higher than elsewhere in town.

Nearly half of the town's labor force is employed at the mill. The success of the other community businesses, which employ the other workers, is interdependent on the success of the Holcomb Mill. It is a commonly accepted economic and political reality of life that as the fortunes of the Holcomb Mill goes, so goes the fortune of Bedford Springs. It is quite natural that the Holcomb family, past and present, are destined to play an important role in the political, economic, and social life of the community. That was the way things were from the town's early beginning when Robbie's great-grandfather built the mill and the town. There is no logical reason why it should not continue to be the same in the future. The Holcombs have been good for the town, and the town has been good for the Holcombs.

The Holcomb name is highly regarded in Bedford Springs. The generations of Holcombs that followed in the footsteps of the old man have done nothing to detract from the family's well-founded image. The care and concern that the old man exercised for the people and for the town is expected of his heirs. They have never let the town down, and the people of the town have never let the Holcombs down. Their leadership and guidance have always been traditional in the affairs of Bedford Springs.

Bedford Springs, nearly midway between New York City and Albany, is named for a series of natural cold-water springs that flow from several hills just beyond town. They are large springs, providing an abundant water supply. This seemingly endless natural resource was the reason that Robbie's great-grandfather built the mill and his home at this location. There is a sufficient supply of pure cold water to accommodate not only the mill, but also provide more than enough water for a town of considerable size.

The elder Holcomb had left nothing to chance. As the mill was built, he made plans for building the town. A mill without a source of labor would be useless. Decent, affordable housing would be needed. He planned everything about the town, including the name. He mapped out the streets, decided which areas would be for business enterprises and which would be set aside for housing. He was determined that Bedford Springs would rival any town in the state of New York for its beauty and appeal. It would be a showcase, and an example of town planning for future generations.

And so it was from the beginning, a town master plan; a masterpiece of aesthetic accomplishments and a great source of pride to its residents. The streets, from the very beginning, were paved with cobblestones. As the town grew and as the residents prospered, the ideals and visions of the generations that followed never lost sight of the old man's wisdom in the initial planning and the future concept for Bedford Springs. Homes and businesses are always kept neat and attractive as is the entire town and all of the public areas.

Great-grandfather Holcomb had not only been a man of wisdom and of great vision, he had also been a man of exceptional generosity. The town had been one of his principal beneficiaries. Profits from the mill were often diverted to finance town improvements. When business at the mill was slow, the labor force was reassigned to perform municipal duties, although they continued to receive their pay as if they were working at the mill.

After the old man died, the citizens erected a large monument in the town square dedicated to his honor and memory. Everyone contributed. Everyone had some part in the project. His body was subsequently laid to rest at the foot of the monument. It was his town, they were his people. It was hallowed ground. The town's respect for the old man never lessened over time. He had taken care of them and they would forever take care of him.

Robbie's eventual inheritance of the Holcomb Mill is an accepted fact of life; it will include many responsibilities and obligations. He seems well on his way to possessing all of the attributes and characteristics necessary to take over the reins of the business and the town when his time to do so arrives.

Chapter Two

Blest Be The Tie That Binds

Opposites attract, or so it is said. Whether it is a law of nature, a truism of history, or pure speculation in the minds of men, it works to perfection, it runs true to form in the lives of Robert Livingston Holcomb and Mary Margaret Hancock. Both are Northerners and had been reared in affluent Yankee families, but their similarities more or less end there. Their dissimilarities on the other hand are many and it is these factors, these characteristics, which seem to be the tie that will bind their lives together; a gravity-like force drawing each of them toward the other.

Mary is an impetuous young lady. She is very impulsive and once moved by an inclination to do something she goes headlong into action. She is not one to look back or to go off on a tangent. When she sets her mind on an objective, it is full speed ahead. She moves decisively forward. There are, in her mind, no valid alternatives or arguments, no other issues or compelling reasons to consider other alternatives or options. Hers is the one and only way to resolve matters.

On the other hand, Robert approaches things methodically. He considers the pros and cons; the best and the worst ways to approach and overcome an obstacle. He contemplates and thinks through the in-between alternatives. It isn't that he does not have strong emotions or opinions about certain matters, it is just that he approaches things differently. He compromises, bargains and works out alternative solutions.

These opposing views, these opposite means and ways of accomplishing a result were apparent to both of them early on in their relationship. Somehow these differences seldom created friction between them. If anything, they created a strange curiosity. They are fascinated by their differences and surprised by the fact that in their own way they both are able to accomplish a great deal. There are no hidden barriers between them.

It was a short courtship. Both were in their early twenties when they met. He was twenty-two, she had just turned twenty. He was Harvard educated and she had graduated from Mount Holyoke College, an upscale women's college in South Hadley, Massachusetts. She had entered college at age sixteen, and it was there that she first recognized the plight that women faced in gaining an equal status with men in a male dominated society. It was the first time that she felt compelled to become involved in promoting women's rights. These concerns propelled her toward other inequities that were prevalent in a male dominated society. She developed an utter contempt for social and political injustices of whatever nature or whatever persuasion, and she vowed that she would be an advocate for whomever these injustices were directed toward. This attitude, this desire to right every wrong, led her not only to the women's rights movement, it also led her to the anti-slavery issue.

Mary had met Robert at the wedding of her cousin. She well remembers the events of that day, nearly two decades earlier, as if it had happened yesterday. She had seen the tall, handsome stranger on the far side of the reception hall. She asked several acquaintances about his identity, but no one seemed to recognize him. Her cousin, of course, knew him, but she seemed totally absorbed with her new husband and his friends. It was socially unacceptable for a young lady to approach a gentleman unescorted. Mary decided to take matters into her own hands. She ignored the formalities of society.

Mary marched directly across the dance floor, leaving her escort for the evening in wide-eyed amazement, breaking all of the social customs, all of the taboos of society, and directly approached the handsome young stranger. "Hello," she announced, extending her hand as she spoke. "I'm Miss Mary Hancock from Massachusetts, and you are?" She left the question hanging.

He was somewhat astonished by her brashness, but he was also amused by her direct approach. "Well, Miss Mary Hancock from Massachusetts, I am Mr. Robert Holcomb from New York, and I am overjoyed to make your acquaintance."

He continued to hold her hand throughout the introduction. She was quite sure that he was not at all disappointed. "Mr. Holcomb," she quipped, "are you just going to stand there for the rest of the evening gawking at me and holding my hand, or are you going to ask me to dance?" He smiled, hesitated for a moment, then replied, "Yes, I may just gawk at you and hold your hand all evening." Then, bowing slightly, he gently raised her gloved hand, kissed it lightly, and led her onto the dance floor.

"Miss Mary Hancock from Massachusetts," he tantalizingly responded, "may I have the honor and the pleasure of this dance?"

She smiled, tilting her face upward toward his, their eyes remained fixed on each other, then replied in her same frank, unabashed manner, "You may, and you may also dance with me for the rest of this evening."

"Do you have an escort for the evening?"

"Yes," she replied, "I am with you."

There was something about her frankness, about her honest, straightforward nature that attracted him to her and it was something that raised his curiosity. On the other hand, he was somewhat piqued because of those same qualities. The unabashed brashness seemed imprudent and unladylike. He responded to her dance-the-night-away proposal with a question. "Did you come to the reception unattached?"

"No, I did not come here unattached," she replied, "but I am no longer attached to the gentleman that I was attached to when I came. It appears to me that you are also unattached, so perhaps we can attach our unattached selves to each other for this evening." She quickly added, "You know the old adage, misery loves company," ending the proposal with a very slight, but appealing giggle. He looked into her eyes, her face remaining tilted upward toward his. It was a pretty face, a very pretty face. She had long, flowing, black wavy hair and deep blue eyes, or so it appeared to him in the dim light of the ballroom. She was, he judged, about five feet, four. A very trim figure. She was absolutely gorgeous.

They danced for what seemed to be an eternity, without either of them speaking a word. Mary could stand the silence, the suspense, no longer and blurted out in a noticeably impatient query. "Not interested? Not interested at all?" He knew that the question dealt with the two of them spending the evening together dancing and enjoying the wedding festivities. It was an opportunity for a bit of fun and to test her own abundant self-assurance. He did not immediately respond.

Again she asked, "Not interested?" This time her tone of voice showed sincere disappointment, as if she feared rejection. She felt foolish. She wondered if she had been too brazen and whether she should have sought a formal introduction. She did not want him to think that she was a trollop.

She was no doubt more aggressive than other ladies of her own age group but she was a lady. She was, in fact, very much a lady and would readily establish that fact if he expressed other ideas or notions.

His continued silence bothered her, and she once again addressed the issue. "Are you offended because I approached you without a formal introduction?" Without allowing him to respond, she continued, "All of the social taboos, all of the social rules of society are established by men. All are man-made. It is a man's world. It is time, however, for things to change. It is time for women to speak up. Time for women to speak for themselves and to set their own rules. I am one of the first rule-breakers. Soon there will be legions of women to follow. The world is going to change." Having firmly stated her piece of mind, she again asked, in a quizzical tone of voice, "Interested?"

He could no longer tease her. Her eyes, her face, showed her let-down feeling. A tear trickled slowly down her cheek. Finally, he jokingly queried back to her, "Not interested in what?"

"In our unattached situation becoming an attached situation for the evening."

He chuckled then teasingly replied, "Oh, that. I was not aware that there were alternatives. I assumed that I was locked into the attachment from the moment of your introduction."

A smile creased Mary's lips, a tear of relief gently inched down her cheek. It was a tear of joy, a tear of happiness. Robert drew her close to him, dabbed the tear from her cheek, and they danced the night away. "I like your spunk. Perhaps we both have much in common."

"Perhaps we do," she responded happily.

Neither of them knew, nor did they even suspect, that their chance meeting on that evening so long ago would eventually bind the two of them together in a life-long journey; a journey with many turns, twists, and pitfalls, with much happiness and occasional sadness. Whatever life offered, whatever fate dished out, whether good or evil, however it was served, as they traveled the road of life, their love and faith and hope would sustain them. There would be challenges and there would be disappointments, but life would go on. Events sometimes would shake them to the very foundation of their trust, but a new day always dawned, raising them from the pits of hopelessness to pinnacles of the promises of a new day and a new hope. Love - their love for each other and for family - would bind them in an unbreakable unity for whatever challenges that lay ahead.

Chapter Three

Measures of Virtue

Robert Holcomb, due to business and town commitments, spends much of his time at the mill and attending town meetings. The mill requires considerable time and effort, nearly ten hours a day, six days a week. He works the same hours and the same days that his employees work. He is a good man, a family man, a caring man. The people and the town and the mill are important to him. Most of all, his wife and his son are important to him, more so than life itself. This is Robert Holcomb. This is who he is. This is what he is. This is what he is about.

Robert never shirks family responsibilities. Family obligations are important. He believes in setting a good example. Even so, family time is limited. He leaves for the mill early on weekday mornings. He arrives at the mill before six o'clock a.m., and he leaves around six in the evening.

After church on Sundays, weather permitting, the horse is hitched to the carriage and the three of them venture off into the countryside. Sometimes it is for picnics or exploring the outdoors, enjoying nature and doing fun things together. Other times they visit friends, walk in the town park, or enjoy a quiet day at home, just being a family, sharing thoughts, ideas and loving their time together. There is no work to be done on Sundays. Not ever. Sundays are always family days.

Mary Holcomb is a good woman, a good mother, and a good wife. She is a caring person, concerned about others, about their rights and about their entitlement to equality and dignity. This is who she is. This is what she is. This is what she is about.

Mary Holcomb assumes all of the household responsibilities. She plans all social affairs and all other functions that are held at the Holcomb house. Although she has two full-time servants, the house with twelve rooms is no easy task to manage - it was not so before Robbie was born, and it never gets easier. She designates most of the domestic chores to the two servants. However, as often as she has time, she works hand in hand with them in accomplishing whatever chores are in need of attention. Mary is not a lazy person, nor does she believe that menial tasks are beneath her dignity. She simply has too many other irons in the fire. She has a burning desire and a commitment for social and political matters. Women are denied the right to vote and many other rights afforded only to men. Her political interests are for those who are disenfranchised from society because of class, gender, or race. She is greatly concerned over the lack of women's rights and the issue of slavery, and she actively pursues the means for righting these wrongs. She is often ridiculed and chastised for her activities. These harassments never lessen her efforts in the fight for equality. She vigorously pursues her mission to right these wrongs.

Robert's personal feelings on social and moral issues closely parallel those subscribed to by Mary. He is not, however, so inclined as is Mary to publicly acknowledge them. This sometimes causes disagreement between the two of them.

"Robert, you are fearful that stating your personal opinions publicly may have a detrimental effect on business at the mill. You also fear ridicule from your male peers if you openly express your true feelings on these matters."

"Mary, you stir up enough consternation over these matters without me getting involved. I have supported you in your efforts - morally and financially. I think that you sometimes forget that the mill hires women and men, whether they are white or colored, and that all employees have the same job opportunities. We treat them all the same. I believe my actions speak louder than words. Besides, the mill is a business, it is not a social function.

"If you will just give these civil matters time - and not continuously harp on them - they will take care of themselves. The opinions of people - and of society - change and so do the laws that regulate us.

"Remember what Plautus said several hundred years ago? Patience is the best remedy for every trouble."

"Robert, how can you say such things? Society has been waiting and struggling for generations, for a thousand years, waiting for people - for men, for society - to change their attitudes on women's rights and the freedom of slaves. Women continue to be second-class citizens and slaves remain as slaves. The slaves are even worse off than are we women.

"Social attitudes, morals, and laws change when enough people cry out - raise their voices - and demand changes. People need to be reminded of these injustices. They need to think about them, to talk about them, and to remind others about them. Then something will be done.

"I remember one of my professors at Mount Holyoke quoting Sir Frances Bacon. He said, 'Silence is the virtue of fools.' I also know that the Bible - in the book of Ecclesiastes - says that there is a time to keep silent and a time to speak.

"The time to speak on these issues is now, Robert. It is now! It is time, and I intend to do so. I hope that your conscience will lead you to do likewise."

"Mary, when has your constant agonizing and bickering over these matters accomplished what you have intended? When have they gained anything? Matters of this magnitude take time and patience. Remember your quote from the Bible - from Ecclesiastes - about a time to speak and a time to keep silent? I remind you that the Scottish writer, Thomas Carlyle, who is still living, wrote that 'Silence is as deep as eternity, speech is as shallow as time.'"

"Well, Robert, you pick a poor source to quote when you use Mr. Carlyle. He also said that 'might and right are the same' and that the 'right of individuals should be denied' and that 'democracy is absurd.' How absurd can a person be?

"Despite the second class standing of women in this male dominated society, slavery is a much greater injustice. An injustice that I perceive to be a blight on the national conscience of America. Slavery is a wicked and shocking blight; it taints both North and South," she laments, adding passionately, "The shackles of bondage and the denial of the inalienable rights of freedom for all people must be broken. Those who are crying for America to shed its ignorance, intolerance and inhumanity towards others and to abolish this sinful and inhuman practice must be heard."

"Mary, I do not disagree with you and with what you stand for. These issues are matters for our government - our national, state and local governments - to resolve. They are probably even now under consideration by them. Write to your government officials if you like. These issues will be resolved in due time. Just be patient."

"Robert, how patient would you be if you were a woman or a slave?"

"Mary, I understand you and I understand the problem. Just be patient. The evils of human bondage and the denial of the rights of womankind will be eliminated throughout America."

Mary takes great pride in her efforts to correct these social evils, not for her own sake, but for the sake of her causes. She personally feels no need for attention. Nevertheless, she humbly accepts the personal recognition, the plaudits, solely because it furthers her causes and her mission.

As her reputation and her influences spread, many political, religious, and secular doors are opened. Politicians begin to take notice. Invitations to speak at women's political meetings and other gatherings increase. She presses her causes on with a vengeance. Even so, her family is never ignored or forgotten.

Robbie's birth years earlier had wrought an astounding change in Mary's life. She was overwhelmed and overjoyed with her infant son. He was her first born and her only child. She became obsessed with love and concern for her child. She hovered over him like a hen over her chicks. Robert worried about her over-protective attitude toward their youngster, especially during Robbie's early developmental years. He fretted over the matter for quite some time. Finally, out of desperation, he confronted Mary.

In a somewhat agitated, although soft, tone he speaks, "Mary, I have been bothered for some time about your over-protective, if not controlling attitude toward Robbie. I realize that you love him dearly. I love him just as much as you do, but I do not constantly smother him with attention and affection. The boy needs room to grow, room to experience things on his own. He needs to learn by doing. Sometimes he needs to discover things on his own, to make mistakes and to learn from them. He needs to be a little boy." He pauses momentarily, then continues, "Mary, you need to let go a bit. For his sake and for our sake."

"Why do you believe I am over-protective and domineering, Robert? I teach him to be a loving and caring child. I teach him to be kind and considerate. I teach him humility and compassion. I try to teach him all of those things that will serve him in life, that will make him the kind of person that we will both be proud of when he is an adult."

"Mary, I am not talking about those things. I am referring to your protectiveness, your constant hovering over him and simply not letting him do things for himself. Let him make a few mistakes and learn from them. Let him be a child; let him be a boy."

Mary stands silently. A slight smile creases her lips, although she does not interrupt him until he pauses. Her response is in a light-hearted, somewhat chastising, tone. "Robert, you are over-reacting. You are making a mountain out of a molehill." Half joking, half caustically, she continues. "I do believe that I have two little boys, and it appears that the older and bigger one is more than a little bit jealous - his feelings are hurt and he is pouting.

"Mommy loves you, too," she teasingly chastises him, patting his cheek. Then playfully she tweaks his nose and embraces him. She has turned the tables on Robert. Her voice is not entirely accusatory, although her message is clear. She is not going to change. Not one bit. Robert blushes. He is angered with her response. "Mary, this is not a joking matter. It is quite important. You need to think seriously about what I have said, for your sake, for Robbie's sake, and for my sake."

"I know what I want my son to be when he is an adult, Robert. I know how I want him to react to other humans, to know how to respect them, to be a highly principled person. I should think that you would think likewise."

"Of course that is what I want, Mary, but I also want him to be a boy - just a little boy, on his way to manhood."

He declines to press the matter further. It does not end his concern. Robert is nonetheless determined that the boy will be exposed to other influences. He wants his son to be well balanced and independent of both his mother and himself in making choices and adopting philosophies. He is not opposed to Robbie adopting his mother's ideals - to do so would be highly acceptable and commendable. Mary subscribes to very high standards - but he wants Robbie's ideals to be his own choices. Neither would he object to his son adopting his ideals - he would be flattered, and very pleased. But again it must be Robbie's choice. He will see to that.

As young Robbie grows and matures he remains the apple of his mother's eye, the joy and passion of her heart. She loves and cherishes her son, and spends as much time with him during his formative years as she can manage. She is determined that her ideals will be indelibly imbedded in his mind; that her attitudes will become his attitudes. She is determined to raise her child to respect and cherish the causes that are dear to her heart. She implores young Robbie to carry her causes of women's rights and the anti-slavery movement into his adult life.

Mary embraces every situation to further her causes. She never overlooks an opportunity to voice her concerns and her contempt for

America's failure to right these wrongs. A door of opportunity opens to her when she is invited to address the Christian Women's Society of New York in the early summer of 1855.

Never has Mary faced such a large audience. She is nevertheless undaunted, nor is she awestruck. "There must be a thousand people here," she murmured half under her breath. "Very few men in attendance but, after all, that is as it should be at a women's conference," she again murmurs. She is excited, but confident. Her mind races in preparation for her presentation. "There are women here from all over the state of New York. Perhaps a gathering of guests from throughout New England," she mused. "This is an opportunity - a great opportunity - to plead the causes of liberty for America's slaves and equality for American women," she whispered to herself, her lips barely moving. She is excited and a little nervous as she awaits her time to speak. There are other speakers scheduled to address the gathering, and some of them precede her to the podium. Waiting her turn is difficult; she paces nervously, listening to the speakers and making mental notes of what they say.

When Mary's time to speak arrives, she reasons that the women's suffrage issue has been addressed in great detail, and it has been addressed with great passion and sincerity. It has been done so admirably. There is nothing more that can be said without duplicating what others have said. "They have stolen my thunder," she mumbles to herself somewhat dubiously, but immediately recovers her composure. "The issue of slavery in America has hardly been mentioned," she muses. "This is my opportunity to state the cause for liberty, for freedom of an oppressed people, for the abolition of slavery throughout America," she half whispers to herself. "I must be ready to meet this challenge."

There is polite applause as she is introduced. She steps confidently to the lectern.

"Thank you, Mrs. Chairman, for your kind and very generous introduction." She turns to face the audience, smiles, and begins to speak. "Distinguished officers, esteemed members, honored guests, ladies and gentlemen. It is indeed an honor and a privilege to address you. I am humbled and excited because we all possess dreams and ideals and compassion for one another and for our fellow members of the human race. All of us have something in common. That something is a Christian concern - a Christian commitment and a Christian brotherhood and sisterhood for all of the human race. We strive and we hope for a better world - for ourselves and for all humanity. For these hopes I rejoice, as each of you rejoice with me.

"I am, nevertheless, saddened that the existence of slavery in some of these United States is an accepted and legal institution. Slavery is the greatest evil that this country has ever embraced; the greatest evil we have ever faced. And we as Christian people have ignored our state, our nation, and our Christian responsibilities by sitting idly by while this evil continues. Slavery is an abomination to Christian people. Slavery is an injustice that casts its shadow of shame over the entire face of America. It is a shame that cuts deep into our Christian heritage; a shame that runs deep, a shame that is cruel and inhuman. The shame of slavery falls on the conscience of all Americans: on those in the Southern states and those in the North. It falls on those who own slaves and those who do not. We, the non-slave owners, are as guilty for this evil as are the slave owners and the slave traders because we silently and passively allow this practice to endure." Interrupted by applause, she pauses then continues. "If we are to have true freedom in America - North and South, East and West - the human bondage of black Americans must end. Our efforts in supporting the cause of freedom must be tireless. We cannot rest, not until freedom rings for all Americans! Slavery of any man, woman or child is incompatible with humanity. It is inconsistent with the ideals and the principles that our founding fathers held dear to their hearts. This cause - the freedom of slaves - is a just cause. It is a human cause. It is a Christian cause."

Again interrupted by applause, she pauses. Mary concludes her address, "The white man's rights are protected and guaranteed by a Bill of Rights; the black man's rights are encumbered and denied by a Bill of Sale." The applause is long, thunderous and vigorous as she leaves the podium. She is satisfied that the evils of slavery have been clearly voiced and that those attending the meeting will be the vessels to spread the word across the state of New York and even beyond its borders.

Back stage a young man approaches her. He identifies himself as a newspaper reporter. "Mrs. Holcomb," he excitedly exclaims as he heartedly shakes her hand, "you have just placed the Trojan horse of Troy within the gates of the slave master."

"I sincerely hope so," she responds, then quickly adds, "We will have to wait and see. I hope that my Trojan horse is filled with men and women of peace, and not with soldiers of war." The reporter - she does not catch his name or the newspaper he represents - asks permission to quote some of her material in a news article he intends to write. She quite graciously gives her approval, then she starts to walk away. "Mrs. Holcomb," he says, placing a hand on her arm, "I believe it was Shakespeare who said, 'Within this wall of flesh there is a soul.' You, Mrs. Holcomb, have given us some of that soul today."

Tears of joy moisten her eyes. "Thank you. Thank you so much for your kind words of encouragement. I do hope that America is awakened." She embraces him momentarily in a spirit of gratitude, then she turns away to depart.

"Mrs. Holcomb," the young reporter again addressed her, "I hope you do not feel that I am being presumptuous, but would you consider dining with me this evening? I assure you this is a professional invitation." The young man is blushing, embarrassed that he has again interrupted her. "I thought it would give me an opportunity to interview you further."

"Would you repeat your name again, Sir? I did not catch it when we initially met. I'm sorry."

"Yes ma'am. I am John Matthews. I work for the New York Daily Tribune."

"I am delighted that you have invited me to dinner, Mr. Matthews. It will be a pleasure to dine with you."

"Is six o'clock alright, Mrs. Holcomb?"

"It's just fine, Mr. Matthews. I'll meet you at the dining room entrance."

She is overjoyed the next morning when she learns that her speech and the interview appear on the front page of the New York Daily Tribune, the Philadelphia Enquirer, the Cincinnati Daily Gazette and dozens of small town newspapers across the East and North. It is gratifying to her that the slavery issue is being laid before the public.

Her address to the convention and the publicity that is generated from the newspaper articles propel her to the forefront of the anti-slavery movement in New York. She continuously voices her displeasures and concerns over social injustices. She hounds political leaders to push the cause of freedom for all people. "America must shed its ignorance, its intolerance, and its inhumanity. It must abolish this disgraceful practice of slavery."

New York officials, prodded by Mary's constant abolitionist efforts, and spurred on by a newly enlightened and aroused citizenry, become more active in social matters. Her accomplishments are mere stepping stones on her pathway, her journey toward the total abolishment of slavery. Vast areas within the United States remain dominions of slavery and unequal rights for women. Her mission of freedom for all people will not be eased by isolated victories. "Slavery," she preaches, "must fall, and the rights of women must be recognized all across America from North to South and from East to West." She will not rest on partial victories. She recognizes the pitfalls of complacency.

Mary is very much aware that she has made enemies because of her abolitionist and women's rights efforts. There are those in high places who are offended. Some oppose her openly and others, the back-biters, pretend to support her causes, but secretly oppose her efforts and conspire against them. There are those who doubt her sincerity and commitment to the cause. She is considered by many to be a rabble-rouser, a woman of financial means with little else to do other than to stir up trouble.

Some oppose her abolitionist ideals because of personal, political or financial interests. Others oppose her on social, religious or ethnic grounds. Those with political or financial interests at stake, those with another axe to grind, are the most vocal and bitter opponents. She takes this opposition in stride. Whatever their reasons for opposing her causes, they quickly discover that she is a vigorous and worthy opponent.

The fight against slavery and for women's rights beyond the borders of New York presents an awesome task. These issues are emotional. They cross geographical lines, political lines, religious lines, social and economic lines. The slavery issue is dividing the nation. In her mind, the slavery issue is foremost on the national scene in America. It has been festering for years, dividing North and South. The chasm between the two sections of America is widening.

Chapter Four

A Turn of Events

The arrival of summer-like weather in the late spring of 1856 is welcomed with much enthusiasm by the residents of Bedford Springs. Winter has been long and harsh, lapping over into mid-spring. Now warm sunny days are beckoning to Mother Nature for a resurgence of new life. Trees are beginning to sport new leaves. The hills and valleys are shedding their drab winter coats in exchange for bright new colors of spring and summer. Flowers are exploding from the sun-warmed earth in an array of bright and beautiful colors. Everyone seems to be busy. Bedford Springs and the hills and the valleys are alive and well after a long and arduous winter. Summer is fast approaching. Excitement and anticipation abound.

Robbie Holcomb, nearing his fourteenth birthday, is not oblivious to all that Mother Nature is changing. He anticipates the onset of summer with all the exuberance of youth. The school year will soon end and he reasons that he will soon be overwhelmed with nothing but free time and lazy effortless days. It is not that the end of the school year assures him of a summer free of responsibilities; it is simply that the regimentation of these daily doses of education - the reading and writing and arithmetic - will once again be cast aside until the coming of fall. He can not help but chuckle aloud at the thought of it.

Mr. Baker, his teacher, hearing Robbie's chuckle, inquires whether there is something amusing that he would like to share with the class.

"No Sir," Robbie replies.

"Is there something in your text book that amuses you?" asks Mr. Baker, who is somewhat annoyed by Robbie's interruption of the silence that is expected during study period.

Again Robbie replies, "No Sir."

Mr. Baker, unwilling to let the issue die, responds, "Mr. Holcomb, please enlighten the class with whatever is more important to you than completing your lesson assignments. Come forward so that your classmates can give you their undivided attention."

Robbie, embarrassed by this confrontation with Mr. Baker, walks slowly to the front of the classroom. His classmates snicker and giggle at his apparent discomfort and make the situation all that much worse. This is very unusual for Robbie. He is well-liked by his classmates, and he is Mr. Baker's favorite student. He never causes trouble.

Robbie clears his throat, the laughter silences, and he begins to speak, "Well, I was sitting back at my desk thinking that the school year would soon be over. I was thinking that I would have the summer off - that there would not be any lessons, no more school work - so I would be able to do exactly what I wanted to do. And then I thought - this is what caused me to chuckle - I thought that school is exactly the opposite of everything else in life and especially it's the opposite of nature. In nature nothing happens in the winter. All things die or become dormant. Trees, at least most of them, lose their leaves. The grass turns brown and dies. The birds quit singing and they fly away. Flowers disappear. And while all of nature is sleeping or hibernating, we come to school and work and study and are alert. Then when summer appears and nature comes alive, we get out of school. We are lazy and lifeless. We don't have to do anything at all. We are alive and active in the winter when nature sleeps and we rest and do nothing in the summer when nature is alive and active. I just thought that it was funny, but it doesn't seem so funny now. That's all there is to it."

Robbie pauses momentarily, looks toward Mr. Baker and in an apologetic tone states, "Mr. Baker, I had finished my lessons, and I apologize for interrupting the class." He is beginning to show signs of his embarrassment. His face is as red as an apple and perspiration sprinkles his upper lip. Normally he would be unconcerned and at ease in addressing the class.

Pausing again for a moment, he is quite aware that his classmates are enjoying his discomfort - not in a mean-spirited way, but rather appreciating the fact that it is Robbie and not one of them who is facing the class and Mr. Baker.

Again addressing his teacher, he asks, "May I return to my seat, Mr. Baker?"

"You may," Mr. Baker responds.

The class applauds and cheers as Robbie returns to his seat. Mr. Baker smiles, then bows to Robbie and says, "Thank you, Mr. Holcomb for your enlightening dissertation on the dissimilarities between nature and education. You have probably enshrined your place in history along with other great thinkers such as Benjamin Franklin and Sir Isaac Newton."

The class, enjoying Robbie's misery and embarrassment more than his story, again applauds and cheers. Mr. Baker smiles, and Robbie, behind a sheepish and embarrassing grin, sits silently through the ordeal.

In spite of the Mother Nature and educational episode and its embarrassing aftermath, which is soon forgotten by everyone except Robbie, he is not unhappy with his schooling. As a matter of fact, he enjoys it. He enjoys the challenges of learning. He appreciates the opportunities of an education. He has always been an exceptional student, always excelling, always at the head of the class and always extremely popular with his classmates and teachers. The up and coming summer vacation, free of classroom activity, is nevertheless for his young mind - as it is for the other thirteen and fourteen year olds - an opportunity for change. An opportunity to experience other matters, other adventures.

Although for the moment, for the beginning of this up and coming summer season, it will just be the good old summertime; nothing more, nothing less. Nevertheless, with school out, life will be less of a hassle, less frantic. It will offer more freedom of choice. A summer free of all obligations has great appeal for a youngster who will not be fourteen until the Fourth of July. He anticipates the freedom of late morning laziness. He can sleep late and at least for a week or so, do whatever he wants to do, even if his desire is to do nothing at all. It sure feels good to think about leisure time. He reasons that this will possibly be his last summer before starting an apprenticeship at the family mill and he wants to make the most of it. He is reasonably sure that his father will have all of his future summers pre-planned. It is time to make the most of this summer.

Robbie is not alone in having thoughts about summer. His father, Robert, also has summer thoughts; thoughts that involve Robbie and the family mill. His father has kept his thoughts to himself. His plans will not only involve himself and Robbie; Mary will also be involved. Robert mulls over his plans time after time, speculating how Mary is going to react when he apprises her of his intention to start Robbie on a summer apprenticeship at the mill.

He knows that Robbie will accept his decision without question. He will neither object nor complain, not even if he is sorely disappointed with his father's decision. That is the way Robbie is, that is the way he has been taught, that is the way he has always been. He never argues, never disagrees with his parents. Mary, on the other hand, can be a different matter. Robert can easily predict her reaction to matters that do not involve Robbie. However, her reaction when anything involving their son is at stake is, at best, unpredictable. She is especially defensive when the two of them differ on matters affecting their son. She, of course, would neither condone nor support Robbie in any wrongdoing or even in small or insignificant indiscretions. The truth of the matter is that he never does or says anything that embarrasses his parents. He is never disobedient in private or in public.

Robbie's demeanor, his conduct, is impeccable. This is not just the opinion of his parents; it is the opinion of others who know him. People in the Bedford Springs community, whether or not they are associated with the Holcomb mill, hold young Robbie in high esteem. He is highly regarded and well-liked by all who know him. He has earned his reputation on his own merits, on his own actions, not through family tradition or heritage.

Robert, nevertheless, can foresee the possibility of resistance from Mary. The degree or intensity of that resistance, he reasons, will depend on how well, how objectively, he presents his case to her. He needs strong and convincing reasons for starting Robbie on an apprenticeship at such an early age.

Robert closes the door to his office much earlier than usual. It is a rare occasion for him to leave the mill before late afternoon. He normally does not leave until the last worker has gone for the day. It is his practice to be the first to arrive in the morning and the last one out in the evening. He owns the mill. It is his duty to set a good example. Today, however, he is going home early. He needs time to decide just how to broach the subject of Robbie's apprenticeship. He needs time to think, time to plan.

As he walks through the mill toward the exit, the workers look first at him and then curiously at the company clock. He knows they are puzzled by his early departure. He waves or speaks to them, but he does not break stride. He is well-liked and respected by his employees, but it would be difficult to get away once a conversation is started. Besides, he does not need any distractions at this time. He needs to keep a cool, clear line of thought. He has a selling job to do at home. He does not stop until the door closes behind him. The refreshing spring air invigorates Robert. He is out of the mill for the rest of the day.

The mid-afternoon sun is high and bright in a cloudless clear blue sky. It is a brilliant blue stretching from horizon to horizon, from east to west and north to south. He does not often see the sky this early in the afternoon, and he is appreciative of the opportunity to do so. To him it lacks the exhilarating beauty of a late evening sunset, but it is nonetheless a gorgeous and spectacular sight on a splendid and magnificent spring day. Surely nothing can go wrong.

He turns his thoughts toward home - to Mary and to Robbie. He will surprise them. He told no one that he was leaving work early or where he was going. It will be several hours before dinner is served and Mary will be flustered by his early arrival. Things are, nevertheless, going to be alright; he feels certain of that. "Yes," he says to himself, "everything is going to be just dandy; I can feel it."

He decides to walk the mile and a half home, even though it is uphill the entire way. In spite of the late spring sunshine, a cool gentle breeze is blowing westward from the river. It is an added bonus to the otherwise warm afternoon. He goes by the livery stable to arrange for the overnight care of his horse and then heads homeward. A very pleasing walk, he thinks to himself as he leisurely trods along the dusty road. He again thinks about his family - he, Mary and Robbie - and about their lives together. He comments as if speaking to someone, "It has been a good life for all of us. Yes, it has been more than good. It has been great; it is wonderful." They are a loving and caring family, a compatible family. They have been abundantly blessed and they have been generous to the community and to their employees: those who work at the mill and those who work in their home. He and Mary are a wonderful match and Robbie completes the family circle. "What more could we want? What more could anyone want?" he half mumbles aloud to himself.

"This walk home is a great idea," he muses. "It has given me an opportunity to reflect on life; to think about Mary, Robbie, and myself. An opportunity to contemplate and to be thankful," he more or less whispers aloud, then quickly glances around to see if anyone is close by. He would be terribly embarrassed and horrified if someone caught him talking to himself. He is relieved to find that he is alone on the road. "Best to keep my thoughts to myself," he half mutters under his breath.

His thoughts again return to his family. "Yes, life has been good. Near perfect. We have never wanted for anything. We have had few misunderstandings and the few disagreements that have occurred we have quickly resolved."

As he continues along, he reassures himself that the current matter of Robbie's summer apprenticeship will be resolved in the same manner as past differences. "Perhaps Mary will totally agree with my decision and there will be no need for further discussion," he says to himself. His emotions are buoyed by the thought and he begins to whistle, convincing himself that things are under control.

As he walks the last hundred yards, he is so convinced that Mary will embrace his idea, he can hardly wait to reach the door.

"Good evening, love. I'm home," he announces enthusiastically as he opens the door, then adds, "and I am right on time," as he strides quickly over to Mary and kisses her gently but lovingly before she has a chance to respond. Surprised by his early arrival, and somewhat breathless by his sudden romantic display, she takes a moment to recover her composure.

"You are not on time Robert Holcomb, and you know it. You are nearly an hour early," she replies, faking displeasure in her voice as she glances at the clock on the dining room mantel. "Why are you home so early? Has something happened at the mill? Is it good news or bad? What is it?" she asks in such rapid succession and without a moment's hesitation that he has no opportunity to reply. When she finally stops to catch her breath, he is so amused over her reaction to his early arrival that he can do nothing but laugh. Piqued by his lack of response to her questions, and due to his silly laughter, she would have thought him to be inebriated were it not for the fact that he was not inclined to indulge in strong drink. She again inquires, in a somewhat irritated mood, "Why are you home so early?"

Robert, continuing to be amused over Mary's inquisitiveness, recovers his composure enough to answer her questions somewhat jovially in the order they are asked. "I am home early because I left the mill early. I came early because I have something important to discuss with you after dinner. Nothing has happened at the mill, and perhaps we will both regard our after-dinner discussion as good news. At least I believe it to be so. It will depend on your personal observations. I am happy this evening because I have a beautiful and loving wife and because we have a handsome and wonderful son. I am genuinely happy. I simply decided to come home early today. A spur of the moment idea. I left the horse at the livery stable and walked every step of the way home. It has been a beautiful day and I have enjoyed every moment of it."

When Robert pauses Mary takes advantage of the situation. Now much relieved from her earlier anxiety, she is, nonetheless, quite inquisitive over the events of the day and the pending after-dinner conversation. "Robert," she retorts, "never in your life have you done anything on the spur of the moment. You do things methodically. You look at things from every possible angle. I am the spur-of-the-moment person in this family. I am the one who jumps first and then looks; but not you, Robert. You always consider the consequences first." She pauses, smiles and looks up into his face - a very handsome face, she thinks. Tilting her face upward toward his, she places her hands on his shoulders, then interlocks her fingers behind his neck, her eyes locked on his. "Robert," she continues, "you are so dependable. You always make the right choices because you consider all the possibilities before you make a decision. You think things through. That's why you never make a mistake. And I love you for it."

She has, without knowing it, reassured his self-confidence. What she has said about him is normally true, especially in matters of business. But this evening's matters are personal, private, family affairs. The rules of normalcy do not always ring true in such matters. He feigns as best he can an air of indifference to her compliment, but a tell-tale smile creases his lips - a dead give-away. He is flattered, and perhaps a bit overconfident. Mary, not aware of the content of the after-dinner secret, is sure that it is the best of news.

They stand silently for several minutes, locked in each others' arms. He kisses her on the forehead, then on her lips. "Mary, my dear," he says, "you could disarm the devil."

Ignoring his back-handed compliment, but well aware that both of them have the after-dinner secret on their minds, she points to the clock. "We have plenty of time before dinner to discuss your little matter, if it is so important."

"It is very important," he responds, "but not so important that it cannot wait."

Curiosity is now gnawing at her patience. "If it is very important," she queries, "shouldn't we discuss it now? You know that I am very inquisitive. To tantalize me with a promised secret is terribly unfair. If you don't tell me now, I will not enjoy dinner and it will be your fault." She looks him directly in the eyes and pleads in her most disappointing and begging voice, her face now drooping and her lips in a disillusioned pout. "Please?" she asks.

"No dear," he responds. "It can wait and you can wait. Quit acting like a child. Dinner is about to be served so call Robbie."

Mary glances over her shoulder at Robert as she is about to call Robbie. "All of this suspense is killing me and it is all your fault," she says, not in the kindest tone of voice. "If you were not going to tell me until after dinner you should not have mentioned it until after dinner." She pauses momentarily, turns and faces him. "Just a hint, just one little hint?" she pleads. For a moment they stand facing each other. He nearly blurts the news out but realizes Robbie and the maid have entered the dining room. Dinner is announced.

Pleasantries are exchanged all around. The maid excuses herself and departs for the day. They remain standing, holding hands, as is the family custom, until Robbie asks grace. Then they take their usual places at the table. The three of them engage in small talk during dinner. Nothing of a serious or important nature is discussed, although Mary can hardly refrain from again broaching the subject of Robert's important news. In spite of her curiosity and constant fidgeting, she enjoys dinner. It is, as usual, a delicious and appetizing meal.

After dinner Robbie excuses himself and returns to his room. Mary excitedly pushes the dishes aside and turns to Robert. "Alright," she quizzically asks, "what is the good news?"

He observes her fidgeting during dinner and now her eagerness, her anticipation to hear the good news, is overwhelming. He does not want to lose the upper hand that he believes he now holds over the situation, nor does he want to overplay his hand. "She," he mentally muses, "is like a child who has been given an unexpected present. She can hardly wait for the wrapping to come off." Robert can not help but gloat to himself. He feels certain that he is in total control of the situation. He now has, or so he believes, convinced Mary that the forthcoming news is good. He is persuaded that she has accepted his apprenticeship plan without even knowing what is about to be told to her. Things are working much better than he had planned. The time is ripe and the situation is beckoning.

Robert takes her hands in his, squeezes them lovingly, and raises her from her chair. He kisses her lightly on the forehead and suggests that they go into the library.

"This must really be important news," she says with anticipation in her voice, although somewhat quizzically and more in the sense of a question than as a statement.

"Yes dear, it is very important," he responds in a serious tone, "but I do not want Robbie to hear us. At least not just yet."

"Shall I close the door?" she asks as they go into the library.

"Yes," he says as he turns to face her, "please close the door."

She detects a slight nervousness in his voice. The happy, carefree expression that seemed to radiate from him before and during dinner is overshadowed by a grimness that she has seldom before seen. Even so, she does not suspect that anything is amiss. She assumes that he is caught by the same excitement that envelopes her. After all, good news is something that excites people. She is nearly bursting with anticipation. Excitedly she blurts out, "Hurry up, Robert. I have waited long enough for your good news. You are intentionally tantalizing me."

"No, I am not, Mary. It's just that I am not sure where I want to begin. I have been mulling over this idea for several days. It has to do with the mill, and I want to get your opinion on the matter." Robert continues to look directly at Mary as he speaks. He is watching her expressions, attempting to anticipate how she is going to react. "The mill," he says, "is our livelihood. Its success is important to us and to the people living here in Bedford Springs. It will be important to Robbie someday."

"Yes, Robert, I know that. Robbie knows it and I suppose that everyone in town knows it," Mary responds impatiently, then adds, "But what exactly does that have to do with what we came in here to discuss? What are you trying to say?"

"What I am trying to say, if you will show a little patience and listen, is that you are going to find that my idea has considerable merit, and you may well be the one that realizes the most benefit from it."

"Robert, you ask me to be patient and listen? I am being patient and I have been listening, but I certainly would like to know what I am being patient and listening for. You have been dilly dallying - beating around the bush - about your so-called surprise ever since you came in from work over an hour early. I think it is time for you to get to the point of the matter."

He stands silently facing her. She is waiting for the promised good news, but silence prevails. It dawns on her that he is trying to speak but words fail him. His self-assurance, his self-reliance has transformed into self-doubt. He has failed to seize the moment. He now suspects that Mary will not be fooled and that she is going to see through his motive for wanting Robbie to spend the summer working at the mill. The prevailing silence jars Mary back to reality. "Is something physically wrong with Robert or has he duped me into a false belief of good news? Does he actually have bad or unpleasant news?" She is seized half by fear and half by anger. Finally, she asks, "Robert is anything wrong? Has something bad happened?"

"Nothing bad has happened, Mary," he responds bluntly. Regaining his composure, he continues. "I have a plan, a new plan for the mill. I plan to assure that the success of the mill will continue for many years to come. Robbie is a part of that plan. You are a part of the plan also.

"I have decided to start Robbie on an apprenticeship at the mill. He is to begin work the day after school is out for the summer. He will continue on the job until school reopens in the fall. I expect him to work the same schedule, the same hours that all employees work. It is important that he knows every worker by name, that he knows their job and how to do it. He is not going to learn everything in one summer, but he will learn a lot. I expect that in a few summers he will know everything about the mill. He will be spending time in every department. I wanted you to know before I told him. It might be a good idea if we both told him."

Mary refrains from interrupting him as he speaks. He is quite pleased, believing that she is in accord with his plan. It has gone much better than he had contemplated. Especially after he missed an opportunity to present a sound reason, a well thought out, intelligent and valid argument for Robbie to begin an apprenticeship at such an early age. When they entered the library, his first reaction was a loss of confidence. Now his self-assurance has returned, perhaps prematurely and perhaps an overabundance of it.

Mary's silence is by no means an endorsement of his plan. She is seething inside. She bites her lip. "So this is the big surprise, the good news that brought you home early today?" she responds sarcastically.

"It's part of the good news, Mary. He will benefit from it, and so will you."

She is incensed. She is perturbed that he has misled her, deceived her about his plans. The more she thinks about it, the more infuriated she becomes. "How can you have the audacity to make such a decision without consulting me?" she responds in a voice so icy cold that it shocks him. She continues, "Mill policy, except in unusual hardship cases, provides a minimum age limit of sixteen years. Robbie is not yet fourteen." Pausing to catch her breath, she softens her response. "I realize that the Thomas boy began working at the mill when he was only fifteen, but his father had died and he had to support the family. That was a hardship case. Robbie is not a hardship case."

Although she attempts to remain perfectly calm in her response, it is becoming extremely difficult to do so. She feels the anger, her face flushing. Her forehead, her cheeks, are crimson red. She can see the whiteness of her knuckles as she clasps her hands tightly together. Finally, taking a deep breath, she looks directly at him with that icy stare. She does not speak in an out-of-control outburst. Rather, it is a soft, controlled, but firm and pointed response.

"You made this decision about our son without consulting me? Without asking my opinion? How could you be so presumptuous, so despicable? Your actions, Robert Holcomb, are hateful and unscrupulous. Robbie is my son - my flesh and blood, the same as he is yours. Do you think for one minute that I am not entitled to an opinion on things that affect Robbie? Am I not to be personally involved in matters that are as important as this? Robert," she continues, in the same controlled and icy, yet soft, firm voice, "I have devoted my entire life fighting for the rights and dignity of those who cannot speak for themselves. I have fought, and I will continue to fight, for the rights of American slaves. I have fought for the rights of women in America and I will continue that fight. You have supported and encouraged me in those missions. Surely you do not think - not for one moment - that I am going to stand silently by and not defend the rights of my own son? My opinions, my concerns for the rights of others is not new to you. You knew this from the very first time we met. I have reminded you of it throughout our marriage. On these issues I will not, can not yield."

Robert realizes that he has miscalculated the circumstances, mischaracterized his wife's intent. He attempts to interrupt her. "Mary, if you will just permit me to say something. . ."

"Please, Robert, just let me finish what I have to say, and I will gladly afford you the courtesy of speaking your piece, uninterrupted. We continue to live in a man's world, a world where men make the decisions. A world where women are ignored. You, Robert, of all people, are attempting to deprive me of the right of making a decision along with you, about what is best, and acceptable, and proper, and right for our child, our only child. Robert, I am not only disappointed in you, I am ashamed of what you are proposing to do.

"I am not going to stand aside and permit you to unilaterally make such an important decision. Robbie is still a child. He is far from manhood. Company policy at the mill has a sixteen-year-old minimum age limit for hirees. I expect to have a say, an equal say, in what he does or does not do during these early years of his life."

She pauses momentarily, looks directly at him and states in a tone of voice so icy cold, so stinging, that it leaves him momentarily speechless. "Furthermore, Robert, you have attempted to skew the facts, the purposes of your little scheme to have me believe that you were doing this for my benefit as well as for Robbie's. Robert, you are attempting to do this for your own greedy purposes. I see very clearly through your plan. You want to get Robbie away from my influences. Do you understand what I have said? What Robbie means to me?" Then in a softer, more relaxed and conciliatory tone of voice she concludes, "Robbie is our son. He is very dear to both of us. He should never be used as a pawn by one of us to gain an advantage over the other or anything or anyone. I love my son dearly, as I love you dearly. We share our son's love and we must share responsibilities and decisions affecting his life and well-being."

Robert has often seen the fire, the intensity of Mary's emotions in her efforts in advocating for the abolition of slavery and for expanding women's rights. He has never before seen her emotions elevated to the height that they have reached tonight. He was totally unprepared for her response. She caught him by surprise. Her reasoning, her feelings disarm him. He realizes that he should not have made the decision of Robbie's apprenticeship without first consulting her. He also knows that his decision was made in large part on his jealous assumptions that she had been overly influencing the boy.

His initial instinct is to fight back, to defend his actions, but for the second time tonight he is speechless, although this time it is self-imposed. He will not in the same evening again make a fool of himself. Her words have penetrated his soul. They have cut like a two-edged sword. That burning desire to strike back is hard to quell.

He stands silent and takes a deep breath. "Mary, I cannot deny that I sometimes feel that your influences on Robbie are excessive, although well-intended. I probably deserve some of the criticism that you have leveled against me. But I do want what is best for him, and for you, and for myself.

"I run the mill. I make the mill decisions. I hire and fire people when it is necessary to do so. I do not seek the approval of their families to do so, nor do I seek the approval of my family. Nor do I interfere with your responsibilities of running this household."

"Yes, Robert, you do run the mill, but those matters are totally different than matters regarding our son, and you know it. Please let us be reasonable and civil about this personal matter involving our son. I would never interfere with things at the mill, but our son is a different matter."

Mary is right. He knows that he has dug himself a hole that is difficult to escape and yet save face. Mary knows it also. She has made her point and it is time to aid him in escaping from the mess that he has made.

"You do have a legitimate argument about Robbie learning about the mill," she says. "Suppose something was to happen to you? He would need to know what to do."

"A good point, Mary."

"Robert, I have been very protective of Robbie. Perhaps I have tried too hard, but my intentions have been good. I know that I will have two men to worry about when both of you are at the mill. I don't know what I would do without the two of you."

"Nor do I know what I would do without you and Robbie."

Tears are welling in Mary's eyes. "Robert, perhaps it is time that we extricate ourselves from this subject - put it behind us."

"That's an excellent idea."

Mary moves closer to him. She touches his face, her index finger over his lips, silencing his speech as if to say enough has already been said. "Robert, we have aired some differences tonight, said things that needed to be said. Now they are over and done with. I believe we have developed an understanding." Having put the finishing touches on the matter, she embraces her husband and gently adds, "We have always settled our differences before bed time and this night is no different from all the others."

"Yes," he responds, "but with one exception. In the event that the apprenticeship issue has not been clarified, I withdraw my proposal. Robbie will not work at the mill this summer."

"We will decide on something tomorrow," she says, adding, "A little work may be just fine; perhaps a day or two a week."

"An excellent solution," he responds.

Chapter Five

Fears and Resolutions

As Mary sits, reflecting on the fleeting years that have so swiftly passed since Robbie's birth, she worries about the future, about his future. The year is 1859, and in a few days, Robbie, his parents, and his friends will celebrate his birthday. In a sense the entire community will be celebrating. July the Fourth not only will mark Robbie's seventeenth birthday, it will also be the eighty-third birthday of the nation; Independence Day, a day of celebration, brass bands, picnics in the town park and an all around good time for everyone. The Holcomb Mill always closes for the day, as do most of the other town businesses. America's birthday is observed as a family day and a community day. A military parade, usually at midmorning, always precedes the Fourth of July ceremonies. Patriotism runs high in Bedford Springs, especially on July the Fourth.

Mary Holcomb looks toward Robbie's birthday with mixed emotions. She is delighted on the one hand, yet dejected on the other. Delighted that Robbie has reached a milestone in his young life. Dejected because he has chosen - against her wishes - to continue his education at a far away southern University. She is fearful for his future - of what it might hold for him in a different part of the country, with different people, beholden to peculiar customs and ideals.

He finished pre-college schooling at the head of his class. He has always been at the head of his class; from his very first year of school to the completion of the current school year. He excels not only academically, but at everything he attempts to do. He possesses a spirit of competitiveness that spurs him onward. He is never satisfied with any result unless he has put forth his best effort. Mary does not attribute Robbie's successes to luck or to some magical or mysterious force. She does not doubt that good luck sometimes plays a part in events nor does she doubt that Robbie enjoys an unusual amount of good fortune. She is, on the other hand, quite aware of his resourcefulness. He is not one to rely on luck. He is one who prepares in advance for both the expected and the unexpected. This, she believes, is the primary source of his accomplishments.

She is happy and quite proud that he shares her concerns for the rights of mankind; for all mankind, for the rights of those with a different colored skin, for the rights of those with a different religious orientation and certainly he shares her concern for women's suffrage. She has laid a firm foundation for him to build his future on. He is her hope for the future. On the other hand, she cannot escape her sadness. It is more than sadness - it is more akin to despair; a fear of losing her son to other factors, to other influences. She has loved and cherished her son for seventeen years. She has been a great influence in the development of his attitudes but now he plans to go south to complete his education.

"Why," she again asks him, "do you need to go to a southern college where you will be subjected to southern attitudes and influences? These influences will change you. Will you forget my teachings? Your upbringing? Will you be ostracized for your northern attitudes? Will you be an outcast? After all," she cautions him, "Virginia is a slave state and the attitudes and philosophies of Southerners differ dramatically from those of people in the North. Southerners are greedy landowners and cotton barons, hungry and conniving for wealth and power. They have gained both through the ownership of other humans; they consider their slaves as property, the same as beasts of burden."

Mary's passionate outburst catches Robbie by surprise. Although he feels compassion for his mother, he is determined to stand firm on his education decision. "Mother, you hardly give me a chance to answer. You ask one question after another without pausing to allow me to answer. I will never forget the things you have taught me, nor will I ever change from the kind of person that I am. Your influences will forever be a part of me - a guiding light. I will always cherish and uphold those principles of equality that you have espoused.

"Furthermore Mother, I am no longer a child. I must stand on my own feet and make decisions for myself. I am confident that my educational choice of going to the University of Virginia is a good one, a proper one.

Please try to look at this as a great opportunity for me, an opportunity to further my education at one of America's greatest Universities, an opportunity to learn about the South, its rich history, its people and its culture. And Mother, most Virginians and most Southerners do not own slaves."

"But, Robbie," Mary insists, "the slave owners stand in ultimate authority and judgment over their slaves, even over their life and death. Slave owners and slave traders are unscrupulous, unchristian and inhuman," she laments. "Their very act of slave ownership is the epitome of hypocrisy. How can these people consider themselves Christian?" she shrieks aloud, wringing her hands and wildly swinging her arms.

"Please, Mother, you are allowing your emotions to run wild. You are judging all Southerners on the basis of the actions of a few. The vast majority of Southerners do not own slaves. I have repeated this to you many times.

"There are slave owners in the North and in the South. That does not taint everyone else. People's attitudes are changing all over the country. The South, just as in the North, has many people opposed to slavery.

"There are good people in the South and in the North. Southerners were very much involved in bringing about our American government: Washington, Jefferson, Patrick Henry and others. America has had fifteen presidents, Mother. Of these fifteen presidents - Washington, Jefferson, Madison, Monroe, Harrison, Tyler, and Taylor - were all Virginians. These men were elected and not just by southern voters. They were also elected by voters from the North.

"Yes, Mother, seven of our fifteen presidents were Virginians. Our country is not perfect. These men were not perfect, but they have given us something to build on - to become a more perfect union of states.

"We should not consider just the negatives. There are many positive factors to consider; and these positives are what have inspired me to go south to continue my education in Virginia. It's an opportunity to learn more about southern people, to meet them, to explore and to reconcile our differences."

"Oh, Robbie, there are differences; slave holding people who believe that owning another human is honorable and Christian and upright. How can you, my only son, my only child, even consider going to a Southern university? You have been raised to loathe the idea, the concept of slavery. You have heard both Robert and me condemn this practice. You have heard sermons from the church pulpit condemning the evils of human bondage.

The thought of arrogant southern slave owners living their debonair and aristocratic life style at the expense of Negro slaves riles me to no end. The slaves live in run down shacks and are forced against their wills to work from daybreak to nightfall for a meager food ration. It riles me into a frenzy."

"Mother, you are permitting yourself to greatly overemphasize the slavery issue in Virginia. Yes, there are slave owners, but most people are not involved in these matters. Education is the answer to most of society's problems, both North and South. Please let me go with your blessing. It would mean very much to me. And furthermore, Mother, separating people - North from South and vice versa - does not solve the problem. We need to know each other."

"Robbie, you are so young, and I know that you have always made the right decisions about everything. Please, please reconsider this matter very carefully. Do it for me, Robbie."

"Mother, I have thought about this matter very seriously. I truly believe it is best for me. We will discuss it again later. I am meeting some friends at the tavern. We are going to discuss our plans for after the July Fourth parade. I really must go."

"Is the Johnson girl going to be there?"

"Yes, Mother, Serena is included."

"Oh, wonderful. She is such a lovely girl."

"Yes, she is."

"Why don't you invite her to your birthday dinner?"

"Good idea, Mother. How about the rest of my friends?"

"I suppose it will be alright. Wouldn't you like to just invite the Johnson girl?"

Robbie is out the door and on his way without answering his mother. Overcome by self-pity and exasperation, Mary falls exhausted onto the couch. She is somewhat angry at Robbie; however, more so at Robert. "Why hasn't he supported me in my efforts to persuade Robbie to attend a Northern college?" she cries. "Why is he punishing me? What have I done to deserve this? I have done everything in my power to persuade Robbie to change his mind. Robert has said nothing - he has done nothing to support me or to dissuade Robbie. He is willingly supporting his son - our son - to go into that Southern den of iniquity where he may be influenced by perverse and sinful ways." Overcome with emotion and exhausted, she feels weak and all alone. Exasperated, she sits on the couch and drifts off to sleep.

The late afternoon sun is low in the sky when Mary awakens. She can hear Robbie and Robert talking, sharing a laugh as they unhitch the horse from the carriage. "How can they be so happy when my life is in shambles?" she moans. She hurriedly brushes the wrinkles from her clothes as she goes to meet them. It is nearly time for dinner.

As usual they are discussing Robbie's educational opportunities at the University of Virginia. It seems that the two of them discuss it endlessly. If one does not bring the subject up, the other does. Either Robert or Robbie seems to bring the University subject up whenever she is present. She wonders whether their ploy is to mention it often enough so that she will finally accept the inevitable. She murmurs to herself, "I'll resist to the bitter end. That Southern town with its Southern attitudes has nothing worthwhile to offer my son." She again murmurs to herself, "I don't care where Charlottesville and the University of Virginia are."

In truth, she knows the precise location of Charlottesville, Virginia. She has a very good geographical knowledge of the entire nation, both North and South. She is an astute and intelligent person, yet she has built mental barriers that resist Southern cultures and Southern ideals to the point that it has skewed and altered her sensibilities of anything related to the South. "Perhaps Robbie's exuberance can be attributed to his youth, but Robert is a grown, adult man," she again murmurs. "He has completely lost his senses. He is supporting and contributing to what will be the moral and social destruction of our only child." She again murmurs in self-pity to herself, "What on God's green earth could cause two male humans of supposedly exceptional intelligence to come to such a decision? It is absolutely mystifying, absolutely baffling." She again feels her anger rising, yet she well knows that this is not a solution to the problem.

She has argued and prayed against the decision for nearly a year, but to no avail. "There are plenty of good, no, plenty of excellent colleges in the North, some of them hardly a stone's throw from our home," she laments. "Colleges in New York City, Philadelphia, and Boston. Why not Harvard where his father graduated? Even West Point, a few miles downriver is more acceptable than a Southern university - even though it is a military school." She cringes at the thought of Robbie becoming a professional soldier. "Certainly many Northern colleges are within a day or two's journey from home." She again moans, "The idiotic decision of our son with the full support of his father has been made." It leaves Mary with a feeling of abandonment. She cannot for the life of her understand the two of them.

She had seen the decision coming. She subconsciously expected it. All the signs were there. They have actually been there for a long time. His fascination with the ideals of Thomas Jefferson began in the fourth or fifth grade. That fascination has never lessened over the years. It has, if anything, grown deeper and more intense as his knowledge of Jefferson increased. The die has been cast, her efforts tossed to the wind when Robert paid his entrance fee at the University of Virginia and arranged for his room and board at a Charlottesville boarding home. Robbie is developing independent attitudes. He is reaching for his own identity. It isn't that he is rebellious. He is quite the opposite. He is loving, caring and considerate, as he has always been. But he is no longer a little boy. He is reaching manhood, becoming his own person. It is time to spread his wings, time to try new things. Time for independence. It will never be the same again.

Mary reluctantly recognizes that she must let loose. She must face the inevitable. It is not going to be easy. It is going to take time. She is determined - for her own sake and the sake of Robbie and Robert; she will do it. The tears come. They are mixed tears; a combination of the sadness of what was past mixed with the uncertainties of the future, with a dash of joy and anticipation of a new beginning for the three of them. She concedes to herself that Robbie's future should be his own. If she cannot be happy for herself, she should at least be happy for him. She is determined to do the best she can for the rest of the summer, and when he leaves for Virginia he will go with her blessings. The love, the loss of closeness between mother and son and his presence in her life will leave a void that can never be replaced.

This time it must be different. She must exercise flexibility. She must make concessions. She, for the first time, lets herself think positively about Robbie's educational decision. She expresses an interest in Mr. Jefferson and the University of Virginia. Robbie is elated over his mother's change in attitude.

"Mother," he explains, "as you know, the brilliance of President Jefferson played a major part in the freedom that this country enjoys. He founded the University of Virginia. It is a great academic village with a superior national reputation.

"Mr. Jefferson's ideas, his concept for a university - was founded on different principles - on unique concepts that had never before been utilized in America. He set about to revolutionize the curriculum in America patterning it after the great universities of Europe. When Mr. Jefferson was Ambassador to France, he became fascinated by the European university educational system. After he returned to America he completed all of his political commitments, then went home to Monticello with the idea of establishing a new university. He was instrumental in designing and overseeing the physical implementation of the buildings and grounds in a quadrangle with the Rotunda at one end and open at the other. Mother, I can hardly wait to walk along The Lawn and gaze at the magnificent Rotunda which is based on the design of the Roman Pantheon. This structure is used as a library and lecture rooms. And on either side of the quadrangle are the Pavilions and Colonnades which house professors and some students.

"Mr. Jefferson had great confidence in the ability of students to regulate their own affairs. This proved to be unworkable and in 1842 it was replaced by an honor system which required students to sign a statement that they neither received nor gave advice to any other student enrolled at the University.

"Initially, Mr. Jefferson was appointed Rector of the University, and he was assisted in these responsibilities by two other former U.S. Presidents, James Madison and James Monroe.

"He wanted to be remembered for three things: one was authoring the Declaration of Independence, the second was authoring the Statute of Virginia for Religious Freedom and the third was for being the Father of the University of Virginia.

"I have chosen the University of Virginia because it is the best place to further my education. I sincerely seek your approval. I am impressed with Mr. Jefferson's accomplishments as president, with his contributions to society. Jefferson authored the Virginia Statute for Religious Freedom; he authored the Declaration of Independence when he was 22 years of age. He was a symbol of progressive American architecture, and a literary historian. He spoke seven languages, was a scientist and a gentleman farmer. He was an ambassador to France. He served two terms as governor of Virginia, and he was an inventor. His legacy will endure throughout history.

"Mother," Robbie continues, "with these attributes, with these credentials, the University of Virginia was founded by Mr. Jefferson in 1819, and the Jeffersonian principles were firmly imbedded in the tradition of the University's educational philosophy when its doors opened to students in 1825. Those traditions will always continue."

Mary is overcome with Robbie's maturity, with his enthusiasm. "Oh, Robbie," she happily cries, throwing her arms around him, "I do want you to be happy, but the thought of losing you haunts me."

"Mother," he replies with tears in his eyes, "you are not going to lose me."

In her heart Mary knows that Robbie has unlimited capabilities; that he has strength of character, that he is wise in many ways - wise beyond his years. She often marveled over his capabilities of comprehending things and events in a manner far beyond what would normally be expected of someone so young. Others also noticed these characteristics and had often spoken about them to both her and her husband. She knew that these comments were not attempts to flatter her; that they were made in sincerity, they were honest, forthright and spontaneous opinions of friends, acquaintances and oftentimes from total strangers.

She truly believes, and with good reason, that her son is a wonderful, capable and special young man; that he is blessed with many natural gifts, and that yes, she has made many contributions, unselfish contributions - toward the development and expansion of these natural gifts. She is proud of her efforts in Robbie's development. Yet she is very careful, very private, in the influences she has had on his young life. She is careful not to bore others with Robbie's accomplishments and capabilities. To do so, she reasons, would have an adverse effect on herself and on her son. This she will not do. These are private matters, not public affairs. She will forever hold them dear to her heart.

It is not going to be easy to give him up - not even temporarily. Four years away from home, away from her, will seem like a lifetime, even though he will have summers at home. It is a disheartening thought. "How will this change his life? How will it affect my life? How will it affect our relationship? Suppose he decides to marry and remain in the South after his education is complete, instead of returning home to assist his father in running the mill? What if the political storm clouds over the slavery issue between North and South erupt into war?" These are perplexing and worrisome problems.

Her mind wanders from things negative to things positive, from periods of near depression to periods of hope and optimism. She sincerely wants to feel positive for her own sake and for her son and her husband. Never has she gone through such turmoil. Never has she deviated or retreated from a course of action. It is time to face the realities of life. Robbie has always made the right choices; always done the right things. He has always been an excellent student and remarkable young man with considerable abilities. She can no longer be a stumbling block on the road to his successes. "Yes," she assures herself, "Robbie will do all right; he will be just fine."

Chapter Six

Love Sublime All Love Excelling

Serena Johnson always was Robbie's best friend. They met on the very first day of first grade, and they were inseparable thereafter. It was, at first, a simple childhood friendship - one of playing together, sharing lunches, doing homework. They climbed trees, swam in the cold waters of the nearby creek, played in the town park, and walked hand in hand on the town's main street. They did all of the things that young friends do together. Early on, Serena was a tomboy. That was just fine with Robbie. At that age, little boys do not much care for girly little girls, and girly little girls do not much care for mischievous and rowdy little boys. Anyway, Robbie never thought of Serena as a girl. She was simply his playmate, his best friend, his pal. That is just the way it was.

Their parents were amused over their children's companionship. Neither Robbie nor Serena seemed to sense a biological difference in the other. They were oblivious to their physical dissimilarities. Of course, as they grew older the differences became obvious to both of them. Even so, the "best of friends" friendship continued unaltered in the same manner that it had existed before. They were always together. Where one went, the other one went. Serena's tomboyishness vanished over a period of time and the pretty little roughneck girl became a beautiful, refined young lady. Changes were also evident in Robbie. He became an astute, sincere and handsome youngster. As strange, as mysterious as it may seem, their physical changes never seemed to faze them. It did not alter their feelings, their companionship whatsoever. Their close personal relationship remained precisely as it always had been.

It is not until the last day of eighth grade that they finally recognize that their relationship, their companionship, is maturing. They nevertheless remain as close, if not more so, than they were before. The change happens almost instantaneously - like a bolt out of the blue. It is a somewhat awkward awakening; a spontaneous happening that hits them both simultaneously. They are playfully teasing, pestering, laughing, and kidding each other, friendly jostling about, when their lips suddenly and accidentally meet. It is unplanned and unavoidable, but that is exactly the way it happens. She blushes, he blushes, faces crimson red, embarrassed, speechless.

But they know, they both know, that in that instant, at that moment, at that time, the old relationship - the childhood relationship - has passed away. It is the start of a new beginning. Boy meets girl, girl meets boy. For the first time in their young lives, they see each other differently. They know, even before a word is spoken, that it has happened. Even so, even though both are secretly overjoyed with the quick and unanticipated kiss, it is an awkward moment; and an awkward truth.

Finally the silence is broken. Serena giggles. Robbie giggles. Then she speaks ever so softly, "Why did you do that, Robbie?"

"Why did I do what?"

"You know what, Robbie."

"No, I don't. Tell me."

"Why did you kiss me?"

"I don't know, Serena. It just happened. But I'm glad it did. Are you angry?"

"Oh no, Robbie. I am glad it happened, too."

Holding Serena's hands, still facing one another, he sheepishly asks, "Want to do it again?"

"Maybe."

After the second kiss, still holding hands, he asks, "Serena, do you remember Mr. Baker's literature class last winter, when we were studying poetry? We were studying Robert Herrick, or rather his poetry."

"Robbie, we read a lot of poetry in Mr. Baker's class. I don't remember one poet from another, or what they wrote."

"Well, you should remember Robert Herrick. He lived during the late fifteen hundreds and the early sixteen hundreds. He was an Englishman, a Cambridge University graduate, and he wrote poetry about love. This is part of one of his poems; now listen.

'Give me a kiss, and to that kiss a score;
Then to that twenty, add a hundred more;
A thousand to that hundred, so kiss on
To make that thousand up, a million,
Treble that million, and when that is done,
Let's kiss afresh, as when we first begun.'"

Serena giggles. "I remember it now when you recite it. I think everyone in class was blushing. I was afraid to look at you."

They kiss once more, very quickly. After the kiss, she again speaks in a very serious tone of voice, "Are we in love, Robbie?"

"I suppose so," he replies after pausing momentarily to think about it. Then he says more seriously, "Yes, I am Serena. I know I am."

"And I am too, Robbie. Should we tell our parents?"

"I don't know, Serena. Parents can act funny and odd sometimes. Maybe we better not, at least not just yet. We need to think about it." The change in the relationship between the two of them does not need to be verbally communicated to their parents. As a matter of fact, it does not require verbalization to anyone in the community. Their parents seem to know almost immediately. At least the mothers do, and they inform the fathers. Friends notice it. Soon it is common knowledge and town gossip, although the gossip is not evil or ugly. It is simply entertaining. It is now a different relationship. She writes Robbie love notes in school, passing them secretly to him. He, too, writes endearing little love notes to Serena, transmitting them to her in the same secret fashion. Their attraction to each other grows stronger. They both know that if they are caught passing notes, they will be called to the front of the class and required to read the note aloud. That would be humiliating to both of them. Unbeknownst to them, their secret relationship is secret only to them.

Mary is not happy over the revelation of the changed relationship between the two youngsters, and she keeps a sharp eye on them. Yet she is hesitant to speak to either of them about the matter, waiting for one of them to broach the matter or for an opportune time to do so herself. A month goes by, and nothing is said to Mary by either Robbie or Serena. Robert is unconcerned about the matter, but Mary is antsy. She has tired of waiting for Robbie or Serena to say something about the matter. Finally, she decides that it is time to air the matter out.

It is Saturday morning, the maid's day off. Robert has left for the mill, Robbie has not yet come downstairs for breakfast. She fidgets around the kitchen waiting for him.

"Good morning, Mother." His voice startles her. She nearly drops the eggs she is about to fry.

"Oh, Robbie, you nearly scared the life out of me. I didn't hear you come in."

"Sorry, Mother," he responds as he walks across the kitchen and gently kisses her on the cheek. It is really just a peck on the cheek, hardly a real kiss at all. "Well," she responds, half teasing and half sincere, "I suppose that someone we know gets a much better kiss than that."

Robbie is caught off guard. His face reddens. He is momentarily flabbergasted. "What do you mean, Mother?"

"The neighborhood gossip is that you and Serena have become quite close."

"Mother, you always told me not to repeat gossip."

"Yes, I have always told you that, and it is good advice. I hope that you always remember it. I do not mean to engage in gossip, but the rumors about you and Serena are all over town. Every tongue-wagging woman in town, and half of the men, are talking about it."

"What are the rumors, Mother? We have not done anything wrong. Yes, we have kissed and hugged and we are very fond of each other. Is that a sin? A disgrace?"

"Oh, Robbie, you and Serena are so young, too young. I don't know what to say. I truly, truly like Serena. She seems to be a very nice young lady."

"Mother, she is nice. She is wonderful. I don't understand why everyone is talking about it. Is it wrong for a boy and a girl - for young people - to have strong feelings for each other? It wasn't something that was planned. It just happened."

"Well, you should have told me. I shouldn't have to find these things out through other peoples' gossip, although I had suspected something had changed between you two. Serena should have told me or she should have told her mother."

"It was not Serena's fault, Mother. She wanted to tell. I told her not to; that her mother - that her parents - wouldn't understand, neither would mine. I am totally to blame if there is anyone to blame."

When Robbie met Serena later in the afternoon, he related the conversation between him and his mother.

"Is she mad at me, Robbie? Oh, I hope not."

"No, she is not angry with you, but she is slightly miffed at me."

"What should I say when I come over to your house?"

"I don't know, but I'll think of something, Serena. The problem is what are you going to say to your mother."

"I am going to tell her exactly what has happened and that we have done nothing wrong. She has been asking a lot of questions anyway." Serena, facing Robbie, asks, "Do you still love me?"

"Of course I do, Serena. Why do you ask that question?"

"I want to be sure. Please go with me to tell Mamma."

Mrs. Johnson, Serena's mother, is very understanding when she is told of the initial kissing episode. Robbie, on the other hand, is extremely fidgety during Serena's explanation of how and what had happened.

"I believe you and I trust you, sweetie," she says to her daughter, then adds as an afterthought, "I believe and trust you too, Robbie. I think you are a fine youngster. I think you respect Serena. The two of you have been friends for a long time."

Speaking again to Serena, but unquestionably addressing both of them, she adds, "There is a lot that both of you need to know, and to learn, about life. Just don't rush into adulthood. It can wait."

Both Robbie and Serena are much relieved after the conversation with Serena's mother. "Wow," Robbie exclaims as they leave her home. "I was a little nervous in there."

"You were more than a little nervous. I thought you were going to faint," Serena responds.

"I would have been happy to faint. At first it was a dilemma between whether I should stay and face the music with you or whether I should dart out the door and run."

"Well, it's a good thing that you didn't. I would never have forgiven you." They both laugh.

They walk down the Main Street, hand in hand, passing and meeting neighbors. "You know what," Robbie says.

"What?" Serena responds.

"We should kiss right down in front of the Town Square."

"Let's do it," she responds.

"Yes, that will give people something to talk about, Serena."

She laughs as they skip off toward the Square, still hand in hand.

"Robbie, will you recite that kissing poem to me before we kiss?"

"Sure will - on bended knee."

They both laugh.

Chapter Seven

Signs of Promise, Signs of Fear

The summer of 1859 vanishes in a flurry of activity at the Holcomb place. It has been a whirlwind of coming and going all season long. The Holcombs, the three of them, have exercised a spirit of compatibility among and between themselves, each of them going out of their way to please the others. They indulge in personal pleasantries. Everything and anything that remotely borders on differences of opinion is avoided. Hospitality overwhelms hostility.

It is not that discord is commonplace in the Holcomb house; it is not. Nor is it a home where differences of opinion are avoided. It is not uncommon for feelings or opinions to sometimes rise to meet the occasion. Self expression of ideas and opinions are always aired freely. Differences are at times heartedly debated, although they seldom, if ever, get out of hand. As a family, the Holcombs are compatible, caring and considerate.

The warm days of summer are now past, having succumbed to an onslaught of cool early September mornings and long afternoon shadows. It is a sure harbinger of the coming of fall. Not a welcome sign to Mary Holcomb. Robbie's impending date of departure is fast approaching. The scheduled opening of the thirty-sixth session of classes at the University of Virginia is set for October first, where Robbie is registered as a first-year student. He plans to leave home two weeks early to allow sufficient time to become acclimated to the new surroundings and his new life.

Mary continues to harbor reservations about the wisdom of this venture, although the harshness and bitterness of her objections has mellowed considerably. She has reluctantly acquiesced to the matter, partly to keep peace in the family and partly because her objections have been fruitless. She sincerely wants harmony to prevail during the short time Robbie remains at home. There are many things left to do, and so little time to do them. Then there are the goodbyes. They will be the hardest of all.

Robbie has goodbyes to share with friends and family. Friends are on the agenda for the evening. He has discussed it with his father, but he forgot to mention it to his mother. He hurries off to tell her. "Mother, I will not be dining at home this evening. I am visiting friends in the village."

"Oh, is Serena Johnson going to be there? You've seen a lot of her lately. She is a lovely young lady."

"Yes, Mother, she is lovely and I am very fond of her. I am meeting her early for dinner and we are meeting the rest of the gang later. I want to tell her goodbye privately."

"Why didn't you invite her to dinner here tonight?"

"Mother, I wanted to have dinner - just the two of us. I wanted it to be private. Just Serena and me.

"Serena has always been my best friend. She always will be. She will be leaving for college a week after I do."

"Yes, I know. I was talking to Mrs. Johnson last week. She is as unhappy about Serena leaving as I am over your departure. Of course, Serena will not be very far from home. She is head strong just like you are, Robbie."

"Why do you say that, Mother? Neither of us are head strong as you say. We just know what we want to do. Serena told me about wanting to be a nun before she told her parents. Her priest knew before I did, but he was the only one that knew. She will be going to the Academy of the Sacred Heart in Purchase, New York, just outside of New York City. It's an all-girls religious college, owned by the Catholic Church."

"Maybe if. . ." Mary says, her voice drifting off and not finishing the sentence.

"Mother, I know what you are thinking. But it wasn't meant to be. Serena and I are extremely fond of each other and we do love each other very much. It's kind of like a brother-sister love. It is not a romantic love. We both are happy. She wants to teach poor children. She will be a teacher, not a housewife. She is dedicating her life to religious service. She will live in a convent, and she will be a wonderful blessing to all she ministers to, and to those she teaches. I am very proud of her, Mother."

"Where will you be having dinner?" Mary inquires.

"At the inn. It's sort of a going away get together. I know you understand." As an afterthought he adds, "I will be taking the horse."

"Did you ask your father?"

"Yes, Mother. I asked him this morning before he left for work. He said it would be alright."

"Why didn't you tell me of your plans earlier? You and your father have too many secrets," she says in a somewhat agitated voice.

"Oh, Mother, it was no secret. I just forgot to tell you earlier. Father reminded me before he left to tell you. It just slipped my mind. I'm sorry." He kisses his mother apologetically as he heads toward the door.

"Father is coming up the lane now. Goodbye, Mother." The door closes behind him as he anxiously runs to the stable.

"Will you be late, dear?" she shouts, but Robbie is already out of earshot. There is no answer. She smiles, happy that he is visiting friends, and especially that Serena will be there, although realizing that it is time that she will not have to spend with him.

She waits at the door to meet Robert. He greets her with a kiss and words of endearment. "How was your day?" he inquires as he drops wearily into the nearest chair.

Mary recites the events of her day, commenting in depth about every detail.

"Wonderful," he responds, unaware of what she has said or done.

"Wonderful yourself," she replies, then adds accusingly, but in a pleasant voice. "Robert Holcomb, you have not heard one word that I have said. I don't know why I bother to tell you things."

They engage in small talk, unimportant happenings during dinner. Afterward they sit in the parlor enjoying the solitude of the evening. They have not been alone for some time and the unbroken silence is relished. Robert, exhausted from the long day at the mill, cat naps. Mary sits quietly, not wanting to disturb her husband; her mind drifting hither and fro. As usual her thoughts settle on Robbie's fast approaching Southern sojourn. It is not something she wants to do. It is something she cannot help doing. The closer the time of Robbie's departure, the greater her preoccupation with it. She does not want to spoil the evening, the tranquility, the solitude. Even so, she can not rid her mind of the thought of Robbie leaving. Nor can she reconcile herself to the finality of the Southern education discussion. It is quite perplexing.

Mary scolds herself silently and hesitates momentarily before she speaks. "Robert, are you sleeping or are you awake?"

"I have not been sleeping. I have been dozing. Sort of cat napping. I have not slept soundly. Is there something on your mind, Mary?"

"No, not really. I was thinking about how quiet it is this evening. Don't you think so?"

"Yes, I suppose so," he answers. "It's always quiet when Robbie is out."

Mary hesitates momentarily then responds sharply. "Robert that is the point of my question. That is the whole problem. Robbie is going to be leaving in a few more days. We are going to have an abundance of silence around here. Silence is all we are ever going to have after Robbie is gone. You will be able to hear a pin drop. That's how quiet it is going to be."

"Mary," Robert replies sympathetically, "I realize it will be different when Robbie leaves; but it will be the same silence whether he goes to a Southern college or a Northern college. Silence is silence. There is no difference between Southern silence and Northern silence," he responds in a chiding voice.

"Oh, Robert, it would be a different silence if he were going to a Northern school. At least it would be a happy silence, a peaceful silence." Mary hesitates, then continues. "Robert, I am so frightened over this Southern education. I am frightened for Robbie, and for you and for myself. Can anything good come out of this?"

"Mary, you need to calm down. You are again making a mountain out of a molehill. You promised that you were going to let this Southern education issue die. The three of us agreed to it."

"Please believe me, Robert. I do not intend to again resurrect the old arguments. That issue has been settled. His tuition has been paid. So have his boarding house expenses. I have caused enough trouble over these matters. I am Robbie's mother. I love him and I cannot help being afraid. It is a mother's right to do so. I was hoping that everything would work out between him and Serena Johnson. She is such a lovely girl. I know he is very fond of her and she just worships him. Oh, why couldn't it happen?"

"Mary, you are punishing yourself. You are punishing me and you are punishing Robbie. I hope you are not trying to resurrect or encourage a romance between them. They both know what they want."

"Robert, I do not want to punish anyone. Not you, not Robbie, not Serena, and not myself. I am afraid of this silence as we sit here. I am afraid of the silence, of the long days and nights, the long weeks, and months, and years, that Robbie will be away. I detest the thought of silence. I am afraid of the rift - the political rift that seems to be widening between the North and the South. I am afraid of Southern influences. Robert, I am afraid of everything - everything Southern!!"

Mary is again near the point of hysteria. She wants to cry. Emotionally, she needs to cry, but she is determined not to yield to her physical and mental impulses. She refuses to permit herself this luxury. Robert recognizes the overwhelming anguish of Mary's frustration, the realness and sincerity of her fears. He feels her emotional pain, the distress and despair that are overwhelming her.

Robert embraces her. He holds her close - lovingly close. Her small lean body trembles with emotion. He feels her tears against his cheek. Silent tears - involuntary tears - that well in her eyes. But she refuses to let them go. Neither of them speak. He holds her ever so gently, caressing the nape of her neck, soothing her doubts and fears. He softly, tenderly responds, "Robbie is going to be alright. He is going to be just fine. We are going to miss him, Mary. We are going to desperately miss him and he is going to miss us. But we must let loose, you and I. We must let loose individually and together. We can help each other, Mary. We can lean on each other."

Mary interrupts, "But how about Robbie? Who is going to help him? Who is he going to lean on? He will be a thousand miles away from home. He doesn't know a soul. He is going to be homesick. I just know it."

"Mary, Robbie is seventeen years old. He is no longer a boy. He is a young man. You also forget that he has two distant cousins who teach at the University of Virginia. James Holcombe is a law professor, and his brother, Thomas, is the college librarian."

"Robert, you know as well as I do that Robbie does not know either of them. You don't even know them yourself. You have never seen them. Except for an occasional letter from them, you know nothing about them. Besides, they have that ridiculous 'e' at the end of Holcomb. They are probably part of the Southern aristocracy and will have little in common with Robbie. They probably own slaves." She pauses momentarily, then adds, "Besides, they might try to teach him those high minded ideas that slavery is an acceptable institution."

"Mary you are permitting your imagination to control you. It is leading you on a wild goose chase. Going to the University of Virginia is Robbie's choice. It is his dream and that is why I have supported him. This is what he wants to do. It is time for him to leave the nest, to spread his wings and to learn new things. He will become a better man, a better person, because of this educational experience. It is time for you to untie your apron strings."

Although Robert's reassurances relieve Mary's fears, she is not fully convinced of the wisdom of Robbie's decision. "I wish I had your confidence, Robert, but I don't. There are so many questions that are unanswered. I cannot help but think of them. What if he should fall in love with a southern girl? What if he should marry? What if war should break out between the North and South? There are so many 'what if's.' "

"Mary, dear, we do not live in a 'what if' world. We live in a day to day world. A world where we move along step by step. Sometimes we move by inches, sometimes by leaps and bounds; but we always move - sometimes backwards, sometimes forward. We need to let each day account for itself. We should account for it after it is over - not before it happens.

"What is that Biblical scripture that the Parson is always referring to? Something about not worrying about tomorrow, that the things of tomorrow will take care of themselves, or something to that effect? It's a good thought, a good lesson for us both. Don't you think so?"

"Yes, Robert, it is a good thought. I know that everything you have said is true; but that doesn't make it any easier. The pain is still there. So are the doubts. The pain and the doubts will always be there. They will be there until all of this is over and done with, until Robbie is home to stay. That is when I will stop worrying. I am aware that Robbie is quite mature for his age, and yes, I am aware that I need to let go of him - for his sake and for mine. This is the most difficult decision of my life. Robert, please believe me. I am not angry with you - or with Robbie - over this Southern education issue. I am disillusioned, I am dejected, but I do not hold you responsible. It is water over the dam. You very well know that I could never remain angry with you or him for any length of time."

"Nor I with you, Mary," he interjects.

"Robert, I do not mean to be critical. I know that you believe in your decision to support Robbie. I know you have every right to do so. But I am different. I cannot disguise my fears and doubts. I try - I really do. I try and then the doubts and fears come flooding, rushing back and I am completely inundated with those same fears and doubts. I have not told you, I do not even like to mention it. I am afraid that something dreadful - something terrible - is going to happen to Robbie. I am afraid that we are never going to see him again."

Each passing day seems to be shorter than the day before. They come and they vanish like dry leaves before a winter storm. Now it is Robbie's last night at home. The three Holcombs sit silently at the dinner table, the same thought on each of their minds. Each of them hesitant to broach the subject. Robbie looks at his mother. As their eyes meet he gently takes her hands and lovingly squeezes them. Tears fill their eyes as they sit silently. Robbie collects his thoughts as he waits for the sizable lump in his throat to subside. He needs to address the issue of his leaving. It is on both of their minds. The task is not easy. Finally, the words come. At times in a controlled, thoughtful manner, at times with much emotion, but always with complete sincerity.

"Mother, please do not cry. I am going to go away for a while. It may seem like a long time to us now, but it will pass quickly. I will be home summers and I will write to you regularly. I love you dearly, you and Father. In thought and purpose we will never be far apart.

"I shall forever cherish the love, faith, and compassion that I have been taught in this household by you and by Father. Mother, I do not profess to be a man. Neither do I admit to being a boy. I am, however, more of a man than I am a boy. I tell you this to ease your mind, to make this transition easier for the three of us."

"Oh, Robbie, you are a boy. You are just a boy," she laments through a flood of tears. Robert rises from his chair, stands behind Mary gently caressing her arms and shoulders while fighting back at his own emotions. Robbie continues to gently hold her hands.

"Mother, please. Please let me finish. It will make it easier for the three of us tomorrow. My time at home is temporarily ending. It is a difficult time for each of us. But there are things I need to say. Things that come from the depth of my soul, from the bottom of my heart.

"I have been blessed beyond measure to have shared seventeen years of life with you. The things that the two of you have taught me will never be forgotten. I shall always live by those standards - by those rules that I have been taught in this household. I hold them dear to my heart, I deeply cherish the principles of equality for all people - man, woman and child - as both of you do. I believe in the Jeffersonian principles of life and liberty. That is why my educational goals are centered on, are fixed on, attending the University of Virginia. Mother, that is why I must go; that is what I must do.

"Mother, please do not blame Father for this decision. It was mine and mine alone. Yes, he supported my decision, and I am grateful for it. But my decision would not have been altered, my hopes and dreams would not have changed if he had not supported me. I would never be happy at any other college or university - North or South. I simply must attend Mr. Jefferson's university. You could have refused to provide my financial resources, but it would never have quenched my thirst for the choice of attending 'Mr. Jefferson's University.' This is my passion. This is my hope."

Robbie's parents, saddened as he began to speak, sat attentive until he finishes. They are seldom surprised at his wisdom and maturity. They are, nevertheless, awestruck with his explanation. They found themselves nodding in agreement to his remarks and occasionally wiping away a happy tear.

"It will be easier tomorrow," Mary agrees.

"It will be much easier." Robert adds his approval with a broad, understanding smile. Much of the tension that had developed over the past several weeks vanishes like a snowflake in July. They are a close-knit, happy and compatible family.

Chapter Eight

The Long Journey

It is near mid-day when the Holcombs awaken. They sleep late enough but hardly long enough. Robbie's farewell dinner and the family discussion the night before had continued late into the night. Much had been accomplished. A better understanding of the matters at hand has developed and family harmony is reunited. It is a wonderful beginning for the day of Robbie's departure. His time of departure is hours away.

Last minute packing remains undone. Parental instructions have not been fully vocalized and those departing good-byes seem as if they are far off in the distance. The three of them are rushing here and there, first in one direction, then in another, each one in each other's way. Nevertheless, good humor abounds throughout the confusion. Mary is in a motherhood tizzy. Everything has to be packed in its proper place. Things that Robbie will need for the next nine months have to be accounted for. She is satisfied - if not totally happy - for the first time in months, irrespective of Robbie's departure. Her new attitude change brings about an upbeat atmosphere to the two most important men in her life.

Robert, pleased with Mary's new found enthusiasm, jokingly chides her. "If you pack anything else for Robbie to take, the boat is going to sink before it leaves the dock."

"If you will help me to get these things together instead of just standing there, you wouldn't have time to criticize," she pleasantly responds.

"Keep a stiff upper lip," he teasingly answers.

She quips back, "And you too."

Packing is completed and they are ready to go. A four day journey to Charlottesville and the University of Virginia lay ahead for Robbie. "It's going to be a long trip, dear," Mary says as she looks directly at Robbie, then continues. "You'll be in New York City by noon tomorrow. The paddle wheeler will probably keep you awake half the night as it churns the water going downriver. Then you catch the train. How many different trains do you change to before you get to Charlottesville?"

"Three I believe. I'll not have any problems," he responds. "I'll be alright, Mother."

"Do you have your tickets, dear?"

"Yes, Mother, I have them."

"Please don't lose them. And watch out for pickpockets. Don't talk to strangers either."

"Mother, I am not a kid. I'll be all right, please don't worry yourself to death. Mother, if I don't talk to strangers, I won't have anyone to talk to."

"Well, be careful anyway," she responds.

Robert stands silently by, smiling as Mary gives her on-going instructions. When she finishes, he interjects. "Mary, if you are confident that everything is ready, I'll fetch the horse and carriage." He hurries to the stable without waiting for a reply. He is back within a matter of minutes. "Robbie, give me a hand with loading your luggage. The boat is at the dock and the Captain likes to leave at the exact departure time. He plans to leave on time irrespective of whether all the passengers are on board. His primary business is hauling freight and those are the customers he caters to. If you miss the boat, it will be another week before he is back."

"I have fixed Robbie a sandwich. He has time to eat it before we leave," Mary shouts. "Anyway the Captain is not going to leave without Robbie and you know it. He has waited often enough for you. As much business as the mill provides to him, he is not going to do anything to jeopardize that. Do you want a sandwich, Robert?"

"Not now, dear," he responds.

The carriage is packed, the sandwich eaten, and they head downhill toward the town and the river. All are aware that it will be their last trip together for a long time. Their jovial attitudes become somber, the only sound is the horse's hooves on the hard dusty road. Not even the sound of a breeze breaks the silence. Robbie's going away is not going to be easy. No one really expects it to be. Last night's family get-together made great strides in soothing Mary's apprehensions and doubts and today has been remarkably pleasant. She is making a gallant effort to consider the bright side of this departure. She thinks about his education, about his enthusiasm for the University of Virginia. She cannot verbalize her thoughts. The words fall silently in her mind.

"Is Serena meeting us at the dock, Robbie?" Mary asks, "Or did you tell her your final goodbye yesterday afternoon?"

"We had our goodbyes in the afternoon, but she is going to meet us at the dock."

As they approach the dock, Serena is waiting. "Hi, Mrs. Holcomb; hi, Mr. Holcomb." She greets them with hugs. She and Robbie embrace in a long hug. There are tears in both their eyes.

"I have been waiting nearly a half hour for you. I believe the Captain is anxious to go. You better hurry."

As Robbie's baggage is checked and loaded, the passenger boarding horn sounds. Robbie turns to his parents. He holds his mother tight - a bear hug embrace. He kisses her lovingly. "Mother," he says, "I love you dearly. I will miss you more than you can possibly know. I will miss you both. I have been privileged to have wonderful, loving and caring parents. You both have taught me many things. You have made me aware of life's greatest values and I cherish your concern and determination for others. Your life commitments will be my life commitments."

He turns to Serena. "And I will always love you. You will always be dear to me."

"Oh, Robbie, you are the hardest part of my commitments to give up; but I must do what I am called to do. My heart is breaking, but all the pieces belong to you. You are my one and only love - it will never end."

Tears fill Mary's eyes. Her heart is breaking - but she does not cry. She does not want to spoil the wonderful day the three of them are spending together. She wants to speak, to respond to her son's earnest comments, but words will not come. She stands mute; if the words come the tears will follow.

"It's all right, Mother. It's all right to cry."

Through sadness and despair she lets go. "Robbie, I love you so much. I am heartsick to see you go; but I know that you must." She can no longer contain her feelings; the tears come; she and Serena desperately cling to one another.

"Mother," Robbie says as bravely as he can summon his voice to cooperate, "you and Serena are my great loves, you will always be. We are going to miss each other. I will write often - every day when time permits

- but I will think about you always. Mother, I will only be one letter away and I'll be home in nine months for the entire summer. Nine months is a short time." Tears well in Robbie's eyes - not because he is leaving, but out of the love and compassion he feels for his mother and Serena. He looks away momentarily, in an effort to regain his manly composure.

Robbie continues to hold his mother and Serena with one arm as he reaches to embrace his father with the other. The four of them stand motionless, silently embracing one another. "I'll write often," he repeats for his father's benefit, "and I'll write to you, Serena, when I get your school address."

The Captain, having paused as long as he can, signals the pilot to sound the final boarding call.

"You better go now, son. The Captain is getting anxious," Robert cautions.

"Yes, I know."

He embraces his mother and Serena again and gives his dad a manly hug. "This is it. Father, take good care of Mother. Mother, take good care of Father. I'll see you both next summer. I'll see you next summer, too, Serena, if you are home from school."

Robbie turns to board the boat just as the Holcomb Mill whistle gives a three blast salute, followed by the company employees giving him a rousing round of applause. He has earned their respect and admiration through hard work at the mill, not just because he is the boss's son. He pauses, faces the employees who are standing and waving from every window on the river side of the mill, then he returns their salute with a wave of his hand. He turns again toward the ship and goes aboard.

"Some send off, son," remarks the Captain. Robbie nods, fearful to acknowledge the Captain verbally. His pent up emotions would rush forth in a flood of tears and embarrassment if he attempted to speak.

As the ship moves away from the dock, the mill whistle sounds one long, final, mournful farewell in tribute to his departure. Robbie is very touched by the employees' display of affection. "Leaving home is not an easy task," he murmurs to himself.

Although they cannot hear him because of the noise of the paddle wheeler, he calls to his friends, "Farewell, farewell good friends and family. I shall long remember you."

Robbie stands silently near the ship's stern waving to his parents, to Serena, and to his friends as the paddle wheeler heads downriver. He watches as his parents' and Serena's silhouettes become smaller, until they disappear in the distance. He watches as the Holcomb Mill and the town and the Holcomb house on the hill vanish from sight. The past is behind, the future lies ahead.

He remains standing at the same place for a long time. He continues to look upriver toward the town and the people and his family. He has fond memories of what is past, but he is not sad. Neither is he homesick. He has no regrets about what is past. He will treasure it always. Now he is alone. Alone with his hopes and his dreams, and his thoughts, and his anticipation for the future.

He watches as the last glimmer of sunlight fades, then disappears behind the western hills. He watches as the moon appears in the eastern sky. He watches the moon-beams dance and frolic in the wake of the paddle wheel as they move farther away from the past, rushing onward toward the mysteries and excitement of the future. He stands traumatized and alone with his dreams.

The late September evening, in consort with the river and the night, brews a crisp cool wind. He feels the chill penetrate his skin, a call to his senses that day is done. Tomorrow his boat trip will end at New York City, then on by train towards his final destination. Once again he turns and looks upriver toward home. There are no tears. He is ready for his cabin and a good night's sleep.

Chapter Nine

The Journey's End

Robbie's southbound journey is nearing its end. He arrives in the nation's capital on the third morning after his departure from home. Tomorrow afternoon the journey will end in Charlottesville, destination: the University of Virginia. He is elated. The long boat trip down the Hudson River and the long train ride from New York City to Virginia will be over. Bedford Springs and his former home on the hill above town seem worlds apart from the present.

Time and distance are beginning to separate the past from the future. He is optimistic and eager to get on with his life, with his education. He welcomes the opportunities and the challenges that he will soon encounter at Mr. Jefferson's Academic Village.

Robbie had never before been to Washington. He had studied about it in school; he had seen pictures of many of its important buildings, but this is his first time in the nation's capital. As he stands before the United States Capitol, seeing it in person for the first time, he is awestruck. A feeling of pride and patriotism swells within him. He stands quietly, looking at this magnificent structure, spellbound over its beauty, over the awesome power and authority that originates through the members of the Congress working within its walls. There is much to see and less than half a day in which to see it.

He wanders the halls of the Capitol. He wanders the streets. He watches men in suits gathering in small groups, seemingly discussing things of great importance. "Probably congressmen conducting the government's business and discussing things of great importance," he muses to himself with a boyish faith in the ability and desire of politicians to put the business of government, and of the people, ahead of political and personal matters.

He marvels at the contrast between the people of Washington and those of New York City, where people were coming and going in all different directions all at the same time, never stopping, always gesturing, always talking. The scene in the nation's capital seems to be the exact opposite. Different cities, different people, different objectives, but all Americans, all united, all of one spirit, he thinks to himself. Both are good American cities. "Charlottesville will be no different," he presumes.

Robbie arrives in Charlottesville on the afternoon train. Unlike the send-off when he left Bedford Springs, where nearly half the town had bid him Godspeed, there is no one to greet him. Not that he expected a reception, nor does he want one. It is, after all, good to be on his own. He does not know a soul and no one knows him. His future lies ahead, not behind him. He stacks his luggage, the only reminder of his past, next to the empty train station. Robbie turns quickly at the sound of a man's voice.

"Son, do y'all need some hep wit yer belongins? I kin tak ya whar whar ever yer goin' if ya got a doller."

Robbie looks the man over quizzically before responding, somewhat startled by his accent. He is black as coal, with a stubble of whiskers on his chin. He is wearing bib overalls and a red shirt, threadbare at the elbows. Even so, his clothes appear clean. He is shorter than Robbie, although he has very large hands; hands, from their appearance, that have been accustomed to hard work. His close-cropped hair is nearly white. A broad smile - almost too large for his face - is full of friendliness. "Do you have a buggy? I have quite a bit of luggage as you can see."

"Yes Sir, son. Ah kin handle yer luggage. Whar ya be goin'?"

"I'm going to Mrs. O'Riley's rooming house. Do you know where it is?"

"Sho' do. Is that whar y'alls a'goin?"

"That's where I'm going. How much did you say you wanted to take me there?" Robbie asks.

"I guess ah kin take ye fo a half-doller."

Robbie smiles and hands the man a dollar. "Let's go," he says.

"Son, ah ain't got no change, and that's the honest truth."

"You don't need change; the dollar is yours."

"Son," the man says, "Ya talk funny, but ah like y'all anyhow. Are ya one of them college boys?"

"Yes, I guess I am. At least I will be in a few weeks."

"Well, son, you'll be stayin' at a mighty fine place at Widder O'Riley's, an' she got a purty daughter. A mighty purty daughter, but she don't hanker much to college boys - sez thar smart alecs."

"That's fine with me. I'm here to go to school, to get an education. I'm not interested in her daughter."

The man chuckles. "Son, y'all ain't seen 'er yet. Just y'all wait an' see. Yesiree bob, jus ya wait an' see."

"The name is Robbie, Sir, not Bob," he answers, unaware that the man is not referring to his name.

Mrs. O'Riley comes to the door when Robbie knocks. He removes his cap and extends his right hand in greeting. "Mrs. O'Riley, I'm Robbie Holcomb from New York."

"Yes, Mr. Holcomb. I've been expecting you. I hope you had a good trip down from New York," she says as they shake hands. "Come in and make yourself comfortable. We want you to feel right at home here. We think of our guests as family. However, we do have house rules. I believe I mailed you a copy some time ago."

"Yes ma'am, you did. I read them. So did my parents. You won't have any trouble with me."

"Thank you, Mr. Holcomb," she responds. "Would you mind bringing your luggage in? Your room is the first door on the left at the top of the stairs. Classes at the University do not start for another two weeks, so we have not yet hired extra help. I hope you understand."

"Oh, yes ma'am, I do. I'll move my things on up to my room."

As Mrs. O'Riley hurries to the kitchen, she calls back to Robbie, "You might want to open a window and let some fresh air into your room. It gets a little warmer on the second floor. You can see out over the University Grounds from your window. It's one of the best views from our house. I thought you might like it."

"Thank you, Mrs. O'Riley. I know it will be just fine."

"If you want to sit in the parlor and rest after you have moved in, please do so. It's very comfortable."

Robbie is exhausted after several trips up and down the stairs. His luggage is in his room and he will have plenty of time to put things away later. He is happy to accept Mrs. O'Riley's offer to relax in the parlor. He barely settles into a comfortable chair when footsteps sound on the front porch. He sees her just as she opens the door; her silhouette in the late afternoon sunlight is stunning. She is absolutely gorgeous. Is this the daughter of Mrs. O'Riley that the carriage driver spoke about on the way from the train station? he wonders.

She is momentarily startled, surprised that a young man is sitting in the parlor. She is certainly a beautiful girl. Her long blond hair dances lightly in the soft afternoon breeze, a halo-like reflection from the afternoon sunlight glimmers in the shadows. Her eyes are a lovely green.

Robbie is stunned. His head spinning, he is speechless. Thoughts of his conversation earlier in the day with the man that brought him from the train station comes rushing back. Something is happening. He can't speak, he can't think. His knees trembling, he is perspiring. He stands when she comes through the door, mechanically, from habit, rather than from a mental reaction. His mother taught him good manners and the lifelong habits have come to his rescue. However, the greater his effort in attempting to speak, the lesser is his ability to do so. He is mortified.

She, too, has not spoken. Not because of an inability to do so. She is simply caught by surprise, startled by the presence of a stranger in the parlor. She blushes, and, regaining her composure, realizes that he is an early student arrival. She walks over to him. "Hi. I'm Mollie K, Mrs. O'Riley's daughter. Are you one of our new boarding students?"

Robbie nods affirmatively, reaches for her hand, and finally manages a half-stuttering "yes." They shake hands for a longer-than-usual length of time. "Yes," he again replies. "I am Robbie Holcomb from New York. I just moved in. Your mother said it would be alright if I sat here in the parlor and rested. I'm sorry if I alarmed you."

He continues to hold her hand. She says nothing, realizing that he is embarrassed. Although she is uncomfortable, she does not make an attempt to withdraw her hand. She does not want to further embarrass him. He tries to say something, anything, but he is speechless. He is totally embarrassed.

Robbie continues to hold Mollie K's hand, unaware that he is doing so; she does nothing to encourage him. She is aware that he is tall and handsome. She is not, however, taken aback by his appearance. She has seen more than her share of handsome young male University students since her mother converted their home into a boarding house. All had been from well-to-do Southern aristocratic families. They often maintained an air, a sense of their own social superiority. She and the other boarding house workers, including her mother, were the commoners and the servants of their masters. Not that the students' attitudes bothered her; their self-centered arrogance was actually amusing. Nevertheless, she had no desire to be a pawn in the love life of a lonesome and homesick student. She had always been polite to the students, but she never felt a romantic attraction to any of them.

She avoids eye contact. He continues to look at her, marveling at her composure. Both of them are embarrassed, both are blushing. Robbie is grateful for the humility and maturity that she is showing. She certainly does not want to embarrass him.

Mrs. O'Riley enters the parlor and is somewhat surprised to see the two of them standing together. "Mollie K, dear, I see that you have met Mr. Holcomb. He is one of our new boarding students. He will be attending the University during this coming session. He's from up North, from New York."

"Yes," Robbie breaks in, finally in control of his speech and mental faculties. "I wish to be called Robbie. Not Mr. Holcomb." He again reaches for Mollie K's hand. She smiles and they again shake hands as if they had not done so earlier. Neither of them mentions the earlier embarrassing moments. He feels comfortable that the experience will not be mentioned by Mollie K. It is over and forgotten. They both smile.

Mrs. O'Riley quickly interjects, "Mr. Holcomb, remember the house rules require that our guests are always to be referred to as 'Mr.' This rule applies to me and to Mollie K, the same as it does to other workers here at our house."

"Mrs. O'Riley, if I must be addressed as 'Mr.,' I would prefer to be called 'Mr. Robbie;' 'Mr. Holcomb' seems so formal and strange."

The three of them look at one another, then all laugh at the absurdity of his suggestion. Mrs. O'Riley, struggling to retain her composure, responds, "If you sincerely desire to be addressed as Robbie, it may be just as well if we drop the 'Mr.' altogether."

The three of them again laugh. Robbie muses to himself that his good fortune or luck, that has been with him throughout his life, must surely have followed him South.

Mollie K has been holding a basket of apples on her left arm the entire time she has been in the parlor, some five minutes or so. As she switches it to her right arm, Robbie notices the basket for the first time.

"Please let me carry the basket, Mollie K. Your arm must be nearly broken. I apologize for my lack of manners. I should have noticed it when you came through the door. I don't know what came over me. It is inexcusable."

Mollie K smiles and hands Robbie the basket. "It was getting quite heavy, but I am alright," she responds. "Please take the apples to the kitchen. Mamma will show you where to put them. The kitchen is through the door at the back of the dining room."

"Yes, I know," Robbie replies. Their eyes meet momentarily. He again experiences the same feelings that overcame him in the parlor. This time they are much milder and he silently scolds himself for being foolish. He turns toward the kitchen.

"Robbie," she says, then hesitates. "Thanks, thanks a lot." She is not aware that he is attracted to her. He feels the same weakness in his knees, the same accelerated heartbeat in his chest. "It's probably the after-effect of the long trip South," he tells himself as he enters the kitchen.

"Mrs. O'Riley, I have brought the apples in for Mollie K. Where shall I put them?"

"On the table over by the wall," she replies, pointing to the other side of the kitchen. "I'm going to bake apple dumplings for Mollie K. It's her favorite dessert. I love to do special little things for her. Do you like apple dumplings?"

"I don't believe I have ever eaten them. Are they something like apple pie?"

"Yes, its something like apple pie, but a lot better."

"It sounds good, Mrs. O'Riley."

"Oh, Robbie, they are absolutely delicious. Why don't you join Mollie K and me for supper tonight? You can go to your room, unpack your belongings, rest a bit from your long train ride and come down to supper. You are our first student border from up North. It will give us all an opportunity to better know one another."

Robbie is aglow over the invitation, yet he feels that he has weaseled the invitation through the series of questions he has asked Mrs. O'Riley. He hesitates momentarily, wanting desperately to accept the invitation. On the other hand, he does not want to interfere with their dinner plans.

"I very much appreciate the dinner invitation and your hospitality. I thank you for your kindness, but I do not want to interfere with the personal time that you and Mollie K have together."

Mollie K has entered the kitchen just as Robbie is declining the invitation. "Please join us for supper. We would love to have you as our guest. Besides, Mamma is fixin' my favorite dessert, apple dumplings. Everybody loves them."

This is an invitation he cannot decline, not from Mollie K. His heart pounds with joy. He has never been so happy in his entire life. "Yes, yes, I accept the dinner invitation. I know that I will like the apple dumplings, too. Is there anything I can do to help?"

Mollie K replies, "You can help me wash the dishes after supper," then she quickly adds in a teasing voice, "I bet you have never washed dishes – never, ever washed them, have you?"

Robbie's face is a crimson red. "No, I have not," he answers somewhat sheepishly. "Mother has housekeepers to assist with the chores, but I will be glad, no, I will be honored to help you with the dishes."

"I'll wash and you dry," she says.

"Agreed," he quickly replies. They both laugh.

"Want to know how I knew that you had never washed dishes before?" she asks.

"I suppose so; how did you know?"

"Because rich folks always say dinner for the evening meal and us poor folks always say supper. Rich folks always pay somebody to do their dishes and poor folks wash their own. I heard you say dinner, and that's how I knew. But its okay if you say dinner, 'cause you're not snobbish like most rich people."

Robbie smiles. "Mollie K, we are not rich. We just say dinner up North. It's simply a Northern custom. Besides, I have worked at our family garment mill. I have done plenty of hard work, even dirty work at times."

"Then you wash and I'll dry," she says kiddingly.

"Either way," he replies, then asks, "Mollie K, what is the 'K' for in your name? Is it for the name 'Kay', spelled K-A-Y, or is it short for Kathryn?"

She pauses, a sad look on her face. He is afraid she is going to cry. Turning away she responds, "It doesn't stand for anything. I do not have a middle name. It's something my daddy added to my name, just the letter 'K'. That's what he called me. Sometimes he just called me 'K'; sometimes he called me 'Mollie K', but he never called me 'Mollie' without using the 'K'. Now Daddy is gone. He's dead. I never want anyone to say my name without the 'K'. It's for him, for my Daddy."

Robbie feels terrible. He knows she is near the point of tears. He wants to take her in his arms, but he is afraid to do so, afraid that if he embraces her, his purpose, his intent in doing so might be misunderstood. "Mollie K, I am sorry, I am terribly sorry. Please believe me."

"It's alright, Robbie. You needn't feel bad. It's not your fault." Mollie K turns and faces him. The sadness is gone. She is smiling again. "Better freshen up for supper . . . for dinner," she adds with a giggle. "The apple dumplings are best when they are served hot with fresh cream. You better hurry."

"I won't be late and I know I will like the dumplings." He is nearly to the kitchen door when he turns. "I want to reciprocate with a dinner invitation to both of you just as soon as I find the best inn in Charlottesville." Then he quickly adds, "Other than here, of course. It'll be the second best place to eat in Charlottesville."

"Robbie," Mollie K responds, "we don't call public places that serve food and drinks inns. They are called 'ordinaries' in the South."

"I'll try and remember that," he responds.

"It's a good thing you added that afterthought," Mrs. O'Riley calls after him.

Robbie is overjoyed as he bounds up the stairs, two at a time. He could not be happier than he is at the moment.

Chapter Ten

A Strange Beginning

The First University Year
1859 - 1860

The thirty-sixth session of classes at the University of Virginia opens as scheduled on the first day of October, 1859. Robbie Holcomb arrives at the Rotunda early, as do most of the more than 600 students who are enrolled for classes. The student body, as expected, is predominantly Southern; only fifteen students are from Northern states, a decidedly small minority.

Irrespective of the overwhelming Southern student majority, the University vigorously maintains a non-sectional, nonpolitical atmosphere by official policy on all University property. The University Board of Visitors and the University professors are cognizant of the sectional disparities between the North and South and are always alert to prevent a hostile classroom environment. Although the doctrine of sovereign states' rights is subscribed to policy-wise, and accepted privately among many of the professors and administrators, there is little, if any, sentiment for disunion of the two sections of the United States.

Northern students, Robbie included, refrain from engaging in north/south discussions of a constitutional nature outside the classroom, preferring to familiarize themselves with knowledgeable discussions in a classroom atmosphere. The legal differences are best left to the authorities in the field of constitutional law.

Robbie is fortunate that a distant cousin, James P. Holcombe, is a professor of constitutional law at the University. He is privy to much of the legal arguments and interpretations from his cousin. Another cousin, Thomas, a brother of James, is the University librarian. Access to the knowledge of these two cousins is invaluable to Robbie as he becomes acquainted with the rigors of college life.

The two weeks in Charlottesville prior to the beginning of classes has afforded Robbie an opportunity to become acquainted with his two cousins. He is curious that their last name, pronounced the same as his, has the letter "e" added at the end.

"Why," he asks them during an afternoon discussion, "did the Southern relatives add the 'e' at the end of their name?" Professor Holcombe chuckles as he responds, "We did not add an 'e'; it was you Northerners that dropped it." He then says that some family members preferred to add the "e" in the pronunciation of their name. "A little French flair. It gives a distinct European polish or aristocratic distinction to the name."

Robbie never pursues the matter further. "I suppose a Holcombe is a Holcomb, regardless of how we spell it or how we pronounce it, don't you think so?"

"You hit the nail right on the head, Robbie," offers Thomas.

The first two weeks of college life go exceptionally well for Robbie. He studies hard, keeps up with his assignments and spends the weekends preparing lessons for the upcoming week. He expected college to be tough, and he intends to work hard at it. Monday, October seventeenth, he does not attend classes. His classes for the day are cancelled.

He awakens early Tuesday morning, dresses and heads for class. The University Grounds are a mass of people. As he approaches them, everyone seems to be excited. People are speaking loudly, waving their arms and assembling in groups of varying sizes. The groups seem to be discussing something of great importance. One or two people in the groups seem to be leading the discussions and the others, those listening, seem to be highly agitated. Curiosity gets the better of Robbie as he approaches one of the groups. Some of the listeners are shaking their fists, cursing and shouting threats against someone or something.

"What's going on?" he asks. "What is happening with all of these people acting as if pandemonium has broken loose?"

"It's worse than pandemonium," says one of the student leaders. "Haven't you heard the news?"

"What news?" replies Robbie. "I just got here. I have no idea what's going on."

The student, looking at Robbie in disbelief, asks, "You haven't heard about John Brown? You don't know about him? What he has done?"

"I don't know who John Brown is, and I have no idea what he has done."

"John Brown is a Northern abolitionist. A rabble-rouser from Kansas or Maryland or someplace up North. He's the leader of a group of men, a small army of trouble-makers, murderers, who attacked and captured a federal arsenal at Harpers Ferry, Virginia. They killed several people in the attack."

"Why did they attack the government arsenal? What do they want?"

"The federal government has 20,000 rifles and large supplies of ammunition stored there. John Brown intends to liberate the slaves. He intends to arm them and to start a war between whites and blacks. He's a religious fanatic."

"How do you know that? How do you know that it's true?"

"It's true alright. A telegram came through earlier this morning. Brown attacked the arsenal late Sunday night; two nights ago, October sixteenth."

Robbie interrupts the speaker. "If it happened Sunday night, why are we just hearing about it today?"

"Because Brown and his men cut the telegraph lines at Harpers Ferry Sunday night before they attacked the arsenal. There wasn't any way that anyone could know what was going on. Not even the federal government knew what was happening. The governor of Virginia did not know either."

"When did the government find out about what Brown is doing?"

"If you'll quit asking questions for a minute, I'll tell you what we know. It appears that some of Brown's men captured a Baltimore and Ohio train Sunday night when it stopped at Harpers Ferry. They killed a black man who worked for the railroad and they wouldn't let the train leave. They kept the train and its passengers there until sometime Monday morning, then they let the train go on its way. Government officials didn't know what was going on until late Monday evening when the train reached Baltimore, Maryland. The conductor called federal officers."

The speaker continues, "The government sent an army colonel - a man named Robert E. Lee and one of his military aides, J.E.B. Stuart - and eighty or ninety U.S. Marines up to Harpers Ferry to quell the Brown uprising. Apparently, the local citizens at Harpers Ferry and men from other small towns in the area had armed themselves and rose up against Brown and his marauders. Brown captured a few local citizens, one of them a descendent of George Washington, and holed up in the arsenal. The citizens apparently have Brown and his men surrounded. Brown is using the captured citizens as hostages. There has, from all reports, been bloodshed on both sides and several deaths."

Robbie interrupts the student. "What has been heard from Colonel Lee and the Marines? What are they doing?"

"We haven't heard anything more this morning. We are waiting for further news from the telegraph office."

"Thanks," replies Robbie. "Could you tell me where Harpers Ferry is located?"

"It's a small Virginia town in the Shenandoah Valley, up near the Maryland border. It's at the junction of the Potomac and the Shenandoah Rivers. It's quite some distance from here, probably no more than fifty miles from Washington."

"Just one more question, please. Is the rebellion spreading? Does it appear to be a general uprising?"

"No one seems to know at this time what exactly is going on or what's going to happen. You can bet one thing, though. It's the work of Northern abolitionists. You can bet that Brown didn't do this on his own." The student looks closely at Robbie. "Aren't you one of the students from up North?"

"Yes," replies Robbie, "but I do not know anything about John Brown."

"I hope not, for your sake," the student says.

Excitement and bitterness against Brown and his men runs high as news of the raid spreads throughout the University area. Students, faculty and local residents congregate around the University Grounds throughout the day. The University administration circulate warnings that violence or civil disturbances of any kind will not be tolerated. Classes are not cancelled, although very little is accomplished academically during the day. By mid-morning, when many students are not attending classes, the University administration announces that telegraph service will be provided during the remainder of the day to keep rumors and speculation under control.

By early afternoon, news of the John Brown raid is again coming across the telegraph wires. Students, faculty, and concerned citizens of the area gather near the Rotunda awaiting the arrival of the telegraph dispatcher. A makeshift platform is erected so that the news can be disseminated to the large gathering of people. Their wait is short.

The dispatcher mounts the platform. "Ladies and gentlemen, if you will give me your attention." He waves his arms furiously, asking for silence. A hush falls over the crowd. "Thank you. I will speak as loudly as possible. I am here to give you the latest news on the John Brown situation. Please refrain from interrupting me. If there are questions afterward, I will try to answer them."

"Get on with the news. That's what we are here for," someone impatiently shouts from the crowd.

Ignoring the rudeness, the dispatcher continues. "Early this morning, I believe about six o'clock, a detachment of twenty-four U.S. Marines under the command of U.S. Army Colonel Robert E. Lee stormed the arsenal at Harpers Ferry. It took the Marines about three minutes to quell the insurrection and to recapture the fort. The hostages that Brown had captured were also rescued. John Brown was wounded before he was captured, a sword wound to the back of his neck and shoulder, which was inflicted by Marine Lieutenant Israel Green. A number of Brown's men were killed - perhaps ten. One U.S. Marine was killed, another was wounded.

"Before the Marines attacked the fort, Colonel Lee sent his aide, Lieutenant J.E.B. Stuart, forward to seek Brown's surrender. Brown refused to surrender. He wanted to be set free, he and his men. At that point, Lieutenant Stuart signaled the Marines to attack, which they did. They battered the door in and entered the fort under heavy rifle fire from Brown and his men. The Marines had been ordered by Colonel Lee not to fire their weapons for fear of shooting the hostages that Brown had captured. They were told to use their bayonets, which they did. This is about all that I know at this time. Thank you."

Robbie extends his arms, waving them back and forth to attract the attention of the dispatcher. "Sir, did John Brown or any of his men make a statement after they were captured?"

"Yes, Brown made several statements. I am not aware of any statements that any of his men made. I will read what Mr. Brown was asked and what he replied.

"He was asked who sent him to Harpers Ferry. His reply was, 'No man sent me here. It was done by my own prompting and that of my Maker, or that of the devil, whichever you please.'"

This embroils many of those in attendance, especially the students. They began to shout in unison, "The devil, the devil, John Brown was sent by the devil." They repeat the expression several times. Someone else in the crowd shouts, "The devil is all of the people up North. They are the root of John Brown and his evil ways."

The crowd begins to stir uneasily, agitated by the hecklers and incensed by the Harpers Ferry incident. There are shouts of "Kill John Brown and all of his followers." "And all Northerners," another person loudly chimes in.

Professor Holcombe, recognizing the seriousness of the situation, approaches the speaker's platform, waves his arms and calls for silence. "Please, gentlemen," he chastises the crowd, "if you cannot refrain from these violent and unruly outbursts, this public announcement will be terminated and there will be no further announcements. Those of you who cannot control your emotions or your anger, we ask you to leave the University Grounds immediately. There are many people assembled here who are interested in what has happened and what is continuing to happen. If you have no respect for yourselves, please respect the rights of those who are interested. We thank you." The crowd, except for a few muted grumblers and hecklers, becomes silent.

The dispatcher thanks Professor Holcombe as he departs, then he continues. "Mr. Brown was asked whether he thought that he was acting under divine authority. Brown responded, 'Yes. I think, my friends, you are guilty of a great wrong against God and humanity. I think it is right for me to interfere with you to free those you hold in bondage. I hold that the golden rule applies to the slave also.'"

There is, again, mild grumbling throughout the crowd, an indication of their disagreement, even hatred, of John Brown and what he represents. The crowd, however, does not get out of hand.

"What else did John Brown say?" someone from the crowd shouts.

The dispatcher pauses to allow the crowd time to simmer down, then responds, "A witness to Brown's arrest shouted to him, 'John Brown, you are a mad man.'

"Brown is quoted as saying, 'You are mad and fanatical, and the people of the South are mad and fanatical. Is it sane to keep five million men in slavery? Is it sane to suppress all who would speak out against this system and to murder all who would interfere with it? Is it sane to talk of war rather than give it up?'"

The hatred of the crowd, already incensed over the audacity of John Brown and his men to pillage the quiet little town of Harpers Ferry, rises to an even higher level of loathing. Tempers are nearing the point of explosion. Shouts of "Lynch John Brown," are heard throughout the crowd. Others are shouting, "John Brown is a murderer. He should be put to death!"

Professor Holcombe again approaches the makeshift platform. In a low but firm voice he cautions the dispatcher, "The crowd is beginning to show signs of excessive and perhaps uncontrollable animosity over this John Brown affair. Their agitation is reaching the point where things may get out of hand. I believe that it might be wise to terminate this news advisory as quickly as possible."

"Professor, I agree with you. But this crowd is so incensed that if I attempt to leave without finishing, I fear they will inflict bodily harm on me. Perhaps if you would stand here with me, the students will be influenced by your presence and they will hold their anger."

"Very well. I am happy to oblige. We certainly do not want you to be harmed in any way. I am sure the anger is not directed at you personally; you just happen to be the messenger."

"Yes. It is unfortunate but true."

Turning again to the crowd, the dispatcher raises his arms, indicating a request for silence. "Gentlemen, the hour is late. If you please, it is time for me to return to the telegraph office."

"One more question, please; just one more," someone near the speaker's platform pleads. The dispatcher is uncertain what to do. The crowd has quieted. Some are beginning to disperse. "Very well, one more question, then I must go."

"What did Colonel Lee do with John Brown? I hope he lynched him."

A great roar of approval arises from the crowd, followed by a unanimous chant, "Lynch John Brown! Lynch John Brown!" A student jumps to the speaker's platform followed by two or three others. The crowd takes up the chant, "Lynch John Brown."

Professor Holcombe again raises his arms, calling for silence. "Gentlemen, please. We ask you to respect your University and respect its founder, Mr. Jefferson. We ask that you desist from further disorder and allow this last question, the final question to be addressed."

A silence immediately falls over the crowd. Professor Holcombe turns to the dispatcher. "Will you answer the question?"

"I believe Colonel Lee and his troops took Brown and the other prisoners some eight or ten miles to Charles Town, which is the county seat of Jefferson County, Virginia. All of the prisoners, including Brown, were turned over to local authorities where they are incarcerated in the county jail. The fate of John Brown, and the others, will be determined in due course, as a matter of law. There was no attempt to lynch John Brown."

The several contentious days of excitement over the John Brown affair have ended. The business of educating the students is once again vigorously pursued by the University. Brown and his men are all but forgotten. Robbie Holcomb and his fellow students are again burdened with educational matters.

Robbie is not, however, so burdened with educational matters that he has forgotten about Mollie K. His infatuation becomes more intense with each passing day. He didn't intend for it to happen. He did not want it to happen, but happen it did. He is hopelessly captivated by her beauty, both her outward and her inward beauty.

It is not that Mollie K has encouraged him romantically. As far as he knows, she is not aware of his romantic feelings for her. She is pleasant and friendly to him, but she is pleasant and friendly to everyone, to people she knows and to people she does not know.

Robbie needs to get Mollie K out of his mind. He came to the University for an education. Girls were the furthest thing from his mind when he left home. It wasn't that he disliked them; they were his friends, just friends. Except for Serena, that's all they had ever been.

Mentally, he hopes to keep it that way; but his heart, with assistance from Cupid, is leading him in the opposite direction.

He discreetly attempts to avoid Mollie K. He hopes that keeping her out of his sight will get her out of his mind. He leaves and returns to the boarding house at different times each day. He alters his meal schedule to correspond with times that she will likely be elsewhere. He sits at inconspicuous places in the dining room, always with his back to the entrances. He attempts to mentally find fault with her.

He tries to rationalize that his infatuation over her is due to homesickness, but he is not homesick. The harder he attempts to avoid thinking about her, the more she dominates his thoughts. Nothing seems to work. He is at his wits end.

Robbie is late for dinner, later than he intended. The dining room is closed. He hears someone in the kitchen. He cautiously peeps through the half open door. Mrs. O'Riley is alone. He calls to her, "Is it alright if I come in?"

"Sure, Robbie. You are awfully late this evening. Is anything wrong?"

"No, Mrs. O'Riley. I was late leaving the library. I'm very sorry. Is it alright if I fix a sandwich? I'm very hungry."

"I'll be glad to fix you something."

"No thank you, Mrs. O'Riley. My tardiness is my own fault. You have been in this kitchen long enough today. If you don't mind, I prefer to do it myself."

"Suit yourself. I am rather tired. Help yourself to whatever you want. Be sure to turn the lamp out when you leave. We don't want a fire in the middle of the night. An unattended lamp is dangerous. Oh, and be sure to close the door. Good night, Robbie."

She starts out of the kitchen door, pauses momentarily, turns and speaks. "We haven't seen much of you lately. Is anything wrong?"

"No, no, Mrs. O'Riley. I have been very busy at school. Everything is just fine. Thank you for asking."

"Don't forget the kitchen lamp."

"I'll be sure to turn it out. Good night."

"Good night, Robbie."

He feels bad that he hasn't been truthful with Mrs. O'Riley. But how can he tell her the truth? He has known Mollie K for less than a month. How could he have fallen for her so quickly, so hard? He sits at the kitchen table nibbling at his sandwich in silence, his head lowered, feeling sorry for himself. He does not hear a sound. He raises his head and there she is, alone, tears in her eyes. A silence falls as they face each other.

"Mollie K. You startled me. Are you alright?"

She does not respond to his question, instead posing a question to him. "Robbie are you angry with me? Have I offended you or hurt your feelings somehow?"

"Oh no, Mollie K. I am not angry with you. You have never offended me. I could never be angry with you." He tries to speak convincingly, although the quiver in his voice reveals that he is not being totally honest. His face is red with embarrassment. He hopes that she will not notice his nervousness in the dim light of the single lamp. He rises from his chair.

"If I have not offended you, Robbie, then why are you avoiding me? What have I done to you?" Mollie K is genuinely hurt.

Robbie is flabbergasted. He stammers and stutters as he attempts to gather his thoughts. It is not his habit to be dishonest or deceitful. Yet he feels that if he tells her the truth she might laugh. He nevertheless decides then and there that there can be no more deceit, no more excuses. Finally, he drops his head. "Mollie K, I might as well be truthful. I have been avoiding you, but it is not because of anything you have done. It is because of my own doings. Mollie K, I have fallen for you. I have tried very hard not to, but I can not get you out of my mind. I have never felt this way about any other girl. Never. Never in my life. I know it sounds silly, but it's the truth."

"You have never had a girlfriend, Robbie?"

"Well, not really a girlfriend. I did have a friend - a girl that was my best friend in school - from first grade on. I liked her a lot and she liked me. But it was never the way I feel about you. She is still my best friend.

"Her name is Serena Johnson and she is going to be a nun - dedicating her life to the service of her church. She's Catholic.

"We will always be the best of friends. We promised each other that. It's a different kind of love."

"Did you ever hug or kiss Serena?"

Robbie's face reddens. "Yes, Mollie K, I did. The first time it was an accident and we were both embarrassed. We kissed some afterwards, but it was not like people in love do. Anyway, it was just friendly. Then she decided she wanted to be a nun. Want to hear something funny, Mollie K?"

"I guess so," she responds.

"Somehow everyone in town was talking about me and Serena - you know, spreading gossip. We decided, as we were walking down Main Street on a Saturday, that we would run down to the Town Square - that's where everybody congregates on Saturdays - and we would kiss right in front of everyone. We did it because of all the gossip - to give them something to talk about."

"Did they talk about it?"

"Certainly, and our parents were furious until we told them why we did it."

"Then what happened?"

"The gossip kind of settled down as it got around that we did it just because people were gossiping. Our friends thought it was hilarious."

"Well, I don't think it is funny at all, Robbie Holcomb," Mollie K responds in a pouting gesture.

"It's the truth, Mollie K. That's the way it happened."

Both of them are blushing, embarrassed. They stand facing each other, not touching, just standing there in the dim light of the kitchen lamp.

"Robbie, I am also fond of you. I have cried every night thinking you did not like me. I did not know why you were avoiding me. I am so glad we have talked. I feel much better."

They hold hands in the innocence of their mutual affection. They do not embrace, their lips do not meet. It is the purity of young affection. It is enough for this night; a night of happiness, a night to remember.

"Mollie K, where have you been? Do you know that it's almost ten o'clock? You should be in bed."

"Yes, Mamma, I know. I was down in the kitchen talking with Robbie."

"With Robbie? What were you two talking about?"

"About why he has been avoiding me."

"And what did he say?"

"Mamma, do I have to tell you? It's kind of personal between the two of us, between Robbie and me."

Mrs. O'Riley looks at her daughter. She trusts her implicitly. "Mollie K, you are all that I have in this world - all that is important to me. I would walk through fire for you. No, you do not have to tell me what you two said to each other, as long as nothing improper went on."

"Oh, Mamma, shame on you. Nothing improper happened. Mamma, he has been avoiding me because he likes me. Mamma, you know that I like him, too. We held hands. That was all. We didn't hug or kiss, Mamma. Honest, we didn't."

"I believe you, sweetheart, but remember that boys will be boys."

"Mamma, sometimes you say the strangest things."

A day or so later Mrs. O'Riley meets Robbie as he is coming up the front walk. "Good morning, Mrs. O'Riley," he greets her pleasantly.

"Good morning Robbie," she responds. "I hear you and Mollie K had a long conversation the other night."

Robbie's face reddens. "She told you about it?" he responds, very disappointed.

"No, she did not reveal your conversation; she said that it was personal between the two of you. I did not press the matter. I do want to tell you about Mollie K, if you have a few minutes."

"Yes, ma'am, I do. But you needn't worry, Mrs. O'Riley - I would not harm one hair on Mollie K's head. I am very, very fond of her."

"I believe you, but I need to tell you about Mollie K."

"Please do, Mrs. O'Riley."

"Mollie K is only sixteen. She will be seventeen on November twenty-fifth, in just over a month. She is my joy, my life. Her father died when she was ten. He was killed in a sawmill accident at work. His death devastated both of us. We were left penniless. I never had a job before, so I turned our home - this home - into a boarding house. The people at the University have been wonderful in referring students to us. For someone so young, she has faced many adversities, more than her share. Through all of these misfortunes, she has never complained, never was cynical, never suspicious. Robbie, I do not want Mollie K to get hurt."

"Mrs. O'Riley, I will never, ever do anything to hurt Mollie K or you. I promise you that. Mrs. O'Riley, it is more than Mollie K's outward beauty - its her inward beauty; she is wonderful."

"Robbie, I feel much better about our conversation. I believe we can keep this private - between the two of us."

"Yes, ma'am, Mrs. O'Riley. I believe we can."

Chapter Eleven

The University Years: A Path to Justice

A week to the day after John Brown's capture and imprisonment, he is once again in the news as he will be facing serious criminal charges. Brown claims to be innocent of wrongdoing; he claims that he acted only in self-defense during the bloody uprising at Harpers Ferry, Virginia.

News of the rumored charges and the almost certain trial of Brown is received by the University of Virginia student body with the same fervor, passion, and hatred that his raid on the U.S. Arsenal and the town of Harpers Ferry had originally caused.

The University administration characteristically refrains from expressing an official opinion on either the charges or the potential trial. Nevertheless, in deference to the intense interest shown by the student body and the faculty, it is decided that a special telegraph service will be provided to assure current coverage of the events developing in Charles Town, Virginia. The announcement is made from the steps of the Rotunda by Thomas Jefferson Randolph, Rector of the University.

"Distinguished faculty, young gentlemen of this University, and other guests assembled here. We welcome you on behalf of the Board of Visitors and others associated with the University. Our purpose in making this announcement is to assure you that the University is totally committed in its efforts to keep you informed about the on-going events concerning the Commonwealth of Virginia versus John Brown and others.

"The University will do so by a special telegraph arrangement between facilities in Charles Town and facilities here at the University. Mr. Thomas

Holcombe, the University librarian, is in charge of the telegraph services. He will report matters of interest relating to the John Brown affairs three times daily from the steps here at the Rotunda. The first report each day will be made at 10:30 in the morning. The second will be at 12:00 noon and the third and final daily report will be made at 4:30 in the afternoon. If news events should occur that are deemed to be of great importance, there may be impromptu announcements at other times.

"For those of you who are unable to attend the regularly scheduled announcements, a verbatim copy of the report will be posted on the Rotunda doors. The same applies to any special bulletins that are received.

"We ask you to refrain from disturbing Mr. Holcombe in the library. He has been instructed not to provide any information from the library, either verbally or in writing, that pertains to the John Brown matter. We expect you to honor these conditions.

"All students are cautioned that your primary responsibility to the University, to your families, and to yourselves, is to attend your scheduled classes. The news is of secondary importance to this academic community, as it should be. Should Mr. Brown be tried - which appears likely - his guilt or innocence will be determined by a jury of his peers in a fair and impartial trial. James Holcombe, the University's professor of constitutional law, is presently in Charles Town to monitor the on-going events and to provide accurate and relevant information to the University community. We trust that the information provided through this arrangement will meet the needs and expectations of all concerned.

"The individuals in Charles Town charged with the responsibility of resolving these legal matters are highly qualified, competent, and dedicated people. We ask all of you to put your trust in the legal system of the Commonwealth and to have faith in those men who will prosecute and those who will defend the accused. If Mr. Brown, and others associated with him, are indicted for crimes they are accused of, we ask all of you to remain calm, to contain your emotions and to have faith in our justice system. Thank you for your attention and courtesy."

Thomas Holcombe is on the steps of the Rotunda the following morning at precisely 10:30 a.m., with brother James' first telegram in hand. He greets those in attendance, a rather small crowd of perhaps fifty students and faculty.

"Good morning. We welcome you to the first in a series of messages relating to the John Brown raid at Harpers Ferry and the events that are now transpiring as an aftermath of that event. These events are not only of a legal nature, but also of a political and social nature.

"We remind you, as Mr. Randolph did yesterday, that these messages are to keep you informed. You are expected to conduct yourselves as gentlemen during and after these presentations." That said, Thomas begins to read:

> *"It is early Tuesday morning, October 25, 1859, a crisp clear morning in Charles Town, Virginia. We are near the Jefferson County Court House in downtown Charles Town. The streets are literally filled with people; overflowing from side to side and from end to end. The entire town, as far as one can see in any direction - from North to South and from East to West - is a solid mass of people.*

> *'People are here from all walks of life: professionals, doctors, lawyers, politicians, newspaper reporters. There are the common people, the farmers, shop keepers, and of course, there are curiosity seekers.*

> *'It is unlikely that there has ever been in the history of this quaint little Southern town, or that there ever again will be, a series of events that will equal those that are about to unfold here. The events that are in the making today and that will continue to unfold for days to come are momentous events that will decide the fate of abolitionist John Brown and those arrested with him.*

> *'Very few people here today will be privileged to witness the trial - if there is a trial. We understand that a preliminary hearing for Brown and the others is scheduled for later this morning. At the hearing, the accused will be officially iinformed of the charges against them.*

> *'The attorneys for the Commonwealth of Virginia are required to establish probable cause, if the legal process is to move forward. If probable cause is not established, Mr. Brown will walk away from here a free man.'"*

The thought of Brown walking away as a free man riles the students among the crowd into a near frenzy. The audience has, to this point during the reading, been rather docile. It has not been a message to inflame them or to raise their ire. Not, at least, until the statement that Brown could possibly go free.

There are sporadic signs of impatience at the slow pace of legal action against Brown, but there have been no outright disturbances. Now the crowd is disturbed. Happily, Thomas reasons that it is a rather small crowd, and it has begun to disperse the moment he finishes with the telegram. A few students are left mingling aimlessly in an effort to stir the crowd's emotions, but they are not inclined to participate in any rowdiness. Most of the students hurry off to class. The first reading session has been successfully completed with no apparent problems.

Robbie misses the first telegram reading. He attends morning classes instead. It is nearly noon when he stops to read the telegram that is now posted on the Rotunda door. He waits on the Lawn near the Rotunda steps for the noon telegram reading. Students and some faculty members began to gather in small groups.

When Thomas appears, Robbie waves. Thomas returns the salutation, then addresses the crowd. "Our second telegram from brother James was received just moments ago. I have not had the opportunity to read it, so we will all share its contents together. Here it goes:

'It is late Tuesday morning and we are witnessing history as it is developing. At 10:30 this morning Sheriff James Campbell escorted John Brown and several other prisoners from the county jail to the Jefferson County Court House. We believe the others are men that were arrested with Brown. They are, we suppose, minor players in this series of events that have brought us here today.

'It is because of these events, because of Brown, that security here in Charles Town is at an astoundingly high level. The town is completely surrounded by some 3,000 heavily armed troops. Other security officers are intermingled with the crowds of onlookers that are wandering aimlessly in the streets. These troops are here to prevent acts of violence for or against the life of Brown, or to prevent acts of violence against those persons conducting or participating in the legal matters for or against the prosecution or defense of Brown.

'There are many Northerners here. They are mostly sympathetic to Brown and his causes. They are the people who wish him well and hope for his release or acquittal, if he should go to trial. There are also many Southerners here that intensely despise Brown. They hope to see him punished for those acts of violence that were committed at Harpers Ferry, and they hope that his punishment is death. Emotions for and against John Brown are running high.

'The citizens of this small town have suddenly found themselves thrust into the forefront of an impassioned and anxious nation; a nation divided over the guilt or innocence of one man.

'Some minutes ago, Brown and his men were advised of the charges against them. Those charges are treason against the Commonwealth of Virginia, inciting a slave rebellion, and five charges of first degree murder. Conviction on any one of those charges is punishable by death.

'All of the accused - Brown and his men - have pleaded not guilty. Brown and the others have been provided court-appointed attorneys to defend them against the charges. John Brown made an emotional and scathingly critical statement to the Court in regard to the legal charges against him. The anger of those in the court room was apparent from the expressions on their faces. We give you, word for word, what Brown said:

"I did not ask for any quarter at the time I was taken. I did not ask to have myself spared. The Governor of the State of Virginia, Governor Henry Wise, tendered me his assurance that I should have a fair trial, and under no circumstances whatever will I be able to attend a trial. If you seek my blood, you can have it at any moment without the mockery of a trial.

"I have no counsel. I have not been able to advise with one. I know nothing about the feelings of my fellow prisoners and am utterly unable to attend in any way to my own defense. My memory don't serve me. My health is insufficient, although improving. There are mitigating circumstances if a fair trial is to be allowed us that I would urge in our favor.

"But if we are to be forced with a mere form of a trial to execution, you might spare yourself that trouble. I am ready for my fate. I do not ask for a trial. I plead for no mockery of a trial - no insult - nothing but that which conscience gives or cowardice would drive you to practice.

"I ask to be spared from the mockery of a trial. I do not know what is to be the benefit of it to the Commonwealth. I have now little to ask other than I be not publicly insulted as cowardly barbarians insult those who fall into their hands."

Hissing and angry slurs are voiced repeatedly during the reading of Brown's caustic and insulting outburst against his nearly certain trial.

Several emotional outbursts erupt during Thomas' reading of the telegram, although he does not hesitate or pause until he has finished.

"When are the officials in Charles Town going to stop all of these unnecessary formalities and get on with the trial?" shouts a student. Another student cries out, "Why should he be given a trial? The people he murdered were not given a trial. What he needs is an 'eye for an eye and a tooth for a tooth' kind of justice. After all the murdering he did in Harpers Ferry, and all of the other crimes that he committed, they should go on and hang him. That's what he deserves."

Someone else shouts, "Why doesn't the University get rid of the Northern scallywags attending classes here? They are here only to stir up trouble. They should either go home voluntarily or the University should expel them and send them home. All Northerners hate us Southerners. They want to destroy the South."

A student stands next to Robbie. They exchange glances. "I'm Jack Simon. I recognize you from Latin class. You're from up North. I could tell by your accent."

"Yes, I'm from up-state New York. My name is Robbie Holcomb." They shake hands.

"Robbie, I want you to know that not all Southerners here at the University are against you because of what John Brown has done; actually there are very few."

"Thanks, Jack, thanks for telling me," Robbie responds, then asks, "Are you from Virginia?"

"No, I'm from South Carolina." He pauses momentarily, then continues. "What is your opinion of this Brown mess?"

Robbie looks at him intently, pausing momentarily before responding. "I think the officials in Virginia are doing what should be done under the circumstances. Individuals or groups of individuals cannot take the application of laws into their own hands. I think it was John Locke who said, 'Wherever law ends, tyranny begins.' As you know, Locke's political theories greatly influenced Thomas Jefferson's ideas when he wrote the Declaration of Independence.

"I think, too, that our University officials are handling the matter properly. Do you agree?"

"I do indeed, Robbie. I also believe that if Brown is found guilty, he should be hanged. I have no sympathy for murderers, for rabble-rousers. I suppose it would have been better if the Marines had killed him in their assault at Harpers Ferry."

Jack again looks toward Robbie. "Your name - your last name is Holcomb. Are you related to Professor Holcombe and Mr. Thomas Holcombe?"

"Yes, we are cousins."

Again looking directly at Robbie, he continues, "But they are Southerners - at least they sound like Southerners."

"They are Southerners," Robbie responds with a chuckle.

"Did you come to the University because of your relationship to them?"

"No, I came because of Thomas Jefferson, because of his ideals, because of his greatness, his influences."

"Robbie, I must go. I have some commitments this afternoon. I have enjoyed talking with you. I hope we can talk again."

"Same here, Jack." The new friends depart, both happy to have met the other.

Some students, the agitators, remain in small groups discussing the content of the telegram that Thomas has just finished reading. They are loud and boisterous. Robbie remains silent. Not that he is afraid to speak; it is simply useless to do so. Anything he might say would further inflame the agitators in the crowd. It would serve no useful purpose. Besides he does not dislike Southerners. Some are very good friends. The O'Rileys, Mrs. O'Riley and Mollie K, and Jack Simon whom he has just met. He is exceptionally fond of them. And his cousins, James and Thomas have become very close friends. They provide the strength and fortitude to keep his ship on keel. Robbie remains silent. He holds his peace. He later tells Thomas, "I thought of the words of Thomas Carlyle when he said, 'Speech is silver, silence is golden.'" Robbie is not sympathetic with Brown for his murderous and illegal escapades.

He is about to slip away when Thomas motions to him. He climbs the Rotunda steps and they go into Thomas' office next to the library. "Robbie, I was hoping that you would not let the agitators draw you into a confrontation over Brown. I'm proud of your restraint."

"Thomas, I knew it would be useless to do so. I also understand the frustrations they are experiencing. As you know, I am a firm abolitionist. Not just because of my mother's strong stand on the anti-slavery issue, but because of my own personal feelings. It is because of my belief that slavery is unjust, un-American and inhuman. It is, in my opinion, sinful."

"We share many of the same ideals. My parents released their slaves and moved to Ohio over the slavery issue years ago. But we need to realize that the issue that is brewing is not one-sided. There is also the issue of the rights of a state to set its own policies, to establish its own laws, and to enforce those laws free from interference by the federal government, or for that matter, to be free from interferences by any outside forces whatsoever. This is the main issue as many Southerners see it."

"Yes, I understand what you are saying, Thomas. I do not understand all of the legal issues or even all of the economic and social issues from a Southern point of view. I just hope this Brown incident does not widen the rift between the North and South. I do believe that Brown deserves a fair trial, an unbiased trial. Laws are the rules of a civilized society. Those societies that fail to live by them, those individuals that fail to live by society's rules, must suffer the consequences. Societies are the benefactors of justice. Societies suffer injustices where justice is inequitable, as in the case of slavery."

"Well spoken, Robbie. Perhaps you will share with future generations some of the Jeffersonian wisdom that you will absorb here at his University." Robbie blushes but does not reply.

At the same time, in Charles Town, Professor Holcombe leaves the court house soon after Brown's preliminary hearing. He plans to interview the attorneys for the prosecution and the court-appointed defense attorneys. He is aware that the afternoon court session is set aside for the Grand Jury to convene. These jurors will decide after the Commonwealth of Virginia presents its evidence, and after questioning some of the Commonwealth's witnesses, whether there is sufficient evidence to indict Brown and the others on the charges they are accused of.

Professor Holcombe waits just outside the courthouse. He does not have long to wait before the prosecutors exit from a side door. He approaches them.

"Gentlemen, I am James Holcombe, a law professor at the University of Virginia. I am here in Charles Town on assignment to keep the University community in Charlottesville apprised of the on-going events in the pending trial of John Brown. The University has arranged for a special telegraph service from here in Charles Town to Charlottesville. We will have the news there almost as fast as it happens here. A quite amazing feat, wouldn't you say?"

"Absolutely, Professor. What can we do for you?"

Gesturing toward one of the men, Professor Holcombe continues, "I believe Sir, that you are Andrew Hunter, the special prosecutor appointed by Governor Henry Wise?"

"That is correct, Professor. And this is my co-counsel, Harpers Ferry Town Prosecutor Charles Harding."

"It's a pleasure to meet you both," acknowledges the Professor. He then continues with his interview. "My question, gentlemen, is whether you are prepared to proceed with the prosecution of John Brown, and do you believe there is sufficient evidence to convict the accused of the charges against him? Would you care to comment, Mr. Hunter?"

"Yes, of course. We are confident that the evidence against Brown is more than sufficient to convict him on all charges. The grand jury is meeting this afternoon to hear the evidence and to question some of the witnesses. We are confident that they will indict him when they are presented with the evidence.

"There is a preponderance of evidence against Brown. He is as guilty as sin. We will call only a few witnesses. That is all that should be necessary.

"We fully expect an indictment, and we are prepared to proceed with our case as quickly as it is possible to do so."

"Do you expect the grand jury to wind things up this afternoon, Mr. Hunter?"

"Professor Holcombe, we have no idea how long it will take these men to wind things up. We don't mind working late this afternoon. However, if it runs over into tomorrow, that is fine with us. Our objective is to see that justice is done. If it takes a little longer than we expect it to, it will be alright. However, our feelings are that the sooner it's done, the better off we will be, the better off society will be, and the better off the Commonwealth of Virginia will be. We plan to seek the death penalty."

"Mr. Hunter, would you comment on how you intend to present the Commonwealth's case against Mr. Brown?"

"Professor Holcombe, we are not going to play our hand publically at this time. The evidence will all come out in due time, and in its proper place, as the trial progresses."

"I certainly understand your position, Mr. Hunter, and I appreciate your comments. As you know, there is great interest in this case, not only in Charlottesville, but all across the country. I thank you both."

The two prosecuting attorneys had been on their way no more than a few minutes when the defense attorneys appear. Professor Holcombe calls to them, "Mr. Botts, Mr. Faulconer."

They turn toward him, "Yes, Professor," Attorney Lawson Botts responds. "It has been rumored that you are here in Charles Town to critique the trial. Is that true?"

"Not exactly. I am here to observe the trial. I am here on behalf of the University of Virginia. My responsibility is to follow the progress of the Brown events here in Charles Town and to keep the University community well-informed about what is happening and when it is happening. I send telegrams back to Charlottesville several times daily."

Mr. Botts then interjects, "Professor, I couldn't help but notice that you said you were following the John Brown events. You did not mention the trial."

"You have a good legal ear, Mr. Botts. I did not mention a trial because Mr. Brown has not been indicted. Do you think that he will be?"

"Professor Holcombe, I do not know what the Grand Jury is going to do. As you are aware, the defense attorneys have no access to the Grand Jury. We will just wait and see. While they are meeting we intend to use that time to build our defense."

"Thank you, Mr. Botts. That leads me to my next question. How do you feel about defending John Brown, and how do you intend to approach his defense? Mr. Botts, would you care to respond?"

"Yes, of course, Professor. As you know, every person accused of a crime in these United States is entitled to a fair and impartial trial; and every accused person is entitled to legal counsel. As Mr. Brown's legal counsel, we intend to defend him to the best of our ability to do so. We believe that there are legal, jurisdictional, and constitutional issues in this case that are favorable to Mr. Brown's defense and we intend to pursue those issues vigorously. As you know, Professor, Mr. Brown is presumed under the laws of the Commonwealth of Virginia to be innocent unless or until he is otherwise proven in a court of law to be guilty."

"Do you believe, as court-appointed lawyers, that you will have sufficient time to prepare your case?"

"Well, we just had an opportunity to converse with Mr. Brown after we were appointed. We will be meeting with him again this afternoon. We are both experienced trial lawyers and we both have had years of experience in criminal law. We - as we have indicated - have some important legal issues to pursue. We recognize that the case is a difficult one, but we have faced legal matters of immense proportions before where the odds seemed to be against the accused. We'll take it a step at a time."

"Well said, Mr. Botts. I am sure you are aware that this is a highly sensitive case. The entire nation, and much of the rest of the world, is going to be reading about it, keeping up with it through their daily newspapers. The Northern newspapers are questioning whether John Brown can receive a fair trial in the South. Southern papers - at least some of them - are questioning whether he even deserves a trial. How do you respond to these people? How do you answer these people? What do you say?"

"Professor Holcombe, we don't respond to these questions. We don't respond to these people. We recognize that there are all kinds of opinions out there. This is an emotion-packed situation. Some of the opinions - and I might add they are only opinions - are honest opinions, whether they are in support of or against Mr. Brown. Some are politically motivated, other opinions may arise from other causes, we don't know why or how.

"What we do know, as we have said before, is that Mr. Brown deserves a fair trial. He deserves to be represented by dedicated and totally committed legal counsel. If I and my co-counsel Charles Faulconer were not willing to put all of our legal knowledge, all of our legal expertise on the line in defending Mr. Brown, we would not be here today. We would have declined to represent him. We have assured Mr. Brown that we are totally committed to his defense. He understands it. And now we need to get on with the task of preparing his defense."

"Thank you, Mr. Botts. Thank you, Mr. Faulconer."

As Brown's attorneys hasten away to prepare for his defense, Professor Holcombe hurries off to send a telegram to the University. He is elated over the success of his two interviews. He muses aloud to himself, somewhat jovially, "I believe that I would have been quite a good newspaper reporter. My legal instincts, however, tell me that the next few days are going to be very exciting. This trial - and I am sure it's going to trial - is going to be a memorable one. A case that is going to be debated for a long time."

The Professor's telegram to the University, reciting the events of his two interviews and his personal observations about a trial, bring a rousing cheer of approval from the University crowd. The attendance at the telegram readings is increasing. The crowds are anxious for a trial, anxious for the blood of John Brown. The opinion of Professor Holcombe that there will be a trial raises their hopes. They are anxious for revenge.

Robbie and Thomas discuss the interviews that Professor Holcombe had with the opposing lawyers as well as the reaction of the University students after the telegram is read.

"It's quite amazing, Thomas, how inflamed and emotional some of the students become after listening to these telegrams. They translate that emotion - that hatred - to everyone that is from the North."

"Yes," responds Thomas, "It seems to be one of the weaknesses of human nature. People become lowliheads through their emotions. People react without thinking and there always seem to be certain people that will inflame others that normally are not inclined to otherwise think and react violently. You had best remain noncommittal during these meetings."

"Yes, Thomas. I expect to do so."

The Grand Jury meets and deliberates late into the evening on Tuesday, then continues their work Wednesday morning. Just before noon they finish their session, voting to indict John Brown. The indictment is read to the court:

"John Brown, together with diverse other evil-minded and traitorous persons, to the jurors unknown, not having the fear of God before their eyes, but moved and seduced by the false and malignant counsel of the other evil and traitorous persons and the instigators of the devil, with other confederates, to the jurors unknown, did feloniously and traitorously make rebellion and levy war against the said Commonwealth of Virginia."

The Professor's assumptions of the previous day prove to be true. There will definitely be a trial.

Professor Holcombe's telegram to the University, a verbatim recital of the Grand Jury indictment, is too late for the noon presentation. It will, however, provide quite a stir for the 4:30 afternoon reading. Anticipating the possibility of trouble, he sends a special telegram to Thomas, advising him of the content of the forthcoming afternoon telegram and to be alert for student celebrations that could possibly get out of hand.

Thomas again warns Robbie that it might be wise for him to avoid the telegram readings for several days because the student agitation level is rising day by day.

"You are a Northerner, Robbie, and the hatred toward Brown may sometimes cause people to do things in anger that they would not otherwise do. You might be attacked simply because you are from up North."

"I suppose that's true. I hope not, but I realize that it is possible. Thomas, you can be sure I will not initiate trouble. I will do everything possible to avoid it. But I cannot be intimidated over John Brown's acts. I cannot hide from it if it happens."

Chapter Twelve

A Question of Reasonable Doubt

Any glimmer of hope that John Brown will not be tried for his alleged crimes at Harpers Ferry are cast to the wind by the Grand Jury's scathing indictment. The charges against him, charges of treason, inciting insurrection, and first-degree murder, are exceptionally serious. Conviction on any one of the charges can be punishable by death. The day of reckoning is near at hand. His trial is now a certainty.

Professor Holcombe, by arrangement from Virginia Governor Henry Wise, is one of the guest attendees. Of the thousands of people visiting Charles Town hoping to attend the trial, he is one of the fortunate few who is guaranteed admittance. The day that an anxious and apprehensive nation has been waiting for has arrived. It is Wednesday, October 26, 1859. The courtroom is filled beyond capacity. Nearly five hundred spectators are crammed into a space designed to accommodate fewer than three hundred people. Emotions are running high. Security is exceptionally tight. Excited voices jumble together, resonating from wall to wall as everyone attempts to speak simultaneously; a mass of indistinguishable words mixed together like the drone of ten thousand angry, swarming bees.

As the judge enters the court from his chamber, the bailiff stands and in a loud, clear, authoritative voice commands, "All rise." An instantaneous silence falls over the courtroom as if the spectators' vocal cords have been severed. The bailiff continues without hesitation, "Oh Yez, Oh Yez, Oh Yez. The Circuit Court of Jefferson County, Virginia is now in session. The Honorable Judge Richard Parker presiding."

The first day of court is rudimentary. A jury is chosen, defense attorney Charles Faulconer withdraws from the case after John Brown expresses a lack of confidence in him. Faulconer is replaced by local attorney Thomas Green.

All three of Professor Holcombe's telegrams on day one of the trial are received by the University and read to the student body. The students show little enthusiasm for the results of day one of the trial. There are no major celebrations and no overt disturbances. It is best described as a wait and see attitude.

Robbie attends the meetings with his newfound friend, Jack Simon from South Carolina. Jack sums up the content of the three telegrams, "Not much to get excited about today."

"Perhaps not, Jack, but it just might be the lull before the storm. It is sure to get confrontational and heated as the prosecutors and the defense present their facts."

Thursday morning, October twenty-seventh, is clear and cool in Charles Town. Professor Holcombe is up early. He expects a busy day with the business of Brown's guilt or innocence finally taking center stage. The professor is not to be disappointed. Unlike the crisp and cool outside temperature, the courtroom environment becomes heated and antagonistic from the opening moments of the second day of court.

Defense attorney Lawson Botts springs to his feet. "Your Honor, if it pleases the court, I request permission to read a telegram that I received early this morning. I believe this to be extremely important to the defense of my client, Mr. John Brown."

Prosecutor Andrew Hunter quickly steps forward and addresses the court. "Your Honor, the Commonwealth of Virginia objects to this highly unusual request by the defense. We have not been privileged to inspect this document. We believe this request is improper."

Judge Parker instructs the bailiff to bring the telegram to him. After inspecting the document, he addresses Prosecutor Hunter. "The Court holds that the Commonwealth's objection is not sustained and is overruled. Mr. Botts, you may proceed."

"Thank you, Your Honor," Botts replies, then turning to the jury, "Gentlemen of the jury, the telegram that I am about to read to this court was sent to me from a man in Akron, Ohio. He is very familiar with the family of John Brown. He has known them for many years. He is well-acquainted with John Brown's parents, and siblings. He has known them all for much of their lives. His intimacy with the Brown family and the knowledge he shares in this telegram makes it most important in the defense of Mr. Brown. The telegram reads:

> *'Insanity is hereditary in John Brown's family. His mother's sister, John's aunt, died with it. A daughter of that sister has been two years in a lunatic asylum. A son and a daughter of his mother's brother have also been confined in the lunatic asylum and another son of that brother is now insane and under close restraint. These facts can be conclusively proven by witnesses residing here, who will doubtless attend the trial if desired.'*

"Mr. Botts, do you intend to introduce this telegram as evidence for the defense?" Judge Parker asked.

"No, Your Honor. Mr. Brown has informed me that he does not wish to plead insanity as a defense."

Brown arises from his cot, where the court has allowed him to lie because of the injuries he received at Harpers Ferry. Facing Judge Parker, he says, "I am perfectly unconscious of insanity and I reject, so far as I am capable, any attempt to interfere on my behalf on that score."

"Gentlemen," Judge Parker retorts, somewhat agitated, "It is time that we get on with the business of this court. There will be no further delays and no more interruptions. Mr. Hunter, is the prosecution ready to proceed in its case against Mr. Brown?"

"It is, Your Honor."

"Mr. Botts, is the defense prepared to defend Mr. Brown against the charges of which the Commonwealth of Virginia has accused him?"

"Yes, Your Honor, we are prepared, but Mr. Brown has indicated that he has received word that out-of-state attorneys are on the way here to defend him. It is his preference that they defend him. We, therefore, request a postponement of this trial until they arrive."

Andrew Hunter springs to his feet. Anger in his voice, he responds to the postponement request. "Your Honor, the prosecution vigorously objects to a further delay of this trial. This is simply a ploy by the accused to delay his trial while his Northern friends and associates attempt to muster forces to free him from facing the justice that he so richly deserves."

"You are sustained in your objection, Mr. Hunter. The court refuses to further postpone this trial. Mr. Brown has had sufficient time to arrange for other attorneys if he desired to do so. He was asked at the time of his arraignment if he had counsel. He responded that he did not. He was offered any two defense attorneys of his choosing from the slate of lawyers qualified to practice before this court. He did nothing. The court appointed two lawyers to defend him. He dismissed one of them before this trial got underway. The court appointed another one, Mr. Green, whom he agreed to. We will have no further delays."

Turning again to the prosecutor, Judge Parker instructs the Commonwealth to address the court. Attorney Charles Harding faces the jury. "Gentlemen, the Commonwealth of Virginia will prove to you that John Brown came to Virginia with criminal intent. He came to commit treason against the Commonwealth. He came to incite and to conspire with slaves and others to rebel against the Commonwealth. And to succeed in those endeavors, he willingly and maliciously committed murder. The witnesses to these crimes will testify to these facts."

Defense attorney Thomas Green presents his opening statement to the jury. "Gentlemen of the jury, I want you to remember that the defendant, John Brown, comes before this court as an innocent man. He is not required to prove his innocence. If there is doubt as to guilt, you must give the benefit of that doubt to the accused. I also remind you that treason cannot be based on a confession that is made outside of the courtroom, only a court room confession can be used for conviction of this crime. With respect to the charge of insurrection, we submit to you that if there was such a crime, it is a federal matter and the Commonwealth of Virginia lacks jurisdiction. Now with respect to the charge of first degree murder, you, the jury would have to find that it was premeditated and deliberate. Otherwise, the most severe finding of guilt would be second degree murder."

Lawson Botts addresses the jury. "Gentlemen, I can add little to what Thomas Green has told you. I am, however, asking you to put aside any prejudices that you may harbor against the North. Put aside the rumors and the hearsay that has circulated in this community for the past several weeks. I remind you, as did attorney Green, that the burden of proof - the burden of proving guilt - falls squarely on the Commonwealth of Virginia. It is not the burden of the defendant to prove his innocence. He is presumed innocent unless proven guilty.

"Now I will address you on the issue of jurisdiction. The Commonwealth of Virginia has no legal right to try John Brown. The state does not have jurisdiction because a crime was not committed on Virginia soil. Everything that happened at Harpers Ferry took place on federal property, at the federal arsenal. One final reminder regarding the Commonwealth's charge of first degree murder. The evidence will show that John Brown treated his prisoners well. He treated them with respect. If he had intended to murder them, he would not have treated them so well.

"I lastly refer to the charge of treason, which Mr. Green brought to your attention. Treason requires that the accused be a citizen of the state in which the charge is made. Mr. Brown is not a citizen of Virginia. He was never a citizen of Virginia and cannot be convicted of such a charge in Virginia."

Andrew Hunter addresses the Court. "Gentlemen of the jury, I am a special prosecutor in this case against John Brown, having been appointed by Virginia Governor Henry Wise. I want you to understand that the evidence against Brown is clear and convincing. I want you to know that the Commonwealth of Virginia has a legal right to prosecute Brown for every crime that he is accused of committing, and this includes the crime of treason. The requirement of a confession in court applies solely to federal law, not to state law. Virginia law on treason applies to all property within the state, regardless of the owner of that property. With respect to the charges of murder, the evidence will show that John Brown personally and willingly engaged in acts of murder. The evidence will show that Brown came to Virginia with murder on his mind. He came - and his men came - heavily armed. They came with malice and ill intent, with ill will on their minds. They came to do evil to the citizens of Virginia. They came - led by Brown - to commit crimes against this Commonwealth, against the citizens of this Commonwealth. He came to wage war, to kill and to maim, and to rob the citizens of this Commonwealth of Virginia."

Pausing momentarily, turning aside from the jury, he raises his right arm, clinches his fist, then points to John Brown. "There is the leader of the pack. There is the traitor; there is the murderer. The Commonwealth of Virginia will present clear and convincing evidence and will present witnesses that will establish the guilt of John Brown beyond any reasonable doubt."

A hush falls over the courtroom as Andrew Hunter returns to the prosecution table. It is nearly noon and the court adjourns for the morning. It is an opportunity for Professor Holcombe to send his second telegram of the day to the University. He rushes to the telegraph office to do so.

Court resumes at one-thirty in the afternoon. The prosecution calls Andrew Phelps as its first witness to testify. The prosecutor addresses the court. "Mr. Phelps was the conductor on the Baltimore and Ohio passenger train that made a stop at Harpers Ferry on that Sunday night of October sixteenth. John Brown's men refused to let the train continue onto its Baltimore destination until late the next morning, Monday, October seventeenth. Mr. Phelps is the usual conductor on the Sunday night train from Wheeling, Virginia to Baltimore, Maryland."

Special prosecutor Hunter directs the questioning of Phelps. "Mr. Phelps, would you tell the Court what you saw when your train stopped at Harpers Ferry on the night of October sixteenth?"

"Well, Sir, we were a little ahead of schedule that night. It was about eleven forty-five p.m. We usually arrive at midnight. As we approached the bridge to Harpers Ferry, the watchman on the armory bridge was not there."

"Was that unusual - the watchman not being on duty?"

"Yes Sir, it was real unusual. It never had happened before. I instructed the engineer to stop the train - then changed my mind and told him to go on, but to go very slow. Just before we got to the bridge, the watchman ran out of the darkness and waved his hands for us to stop. We did. He looked really scared. He said that a bunch of armed men had attacked the armory, that they were there, that they had captured some men and were holding them prisoner. The watchman said that the men were heavily armed and that they had cut the telegraph wires."

"What did you do, Mr. Phelps?"

"I decided that we should continue on with the train. I instructed the engineer to proceed on across the bridge, but to go slow. I got off the train to walk in front in case something was wrong with the tracks. The fireman also got off to walk along with me. As we started to move onto the bridge, a voice coming from the other direction yelled for us to stop."

"Could you see who it was that was telling you to stop?"

"I couldn't see who it was, but I saw four rifle barrels shining in the train's headlight beam. I shouted for the engineer to stop, then told him to back up, which he did. At the same time, I ran to the other side of the train away from the men with the rifles."

"Then what happened?"

"I heard shots coming from the direction of the men with the rifles. I looked back and saw Hayward Shepherd, a railroad porter - a black man, running toward me. I heard someone holler 'Stop,' but Hayward kept running toward the train; then I heard shots again and Hayward fell. I ran out and picked him up and carried him to the safety of the train. A bullet had gone clear through him. Shot in the back. He was alive - kind of gurgling blood - but he didn't die until later in the morning - never did say anything - not a word. He had done nothing to those men, not one thing. They just up and shot him."

"Did you see the men who fired the shots that killed Mr. Shepherd?"

"No Sir, I did not see them clearly, but I could hear them; one of them hollered and said the train could cross the bridge now. I yelled back and said that we were not going to cross the bridge now. I was afraid the bridge timbers had been cut and we would crash into the river below."

"Did you have any further conversation with the men on the other side of the bridge?"

"Yes. I shouted and asked, 'What do you want?' He - the one doing the talking - shouted back, 'We want liberty, and we intend to have it.' I did not know what he meant, so I called back to him, 'What do you mean?'"

"'You will find out in a day or two,' he replied."

"What did you do then, Mr. Phelps?"

"I went back to the train to make sure the passengers were alright. They were alright, but they were plenty frightened. I told them to remain as calm as possible. I did not want to cross the bridge until it was good daylight. I wasn't sure the bridge had not been damaged. I just could not take that chance."

"Did you leave as soon as it got daylight?"

"I did not leave until sometime later. I got off of the train and sat up near the front of the engine. I could see men up near the firehouse at the arsenal doing something, I couldn't tell what. When it got light enough that they could see I was unarmed, I approached them - told them I was the conductor. One of them said he was John Brown. He said they were there to free the slaves. Then he apologized for what happened during the night. He said that he never intended that there would be bloodshed."

"You said that the man you were speaking to said his name was John Brown?"

"Yes Sir, that's what he said."

"Do you see that man in this courtroom today? If you do, would you point him out?"

Looking toward the accused, Mr. Phelps points directly at him and says, "Yes Sir, that is John Brown sitting on the cot. That's him."

At that moment Brown gets up from the cot, faces the court, and replies, "I am John Brown, and the man speaks the truth." He then sat down again and remained quiet.

Andrew Hunter continues his questioning of Mr. Phelps. "Did John Brown say anything else to you at that time?"

"Yes Sir. He told me that I could take the train and continue on the way at any time I wanted to. He said that it was safe to do so, that no harm would come to the train or to the people on it."

"So you boarded the train and resumed your trip to Baltimore?"

"That is correct, Sir."

"What time of the day was it when you left Harpers Ferry?"

"It was late morning when we got on the way. The fireman had to fire the engine up and had to get the steam built up so we could get moving. It was about 9:15 a.m. Monday morning when we finally left. We went on to Baltimore without further delays. We arrived in Baltimore at exactly twelve o'clock noon. I immediately notified the B&O officials of what happened."

"Mr. Phelps, when you left Harpers Ferry on Monday morning, October seventeenth, that was the last time that you saw Mr. Brown until you saw him here in court today. Is that correct?"

"No Sir. I saw Mr. Brown the next day."

"You saw him the next day - the very next day? That would be Tuesday, October eighteenth. Is that correct?"

"Yes Sir, Mr. Hunter, that is correct. That is when I saw him again."

"Mr. Phelps, would you please tell this Court under what circumstances this second meeting with John Brown took place? Would you tell us who was there and what was said?"

"Well, my boss on the B&O Railroad summoned me to his office early Tuesday morning. He told me that I was to return to Harpers Ferry immediately; that a train was dispatched to take me and some others there. He said that the U.S. government had recaptured the U.S. armory there. When I got to Harpers Ferry, I learned that Mr. Brown and his men had been captured early that same morning."

"Mr. Phelps, when you say the same morning, you are speaking about Tuesday morning, October eighteenth. Is that correct?"

"That is correct, Mr. Hunter."

"Thank you, Mr. Phelps. Please continue with the events that took place that day while you were present."

"Well Sir, when I got to Harpers Ferry that day, the Governor of Virginia, Mr. Henry Wise, was there. I was introduced to him and he was asking me some of the same questions that you are asking. Then someone said that they were bringing Mr. Brown in. He was lying on a pallet with a blanket over him. He had a bloody bandage around his neck. He looked tired. His eyes were open, but he didn't look scared. He kind of nodded as if he recognized me, and I nodded back to him."

"Then what happened, Mr. Phelps?"

"Governor Wise introduced himself to Mr. Brown. He told him that he was the governor. Then he started to ask Mr. Brown some questions."

"What kind of questions did Governor Wise ask and what answers did John Brown give? Can you tell us, Mr. Phelps?"

"Yes Sir. Governor Wise asked Mr. Brown why he attacked the Harpers Ferry armory. Mr. Brown said he captured the armory to obtain the rifles and ammunition that were stored there. He said that he was going to use them to arm the slaves that he thought would join his cause."

"Mr. Phelps, did John Brown say what his cause was?"

"Yes Sir, Mr. Hunter. He said that he had come to free the slaves. He said that he was the commander-in-chief of a new provisional government that he had established."

"Mr. Phelps, when you use the terms 'he' and 'Mr. Brown,' you are referring to the accused, John Brown. Is that true?"

"Yes, Mr. Hunter, I am speaking about John Brown," Mr. Phelps replies, and at the same time points toward Brown, who is now reclining on the cot. Mr. Phelps continues, "That John Brown."

"Thank you, Mr. Phelps. Now a few moments ago you stated that Mr. Brown had established a new government. Where was that new government located?"

"Right here in Virginia. He told Governor Wise that the new government had a new constitution. I remember exactly what he said. He said that he planned to reorganize the United States government with a new constitution and ordinances for the people of the United States."

There is considerable murmuring among the spectators in the courtroom following these revelations. Judge Parker gavels the bench for silence and in a loud voice calls for order in the court. The courtroom becomes silent.

"Mr. Phelps, I have one more question. You sometimes refer to the place where these events are taking place as the Armory and sometimes the Arsenal. Could you explain the difference in these two terms?"

"Yes Sir, Mr. Hunter. The terms are used interchangeably. The Arsenal and the Armory are one and the same place."

"Thank you, Mr. Phelps. Your Honor, the prosecution has no further questions for this witness."

The judge then asks the defense if they wish to cross-examine. Defense attorney Thomas Green responds affirmatively. He is keenly aware that damaging testimony has been given; testimony that directly implicates John Brown to the charges of treason and insurrection. He knows that Phelps is an honest witness. A fact that Brown has acknowledged standing before the court.

"Mr. Phelps, you testified that you spoke with the defendant, John Brown, on Monday morning, October seventeenth. Is that correct?"

"Yes Sir, it is correct. It was on a Monday morning."

"Did Mr. Brown seem to be belligerent or hostile toward you, Mr. Phelps?"

"Oh, no Sir. He seemed friendly. He was apologetic for what happened the night before, for stopping the train, and for the gunfire."

"Did he say who ordered the gunfire?"

"No Sir, Mr. Green, he did not. He did not say that he did or that he did not order it. He apologized for the bloodshed. He said that there would be no more gunfire unless he was attacked."

"Mr. Phelps, you testified that you heard the voices of gunmen on Sunday night, October sixteenth. Is that correct?"

"Yes Sir, that is correct."

"And you spoke with John Brown on Monday morning, October seventeenth, several hours after the incident on the railroad bridge. Is that correct?"

"Yes Sir, that is a correct statement."

"Can you say, Mr. Phelps, whether one of the voices on the bridge on that Sunday night was that of John Brown?"

"Mr. Green, John Brown's voice was not one of the voices on the railroad bridge on that Sunday night. Of that I am certain. I am also certain that Mr. Brown was not on the bridge that night. I could see the men well enough to know that none of them had a beard. John Brown has a long beard. He was not on the bridge. He was not involved in the shooting."

"Thank you, Mr. Phelps. I have no more questions."

Witness Phelps exits from the witness stand and the prosecution calls its next witness, Colonel Lewis W. Washington, a local plantation owner and the great, great nephew of former President George Washington. Lewis Washington, along with several of his slaves, had been captured the Sunday night of the raid on the arsenal by some of Brown's men. Several other prominent citizens of Jefferson County had also been placed under arrest, under order of Brown. All of the prisoners were brought to Harpers Ferry and held captive at the arsenal.

Prosecuting attorney Hunter questions the witness. "Colonel Washington, do you recognize the defendant - the man sitting on the cot?" Mr. Hunter points toward Brown.

"Yes Sir, I do."

"And do you know his name?"

"Yes Sir. His name is John Brown."

"Do you know him by any other name?"

"Yes Sir, Mr. Hunter, I know him by the name of Osawatomie Brown of Kansas."

"And how, Colonel Washington, do you know him by the name of Osawatomie Brown of Kansas?"

Before the witness can answer, defense attorney Lawson Botts is before the bench, hands waving emotionally above his head. "Your Honor, the defense objects to this line of questions. It is irrelevant to this case and it is used simply to inflame the jury against the defendant."

"Your Honor," Andrew Hunter interjects, "the question has much to do about this case. It is very relevant to the issues before this court. May I proceed with the questioning?"

"Very well, Mr. Hunter, you may continue with the question. However, if it does not quickly establish some relationship to the case at hand, I shall sustain Mr. Botts' objection."

"Yes, Your Honor, I understand." Then turning to the witness, he repeats the question. "Colonel Washington, how is it that you know the defendant by the name of Osawatomie Brown of Kansas?"

"Well Sir, that is the way he introduced himself when I was brought before him."

"Had you ever heard the name, 'Osawatomie Brown' before?"

"Yes Sir, I recognized the name. It was notorious a few years back, out in the Kansas territory. An abolitionist named John Brown attacked the homes of several men who lived at Osawatomie, Kansas, and who supported slavery, although they did not own slaves. He dragged them from their homes and murdered them. Hacked them to death in cold blood in front of their screaming and hysterical wives and children."

"Did his introducing himself as Osawatomie Brown frighten you?"

"Yes, it did. I was already nervous, having been called from my bed at eleven o'clock at night and taken captive by six heavily armed men. It was a frightening and intimidating experience. I believe Mr. Brown introduced himself as Osawatomie Brown to cause me to fear him; to let me know that he might kill me."

"Colonel Washington, did the men Brown sent after you do any damage to your property, or take anything of value?"

"Well, they did not do damage to my property, but they did take two valuable family heirlooms that had belonged to President Washington."

"What were the heirlooms?"

"One was a magnificent sword presented to General Washington by Frederick the Great, and inscribed on the blade was, 'From the oldest General in the world to the Greatest.' The other item taken was a set of two pistols, a gift to General Washington from General Lafayette."

"How did they find the sword and pistols?"

"Well, that is something of a mystery. They knew about the sword and pistols and they knew where they were kept."

"Did they say why they wanted them?"

"They said that John Brown wanted them. They were to be ceremonial objects in the new government that Brown had established. Brown was the commander-in-chief."

"Was that new government located in Virginia?"

"Yes Sir, right here on Virginia soil."

"Now, Colonel Washington, tell the court what happened after you and the other captives were taken to Harpers Ferry."

"We were told that we were hostages. Our slaves were armed with pikes. Pikes are long like a spear with a razor sharp, knife-like object on the end. The slaves were told to guard us."

"Colonel Washington, you say that the slaves were to guard 'us.' Are you stating that there were other prisoners or hostages other than you?"

"Yes Sir. They had captured several other plantation owners, neighbors and friends of mine, and some of their slaves, and they had also captured several of the arsenal workers who had been caught by surprise."

"Did the slaves mistreat you?"

"No Sir. They were kind and gentle. Brown told them that they were now free. He told some of them to go out into the countryside and tell the slaves they were free to go. That they should come to Harpers Ferry and he would give them weapons."

"Did the slaves follow John Brown's orders?"

"No Sir. Not that I am aware of."

"How were you treated by John Brown and his men?"

"Well, we were not treated unkindly. That is, we were not physically abused. We were, however, under a terrible mental strain. None of us knew what they were going to do to us. They certainly let us know that we were their prisoners and that they were in charge. I knew what he had done in Kansas."

"Were there attempts to rescue you and the others?"

"During the night - off and on - there was sporadic gunfire."

"Can you remember a time frame - an approximate time that you heard gunfire?"

"Well, I was brought to the armory by John Brown's men fairly close to midnight. I heard the B&O train come into the station. It usually arrives about midnight. About that same time I heard shouting and then gunfire."

"Did the gunfire continue throughout the night?"

"No. It was along about daylight when the gunfire began to really get heavy. There was lots of shouting and firing of guns."

"What was John Brown doing at the time?"

"He appeared to be surprised. He said something about the town residents getting all riled up and that he and his men's escape out of town did not look promising."

"Did the gunfire between the townspeople and Brown's men continue?"

"Yes. It continued all day Monday. There were shouts that men were killed. Some were local people and some were Brown's men."

"Was there any talk of escape by Brown and his men?"

"There was talk early Monday morning, but reports were coming in that neighboring communities were sending in militia to help the local folks. They kept coming all day and the fighting continued. Brown told his men there was no way to escape."

"What did Brown do?"

"He tried to negotiate a peace with the locals to let them go."

"What did the locals do?"

"They refused to let him go, so Brown and some of his men took nine of us prisoners and moved into the fire engine house. It has thick walls and is built like a fort. He said they would be safe there until they decided how to get away."

"Apparently he was unsuccessful. Is that true?"

"Yes Sir, Mr. Hunter, that is true."

"How long did Brown keep you and the other prisoners in the fire engine house?"

"Well, the next morning, Tuesday morning, October eighteenth, a regiment of U.S. Marines under the command of Colonel Robert E. Lee arrived at Harpers Ferry. Brown and his men were told to surrender. Brown asked to be allowed to cross the bridge into Maryland without further bloodshed to him and his men."

"What did Colonel Lee do?"

"He informed Brown there would be no deal. He promised to protect them from further bloodshed if they surrendered, but he would have to arrest them for their illegal seizure of the U.S. arsenal."

"What did Brown say?"

"He refused to surrender, so Colonel Lee ordered the Marines to attack. They did and the battle lasted about three minutes before the Marines were in complete control."

"Thank you, Colonel Washington. We have no further questions."

Defense attorney Thomas Green cross-examines. "Colonel Washington, before the U.S. Marines attacked, were you aware of what they were going to do?"

"Yes Sir, I was. They told John Brown that if he and his men did not surrender, they would assault the fire house."

"And you testified that they did attack. Is that correct?"

"Yes Sir. That is correct."

"Did John Brown use you and the other prisoners as shields to protect themselves from harm?"

"No Sir. When it was apparent that the Marines were going to attack, Mr. Brown told his men to put all of us prisoners in a safe place in the back of the building. That is what they did."

"Could you see what was going on, what was happening?"

"It was rather dark in there, but I could see. I could also hear the noise. The engine house doors were thick and the Marines were trying to batter the doors down. They finally battered a hole about three feet around and the Marines were jumping in as fast as they could."

"Did Brown order his men to fire their weapons at the Marines?"

"I am not sure. Anyway, they were firing their guns as fast as they could and the Marines were firing back. The first man through the hole appeared to be their leader. I pointed to John Brown, and the Marine; I later learned that he was Lieutenant Israel Green. Anyway, he drew his saber and struck John Brown a crushing blow, causing a deep gash across his shoulder and the back of his neck. John Brown fell to the floor unconscious. Two of Brown's men were killed and one of the Marines was killed. When Mr. Brown fell to the floor, Lt. Green ordered his men to stop firing their weapons and to use their bayonets. The fight was then about over."

"Colonel Washington, before the assault, and during the battle, John Brown did everything possible to guarantee your safety and the safety of the others with you. Is that correct?"

"Yes Sir, that is correct."

"Thank you, Colonel Washington, I have no further questions."

Commonwealth attorney Andrew Hunter again questions the witness to establish that Colonel Washington was present when Brown admitted to Governor Wise that Harpers Ferry was chosen as the headquarters for his new provisional government and that the purpose of that government was a free society for all people, black and white. After Attorney Hunter finishes questioning Colonel Washington, the court adjourns for the day.

The telegraphed results of day two of the John Brown trial prove to be more interesting to the University students than those of the first day. Some of the fire is re-ignited, although student agitation is at a minimum. There are no physical confrontations.

"What do you make of the more or less passive attitude of nearly everyone?" Jack asks as he and Robbie walk across the Lawn.

"I have no idea, Jack. I suppose that most of the students here believe that the trial evidence is strongly against John Brown and that he will be convicted. We have no way of knowing until a verdict is rendered."

The third day of the trial began Friday morning, October twenty-eighth. Defense attorneys Lawson Botts and Thomas Green appear in court accompanied by George Hoyt, a young Boston attorney hired by Northern interests to assist in the defense of John Brown. Prosecutor Hunter objects to the admission of Hoyt on the defense team, an objection which is overruled by Judge Parker.

The defense team recalls Colonel Washington to the witness stand. Attorney Botts questions the witness in an attempt to establish that Brown wished to reach a peaceful solution to the hostilities, that he wanted the hostages to go free. This attempt backfires. Washington testifies that Brown wanted to get himself and his men out. His primary objective was the freedom of himself and his men. Washington testifies that he and the other hostages could have been released by Brown at any time, but it was not done. They were, he testifies, useful to Brown for whatever benefit he could reap for their release. It was not his ultimate concern for them, it was, rather, his concern for himself and his followers. He testifies further that Brown and his men continued to resist, continued to fire their weapons as the Marines battered their way into the fire house, that John Brown was holding a rifle at the moment Lieutenant Green struck him down with a blow from his saber. Resistance continued by Brown and his men amid the Marines' continuing call for their surrender. When Lieutenant Green ordered his men to cease firing for fear of injuring or killing Brown's prisoners and to fix bayonets for a final assault, there was a mass surrender by Brown's men.

After Colonel Washington's testimony, the prosecution introduces Brown's provisional constitution as evidence of his treasonist and insurrection activities. Sheriff Campbell has frequently witnessed Brown's signature on letters and documents. He is called to substantiate the authenticity of Brown's signature. The sheriff verifies Brown's signature and Brown loudly proclaims that it is in fact his signature.

Other witnesses are called throughout the day. Their testimony parallels that of the earlier witnesses. Late Friday afternoon Brown stands and faces the court.

"May it please the court, I discover that notwithstanding all the assurances I have received of a fair trial, nothing like a fair trial is to be given me, as it would seem. If I am to have anything at all deserving the name and shadow of a fair trial, that this proceeding be deferred until tomorrow morning, for I have no counsel, as I before stated, in whom I feel that I can rely, but I am in hopes counsel may arrive who will attend to seeing that I get the witnesses who are necessary for my defense. I stand before this court to witness, to proclaim that I have no confidence in Attorneys Botts and Green. I do not believe that they have my best interests at heart."

Having so stated, Brown sits down.

Botts and Green are shocked. They have diligently worked in defense of Brown. They have attempted to obscure the testimony, animosity, and the hostility against Brown. They have inferred that the laws of Virginia on treason and insurrection were inapplicable to Brown's situation; that, if anything, it is a federal matter. They argued that any murder - if Brown's acts were deemed to be murder - was not premeditated, and in the worst case scenario would constitute a conviction of second degree murder, a crime not punishable by death.

Having no alternatives, Botts and Green face the court and request dismissal from the defense of Brown's case. Their request is granted.

George Hoyt, the Northern attorney sent to aid in Brown's defense, is surprised by Brown's action. He has been impressed by Botts' and

Green's defense efforts. Brown, with his outburst, has further alienated the jurors. He has angered the court. Hoyt is unfamiliar with Virginia law. He has no knowledge of the testimony that has already been given. Representing Brown under the best of circumstances would be an awesome task. Representing him under the present circumstances is a hopeless and thankless situation.

Judge Parker, at the request of Hoyt, adjourns the court for the day. Hoyt asks Botts and Green if they will assist him in preparing to represent Brown. They agree and work with Hoyt throughout the night.

The third day's telegrams of events of the trial of John Brown are received by the University students with hopeful anticipation that the end of the trial is near. They see Brown's dismissal of his court-appointed lawyers as an act of panic, that his actions will alienate most people in the court. They see it as especially detrimental in the eyes of the jury - and those are the opinions that count. The testimony of the witnesses has been unfavorable to him; and yet on several occasions Brown has stood and faced the Court and proclaimed that the witnesses were truthful. The day of reckoning is at hand. Time is running out.

Although most of the Southern students are peaceable and hold no ill will against the northern students, there are those that harbor anger, and even hatred, toward the northern students. Robbie and Jack have continued to attend the telegram meetings together.

The trial reconvenes the next day, Saturday, October twenty-ninth. Attorney Hoyt, assisted by two other Northern attorneys who are now on the scene, request a further trial postponement. The court denies their request; the trial continues. There are no new revelations from either the defense or the prosecution.

On Monday, closing arguments are made by the attorneys from both sides. Andrew Hunter has the last say for the prosecution.

"Gentlemen, administer justice according to Virginia law. Acquit the person if you can; but if justice requires you by your verdict to take his life, stand by that justice uprightly and strongly, and let retributive justice, if he be guilty, send him before that Maker who will settle the question forever and ever."

The outcome of the trial is in the hands of the jurors. After conferring for less than an hour, they are back in the courtroom.

The bailiff reads the charges against the accused, then faces the jury and asks, "Gentlemen of the jury, what say you? Is the prisoner at the bar, John Brown, guilty or not guilty?"

The foreman of the jury responds, "Guilty!"

The bailiff inquires, "Guilty of treason?"

"Yes," replies the foreman.

"Guilty of conspiring with slaves and others to rebel against the people of the Commonwealth of Virginia?"

"Yes" is the reply.

"Guilty of murder in the first degree?"

"Yes" is again the reply.

Except for several surprised gasps from the audience at the initial guilty response from the foreman of the jury, the crowd holds their silence. There is not another sound; no gloating from the predominantly Southern audience. There is no wailing and no tears from the Northern sympathizers. There is not a sound. Nothing. John Brown seems oblivious to the announced verdict.

Chapter Thirteen

Winds of Unrest

A hushed silence like a mantle of stillness settles over the courtroom at the announced guilt of John Brown. There are neither shouts of joy or cries of despair, neither signs of gloating or signs of grieving. Not a word, not one single word escapes from the lips of the spectators in the over-crowded courtroom. Lips are sealed in silence, a silence that is not quick to be broken.

Brown's reaction is no different from that of the spectators. He says nothing, he does nothing. He shows no signs of surprise, no signs of anger, and no signs of fear. The dead silence prevails for perhaps a minute or more. It ends in a soft voice reciting from the Old Testament Book of Ecclesiastes:

"To everything there is a season, and a time to every purpose under heaven.
A time to be born, and a time to die;
A time to kill, and a time to heal;
A time to weep, and a time to laugh;
A time to keep silent, and a time to speak;
A time to love and a time to hate."

Professor Holcombe immediately leaves the courthouse. He proceeds to the telegraph office and dispatches a six-word telegram to the University: *"John Brown convicted on all charges."*

The short message is all that is necessary. It says precisely all that needs to be said. It tells the story that needs to be told.

The professor thanks the telegraph operator for the courtesy he has shown him, then adds, "The Harpers Ferry incident should now be avenged in the minds of the South. The score is settled. Tomorrow John Brown will be sentenced for the crimes of which he has been convicted. That will be my final telegram to Charlottesville. I will then be heading home, back to my family and back to teaching law."

"I wish you well in your endeavor Professor, but remember, most of the people here in Jefferson County will not be satisfied until the sentence is handed down and has been carried out. If Brown is not sentenced to death, if he is not hanged for his murderous crimes, the people in this county, and perhaps throughout the Commonwealth of Virginia, will not be satisfied. I am well aware from the telegrams I send up North that the feelings up there are that Brown has done nothing wrong and that he should be set free."

"Yes, you are absolutely correct," the Professor responds. "There are social and political rifts between the North and South that are going to take time to heal. All of us, North and South, need to work for a peaceful solution to our differences. We are all Americans."

As Professor Holcombe walks the short distance to the hotel, he is relieved that the trial is over. He hopes that the students' pent-up feelings against Brown and the North will now subside and that their educational pursuits will again be vigorously pursued.

The initial student reaction to the professor's telegram announcing John Brown's conviction is one of jubilation. There is dancing on the University Grounds and on the steps of the Rotunda. There are shouts of joy, a contrast to the courtroom silence in Charles Town following the announcement of Brown's guilt. Generally, the student body is satisfied, relieved that the trial is over. Most of them are ready to put the matter behind them, ready to move on with their lives and their education. They are satisfied that justice will prevail.

A small minority of students are, however, inclined to do otherwise. They are not of a mind to permit this matter to die. The guilty verdict and the almost certain death penalty awaiting John Brown does not quell their thirst for further vengeance. They are intent on rendering their own brand of justice. These dissidents spread out among the other students in the crowd, sowing seeds of hate, seeds of revenge, not just for the punishment of John Brown, but for the punishment of all Northerners. They fan the flames of hostility, the winds of unrest aimed at the Northern students.

The cheers for the conviction of Brown turn to jeers for the Northern students as the hecklers continue to spread their brand of hatred among the crowd of students. The guilt of John Brown becomes the guilt of the North and the guilt of the Northern students. The inflammatory rhetoric of the antagonizers, bolstered by free-flowing alcohol, incites others to join their unfettered crusade. Having sufficiently aroused some among the crowd, the hecklers and dissidents divide into groups of eight or nine students, then spread out over the University Grounds in search of Northern prey.

Traces of an orange-red sunset remain in the western sky separating the daylight hours from nighttime blackness as Robbie leaves his cousin Thomas' home. It is a short walk across the University Grounds, then down the street to Mrs. O'Riley's boarding house. It is normally a fifteen-minute stroll. He has walked the path numerous times since the start of classes a month earlier. He knows every step of the way. He could walk it blindfolded.

The evening air is cool, although not uncomfortable as he walks along the path. The sun has now set behind the Blue Ridge Mountains, its brightness yielding to a darkened sky. The dim light of the moon peeping over the eastern horizon casts eerie and grotesque shadows dancing about on the Lawn. The cool breeze rustles the remaining dead leaves that continue to cling precariously to the trees. The wind rustling the leaves adds a spookiness to the already eerie evening. Robbie chuckles to himself as he realizes for the first time that it is Halloween. "I wonder where the ghosts and goblins are tonight," he murmurs half aloud.

The cool October breeze begins to chill him as he continues across the Lawn on the well-worn path. He rubs his hands briskly, then blows his warm breath on his cupped hands to warm his fingers. He hurries his pace as he thinks about the warm kitchen stove at Mrs. O'Riley's. Just the thought of Mollie K warms his heart.

In the distance he can see a group of students approaching from the opposite direction. They are directly in his path, talking loudly and cursing. As they draw near, he politely steps aside to allow them unobstructed passage. One of the group hesitates and looks closely at Robbie. "Wait a minute," he says to the leader of the group. "I think he's one of 'em."

"Are you sure?" the leader asks.

"Yes, I'm sure."

At the same time Robbie speaks, "One of who?"

Ignoring Robbie's question, the leader of the group speaks directly to Robbie, "Look, I ask the questions around here. You only speak when you are spoken to." Again turning to the group member, the leader asks, "Are you sure about him?"

"Yes Sir, he's one of 'em. One of them Northern scallywags. I see him in some of my classes. Yeah, I'm sure. Ask him."

The other members of the group have formed a circle around Robbie. He senses that trouble is brewing, although he wants to avoid a confrontation if possible. He tries to count the number of those in the group. He estimates about eight to ten young men.

The apparent leader, a big guy, taller than Robbie, about 250 pounds and muscular, again faces Robbie. He outweighs Robbie by perhaps seventy pounds. Big Guy looks directly at him. They stand silently facing each other. Robbie does not flinch. He looks Big Guy directly in the eyes. They are inches apart. He can smell the alcohol on Big Guy's breath.

Big Guy finally speaks, "Are you one of them contemptible Yankees?"

"I'm from up North," Robbie answers without further comment. He feels it is best to keep his comments short. His objective is to avoid a physical and verbal confrontation if it is possible.

Big Guy asks, "What are you doing down here in the South?"

"I'm here to complete my education. I attend classes at the University. Your friend attested to that fact - we attend some of the same classes."

Big Guy turns toward his fellow group of agitators. In a mocking voice he says, "He's down here to get an education. Do you think we should teach him a lesson or two?"

The group snickers mockingly. "Yeah, let's teach him a Southern lesson. He needs to learn about Southern manners."

"I'm not looking for trouble," Robbie responds. "If you will just allow me to pass, I'll be on my way. Please. If you will just step aside, I will be on my way."

The leader again turns to his group of friends as they tighten the circle around Robbie. "He wants us to step aside for him to pass by," the leader says half mocking and half seething with anger. "Yankee boy wants us to bow down to him. Are we going to bow down to him, to this Yankee?"

Without waiting for his friends to reply he again turns to face Robbie, his anger now intensifying, his face so close to Robbie's that their eyebrows are touching. "Are you one of those John Brown sympathizers? One of those Northern abolitionists that is down here to free slaves?"

The crowd around the two of them are snickering and encouraging Big Guy in his aggressiveness. They want a physical confrontation. They want to be a part of the melee, but they want Big Guy to initiate the action.

Robbie knows that the odds are against him. He is determined to remain as calm as possible. It is no time to panic. If a confrontation is inevitable, he is determined to time it at the most opportune moment. He pauses before answering. "I do not sympathize with Brown for the violent and unlawful methods he has employed in his fight against slavery. I do support his abolitionist causes. Yes, I am an abolitionist. Yes, I believe the slaves should be freed."

The crowd is enraged by Robbie's response and begins to further close in on him. He raises his hand, palm open. "Please, if it is your purpose to punish me for my beliefs, to punish me because I am a Northerner, allow me the courtesy to state my cause."

"Let him have his say," Big Guy says. Then with a broad grin stretching across his face, he continues, "then we will beat the living tar out of him." Big Guy's comrades applaud and cheer, then fall silent.

Knowing full well that the odds of resolving the matter peacefully are extremely slim, Robbie began to speak, "Gentlemen, I suppose that each of you came to Mr. Jefferson's University in search of the principles that he espoused; the ideals, the vision that he endowed to this great University and to mankind.

"You need to look no further than the Declaration of Independence, which he authored. There is no uncertainty of purpose in that document about these rights of freedom - of personal freedoms. It states emphatically that all men are created equal; that among those rights, all men are endowed by their Creator with certain inalienable rights; that among these rights are life, liberty and the pursuit of happiness.

"Mr. Jefferson never said that these rights were to be given to some people and not to others. He never said that these rights were to be given to the white man only, or only to some of the people of America. These rights are given to all Americans."

The big guy is now more incensed than ever. "Listen to me, Yankee boy. You are a liar. The Declaration of Independence was written by white men for white men. It does not apply to the ignorant Negro. Thomas Jefferson owned slaves. Slaves were the property of their owners when Jefferson lived and they are the property of their owners today. All of you Northerners are of the same mold. You are here to stir up trouble just as John Brown has done."

"You are incorrect to say that I am here to stir up trouble," Robbie responds. "You, Sir, are correct that Mr. Jefferson owned slaves. It is also true that he did not approve of slavery. Thomas Jefferson said of slavery, and I have memorized his exact words, 'The abolition of domestic slavery is the greatest object of desire in these colonies, where it was unhappily introduced in their infant state.'

"Jefferson further stated that 'the hour of emancipation must come; but whether it will be brought on by the generous energies of our own minds, or by the bloody scenes of St. Domingo, is a leaf of our history not yet turned over. The Almighty has no attribute which can take sides with us in such a contest.'

"Thomas Jefferson, as we all know, was a great American. He was a great Virginian. We should heed to his wisdom. Thomas Jefferson, you see, was at heart an abolitionist."

The big guy is now infuriated beyond reason. Robbie hoped that his comments would bring the group to a realization that their passions for revenge against the acts of Brown are misguided when applied against all Northerners. That is not the case. Again Robbie speaks, "I have done nothing to interfere with any of you. If you will allow me the courtesy to pass by, we can all be on our separate ways. I have done nothing to offend you. I do not intend to offend you. I ask only that you allow me to go on my way."

With fists clinched and anger in his voice, Big Guy responds, "You ain't goin' no where, Yankee boy. We're going to beat the tar out of you like I promised. Ain't we boys? You came down South with your fancy Northern ideas. You came here to make trouble. Well, you've found it. That's my middle name - 'Trouble.'"

Big Guy steps forward, just inches from Robbie. "Take a shot at me if you've got nerve enough." Big Guy points at his chin. "Right here, right on the button," he sneers. At the same time he grabs Robbie by the shirt. "Jefferson never said any of that freeing the slave stuff. You are a liar."

Robbie knocks the big guy's hand away but says nothing. Big Guy responds by spitting in Robbie's face then stepping back. "You are a yellow coward."

Robbie slowly extracts the handkerchief from his pocket, wipes the spit from his face in silence, his eyes fixed on Big Guy. Big Guy's accomplices are laughing, jeering at Robbie and tantalizing Big Guy, "Tear the coward apart!"

The moment of truth has come. There is not going to be a peaceful solution. A lightning-quick punch with the force of a brick hits Big Guy flush in the mouth. Blood spews like an erupting volcano. Big Guy hits the ground with a thud, flat on his back. He squeals in pain. He makes no effort to get up.

Big Guy's accomplices swarm over Robbie like a pack of hyenas devouring the carcass of a helpless prey. Robbie is hit, kicked and beaten over all parts of his body in the melee that follows. He attempts to fight back as best he can. It is useless. He folds his arms around his head for protection. Big Guy, finally on his feet, kicks Robbie unmercifully. His body yields to the punishment and he sinks to the ground in unconsciousness.

Thomas Holcombe has a premonition that something is amiss soon after Robbie leaves for Mrs. O'Riley's boarding house. He at first pushes the thought aside, attributing it to his imagination. It nevertheless keeps recurring in his mind. "Perhaps," he reasons to himself, "I should walk across the Lawn toward the O'Riley's. Anyway, the walk will be refreshing."

He takes a light coat in case it will be needed. The night air is quite cool. The moon is sufficiently bright so that he can see his way without trouble. As he walks silently along, he hears voices off in the distance. He is not yet close enough to ascertain what is being said. As he draws nearer to the sound of the voices, he detects anger or excitement in the sounds. He calls in a loud voice, "Robbie, Robbie Holcomb, do you hear me? Are you there?" The voices that he had heard subside. There is no answer to his call.

He again calls, "Robbie, is that you? Where are you?" He begins to trot toward the sound of the voices. He can see the silhouette of several people in the moonlight, perhaps a half dozen or more. They are no more than a hundred yards away, although much too far to recognize any of them. Thomas now slows to a walk, winded from his accelerated trot toward the group of men. Again he calls out, "Robbie Holcomb, is that you? Are you there?" There is no answer.

A hushed voice from someone in the group cautions the others. "Someone is coming. Let's get out of here." Thomas instinctively heads toward the group as they hurriedly began to depart.

"Wait a minute," he calls. "I need to talk to you. Have you seen a young student? His name is Robbie Holcomb." Thomas is now approaching the spot that the group of men has hastily abandoned. He is running at full speed. The men intensify the speed of their departure and never look back.

Thomas nearly stumbles over the crumpled body on the ground. "Robbie, is that you? Are you alright?" His intuition tells him that it is Robbie, but there is no answer. The only response is a faint groan. Robbie is unrecognizable. His face is bruised, bloodied and swollen. Thomas places his coat over him. There is blood, lots of blood. He leans over and whispers, "You're going to be alright. They're gone. I am going to find help. I won't be long. Don't try to answer, don't try to get up. If you understand what I am saying, can you nod your head?"

There is an ever-so-slight movement of Robbie's head, enough for Thomas to recognize it. "I won't be far away. I'll be back in no time at all."

Thomas hurries toward the street. Within minutes he meets several students whom he recognizes. One of them, Robbie's friend Jack Simon, he sends to Mrs. O'Riley's with a message of what has happened. Another is sent for the doctor. "Tell him to meet us at the O'Riley's."

Thomas and the other students return to aid Robbie. "I'm back and I have help. Can you hear me?" Again, there is a faint nod of his head, but no other response. Anxious steps are heard on the path behind them. For a frightening moment Thomas fears that the assailants are returning. It is two men with a make-shift litter board and blankets. They gently shift Robbie to the board, cover him with warm blankets, and carefully carry him to the O'Riley's boarding house.

Mrs. O'Riley meets them at the door and ushers them into the parlor. "Lay him on the couch," she instructs the men. She is a strong-willed woman, yet she turns ghostly white at the sight of Robbie. It is not a pretty site. He lay as silent as death. There are few visible signs of life. Mollie K is clinging frantically to her mother's arm, sobbing hysterically, "Is he dead, Mamma? Is he dead?"

"No, child, he is not dead. He is going to be alright," she reassures Mollie K, although unsure herself of the extent of his injuries.

Robbie half opens an eye. "Thanks, Thomas," he murmurs through swollen lips. "If you hadn't gotten there when you did, I believe they would have killed me." He looks toward Mollie K. In a pained voice, hardly audible, he says to her, "Don't cry, Mollie K. Please don't cry. I'll be alright."

Dr. Cabell from the University infirmary arrives. He looks at Robbie, then turns to the others. "Out, everybody out. This young man needs my attention. Mrs. O'Riley, I am going to need hot water, lots of hot water and warm cloths. Please hurry."

Except for Mrs. O'Riley's constant trips in and out of the parlor with pans of steaming water, no one else is allowed in. It is an anxious group waiting in the hallway. Mollie K continues to sob quietly, the men pacing the floor and whispering to one another.

In just over an hour Dr. Cabell has completed his examination and diagnosis of Robbie's condition and allows the others to come in. "Robbie is a tough young man. He has survived a terrible beating, an inhuman beating. He does not have any broken bones, but he is severely bruised over his entire body. He is not yet up to talking. He is sore from head to foot. He does not want to be removed to the University infirmary, however, that is a decision that must be made by Mrs. O'Riley. He is going to need some help for the next four or five days. Perhaps for a little longer. I will leave some pills with Mrs. O'Riley in case he experiences excessive pain."

"Oh, please let him stay here, Mamma. I will look after him. Mamma, he will not be any trouble at all." Mollie K is nearly in tears again.

Mrs. O'Riley consoles her daughter. "We will take good care of him, Doctor. If you will leave instructions, we will follow your orders. We want to do what is best for Robbie."

"Mrs. O'Riley, I have no doubt that the care he gets here will be just as good as what he would receive at the infirmary. I will come by tomorrow and for the next several days to check on him." The doctor excuses himself and leaves.

Thomas assures Mrs. O'Riley that he, too, will be back in the morning, having first offered to spend the night looking after Robbie. "Mrs. O'Riley, the telegraph office is now closed for the night, but in the morning when it opens, Robbie's parents need to be alerted to what has happened. I'll take care of the matter in the morning."

"Thank you, Mr. Holcombe."

Robbie, overhearing the conversation, motions to Thomas to come closer. In a broken whisper he asks Thomas to come by before the telegram is sent.

"That's a great idea, Robbie. Perhaps you will feel better in the morning." After the others leave, Mollie K sits near Robbie. She holds his hands lovingly, then kisses him on the forehead. "There," she says, "our first kiss; our very first kiss." She feels a slight pressure on her hands as he squeezes them as best he can, happy indeed for her affection.

The news of the cowardly attack spreads rapidly throughout the University community early the next morning. The University faculty and the administrators are shocked. The student body is angered. The

University issues a statement announcing that the perpetrators will be found and expelled from the University. They will not go unpunished. Such acts of violence will not be condoned.

True to his word, Thomas is at the O'Riley's soon after 9:00 a.m. Robbie's condition is much improved, even though he remains sore and swollen. His speech, through bruised and swollen lips, is somewhat slurred, although understandable. Robbie's efforts to dissuade Thomas from sending the telegram are unsuccessful.

"It is going to upset Mother, and she is going to insist that I move back to New York. I know how she reacts. Tell her the answer is an emphatic 'no.' Father will be at the mill - the only telegraph service in Bedford Springs. Please wait for his reply - and tell him I will send a telegram tomorrow. And Thomas, thank you for all you have done."

Thomas' telegram reports that Robbie's injuries appear to be superficial and healing quickly and that the injuries are the result of an altercation with several inebriated students who have now been expelled from the University. Robbie is not going to withdraw from the University - Mother is not to come here, he had told Thomas to relay the message.

Several telegrams are exchanged between Thomas and Robert. Results are satisfactory. Robbie is to wire his mother tomorrow at the mill. She will be waiting. The University's decision to expel the guilty students in the brutal beating of Robbie Holcomb is announced almost simultaneously with the court's announced punishment in the John Brown trial in Charles Town. Brown has been convicted on all charges. Now his fate - the punishment for his crimes - is in the hands of one man, Judge Richard Parker. The Judge looks directly at Brown, who now stands facing the court.

"Mr. Brown, is there anything you wish to say to this court? Is there any reason why sentence should not be pronounced against you?"

Brown appears surprised, but shows no signs of fear. Looking squarely at Judge Parker, he replies, "I have, may it please the court, a few words to say. In the first place I deny everything but what I have all along admitted - the design on my part to free slaves. I intended certainly to have made a clean thing of that matter, as I did last winter, when I went into Missouri and there took slaves without the snapping of a gun on either side, moved them through the country, and finally left them in Canada. I designed to have done the same thing again, on a larger scale. That was all I intended. I never did intend murder or treason, or the destruction of property, or to incite slaves to rebellion, or to make insurrection.

"I have another objection, and that is that it is unjust that I should suffer such a penalty. Had I interfered in the manner which I admit, and which I admit has been fairly proved, - for I admire the truthfulness and candor of the greater portion of the witnesses who have testified in this case - had I so interfered in behalf of the rich, the intelligent, the so-called great, or in behalf of any of their friends, either father or mother, brother or sister, wife or children, or any of that class - and suffered and sacrificed what I have in this interference, it would have been all right; and every man in this court would have deemed it an act worthy of reward rather than punishment.

"This court acknowledges too, as I suppose, the validity of the law of God. I see a book kissed here which I supposed to be the Bible, or at least the New Testament. That teaches me that all things 'whatsoever I would men should do to me I should do even so to them.' It teaches me, further, to 'remember them that are in bonds as bound with them.' I endeavored to act up to these instructions. I say, I am yet too young to understand that God is any respecter of persons. I believe that to have interfered as I have done, in behalf of His despised poor, was not wrong, but right. Now, if it is deemed necessary that I should forfeit my life for the furtherance of the ends of justice, and mingle my blood further with the blood of my children and with the blood of millions in this slave country, whose rights are disregarded by wicked, cruel and unjust enactments, I submit. So let it be done!

"Let me say one word further. I feel entirely satisfied with the treatment I have received on my trial. Considering all the circumstances, it has been more generous than I expected, but I feel no consciousness of guilt. I have stated from the first what was my intention, and what was not. I never had any design against the life of any person, nor any disposition to commit treason, or incite slaves to rebel, or make any general insurrection. I never encouraged any man to do so, but always discouraged any idea of that kind.

"Let me say also, in regard to the statements made by some of those connected with me. I hear it has been stated by some of them that I have induced them to join me. But the contrary is true. I do not say this to injure them, but as regretting their weakness. There is not one of them but joined me of his own accord, and the greater part at their own expense. A number of them I never saw, and never had a word of conversation with, till the day they came to me, and that was for the purpose I have stated. Now I have done."

As John Brown finishes speaking, Judge Parker gavels the bench for silence, as there is considerable murmuring in the court. As the audience silences, Judge Parker once again speaks.

"John Brown, you have been tried for crimes against the Commonwealth of Virginia in this the Circuit Court of Jefferson County, Virginia. The evidence against you has been considered by a jury of citizens of this county, and they have found you guilty on all charges. By the power vested to me by this court, I sentence you to death by hanging on the date of Friday, December second, in this year of our Lord, one thousand eight hundred fifty-nine."

Chapter Fourteen

And the Greatest of Gifts Is Love

Young Robbie Holcomb is once again blessed by that ever-present good luck omen that always seems to embrace him in his time of need. Within days of the brutal beating that he endured, he is again back on his feet.

"Nothing short of a miracle," offers Dr. Cabell, the University doctor who is somewhat astonished by Robbie's miraculously speedy recovery. "Come by the infirmary one day next week and I'll check you over. Those bruises should be healed by then and most of the soreness should be gone. You're a lucky young man."

"Thank you, Doctor," Robbie responds. "I'll come by next Tuesday afternoon after my classes are finished, if that is convenient."

"I'll see you then," the doctor replies.

Mollie K smiles. She, too, thanks Dr. Cabell as he departs. She has been Robbie's constant companion and nurse during his convalescence, and she feels a sense of pride for the part she has played in his recovery. Their budding affection for each other, under the watchful eyes of Mrs. O'Riley, has blossomed into a somewhat unconscious romance. A romance that neither Mollie K nor Robbie has verbally communicated to one another, although it is quite evident to others.

Mrs. O'Riley is amused over their apparent verbal shyness, although she does not mention it to either of them. "Actions speak louder than words," she muses to herself. "I'll just stand aside and let nature take its course." She is quite fond of Robbie. He is a fine young man, a principled young man. She has no problem with the developing romantic interest between

Robbie and Mollie K. Nevertheless, she is determined not to interfere in the matter. "It's something they will have to work out between themselves," she mumbles aloud, then adds in a determined voice, "Nobody has asked my opinion anyway, and I am just going to keep my nose out of it."

Although Mrs. O'Riley may be determined not to interfere in any budding romance between Mollie K and Robbie, it would be a completely different matter if Robbie's mother were suspicious of such a happening. Should Mary have the slightest inkling that a romance was brewing, wild horses could not prevent her from attempting to interfere - to throw cold water on any romantic notions. Robbie often mentions Mollie K in his letters home, but Mary assumes it is simply a platonic relationship. She has no reason to think otherwise.

While Mrs. O'Riley is very comfortable with Mollie K and Robbie's close and growing relationship, she is nonetheless concerned about the potential danger to her daughter - as well as the danger to Robbie - due to his Northern leanings on social and political matters. It is not that Robbie is ever aggressive or that he would ever assail someone for disagreeing with him - he would not. He is, however, one to stand by his principles, even if it causes trouble. "Had he been less truthful, had he pooh-poohed his abolitionist leanings, or soft-pedaled them, he might not have been harmed. A little white lie now and then, if it is done for a good purpose, can do no harm," she muses to herself. "Of course, Robbie will not do that. He is going to stand firm on what he believes," she whispers to herself. "I worry about him and Mollie K."

As mid-November approaches, Mollie K's seventeenth birthday draws ever so near. She says nothing to Robbie about it, and he has said nothing to her. She is sure he has forgotten it. After all, she had casually mentioned it to him only once, as kind of a passing comment, and there was really no reason for him to remember it. Nor had her mother mentioned it. She is sure that the anxiety over Robbie's beating and the excitement over his recovery has overshadowed her birthday. Even so, she is disappointed that it has not been mentioned.

Robbie has not forgotten. He purposely has not mentioned it to Mollie K. He wants to surprise her. He has waited for an opportune time to approach Mrs. O'Riley about his plans.

When Mollie K leaves the kitchen, Robbie seizes the opportunity. "Mrs. O'Riley, do you have a minute to discuss a very important matter?"

"Well, if you can discuss it while I am preparing supper, it will be just fine."

"The University's Jefferson Club is sponsoring a Christmas dance at the Midway Hotel ballroom on Saturday night, December tenth. I would like to invite Mollie K to go with me. It will be for her birthday."

"Have you said anything to Mollie K?"

"No ma'am, I have not. I wanted to ask your permission first."

"Thank you, Robbie. That is very thoughtful of you. Yes, you have my permission. This will be Mollie K's first date. You are a fine young man - a gentleman - and I trust you."

"Thank you, Mrs. O'Riley. It will be my first real date, also. I already bought the tickets hoping you would say yes. I will not violate your trust in me, Mrs. O'Riley."

Mrs. O'Riley smiles as she hurries from place to place in the kitchen, Robbie following closely along as she prepares supper for her boarders.

"There are several conditions to my approval. I want Mollie K to be home soon after the dance is over, and I want you to arrange transportation with Old Ben to pick you and Mollie K up here at the house and to bring you both home after the dance."

"Who is Old Ben?"

"Old Ben is the man who brought you and your luggage here when you first arrived. He is a former slave that has been given his freedom. He is honest, trustworthy, and dependable."

"Where can I find him?"

"Just run down to the railroad station any afternoon when the train is due in. Old Ben will be there."

"I'll do it tomorrow."

"Hadn't you better ask Mollie K first?" Mrs. O'Riley responds, trying very hard not to laugh. "When are you going to ask her?"

"As soon as she comes back in the kitchen," Robbie responds exuberantly.

"Why don't you wait until Mollie K's birthday? You can ask her then. I plan to have a private little birthday supper for her - for the three of us, after the other students have been fed."

"That's a fine idea, Mrs. O'Riley. When is it? I mean, I know it's November twenty-fifth. But what day of the week is it?"

"It's on a Friday. Just two more Fridays."

Robbie is elated. The days rush by. He is totally over the effects of his beating and he has put the matter behind him. He and Mollie K talk nearly every afternoon. He is well aware that she is disappointed that her birthday has not been mentioned. He can hardly keep the secret from her. Anyway, it is just a few more days until her surprise birthday supper.

It is now time. Mrs. O'Riley secretly has baked Mollie K's favorite dessert - those delicious apple dumplings with fresh cream and a scrumptious birthday cake, complete with seventeen candles. Mollie K has gone to her room to freshen up. She is disappointed that her birthday has not been remembered. Nevertheless, she is not going to mention it. She is noticeably dejected as she enters the kitchen.

"Surprise! Surprise!" both Robbie and Mrs. O'Riley shout as they beat on tin pans to add atmosphere to the occasion. The light from the birthday candles adds to the festivities. Mollie K is taken completely by surprise. Tears of joy fill her eyes as her mother and Robbie hug her. "Oh, Mamma, you didn't forget my birthday, after all!"

"No, child, I did not forget. You are my precious love and joy."

"Mine, too," Robbie responds, then blushes at the thought of his romantic implication. After all, they have never even dated, not even once. Mollie K also blushes over Robbie's comment, although she is very happy that he said it.

"Thanks, Robbie, for coming to my birthday supper. . .I mean my birthday dinner, as you would say." Robbie again blushes with embarrassment. He knows that she is teasing him, that she would not hurt his feelings intentionally. She again hugs both of them and kisses him lightly on the cheek. "Let's eat," she says as they walk over to the table. "I am starved!"

"Blow the birthday candles out, sweetie," Mrs. O'Riley says to her daughter, "and don't forget to make a wish."

Robbie interjects, "Take a big, deep breath first, because if you don't blow all of them out with the first breath, the wish will not come true."

"Alright, here goes." She takes a deep breath and easily extinguishes the candles. "I am exhausted." She fakes total exhaustion, limply falling into Robbie's welcome embrace.

"Con amore," he says.

"What does that mean?"

"It's Italian for 'with love.'"

They both laugh but neither of them pursue the matter further. Robbie, anxious to change the subject as both of them are blushing, asks, "Mollie K, what was your birthday wish?"

"Why do you want to know?"

"I don't know. I'm just curious, I guess."

"I can't tell you what it is or it won't come true."

"Well, can you tell me what it's about?"

"No, I can't tell you that either."

"Is it about me?"

"I'm not going to tell you anything. If it comes true, I'll tell you. So don't ask any more questions."

"Case closed," Robbie respond.

"Robbie, you are not a lawyer yet. You sound just like your cousin James."

"Now, now," Mrs. O'Riley intercedes jokingly. "This is supposed to be a happy affair. Let's not have a family squabble."

The birthday meal is delicious. The three of them engage in conversation about Mollie K's birthday and how they managed to keep the secret from her. After dessert is served, Mrs. O'Riley looks at Robbie. "Isn't there something you were going to ask Mollie K?"

Robbie somewhat shyly looks at Mollie K. She is blushing, as she is completely unaware of what is happening.

"Mollie K, there is a Christmas dance at the Midway Hotel on Saturday night, December tenth. Would you go to the dance with me?"

"Oh, yes, yes, yes," she happily responds, then jumps from her chair and kisses Robbie on the check. She then turns to her mother. "Can I, Mamma, please, can I?"

"Well, you leave me little choice since you have already accepted," Mrs. O'Riley responds teasingly, then adds "Of course you can, dear."

Robbie pulls two dance tickets from his pocket. "I already have the tickets, Mollie K." He waves them triumphantly back and forth as Mollie K playfully tries to catch them. She teasingly asks Robbie, "Who is playing the music at the dance? Is it the Calathumpians from the University?"

"Of course not, Mollie K," he responds seriously. "It's a real dance band from Washington, a high-class band."

Mollie K shrieks with joy.

Mrs. O'Riley, who had left the room, returns with a large box. "For your birthday, sweetie," she says as she hands it to Mollie K.

"What is it, Mamma?" she excitedly asks.

"Open it, dear."

"Oh, Mamma, a dress, a beautiful dress. With ruffled sleeves, and it's trimmed with embroidered flowers, and it's my favorite color, lavender. What are these things at the bottom of the dress, Mamma?"

"They are called flounces. They spread and move when you move suddenly. It will look nice when you dance."

"I have never seen anything so lovely. Thank you, Mamma, thank you. I am going to wear it to the dance. Can I, Mamma?"

"Yes, dear. I made it especially for that occasion. It's called a tea gown."

Robbie hurriedly adds, "And you will be the prettiest and loveliest of all the girls - young ladies - there."

Everything for the dance is taken care of except for the arrangements with Old Ben. Saturday afternoon Robbie heads for the train station. The train is due to arrive in half an hour; plenty of time to dicker with Old Ben for transportation to and from the dance. Robbie wonders whether Ben will remember him.

Ben's old nag is tied to a post near the train station. It is hitched to the same old wagon that had taken him to the O'Rileys when he arrived in town. "A sorry looking heap for a pretty girl with a pretty dress to ride in," he mumbles, somewhat dejected with the thought. As Robbie rounds the corner of the train station, he spies Ben dozing on an old wooden bench. He walks over to Ben, who is watching him with a half-open eye.

"Good afternoon, Ben. How are you? Do you remember me?"

Ben studies him for a moment, then with a grin spreading across his face responds, "Well, danged if it ain't the young feller from Noo York. Yes siree bob, I remember you."

"The name's Robbie. Not Bob."

"Is that a fact? What kin I do for ye, son? Ye ain't leavin' town so soon, are ye?"

"No Sir, Ben. I'm not leaving town, but I need to arrange for your services - you and your horse on the evening of December tenth. It's a Saturday."

"Well now, we's available. Watcha need me an' ma hoss fo?"

"I'm going to a dance at the Midway Hotel."

"Why don' ya walk? It's a dang site cheaper than rentin' me an' ma hoss."

"Yes, I know, but I'm taking a young lady to the dance, so I need transportation. Say, Ben, don't you have a carriage or something nicer than that old wagon?"

"Yep, ah sure do. I got a nice carriage. It has a roof an' doors an' ever thing. But it'll cost ye."

"How much is it going to cost me?"

"Well, where am I gonna pick ye up to go to the dance and when am I gonna pick ye up to take ye home?"

"You can pick us up at the O'Rileys around 7:00 in the evening and bring us back a little after midnight."

That wide grin again crosses Old Ben's face. He chuckles aloud. "Son, yo' takin' Miss Mollie K t' the dance, ain't ye?" Old Ben hee-haws to the top of his voice and slaps his legs amusingly. "Son, ah done tol' ya 'bout the widder O'Riley's purty daughter when ye came to town. Y'alls the one that said ye weren't interested in her daughter." Old Ben again commences laughing so hard he nearly falls off the bench.

Robbie is embarrassed. He cannot deny that Ben had warned him, nor can he deny that Ben is speaking the truth. Good naturedly, he accepts Ben's ribbing then adds, "Ben, you are absolutely right. You warned me. I should have listened to you. Yes, she is mighty pretty and she has stolen my heart away. Now, how much is it going to cost for you and your horse?"

"Son, ah was goin' to charge ye two dollars. Since the carriage is for Miss Mollie K, I ain't goin' to charge ye but one dollar and a half, and I'll wait right there at the hotel so as when y'all get ready to leave, I'll be right there. I'm also gonna give ye all a free ride down thru Charlottesville and back. You tell the widder O'Riley that I'm gonna take care of ye all and not to worry."

"Thanks, Ben. Do you want me to pay you now?"

"No siree bob. Y'all pay when ah dun finish' the work."

"Thanks again, Ben, but I'm going to pay you the two dollars. It's worth that much to me."

"Son, I sure thank ye. That's mighty kind. Miss Mollie K, she shore is purty, and she's a mighty fine lady. She'd make ye a mighty fine wife. Yes siree bob, she shore would."

"Ben, we are just going to the dance together. We're not thinking about getting married or anything like that. Now don't say anything more about that marrying stuff."

Old Ben again laughs, "Son, if ye remember, ye told me ye weren't interested in Miss Mollie K when I told ye how purty she was. Yes siree, I know a thing or two. I shore do."

"Everything is set then for Saturday, the tenth. Agreed?"

"Sonny boy, ye can count on me. Ah ain't gonna ferget Saturday th' tenth, and Ah ain't gonna ferget what I told you 'bout Miss Mollie K. Yes siree bob, she'd make ya a fine wife."

Old Ben is right on time, seven o'clock sharp. The carriage is as clean as a pin. Ben is dressed in his finest, complete with a top hat. He jumps from the carriage seat and opens the door for Mollie K and Robbie to enter. He removes his hat. "Evenin', ma'am, evenin', Sir."

"Good evening, Ben," Mollie K answers.

"Good evening, Ben," Robbie responds. Mrs. O'Riley is standing on the porch watching approvingly as the carriage moves away.

It is a lovely evening although rather cold for early December, and the closed-in carriage provides adequate warmth for them. Mollie K is absolutely beautiful in her new dress. They sit facing each other, Robbie holding her hands in his.

They dance the night away. It is a Cinderella-like evening. Even so, Robbie is seldom permitted to finish a dance with Mollie K. His classmates cut in on nearly every dance, waltzing, polkaing, or dancing some other popular dance with her. She is lovely and graceful in her beautiful gown. Jack Simon, his best friend, dances several times with Mollie K. Jack came to the dance unescorted and teases Robbie about stealing Mollie K. Midnight comes all too soon, and it is time to go. Old Ben is dozing in the hotel lobby but awakens easily. True to his promise, he drives them through downtown Charlottesville, then heads toward home. The night has gotten much colder and they snuggle closely together in a horse blanket in the carriage.

"Robbie, do you remember my birthday dinner?"

"Certainly, Mollie K. It was only two weeks ago."

"Well, do you remember my birthday wish?"

"Mollie K, you wouldn't tell me what your wish was or what it was about. Don't you remember that?"

"I told you that I would tell you if it came true, don't you remember?"

"Yes, I remember that. But you never told me anything else so I thought that it never came true. Anyway, birthday wishes are just something we do for fun. They are just make believe. They aren't supposed to come true."

"Yes, they are supposed to come true, and they do so come true, Robbie Holcomb. Don't you forget it."

"Don't get so huffy, Mollie K. Did your birthday wish come true?"

"Oh, Robbie, it came true and it's still coming true. I wished that you would ask me to go to a dance or someplace with you. And my wish has come true. I feel just like Cinderella. Oh, Robbie, I am so happy. I have never, ever been so happy. Birthday wishes do come true."

Robbie embraces Mollie K. "You are the most beautiful, the most precious girl in the world. I knew it from the first moment my eyes fell on you, the first time that I saw you. Mollie K, I do love you."

"And I love you, Robbie." Their lips meet for the first time.

Ben is tapping on the carriage door. "We're home. Back here to the widder O'Riley's place. It's time to go in."

"Thanks, Ben," they say in unison as Robbie hands Ben his fee and an extra half-dollar.

Mrs. O'Riley is waiting at the door. They hurry in, anxious to share the events of the night and to relish the warmth of the house.

"Mamma, I have had the most wonderful time of my life. I have never, ever been so happy. We had dinner at the hotel." She turns to Robbie and chidingly adds, "See, I said dinner, not supper," then continues to excitedly address her mother. "After dinner we danced and we danced and we danced. Other boys kept wanting to dance with me and Robbie was jealous."

"I was not. I wanted you to have a good time."

She runs over to Robbie and embraces him. "Robbie, you are so wonderful. Thank you for a wonderful evening. You know I really wanted to dance only with you and I did not like it when you danced with the other girls." Mollie K then runs back to her mother and hugs her. "Mamma, you are so wonderful. I just wish that Daddy could have seen me tonight."

A lump forms in Mrs. O'Riley's throat. Tears well in her eyes. She holds her daughter ever so close, but she does not surrender to her emotions. This is Mollie K's night; nothing is going to spoil it.

Chapter Fifteen

Something Old, Something New

The O'Rileys plan a quiet New Year's Eve at home. They invite Robbie to join them. "Nothing fancy," Mrs. O'Riley explains. "We will just relax and wait for the old year to end and the new one to begin. If we can stay awake that long."

Robbie is pleased with the invitation and graciously accepts.

The old year will be slipping away in a matter of hours, fading into oblivion. The year 1859 will be history. In many respects, it has been a good year; in many respects, it has not. It has had its ups, it has had its downs. The year has brought many changes in Robbie's life. Some are memorable, some are not. It is a year to remember; it is a year to forget.

Robbie had left a loving and caring family in New York; he has found a loving and caring family in Virginia. Things have gone quite well for him. He has experienced respect and compassion at the University. He has experienced a wealth of knowledge and excellence, the virtues and the zeal of the professors who are anxious to share their experiences, their knowledge, and their honor with the student body. He has also experienced elements of hatred and cruelty in the University community. Nevertheless, the good experiences far outweigh the bad at Mr. Jefferson's University. His decision to come South was right. He has no regrets, not one.

He leans back in his chair, his eyes closed, and continues to silently reflect on the pros and cons of the year. On the positive side are the O'Rileys. He is especially fond of Mollie K, and Mrs. O'Riley is like a second mother. The Southern Holcombes - his cousins James and Thomas - are more like brothers. All of the good things that have come about are

129

due solely to the University of Virginia, he reasons. After all, the University was the one single factor that brought him South.

The down side to his Southern life is totally attributable to the unpleasantness associated with the John Brown raid on Harpers Ferry and the aftermath of that affair. Brown's arrest, his trial, and his execution has widened the rift between North and South. It isn't that Robbie disagrees with the abolitionist ideals held by Brown; it is simply the methods that Brown employed to reach his objective that he disapproves. Two wrongs do not make a right. And of course, Robbie can hardly forget the horrendous physical assault that was waged against him by a few hostile University students. Even so, he harbors no ill will against them.

As the midnight hour draws near, Mrs. O'Riley prepares hot spicy cider and fresh-baked cookies. The night has turned extremely cold, although the parlor is more than comfortable, warmed by the roaring fireplace. Robbie stirs from his daydreams as Mollie K tickles his nose with a feather.

"Sleepy head," she teases, laughing gleefully at his startled look.

"I wasn't sleeping, just resting my eyes," he responds, somewhat agitated.

"Yes you were sleeping, Robbie, 'cause I was watching you. You were dreaming, too. I could see you smile and then I could see you frown. What were you dreaming about?"

"I was daydreaming, not sleep dreaming. When I was smiling, I was thinking about the good things that have happened this year. When I was frowning, I was thinking about the bad things that happened."

Mollie K becomes serious. "Was I in any of the dreams? Was I in the good ones or the bad ones?"

"You were in the good dreams, Mollie K. You're always in the good dreams."

"Oh, Robbie, tell me about the dreams, about the good dreams. Please tell me."

"Mollie K, don't you know it's bad luck to tell about a dream. If you tell anyone about a dream, it will bring bad luck. I'll tell you this much: it was about us and it was all good. Just take my word for it."

"When can you tell me about it, Robbie?"

"I'll tell you about it when we are old and gray," he responds with a laugh.

Mrs. O'Riley re-enters the room with the refreshments.

"Mamma, Robbie is teasing me. I was in his dream and he isn't going to tell me about it until we are old and gray. Mamma, make him tell me now."

"Mollie K, I am not going to get involved in your and Robbie's silly discussions. The two of you will have to settle them among yourselves. Anyway, it's time for hot cider and cookies."

The three of them sip the hot cider and munch on the cookies. They gaze at the open fire in silence, each with their own thoughts. They watch the flames as they flicker, momentarily die to just a glimmer, and then with a new breath of life, rekindle themselves, leaping forth from the logs and again illuminating the room.

The clock on the mantle shows that it is nearing the midnight hour, less than a minute remaining in the old year. The end comes quickly; as the seconds tick away, the three of them join in the count.

"Ten, nine, eight," they count, right down to the final tick of the clock. "Four, three, two, one."

"Hello new year! Hello year 1860!" Mollie K gleefully shouts, her cider cup held high in the air.

"And goodbye to 1859," Robbie responds as he clicks his cup against Mollie K's.

"Now it's my turn," interjects Mrs. O'Riley as she clicks her cup against those held by Mollie K and Robbie. "Time to sing 'Auld Lang Syne,'" she announces as she begins singing and the other two respond simultaneously.

When the singing ends, the three of them join in a three-way embrace and again toast the new year and each other.

"Last kiss of the old year," Mollie K announces as she kisses Robbie on the cheek, then turns and kisses her mother.

Robbie playfully whirls Mollie K around and kisses her.

"First kiss of the New Year," he triumphantly announces. Mollie K blushes. She is surprised at Robbie's kiss, but not disappointed. She glances toward her mother, anxious to see her reaction.

Mrs. O'Riley forces a faint, if somewhat disapproving smile, although she says nothing. "I'll speak to her about it tomorrow," she half murmurs. Again, she keeps her thoughts to herself.

Realizing that it is New Year's Day, she announces, "Enough of this evening for me. I am having a difficult time staying awake." She hugs her daughter. "Good night, sweetie. Good night, Robbie. It's off to bed for me."

She turns to leave, then again turns and faces Mollie K. "Be sure the fire dies all the way down before you come to bed. You know how afraid I am of fire. The wind is getting up tonight and it takes only one spark to set the house afire. You cannot be too careful."

"Yes, Mamma. I will be careful. I will wait until every last spark has gone out. Robbie will wait with me. Won't you, Robbie?"

"Yes, Mrs. O'Riley. I'll stay up with Mollie K. I wouldn't think of leaving her here by herself. I would never do that."

"Thank you, Robbie," Mrs. O'Riley says. She then turns again to Mollie K, hesitates a moment, and looks directly at her with all the love and concern that a mother could possibly have for a daughter.

"Mollie K, you are my precious love, my only child. You are all that I have. You know how to behave. You both know how to behave. I trust both of you." She turns and leaves the room. Enough has been said.

Mollie K's face is bright red. She is embarrassed. Robbie shares her embarrassment. She turns away from Robbie, too humiliated to look at him. She is near tears.

Robbie goes to Mollie K. He gently embraces her.

"Mollie K, please don't be sad; don't be embarrassed. I understand. What your mother said was done in love for you. She did not intend to admonish you or me. It was simply meant, simply said as an act of sincere love, an expression of her love, her care, and her concern for you."

"Oh, Robbie, thank you for being so understanding. You mean so much to me and to Mamma, too."

Robbie and Mollie K sit by the fire in silence, hand in hand, watching the dying embers in the fireplace. They are absorbed in thought, each of them thinking about the other. It is nearly one o'clock in the morning. A slight chill begins creeping into the room as the fire consumes the last log. Nothing remains but a few hot coals. Robbie breaks the silence.

"Mollie K, you are shivering. Are you cold?"

"I'm not exactly cold; just a little chilly, but I am alright. I am more sleepy than I am cold, but I promised Mamma that I would stay up until the last hot coal is out, and I am going to do it."

"Mollie K, the old year has passed away and the old fire is about to join it. You can hardly keep your eyes open. Go to bed. I'll stay up until the fire is all the way out. It's a new day and a new year and I feel fine."

"Thanks, Robbie. I am sleepy. Tomorrow will be Sunday. A new Sunday morning and a new year."

"Mollie K, it's already Sunday morning. The new day and the new year are already here."

"I know that, but it doesn't seem like morning when I haven't even gone to bed or gone to sleep. This is only the second time that I have stayed up past midnight, and the first New Year's Eve. Have you stayed up for New Year's Eve before?"

"Yes, I've stayed up a few times, but not often. My parents always host a New Year's Eve party. It was mostly for Father's business associates and for Mother's abolitionist friends and supporters. I usually went to my room early because there wasn't anyone my age there."

"I bet the party was for rich people, wasn't it, Robbie?"

"Mollie K, stop that. Why do you always think that everyone from the North is rich? I have told you before, we are not rich. Some years the mill hardly makes a profit. Other years it does quite well. That's all there is to it. Besides, I bet there are more rich people in the South than there are in the North, all of those plantation owners."

"Well, it sounds to me like Northerners are rich. Your father owns a mill and you live in a big house, and you have servants. Anyway, I don't care."

"If you are so interested in where I come from and how we live up North, why don't you come home with me next summer after school is out and see for yourself?"

"Do you mean it, Robbie?" Mollie K asks excitedly. "Do you really mean it? Oh, Robbie, say that you do. I have never been any place away from home; never in my life."

"Of course I mean it, Mollie K. Would I invite you to my home if I didn't mean it? You better ask your mother first, before you get all excited."

"Robbie, I am excited." She jumps up and hurriedly starts out of the room. "I'm going to ask Mamma right now."

"Mollie K, come back here. Don't go and wake your mother now."

"I'll ask her the first thing in the morning. Are you going to church with Mamma and me in the morning? It will be Sunday morning tomorrow."

"Mollie K, I keep telling you it is morning right now. It's already Sunday. Yes, I plan to go to church with you. Now you better go to bed, or you'll go to sleep in church."

"I'm not sleepy now. I can't wait for summer and to go visit your folks. Robbie, I am so excited."

"Mollie K, you haven't gotten permission from your mother yet. She doesn't know anything about it, about you going home with me."

"Robbie, will you ask Mamma, too?"

"If it makes you happy."

"It will make me happy. I am already happy. Oh, Robbie, I am happier than I have ever been."

"Why don't you go on to bed now or your mother will never be able to wake you in time for church." He grins and teasingly says, "Mollie K, you're a sleepy head, a lazy bones."

"I am not," she replies, trying hard to fake a pout or to look hurt.

He draws her close to him and kisses her on the forehead. "I love you, Mollie K."

"And I love you, too - except when you tease me. Do you mind if I go on to bed, Robbie?"

"No, sweetheart, I do not mind."

"Robbie, I hate for you to sit up by yourself."

"Go on, Mollie K. I'll be alright. I won't go to bed until the fire is completely out."

"Thanks." She kisses him, runs to the door, then teasingly asks, "How many kisses is that already this year?"

"Not enough," he replies, then adds, "I love you."

"You, too," she replies. Then she is gone.

The new year begins with promise. The early months of 1860 are academically busy at the University. The professors are intent on keeping the students so overwhelmed with class assignments that they will have little time for other matters. The University administration is determined to avoid a repeat of the circumstances that happened during and after the John Brown affair. Nevertheless, the widening social and political chasm between the North and South becomes a matter of daily discussion in nearly every classroom meeting. The forthcoming presidential election campaign promises to add intense agitation to the already volatile political atmosphere.

Robbie is especially perplexed over the widening political and social division between the two sections of the country. He is emotionally attached to both North and South. He listens intently during the classroom discussions, usually remaining silent. Professor Holcombe, during a particularly heated discussion, calls on Robbie.

"Mr. Holcomb, you have been especially quiet of late. Would you care to address the class and share your views with us?"

Momentarily startled, Robbie pauses, then addresses the class.

"As all of you are aware, I am from New York, a Northern state. I have lived here in the South only since early last fall. I consider myself neither a Northerner nor a Southerner. I consider myself an American. I am, as many of you are, concerned over the widening rift between the states, between the North and the South. It is my hope, my prayer, that these United States - through the wisdom of our national and state leadership, our elected representatives - that this divided nation will resolve its differences peacefully and permanently.

"I am perhaps too young to know, or too young to understand, how to resolve the critical matters at issue. I am not too young to share my concerns with others about the differences that are separating North and South. I am not too young to know that there are many factors contributing to these sectional differences; that included in these differences are social, political and economic factors.

"Much of our hope, for the present and for the future, lies not only in the hands of the politicians; that hope, and the responsibility for that hope, also falls into our hands. That hope is perhaps within our very grasp. The politicians in Washington and in Richmond, Virginia - and in the other state capitals in our great nation - have an awesome task before them. Our leaders here at the University of Virginia and in the other colleges and universities throughout America, have an awesome task in educating its students - you and me - as Americans and not as Northerners or Southerners.

"Our future, and our children's future also, lies within these academic halls, within this Rotunda; with the vision of a great nation fashioned by Thomas Jefferson, James Madison, James Monroe, and other great visionaries of an earlier time.

"This, Professor Holcombe, is my wish, my prayer, and my hope for today, tomorrow, and for the coming future."

Robbie pauses momentarily, then continues. "Our voices, the voices of the common people, must be heard - must be heeded - or the greatness of our nation will end in folly through the foolishness of misguided leaders." That said, Robbie sat down.

The students sit silently and attentively through Robbie's presentation. When he finishes speaking, they stand in unison and enthusiastically applaud, long and earnestly.

"Well said, Mr. Holcomb. Well said," Professor Holcombe offers.

"Thank you, thank you very much," Robbie responds to the class and to the professor. "And now Professor Holcombe, may I ask a question of you?"

"You may."

"The question is, do you believe that a state - any state, whether it be North or South - has a legal right to secede from the Union if it desires to do so? And, what is meant by the doctrine of 'State's Rights'?"

"Mr. Holcomb, your question, or questions are difficult ones. There are many opinions on the answers to those questions. A state's right to secede has been answered yes and it has been answered no by some of the ablest constitutional lawyers in the country. There have been threats of secession by some states in the past, but these threats have never materialized, so no one knows the answer for sure. The true answer may be a legal answer, or it may be a military answer. That is, the answer may be settled only by the Supreme Court or by war.

"My opinion is that a state does have a legal right to secede if the people of that state - the majority of the state's people - desire to do so.

"The doctrine of 'State's Rights,' in its simplest terms, is a policy that is aimed specifically at protecting the rights and powers of the various states within the Union from infringement of those states' rights by the federal government. The Virginia Nullification Resolution is identical to such resolutions of other states. It asserts that within the borders of this Commonwealth the State can nullify acts of the federal government if those acts are an invasion of the rights of this Commonwealth."

"Professor Holcombe, does this mean that, if the Commonwealth of Virginia - its state government - believes that the federal government is oppressive, that it is infringing on the rights of the state, and the state has the support of its citizens, that Virginia would have a legal right to secede from the Union?"

"I believe that to be true; that Virginia would have a legal right to do so. I also believe that the federal government would have no legal right to interfere with the state's right to secede.

"You see, Mr. Holcomb - and the rest of you - the federal government is merely a league of independent sovereign states. Therefore, any state, be it Northern or Southern, has a legal right to withdraw from the Union at any time if it should desire to do so, and its decision to do so should be free and without fear of oppression or interference from any other state or from the federal government.

"Of course, Virginia is not, or for that matter there is no other state that I am aware of that is advocating such a policy at this time. We sincerely hope that the differences between North and South are resolved in a mutually acceptable fashion. Differences between the various states and the federal government, and differences between geographical sections of the country, have always been resolved through negotiations, through political give and take. I have no reason to believe that present differences will not be resolved in a like manner."

Chapter Sixteen

Standing on the Promises

The new year is moving steadily onward, the cold winds of winter grudgingly yielding their harsh grip on central Virginia and the University community. A warm Southern spring is emerging, ushering in the presidential election campaign of 1860. The early election rhetoric offers little encouragement for the South. It provides few conciliatory promises designed to mend social and political fences. A long, hot summer is promised in the political arena.

By mid-May, the presidential candidates have been nominated. The Democratic party is in disarray, split into two factions. One candidate, Steven A. Douglas, is running as a Northern Democrat for president on an anti-slavery platform. The Southern Democrats nominate John C. Breckenridge on a pro-slavery platform. Abraham Lincoln, the chosen candidate of the anti-slavery Republican party, is a staunch abolitionist. Lincoln's popularity is centered in the North and West. He is neither widely known nor admired in the South. His rise to become the standard-bearer of the Republican party is hinged on several speeches he has made condemning the institution of slavery. Not to be outdone by the Democrats and Republicans, a fourth presidential candidate, John Bell, is nominated by the American Union party.

The statements and speeches, every word spoken by these candidates, past and present, and up to the very time of the election on November sixth, will be weighed and re-weighed during the coming months.

Southern newspapers, as do the newspapers from the North, print the utterances of these men - what they say and when they say it. These newspaper articles are critiqued and debated with great passion and emotion. Rumblings of agitation and threats of secession again arise in the deep South.

Students and faculty at the University of Virginia are not immune to the rumblings advocating secession that are coming from the deep South, nor is there a lack of sympathy for the Southern cause among many of those associated with the University. Opinions, however, are varied. Abraham Lincoln's stand on the issue of slavery and on the issue questioning a state's right to secede from the Union are brought to the public's attention through newspaper reprints of his earlier speeches. During a constitutional law class, Robbie raises his hand.

"Professor Holcombe, I have here a Richmond Examiner newspaper, which has reprinted several of Mr. Lincoln's speeches. Speeches he made some time ago."

"Yes, Mr. Holcomb. What is the point of the newspaper article? Does it have some relevance to this law class?"

"Yes Sir. It does. If you will allow me a few minutes of explanation, I will get to the question."

"Please proceed, Mr. Holcomb."

"Thank you, Professor. Mr. Lincoln had this to say about slavery - and I am paraphrasing what he said. He says that in his opinion slavery will not end in the United States until there is a crisis in this country; that a house divided against itself cannot stand; that the country will have to be all slave or all free. He goes on to say that he does not expect the house, meaning the United States, to fall."

"Yes, Mr. Holcomb. I am familiar with Mr. Lincoln's speech. I believe he made that speech in the summer of 1858 at the Republican State Convention in Springfield, Illinois. It is called the 'house-divided against itself' speech. Mr. Lincoln was at that time preparing to challenge Senator Steven Douglas for the Illinois senatorial seat. Mr. Douglas is one of the candidates now seeking the office of President of the United States. Mr. Lincoln, as you know, is seeking the same office."

"Yes Sir, Professor. I am aware of that. Mr. Lincoln went on to say in that speech that the 'result,' meaning slavery, or I should say the end of slavery, is not in doubt; that, and I quote from the newspaper article, 'We shall not fail. If we stand firm, we shall not fail.'"

"Yes, Mr. Holcomb, I believe that is precisely what Mr. Lincoln said, but it is not clear what your question is."

"I have not yet asked my question. I have not yet reached the point of the question."

"Sorry, Mr. Holcomb. Please proceed."

"Thank you, Sir. My question is based on the above speech, the house-divided speech, and on a second speech that Mr. Lincoln made in February of this year at Cooper Institute in New York."

"Proceed with your question, Mr. Holcomb."

"Yes, Sir. I am almost there. Anyway, in this other speech Mr. Lincoln said, 'Wrong as we think slavery is, we can yet afford to let it alone where it is.' Does this mean that Mr. Lincoln, if he should be elected president, does not intend to interfere with slavery where it presently exists anywhere in the United States?"

"Yes, I am familiar with that speech. I believe that is what Mr. Lincoln is saying. I believe his policy, his stated policy, is as he has indicated: that he will not interfere with slavery in any state where it presently exists, but he will prohibit slavery from spreading into any new territories or into any non-slave states already within the Union. Nor will he allow it in any new state that becomes a part of these United States.

"Some people believe that this speech at Cooper Institute propelled Mr. Lincoln into the forefront of the Republican nomination for president. He was not well-known throughout the North prior to this speech."

"Well," Robbie inquires, "if Mr. Lincoln is not going to interfere with the existence of slavery in the Southern states, then why are some of the Southern states advocating secession if Mr. Lincoln is elected president?"

"That is a difficult question. It can be answered only by the leaders - by the people of those states. I have stated before that I believe that a state has a legal right to secede if the government of that state, with the consent of its citizens, desires it to do so.

"I have also informed you and the class that there are others within these United States who believe otherwise. Mr. Lincoln, a lawyer himself, is one of those who believes otherwise. That is, he does not believe that a state has the legal right to secede from the Union.

"Mr. Lincoln stated during a speech at Galena, Illinois, I believe it was in the late summer of 1856, that if he were president, he would not permit a state to secede from the Union. I have a copy of that speech somewhere here in a desk drawer."

Professor Holcombe pauses, searching through his desk drawer. "Here it is," he announces, then begins reading what Abraham Lincoln had said:

"But the Union, in any event, will not be dissolved. We don't want to dissolve it, and if you attempt it, we won't let you. With the purse and sword, the army, the navy and the treasury in our hands and at our command, you could not do it. This government would be very weak indeed if a majority with a disciplined army and navy and a well-filled treasury could not preserve itself when attacked by an unarmed, undisciplined minority. All this talk about the dissolution of the Union is humbug, nothing but folly. We do not want to dissolve the Union; you shall not."

"In this recital which we have just read, it is emphatically clear where Lincoln stands on the issue of state's rights. He is opposed to disunion. He does not believe that a state has a legal right to leave the Union. He has also made it clear that he is opposed to the institution of slavery within the geographical boundaries of the United States as it exists today and as it might exist in the future.

"Even so, Mr. Lincoln has stated that should he be elected president of these United States, he will not interfere with slavery in these states where it now exists. He will not, however, condone it in any state or territory where it does not now exist - nor will he allow it to spread into new territories or new states that may be admitted into the Union.

"Mr. Lincoln, in speaking of slavery, in speaking of his personal objection to slavery, also said, 'As I would not be a slave, so I would not be a master. This expresses my idea of democracy. Whatever differs from this, to the extent of the difference, is no democracy.'"

Professor Holcombe pauses momentarily, then continues, "It is important that we recognize that there is a difference between the state's rights issue and the issue of slavery. They are separate and distinct issues, separate and distinct questions. There are too many people, North and South, who believe the two issues to be one and the same. Nothing could be further from the truth.

"I would like also to make one final point concerning the Southern states; the leaders of those states that are now, so to speak, 'waving the bloody shirt' for secession from the Union.

"You need to keep in mind that politicians, and I speak of politicians from all political parties, do not always do, once they are elected, what they promise they will do when they are seeking to be elected."

Robbie quickly interjects, "But Mr. Lincoln is known as 'Honest Abe.'"

"True," Professor Holcombe retorts, "All politicians have an axe to grind." Then, smiling wryly adds, "Mr. Lincoln is also known as the rail splitter candidate. No pun intended."

The class roars with laughter, releasing whatever tensions or animosities that may have been brewing.

The pleasant days of spring, having run their course, surrender to the coming of summer, a season beset by hot, humid weather in the South. The academic year of 1859-1860 at the University is nearing its end. The faculty and the student body have weathered the academic storm. July-the-Fourth ceremonies closing the scholastic year are over. Robbie has done well in his first year of college. He has accomplished much. He has earned the respect and friendship of his Southern classmates. Differences of opinions and of customs, although often at odds, are mutually respected.

Now it is time to head North, time to temporarily say goodbye to the South. One piece of unfinished business remains. Mrs. O'Riley has not yet acquiesced allowing Mollie K to accompany Robbie. Neither has she said no. She meets Robbie as he comes through the front door.

"Well, Robbie, your school year is finished. I suppose you are aching to head for home."

"In a way, yes; in a way, no. I have not seen my family since last September. I am anxious to see them. I also need to again work in the mill until September. There's a lot to do at the mill this time of year. I know that my dad will have a full work schedule for me.

"I am sad about leaving. I am going to really miss Mollie K; and I am going to miss you, Mrs. O'Riley. I can never forget how kind and generous you have been. I will surely miss you both."

Mrs. O'Riley has already made a decision to allow Mollie K to go North with him. She has told neither of them.

"Oh, have you decided against Mollie K going with you?"

"Oh no, Mrs. O'Riley. I thought that you were not going to permit her to go."

"Robbie, I have said neither yes nor no."

"Have you decided to let her go?" Robbie's face is aglow as he waits anxiously for an answer.

"Robbie, go call Mollie K. I will answer the question for both of you. I have kept the two of you waiting long enough."

Mollie K comes running, almost breathless with excitement. "Mamma, Robbie said that you wanted to see both of us; that you are going to tell us whether I can go with him to visit his parents."

She throws herself into her mother's arms. "Please say yes, Mamma. Please, please say yes."

Mrs. O'Riley hugs her daughter. She draws her ever so close. "Oh, sweetie, the answer is yes. How could I say no to you? How could I break your heart? Of course you can go."

Robbie, in uncontrollable glee, hugs Mrs. O'Riley. He has never before permitted his emotions to reach such a state of excitement. He is overjoyed.

"Mrs. O'Riley, I am so happy, so excited. Please be assured that I will take good care of Mollie K. I promise you that. I know my parents are going to love her, too."

"Children, please," she responds laughingly, then continues. "There are conditions to my yes answer. Conditions to which we must all agree."

Robbie and Mollie K interrupt her, almost simultaneously, "We agree, we agree."

"Just a minute, you two. You have not yet heard the conditions. I have spoken with Reverend John Granberry, the University chaplain, about this matter. He has suggested that the trip North would be good for Mollie K. He does not think, however, that it would be proper for her to go without a chaperone. John's wife has agreed to go along as chaperone if it meets the approval of you both."

"Yes, yes, yes Mamma," Mollie K responds, tears of happiness flowing uncontrollably down her cheeks.

Robbie is all smiles. "Yes, Mrs. O'Riley, I think it is a wonderful idea; I agree whole-heartedly."

Mrs. O'Riley, herself excited for Mollie K, again interjects, "Not so fast, you two; you have not let me finish with the conditions. Hold your approval until I have finished."

They both nod in agreement.

"You two must agree that Mrs. Granberry and Mollie K will return to Virginia within three weeks. That is, they must be back in Charlottesville three weeks to the day after the day you leave here on the trip North. This is a condition that the Granberrys insist on. I think it is very fair and very considerate of the Reverend and his wife."

Robbie and Mollie K nod in agreement, keeping silent until Mrs. O'Riley finishes her instructions.

"One final condition - and this applies to you, Robbie. You must send a telegram to your parents seeking their approval. This is going to place a burden on them. I cannot let Mollie K go without their approval."

"Mrs. O'Riley, I'm going to the telegraph office right this minute, just as fast as my legs will carry me."

"And I am going along, Mamma," Mollie K adds as they rush for the door.

Chapter Seventeen

It's A Big, Big World

An exchange of telegrams between Robbie and his parents set the stage for the pending trip North. His parents extend a cordial invitation to Mollie K and Mrs. Granberry. Mollie K is deliriously happy. They are to leave Charlottesville the following Wednesday, July eleventh. The week flies by for the three of them. Their itinerary is planned, baggage packed, and tickets purchased.

Old Ben is at the O'Riley's house at the arranged departure time to transport them to the train station. Mrs. O'Riley and Reverend Granberry ride along to say their goodbyes before they board the train.

"Takin' 'er home to meet yer folks, are ye son?" Ben asks Robbie, pointing directly at Mollie K. His question followed by a half-snicker. "She shore is mighty purty, ain't she, son?" Ben continues, meaning no harm by his comments.

Robbie and Mollie K are blushing and Robbie simply responds, "Yes, Ben."

Mrs. O'Riley, in an effort to rescue Robbie from his embarrassment, turns toward Ben. "Here comes the train, Ben. You better get ready to load the luggage."

"Yesum, Widder O'Riley, they knows me here at the station," Ben replies. He means no disrespect by addressing Mrs. O'Riley as 'Widder O'Riley'. Ben is, in his way, a polite, accommodating servant. Nor does Mrs. O'Riley take offense to Ben. She has known him for many years. He is honest and dependable.

Tears of happiness are shed freely as the goodbyes are exchanged. The whistle blows, the train moves down the track. Mrs. O'Riley, Reverend Granberry, and Old Ben stand waving until the train disappears from sight.

Mollie K is the first to speak. "This is my first train ride. The first time I have ever been away from Charlottesville. I hardly slept at all last night thinking about today. I am going to stay awake until we get to your parents' home. I don't want to miss anything." She hardly takes her eyes from the passing scenery as the train rushes onward toward the next station and toward their destination.

Robbie smiles as he watches Mollie K. He is happy that she is going home with him. "Mollie K, I bet you're asleep in less than half an hour. You will soon tire of watching the scenery, and don't forget, we are going to be on a train, and then on a river boat for the next two and a half days. You'll be sleeping half of the time. We all will, won't we, Mrs. Granberry?"

"Robbie, I am just like Mollie K. I am pretty excited about this trip myself. I have been as far away as Washington, and a little beyond there. But I have never been North of the Mason and Dixon line."

"What's that?" Mollie K asks.

"It's an imaginary line that separates Pennsylvania and Maryland, and part of western Virginia," Robbie interjects. "It's also known as the dividing lines between the North and South. Mollie K you must not have paid attention in History class."

"Yes, I did. I knew that. I didn't know what you all were talking about. I thought you were talking about something else." She again turns to gazing out of the window.

"Mrs. Granberry," Robbie inquires, "have you always lived in Charlottesville?"

"No. I was born in Staunton, Virginia. It's a small town in the Shenandoah Valley, west of the Blue Ridge Mountains from Charlottesville. Have you ever been over there?"

"No, I have not, but I want to cross over the Blue Ridge. I know the view from the top of the mountain must be awesome."

"Oh, it is just beautiful - and so is Staunton."

"When did you move to Charlottesville?"

"Quite a few years ago, soon after John and I were married. I was attending Mary Baldwin College, a Presbyterian girls' college in Staunton, when we met. We married after my second year of college, and John's ministry brought us to Charlottesville."

"Do your parents still live in Staunton?"

"Yes, my father's business is in Staunton. He owns a local gristmill. That's where the local farmers bring their corn and wheat and oats to be ground into flour or meal."

Mollie K, who has been quietly watching the changing scenery through the train's window, apparently uninterested in their conversation, suddenly turns toward them. "Oh cool," she interjects, "both of your fathers own mills. Robbie's father owns a garment mill, and Mrs. Granberry, your father owns a mill that makes food. That's really exciting."

Robbie reaches into the large paper bag filled with food that Mrs. O'Riley had packed. He pulls out a biscuit. "Breakfast anyone? This looks like bacon and egg."

"Yes, I'll have one, thank you," Mrs. Granberry answers.

"What about you, Mollie K?"

"I'm afraid that if I eat now, with the train moving and everything, that it will make me sick."

"It'll make you sick if you don't eat," Robbie replies.

"Well, can I have a bite of your biscuit?"

"Alright, you big baby," he teases as she takes a bite of his biscuit.

Mrs. Granberry smiles, but says nothing. She finishes her biscuit, lays her head back and closes her eyes.

"Robbie, if I go to sleep, will you wake me up?" Mollie K asks. "I don't want to miss anything."

"I'll awaken you if anything important happens."

The three of them doze intermittently, mesmerized by the clickety-clack of the train wheels rolling over the railroad tracks. They half awaken at each little village where the train stops to discharge or take on passengers. They do not completely awaken until the train pulls into Washington, where they have a several hour delay before catching their next train North. It is an opportunity to see some of the nation's attractions.

"It's a fairly large city," Robbie offers. "About 75,000 people live here. Mollie K, do you know who decided where the city of Washington would be built?"

"George Washington, our first president," she responds, then adds, "You thought I didn't know, didn't you?"

"I was just seeing if you were wide awake. I bet you don't know who designed the city - who drew the plans for it."

"Robbie, I don't care who did it."

"It was Pierre L'Enfant, a French engineer hired by George Washington. Do you know why the capitol dome is only half finished?"

Mollie K puts her hands over her ears. "I don't know, and I don't care."

"Our capitol was captured and burned by the British during the War of 1812 - and it's only half restored now."

"Well, I don't want another history lesson, Robbie. I want to enjoy myself."

"Mollie K, I would think you would enjoy it a whole lot more if you knew something about it."

Robbie hires a carriage and a guide to show them around the city. Some streets are paved with cobblestones, but most are dirt. It is not at all what Mollie K had imagined. Still, it is the nation's capital and that fact alone makes it a heart-warming site to see.

It is soon time to catch their next train on the journey northward. It is a short ride on the B&O Railroad to Baltimore, where they will spend the night.

Morning comes all too soon. They hurriedly gather their things and leave for the train station. "Mollie K, we are in another American city with a lot of history, did you know that?" Robbie asks.

"Robbie I don't want a history lesson. I'm tired."

"Well, you shouldn't be. You got more sleep than anyone else. Didn't she, Mrs. Granberry?"

"I believe she got her share," she responds, patting Mollie K on the arm.

Robbie continues, "Did you know that Francis Scott Key wrote the words to 'The Star Spangled Banner' on a ship in the harbor here in Baltimore during the War of 1812? And did you know that Baltimore was once the capital of our country during the Revolutionary War?"

"I didn't know that," Mrs. Granberry offers. Mollie K remains silent.

"Well, it was the capital for only about two months, but it's still an important historical fact."

"Robbie, will you please stop talking about those history things. It gives me a headache this early in the morning. Don't you think so, Mrs. Granberry?"

"I believe Robbie is just trying to enlighten us about some of the history that has taken place in the cities we stop in. Maybe we can get some coffee at the train station. That should liven us all up a bit."

"Mollie K," Robbie says teasingly, "you're a grumpy, sleepy head, but I love you."

"I love you, too." She smiles, hugs him, then kisses him lightly on the cheek. They both giggle.

"No more of that, now. I am supposed to be chaperoning you two," Mrs. Granberry intones good-naturedly; then she, too, joins in the giggle.

The train speeds onward, through small villages and past fields of grain. Farmers occasionally wave or salute the passengers by tipping their hats. Mollie K acknowledges the favor by happily and vigorously returning every wave.

"Mollie K, your arm is going to be sore if it doesn't drop off by the time we arrive in New York," Robbie says.

"Oh, Robbie, this is so much fun. I can hardly believe my eyes. I can hardly believe that all of this is happening, and that it's happening to me. I never knew that anything can go as fast as this train is going, and to see all of these people and all of these places. It feels like a dream, but it's not a dream. It's really real. It's really true, and it's happening to me, and to you, and to Mrs. Granberry."

"You know what else has happened, Mollie K?"

"No, but please tell me, Robbie. What is it?"

"You are now a Northerner. We just crossed over into Pennsylvania."

"We crossed the Mason and Dixon line?"

"Yes."

"Hooray! Hooray! Come on, Mrs. Granberry. Come on, Robbie. Shout hooray!"

"Mollie K, these other passengers will think we are crazy."

"I don't care if they do."

As the day wears on the excitement subsides. The small villages begin to look the same. The hat-waving farmers are simply duplicates of the ones they had left behind.

"How much farther is it to New York City, Robbie?" Mollie K asks.

"I'm not sure. I have been dozing a little."

"You call me a sleepy head and a lazy bones, and I haven't dozed at all, have I Mrs. Granberry?"

"No, you haven't. At least I haven't seen you if you have. I must confess I have drifted off to sleep a time or two."

"Well, I haven't slept at all; and that's the gospel truth," Mollie K responds in a solemn tone of voice, then adds, "I don't want to miss a thing."

"You better take a little nap. If you don't, you're going to be too tired to see New York City when we get there. We will put you in your room at the hotel and Mrs. Granberry and I will go out on the town without you."

"Can I lay my head on your shoulder, Robbie?"

"If that will get you to sleep, it's OK."

Mollie K awakens as the train slows to enter the suburbs of New York City. It is a big city; nothing but city as far as she can see. "W-O-W." She stretches the sound of the word to fit the amazement of the scene that falls before her eyes, totally consumed by the awesome sight of never-ending houses and buildings stretching forth beyond the range of her vision. She again, in astonished amazement, murmurs, "W-O-W. We sure live in a big, big world."

"New York City. This is New York City, Mollie K," exclaims Robbie, "and yes, we do live in a big, big world."

"Yes, I know. Somehow I knew it when I opened my eyes," she responds.

"There's more than eight hundred thousand people living here in the city," Robbie explains, "and 60 years ago there were only 60,000. Isn't that something?"

"Wow," she again exclaims, "where did they all come from? Did the people have that many babies?"

"No, Mollie K. It was waves and waves of immigrants mostly from Europe and others from Asia and from who knows where else."

Mrs. Granberry laughs heartedly. "Yes, that would be a lot of babies!"

After checking into their hotel, the three of them take a carriage ride through part of the downtown business section. They return to the hotel, have dinner, and prepare to retire for the night.

"Tomorrow is the last leg of our journey," Robbie says. "We should be in Bedford Springs by mid or late afternoon. The trip upriver is going to be cool, so wear warm clothing. Also, take a coat along. I'll call you two early in the morning."

"Robbie will we be on a big boat?" asks Mollie K.

"Yes. It's a paddle-wheeler. It's right large. The Captain is taking a load of cotton, Southern cotton, to my parents' mill. He is letting us ride along for free. We will have access to a cabin where we can rest and to keep out of the weather if we like. Good night, Mollie K." He kisses her on the forehead. "Goodnight, Mrs. Granberry," he says politely.

Chapter Eighteen

An Uncertain Course

Mollie K is over-awed by the long boat trip upriver. She spends hours on the stern mesmerized by the steady rotation of the paddlewheel as it propels them toward Bedford Springs. While they are yet some distance away, Robbie calls to her.

"We are nearing home. Soon our house will appear on the landscape above the river. Then you will see the mill and the town. Come up and stand on the bow of the boat. I want you to see Bedford Springs from the river when it first appears in sight."

"Robbie, I am so excited! Will your parents meet us? I am so afraid that they will not like me."

"Mollie K, I like you and my parents will like you. Everything will be just fine. Don't be so nervous and fidgety."

The three of them stand arm in arm, Robbie between them. He points to the far hills on the left of the river bank. "See the white spot on the hill?" he asks, pointing in the direction they are approaching.

"What is it?" asks Mollie K, unable to clearly identify the object.

"Why, it's a building!" Mrs. Granberry exclaims. "I believe it's a house," she continues, "a very large house."

"Yes!" exclaims Robbie. "That's our home and soon the mill and the town will also be visible."

Within minutes the town comes into view. At first it appears like a miniature village, growing larger and larger as they near their destination.

"Is that your mill?" Mollie K asks, pointing toward the large waterfront building with the words 'Holcomb Mill' painted in large letters on the side.

"It belongs to my parents," he responds matter-of-factly.

Looking again toward the colossal structure on the hill, she continues, "And that's where you live?"

"Yes, Mollie K. It's where you are going to live for the next several weeks. That's where we live. It's been in the family for years. It's just a big old house."

"It looks like a rich person's house to me. Don't you think so, Mrs. Granberry?"

"It's a very fine home, Mollie K," replies Mrs. Granberry without further comment.

"Mollie K, please stop using that 'rich person' phrase. It embarrasses me, and it would embarrass my parents. Now promise me you won't say it again."

"I'll try not to, but I don't know why it makes you so huffy," she replies, her tone of voice definitely showing that he has hurt her feelings.

"Mollie K, I'm sorry. I did not intend to hurt your feelings. You know I love you dearly." He embraces her lovingly. "Cheer up, now. We will be at the dock in a few minutes. I want you to look happy and give my parents a big smile."

Pointing toward the dock and speaking to Mollie K and Mrs. Granberry, Robbie happily announces, "There's my mother and father. Wave to them. The other people on the dock are mill workers. Wave to them, too. They are through working for the day."

All of them are waving and applauding. The mill whistle sounds three short welcome home toots for the three of them as a large banner unfurls from one of the factory windows with a 'Welcome Home Robbie and Friends' emblazoned in large letters.

"See, Mollie K. I told you that you would receive a warm Northern welcome. How do you like it?"

"I love it, Robbie. And I hope your parents like me, too. Do you really think they will?"

"Mollie K, don't be a pessimist. I told you. Everything will be just fine. Just act naturally; be yourself."

"Oh, Robbie, your Mamma is so pretty. I can see her waving to us again." Mollie K smiles and returns the waves to Robbie's mother.

The boat has hardly docked when Mary and Robert come aboard. Tears of happiness stream down Mary's face. She literally falls into Robbie's outstretched arms.

"Robbie, you will never know how much I have missed you. I hope you never go away again. I could not stand it. I know I would just die."

"Mother, I have missed you, too. Now regain your composure and welcome my friends."

She turns to the two visitors. "Please forgive my rudeness. It has been such a long time since I have seen Robbie. He is the light of my life.

"You must be Mollie K. Robbie has written so much about you. Welcome to our home and welcome to Bedford Springs." She politely hugs Mollie K.

Mary then turns to Mrs. Granberry. "And a pleasant welcome to you, Mrs. Granberry. We are so grateful to you for chaperoning them. We sincerely thank you. It is a privilege to have you as our guest." She turns to her husband. "This is Robert, Robbie's father." Robert smiles and shakes hands with Mrs. Granberry and then with Mollie K.

After introductions and pleasantries are exchanged, Mary again addresses the two guests. "I hope you are not overly tired. Dinner will be served soon after we arrive at the house. Our maids have agreed to stay late for this occasion. We do not have slaves in the North, you know."

Robbie's face reddens; partly from embarrassment and partly from anger. Although he makes no comment, he gives his mother a disapproving look. Then he takes the hands of his two guests and walks with them over to the group of workers that have welcomed him home.

"Thank you, my good friends. It is very kind and generous of you to take the time to welcome me home and to also welcome my friends who have come all the way from Charlottesville, Virginia to visit Bedford Springs. This is Miss O'Riley and Mrs. Granberry. I know they appreciate your kindness. My guests will be here for about two weeks and then I will be working with you at the mill for the rest of the summer."

Conversation on the carriage ride home is, at first, limited to an exchange of a few words. Robert also heard Mary's caustic remark about the slavery issue but felt that to pursue the matter would create more of an issue than just letting it drop. He will mention it to Mary later when they are alone. Mollie K unwittingly saves the day with her excited chatter. She asks many questions about Bedford Springs and about the Holcomb Mill and their home. She relates events of her own life to them. Soon all are engaged in an exchange of happy conversation. The stalemate is broken.

If Mollie K did not win Mary over to her side, she certainly did so with Robert. He is captivated by her forthrightness and honesty.

Robbie escorts the two guests to their rooms so they can freshen up and rest a bit before dinner. Neither Mollie K nor Mrs. Granberry has ever seen such a lavish and exquisite home. Their rooms on the front of the house face the river. The view is spectacular.

"Oh Robbie, your home is so beautiful. It's just like I dreamed it would be. It's even more beautiful than I dreamed." She runs to the window. "I can see a hundred miles down the river - the Hudson River you said?"

"That's right, Mollie K. You will have lots of time to look out of the windows later. You had better rest a while. Dinner will be served at seven o'clock. I will call you and Mrs. Granberry about fifteen minutes before dinner."

"Robbie, I am so excited. Do your Mamma and Daddy like me? Have they said anything? I hope they do."

"I am sure they do, Mollie K. I believe you have stolen my father's heart away. Relax and just be yourself."

"Oh, I hope they like me, Robbie. I am so happy."

Robbie hugs her. "Mollie K, do you remember the one thing I asked you not to do?"

"What is it, Robbie? What am I supposed to remember?"

"Remember that you are not to say that 'rich' word."

"I promise, Robbie. I won't ever say it again; but poor people don't live in a house like this."

"Mollie K, I never said that we are poor; I simply said that we are not rich."

"Golly sakes, Robbie, don't have a kitten, 'cause I don't care anyway."

Dinner is served precisely at seven. It is a scrumptious meal of fresh fruit, vegetables and roast beef. Dessert consists of apple dumplings with cream, followed by a birthday cake with eighteen candles.

"Mother, I asked you to have the apple dumplings for Mollie K. It's her favorite dessert. But what is the birthday cake for?"

"Robbie, the cake is for you. Surely you did not forget that you were eighteen years old on July the Fourth?"

"No, Mother, I did not forget. It was the day for closing ceremonies at the University. I was very busy that day."

"Well, you are not busy now and everyone must have a piece of birthday cake."

After dessert they all retire to the parlor. Mary is very pleasant, anxious to make amends for her earlier comment at the dock.

"Mrs. Granberry, would you mind if we address you by your first name? It seems so formal to call you 'Mrs.' We are going to be living under the same roof for the next couple of weeks."

"Yes, that's a wonderful idea. My first name is Esther. It's a Biblical name. It's from the Old Testament - from the Book of Esther. Esther had become the Queen of Persia and through her influences with the King, her people - God's chosen people - are delivered from exile. The Book of Esther is right gruesome in places. I believe that my Biblical name is what first attracted my husband. He is the University of Virginia chaplain. Yes, please call me Esther."

"Thank you, Esther. And I hope that you will call me Mary. With that problem settled, would you and Mollie K care to have a tour of the house before you retire for the night? I suspect that you both are quite tired from your long trip. Tomorrow Robbie can show you around the village and the mill."

"Thank you, Mary. That is a great idea. Don't you think so, Mollie K?"

"Oh, yes. Thank you Mrs. Holcomb."

Mary and Esther bond instantly. Mary half-way attempts to be cordial to Mollie K. It is nothing personal that causes her coolness, other than the apparently close relationship that exists between her and Robbie. His infatuation with Mollie K is evident. He spends as much time with her as possible. They laugh, they tease, and they talk. They are happy and affectionate. Mary's irritation is caused by her perception that Mollie K is stealing Robbie's heart away. It is a simple case of jealousy, and this jealousy is gnawing at Mary's heart. Mollie K is simply a rival. A very formidable rival.

Mollie K is not oblivious to Mary's rudeness. She earnestly attempts to be pleasant and helpful, hoping that Mary will warm to her friendliness, that her efforts will at least lessen the tension between them.

"Is there anything I can do to help, Mrs. Holcomb?" she eagerly inquires.

"No, the maids will take care of things tomorrow," is Mary's dour reply.

At Robbie's suggestion, Mollie K cuts fresh flowers from the garden, arranges them in a lovely vase, and places them on Mary's piano. "There," she says to herself, "this should make Robbie's Mamma happy."

Mary, well aware that Mollie K arranged the flowers and placed them on the piano, feigns disappointment and comments in Mollie K's presence, "Now why did the maid place those hideous flowers on my piano? She is well aware that they are not my favorites."

Mollie K is devastated - heartbroken. She says nothing, turns away, and goes to her room. Mary would normally never say or do such a thing. She is quite aware of what she has done. In her mind she is fighting for her son's love - for sole possession of his love. She cannot be sorry for what she has said or done.

Robbie attempts to explain his mother's jealousness to Mollie K the night before she and Esther are to leave on their return trip to Virginia. As they walk through the garden behind the Holcomb house, he holds her close.

"Mollie K, it is going to be dreadfully lonesome here after you leave. I am going to miss you. I'll be back to Charlottesville and the University in less than two months, but it's going to seem like two years."

"Robbie, I am going to miss you, too. I'll miss you terribly, but I am not unhappy to go home."

"Why do you say that, Mollie K? Why are you so unhappy here?"

"Robbie, you know very well why I am unhappy. It's because of your mother's attitude. She does not like me. I have tried very hard to please her. I have tried to do things that would cause her to like me, but she doesn't. She just refuses to like me."

"Has she said other things, other than the flower arrangement episode, to offend you? Because I told her that it was my idea to cut the flowers, but she turned a deaf ear. I am at my wits' end with Mother."

"Robbie, she has said many things and did many things in my presence pretending as if the maids had done them, knowing that I had done them and that I did them trying to please her. I have desperately tried to please her, and she finds fault with everything I do.

"I have said nothing. I do not want to come between you and your mother. Yes, she has said plenty to offend me, but she does it as if she is talking about someone else. Lately, she has hardly said a thing to me."

"Mollie K, Mother's attitude is indefensible. She is jealous of you and I don't know why. I suppose she has fears that I may never come back to Bedford Springs after college. She probably thinks you are the problem."

"Robbie, are you sure you are coming back to the University - back to Charlottesville for your second year of college?"

"Of course I am, Mollie K. Why do you keep asking that question? You know I am coming back because of you, and I'm coming back because of the University. I would come back to you even if I was not going back to the University. Don't you understand that you are the most important person in my life?"

"Robbie, I know that your Mamma does not want you to come back to Charlottesville. She said so when you got off the boat, and she has said it often since then. And now she doesn't like me and that's all the more reason to keep you from coming back."

Mollie K's eyes fill with tears. She continues speaking. "Your mother does not like Southerners. I suppose she likes Mrs. Granberry, but she's the only one. Robbie, she asked if Mamma has slaves. I told your mother that we don't own slaves, that we don't even know anyone that owns slaves."

Robbie does not dispute Mollie K's assessment of his mother's coolness and rudeness towards her. Robbie's father also noticed it. He goes out of his way, makes extra efforts, to be accommodating to Mollie K. Robert's affection for Mollie K is not a put-on. He genuinely cares for her. He is not displeased over their budding romance. His acceptance of the romantic interest brewing between the two youngsters further infuriates Mary.

In spite of her outward coolness toward Mollie K, Mary joins Robert and Robbie on the carriage ride to the dock when the guests leave for home. She makes a special effort to be cordial to Mollie K and bids her a pleasant farewell. She also bids Esther a fond farewell. She says nothing when Robbie and Mollie K embrace and the parting tears flow. He holds Mollie K as long as he can before releasing her to the long trip home. The remaining days and nights of their separation will be painful for both of them.

Chapter Nineteen

Hopes and Fears

Mary's summer-long hope that Robbie would enroll at a Northern university for his second year of college proves to be fruitless, an empty dream. The summer is over and he has again gone south, back to the University of Virginia, back to the O'Riley's boarding house, and back to Mollie K. The old doubts and fears that haunted her when Robbie first developed the notion of a Southern education come flooding back. The old angers resurface. She is again at wits' end.

"Mollie K is definitely the problem; of that I am sure," she confides to Robert. "I thought, from the letters that Robbie had written home last year, that their relationship was simply platonic. He did not say so. He mentioned her in nearly every letter. Still, I thought that the two of them were just good friends. I was quite happy when Robbie telegraphed that Mollie K was coming to visit for several weeks. I again assumed that it was just a friendship. After all, he had many friendships with young ladies he had grown up and attended school with right here in Bedford Springs. There had never been any serious romantic relationships with any of them. Not even with Serena Johnson. Nevertheless, the moment I saw Robbie and Mollie K standing with arms around one another as the boat neared the dock, I recognized that their relationship was more than what I had supposed. My attitude toward her instantly changed. Mollie K is an adversary. She has become the primary Southern nemesis. She is my most pressing Southern fear."

"Mary, you jump at too many conclusions - putting the cart before the horse, as the old saying goes."

"No, Robert, I am not putting the cart before the horse. I could see what was going on. You could see it too, if you would open your eyes."

"What I saw, Mary, was two young people that are fond of one another. That's all I saw. It's just natural."

"Robert, sometimes you make me so angry. You never seem to see things the way I do."

"Well, even if I saw things the way that you do, what is wrong with a young boy and a young girl being fond of one another? It certainly happened to us when we were young. Or have you forgotten?"

"No, I haven't forgotten. We were both Northern. She's Southern - he's Northern. That's what's wrong. There are all kinds of differences."

"Mary, you are the one that preaches equality. You shouldn't be judgmental. Besides, I thought Mollie K was a fine young lady. Anyway, North or South makes no difference."

Robbie was not angry with his mother when he returned to school, although he was terribly disappointed with her failure to politely and warmly welcome Mollie K into their home. She had, by her attitude, driven a wedge between herself and him. He, nevertheless, half-way patched things up with his mother before leaving for Virginia.

It is now early October. Mary and Robert are alone. She has not heard from Robbie. Not a letter, not a word.

"Robert, what do you think is wrong that Robbie has not written?"

"He is probably busy with the new school year and hasn't had time to write."

"Perhaps so. I know that Robbie is infatuated with Mollie K. Perhaps he gets lonely down there in the South. I think he has fallen for her southern accent and that so-called southern charm. Do you think so?"

"Mary, Mollie K has a southern accent because she lives in the South, grew up in the South. You and I have northern accents because we grew up in the North. Do we judge a person's worth because of the way they speak or where they come from? This is totally inconsistent with your belief, with your philosophy, Mary. I just don't understand you."

"Robert, don't you understand the seriousness of what's going on? Do you want your son to come back here to live? Can't you see the storm clouds brewing over this presidential election thing? Now we have two critical problems. Our son is living in the South. The South is threatening to leave the Union, and he could marry that Southern girl."

"Mary, you are overstating the seriousness of these issues. You are getting the cart before the horse again. Besides, I found Mollie K to be very charming. She is a very beautiful girl. I can certainly understand Robbie's interest in her."

"Robert Holcomb, you are no help at all. I do not get any support from you. Yes, I agree she is very pretty and that scares me. It scares me almost as much as the prospects of war."

"Mary, you have been harping about a North-South war for the past three or four years and nothing has happened."

"Robert, if you would read the papers, you would know what I am talking about. Southern political leaders are threatening to leave the Union if Abraham Lincoln is elected President. They want to establish a new nation. Oh, Robert, I worry constantly about these matters. Will anything good ever come out of the South?"

She pauses momentarily, then continues. "War is inevitable, Robert. I fear it is coming. It is coming sooner than most people suspect. I will not be surprised if it happens before the November election. There is so much bitterness in this country."

"Mary, there is always bitterness at election time. Politicians purposely create bitterness and division. They do this to excite and stir up their constituents so that they will get out and vote. It's an old political ploy."

"I hope you are right. Robbie is down there in Virginia. I just don't know what is going to happen."

"Mary, you cannot sit around and speculate about what might or might not happen. Yes, some Southern states have been threatening to secede from the Union. They have been making the same threats for the past fifty years. It has never happened before, and it is not going to happen now. You can mark my word on that. Anyway, Mary, I believe your fears are due more to a pretty little blonde beauty than they are to fighting a war."

"Robert, please don't get me started on that subject again. Perhaps if it wasn't for her, he might have enrolled in a Northern college this year. I hope we don't live to regret his going South."

"Mary, Mollie K had nothing to do with his initial decision to enroll at the University of Virginia and it is not fair to place this year's blame on her either. I believe he would have gone back, even if he had never met her. I believe he is much happier since he met her, but he had his heart set on attending the University of Virginia for years. It was the right decision for him then, and I believe it is the right decision now.

"Perhaps if you are looking for someone to blame, you should accuse Thomas Jefferson. He was the initial instigator. Regardless of who is or who is not to blame, Robbie is there for his second year of college. It was his choice the first year, and it is his choice this year.

"I can see no reason to cast blame on Mollie K for anything. I suppose, from all indications, she is happy that he is back and he is happy that he is back. From my observations, she appears to be a very nice young lady. I cannot understand your resentment. She was pleasant and always a lady during her visit. She was friendly and polite even though you were sometimes not so cordial."

"Robert, I wanted to be nice to her. I wanted to be friendly, but I did not want to encourage a romantic relationship between the two of them. I could just not bring myself to develop a close relationship with her. Maybe I should be ashamed, but I am not. I simply avoided her as much as I could. She has been brought up to be Southern, and she talks Southern. I resent the fact that our friends that met her thought that she was so precious, that her Southern accent was so cute. Yes, Robert, and I resent the fact that you liked her and that she liked you. Furthermore, would you want our son to marry that Southern girl and to live the rest of his life in the South? Well, I don't. These are the reasons I oppose a romantic relationship between them. It is all the reason I need. I do not need any other reasons. Can't you understand that?"

"Shame on you, Mary. You are acting childish and vindictive. You, Mary, of all people, showing prejudice against another person. You advocate the abolishment of slavery. You fight discrimination against women. You speak out against those practices both publicly and privately. Now you are practicing the very evil that you preach against. What reason can you give for your resentment of this young lady, other than your prejudice and jealousy? You can point to no other reason. Mary you need to re-evaluate your own personal concepts. You need to practice what you preach."

Chapter Twenty

Unsettled Times

As election day 1860 draws ever so near, the political agitation between North and South rises to an alarmingly high level of hostility. Provocative sectional insults are hurled across the aisles of the U.S. Congress by the legislative bodies; not because of partisan political affiliation, but due solely to the geographical areas - North or South - that the other party represents. The same tainted tones of hostility are repeated by those politicians currently seeking public office and by the poisoned pens of many of those in the newspaper profession. Conciliatory efforts to resolve sectional differences fail to materialize. Responsibility is always deemed to be the obligation of those on the other side of the argument.

And then it is time. And so it comes. It comes to every household across America, to every door in every hamlet and in every city. It is election day, Tuesday, November 6, 1860.

When it is over, when it is all over, when the votes are all counted, Abraham Lincoln is declared the winner. He is now the President-elect of the United States of America. The election is far from a landslide victory for Mr. Lincoln. He receives less than forty percent of the popular vote. He does not receive a single popular vote in ten of the fifteen Southern states. He does not receive any electoral votes in the fifteen Southern states. He nevertheless receives a sizable electoral vote; more than fifty-nine percent nation-wide. It is more than enough votes to elect him President of the Union and more than enough votes to unfurl the threatening flag of secession flying anew through the deep South states. The abounding mood of jubilation in the North becomes a sullen mood of rejection in the South. To Southerners in general, the election of Lincoln is the straw that breaks the camel's back. Their hopes are now in vain.

Sunrise on Wednesday morning, November 7, 1860, casts shadows of fear and uncertainty across the South. The impossible has happened; the unthinkable has occurred. In the minds and hearts of nearly half a nation there is little hope left for the survival of this Union. One hundred and eighteen days remain until Lincoln will become the sixteenth President of the United States. As President-elect, Lincoln has no authority. He can do nothing but wait. Nothing. Lincoln does not expect war, nor do the vast majority of people, North or South. Nevertheless, there are rumors of war; rumors of war that are rising from prominent and powerful men in high government places.

In Charlottesville, at the University of Virginia, attitudes are somber, but they are not hopeless. There are differences of opinion from those of the President-elect. One of those differences is the Southern belief that under the United States Constitution, the nation is a confederation of sovereign independent states. "As such," states Professor Holcombe, "each state has a legal right to peacefully leave the Union if its citizens desire to do so. It has the right to do so unmolested by any other state or by the federal government. You should remember having discussed this very issue last college year when the same question came up."

Robbie raises his hand for recognition.

"Yes, Mr. Holcomb, you have a question?" asks the Professor.

"Yes Sir. It's kind of a combination question and comment, I suppose."

"Proceed, Mr. Holcomb."

"Thank you, Professor Holcombe. My comment or question deals with President James Buchanan's final address to Congress on December third. According to a Washington newspaper, he had this to say, and I'm reading directly from the news article:

'The Union, as some seem to believe, is not a mere voluntary association of states to be dissolved at pleasure by any one of the contracting states. When "We the People" adopted the Constitution to form - as we so pledged - a more perfect Union, than what had previously existed under the Articles of Confederation, which had stated that the Union shall be perpetual, has adopted that same condition into our present Constitution. That is, the framers of our national government never intended to implant in its bosom the seeds of its own destruction, nor were they guilty of the absurdity

of providing for its own dissolution. State sovereignty is not superior to national sovereignty. The Constitution bestows the highest attributes of sovereignty exclusively on the federal government and this Constitution is the law of these United States and it shall be the supreme law of the land.'"

Robbie pauses, looks away from the newspaper at his classmates, then continues. "According to this newspaper article, President Buchanan, with uncharacteristic passion in his voice, admonished the joint session of Congress with these final words:

'Anything in the Constitution or laws of any state that is contrary to the intent of the United States Constitution is unlawful and unenforceable.'

"Then the newspaper states that the President again paused, pointed toward the Congress, and with a sweeping wave of his right hand, pointing at no specific group of the Congressmen, but intending to include them all, concluded with this warning:

'If secession is legitimate, the Union becomes a rope of sand and our thirty-three states may resolve themselves into as many petty, jarring and hostile republics as they so desire, and by such a dreaded catastrophe the hopes of all of the friends of freedom throughout the world will be destroyed. Our example to the world for more than eighty years will not only be lost, it will be quoted as conclusive proof that man is unfit for self-government.'

"My question, Professor Holcombe, is what do you make of President Buchanan's speech?"

"Mr. Holcomb, I believe that is the most eloquent speech that Buchanan ever made. I read it earlier today. It is certainly thought-provoking. I do not agree with the President's assessment of what a state's rights are under the Constitution. One of the great freedoms under our American Constitution, under our system of government, is the right of men to peacefully disagree with one another. You have heard my assessment of state's rights many times, and I stand solidly behind it, as do many Southern scholars, jurists, and our elected Southern officials. It is our hope, Robbie, regardless of the public posturing and threats of secession by the public officials of certain states, that it will not be necessary to test the legal status of the state's rights doctrine. And if there ever should be such a challenge, we hope that it shall be done by due process of law and not by armed aggression. It is for these reasons that we have a court system and it is why we have a Supreme Court of these United States to decide the final legal issue on such matters."

Jason Miles, a student from Virginia, raises his hand, eager to be recognized.

"Yes, Mr. Miles, do you have a question?"

"Yes Sir, Professor. I suppose that it is, like Mr. Holcomb's, half question and half comment. There seemed to be a difference of opinion among the original signers of the Constitution as to what the intent of the document meant, or perhaps what some of them thought it actually meant or believed that it meant.

"That is, there was a belief, an understanding among some of those men that the Constitution and its Preamble - that the 'more perfect union' clause dealt primarily with the act of defending themselves - that is as jointly defending the various states against an outside or foreign aggressor. Therefore, they - the separate and independent states - were not giving up any other rights other than the defense of themselves on a unified basis. Isn't that true, Professor Holcombe?"

"That is basically correct, Mr. Miles. As a matter of fact, objections were voiced by some of the states within a short period of time after Congress began to pass laws that the officials of some states believed to be treading on the states' separate and distinct rights.

"The Commonwealth of Virginia, as did the Commonwealth of Kentucky, passed resolutions in 1798, objecting to the federal government's intrusion into 'states rights'. I want to make one point clear, that even though these resolutions were not signed by their originators, Thomas Jefferson was the preparer of the Kentucky resolution, and he probably had a hand in the Virginia resolution that was prepared by James Madison."

Robbie again raises his hand for recognition.

"Yes, Mr. Holcomb, do you have something to add to the discussion?"

"Yes, Sir. I just want to point out that none of the other states joined Virginia and Kentucky in supporting the resolutions."

"That is true, Mr. Holcomb. But what we are talking about here today is the intent factor, the original intent of the various states at the time they created a 'more perfect Union'. What did the leaders of the individual states believe - what did they intend to agree to when the Declaration of Independence was signed? What was their intent? The issue of intent, of understanding, of purpose, was made quite clear by Jefferson in the Kentucky Resolution of 1798, which provided that each state,

165

under the federal coalition, is a sovereign and substantially independent nation in and of itself. This is the Jefferson that authored the Declaration of Independence. If anyone understood its meaning, its purpose, its intent, who else but Thomas Jefferson could it be? Sovereignty was retained by the individual states. That was the intent of the Father of the Constitution. That was the intent of the 'framers' of the Constitution - including James Monroe, our fourth president.

"There are other instances in our past history to support the doctrine of states rights. There have been few legal challenges. Nullification - the process of abolishing a law by declaring it null and void - was the principle factor involved in the Kentucky and Virginia Resolutions of 1798, but they were never tested in the Courts because, as Mr. Holcomb pointed out, none of the other states were willing to support the resolutions. It was not again seriously proposed until 1828, when John C. Calhoun proposed what was known as the 'South Carolina Exposition' opposing a Tariff Act. It resulted in the famous Congressional debate between Senator Robert Hayne and Daniel Webster in 1830. President Andrew Jackson riled against it, and it never came to a more serious or legal challenge. Let us hope our present circumstances will not result in anything more serious than what it is at the present."

There are rumblings of discord toward northern ideals and opinions, and even though they are heated and antagonistic, they are not directed at Robbie personally. He is well thought of and respected by his classmates.

The practical question of the state's rights issue, the challenge of a state's right to secede from the Union is not long coming. A State Convention in South Carolina meets on the 17th of December, 1860, to consider these consequences. The axe of secession falls on December 20th. The people of South Carolina declare themselves a free and independent state. They elect to go their separate way.

In rapid succession, the states of Mississippi, Florida, Alabama, Georgia and Louisiana follow suit before the end of January 1861. On the first day of February, Texas joins the confederation of secessionist states.

Senators and Congressmen from the seceded Southern states return home destined to fill similar political roles in a new government, in a new nation. One of those men returning South is Jefferson Davis, a Southern politician and statesman. Mr. Davis, a Mississippian, a West Point graduate, a veteran of the Mexican War, had also held numerous other high civilian posts in the United States government. He had served as a member of the

United States House of Representatives, as a United States Senator and as a Secretary of War.

Upon resigning from the U.S. Senate, Senator Davis addresses his Union colleagues, not in anger, but in a spirit of hope. "Gentlemen, I leave this office with many regrets and with many hopes. I am sure that I feel no hostility to you Senators from the North. I am sure there is not one of you, whatever sharp discussion there may have been between us, to whom I cannot say in the presence of my God, I wish you well and such is the feeling, I am sure, of the people whom I represent and those whom you represent. For whatever offense I have given, I have, Senators, in this hour of parting, to offer you my apology.

"My sincere hope is that as I go in peace that our two nations will coexist in peace."

The United States shrank from a nation of thirty-three states to a nation of twenty-six states. The U.S. federal government makes no immediate forceful challenge to the seceded states. What the North believed to be a dubious threat from the South is now a distinct reality. American history is on a rampage. The nation is at a crossroads.

A new nation, the Confederate States of America, is born. By February 18th, Jefferson Davis, the former U.S. Senator from Mississippi, is inaugurated as its president. Its leaders express its desire that the new Confederate nation be allowed to go in peace.

Students and faculty at the University of Virginia, as is the situation at other colleges and universities throughout the country, both North and South, are plagued by uncertainties after the secession of the deep south states. Sentiment at the University of Virginia remains predominately loyal to the United States government irrespective of its strong Southern ties, and even in the face of secession by other Southern states. By and large they support the only central government they have ever known. Their national history, and their family history, is rooted in the freedoms won by their forefathers in the not-too-distant past-Revolutionary War battles.

President James Buchanan refrains from taking any action against the seceded states. It is, however, now time for a changing of the guard. Lincoln's inaugural address is anxiously awaited. The day, Monday, March 4, 1861, has arrived and his address will be headline news in tomorrow's newspapers.

The University classes open on Tuesday, March fifth, with great excitement. Professor Holcombe greets his class, then addresses Robbie.

"I see you have the morning paper. Would you care to share some of the new President's thoughts with the class?"

"Yes, Sir," Robbie replies as he unfolds the paper. "I will read what I believe to be the key statements from the inaugural speech." He began reading portions of what the new President said.

'I shall take care, as the Constitution itself expressly enjoins upon me, that the laws of the Union shall be faithfully executed in all the states. Doing this, which I deem to be only a simple duty on my part, I shall perfectly perform it, so far as is practicable, unless my rightful masters, the American people, shall withhold the requisition, or in some authoritative manner, direct the contrary. I trust this will not be regarded as a menace, but only as the declared purpose of the Union that it will constitutionally defend and maintain itself.

'In doing this, there need be no bloodshed or violence, and there shall be none, unless it is forced upon the national authority. The power confided in me will be used to hold, occupy, and possess the property and places belonging to the government, and collect the duties and imports.

'But beyond what may be necessary for these objects there will be no invasion, no using of force against or among the people anywhere.'

Robbie pauses, then asks the Professor, "Sir, would you prefer that we pause here for a few minutes and discuss the meaning of the speech up to this point?"

"I assume you have not finished your reading yet, Mr. Holcomb?"

"No, Sir, I have not."

"Then I suggest you continue until you have finished and we will discuss it at that point."

"Yes, Sir, Professor Holcombe. I have just two other portions of President Lincoln's speech that I should like to read. In one place, he says, and I quote, 'No state, upon its own mere motion, can lawfully get out of the Union.'

"Then in conclusion, President Lincoln said,

'In your hands my dissatisfied fellow countrymen, and not in mine, is the momentous issue of civil war. The government will not assail you. You can have no conflict without being yourselves the aggressor. You have no oath registered in Heaven to destroy the government, while I shall have the most solemn one to preserve, protect and defend it. I am loath to close.

We are not enemies, but friends. We must not be enemies. Though passion may have strained, it must not break our bonds of affection. The mystic cords of memory, stretching from every battlefield and patriot grave to every living heart and hearthstone, all over this broad land, will yet swell the chorus of the Union when again touched, as surely they will be, by the better angels of our nature.'

"Professor Holcombe, that concludes the portions of President Lincoln's address that I planned to read."

"Very well, Mr. Holcomb. Now does anyone in the class have a question or comment?"

A voice from the back of the classroom inquires, "Do you think President Lincoln means what he says, Professor?"

"Yes, I believe he means exactly what he says. We should keep in mind that what he has said heretofore was said as a candidate for public office, not as President of the United States. What he has just said in his inaugural address he has said as President of the United States. Yes, I believe he means what he has said."

Another voice from the class interjects, "Lincoln has said that the government will not attack - I believe he used the word 'assail' - those states that have left the Union unless those states are the aggressor - that is, unless they attack first. Is that correct? Do I understand this correctly?"

"Yes," replies Professor Holcombe, "you have heard it correctly."

"Well, Sir," the student continues, "since Jefferson Davis, the new president of the seven confederate states that have left the Union, has stated that all they, the Confederate states, ask is that they be allowed to go in peace, then does this mean that there will be no civil war?"

"Let us hope so. Let us pray so."

"Professor Holcombe," inquires Robbie, "where does that leave the question of 'state's rights?' Remember that in his inaugural address President Lincoln also reiterated an earlier statement made before the election that 'no state, upon its own mere motion, can lawfully get out of the Union.'"

"Mr. Holcomb, I wish that I knew the answer to your question. President Lincoln also said yesterday in his address to the nation that the laws of the Union shall be enforced and executed in all of the states; that it is his duty to do so; that there need be no bloodshed or violence unless it is forced upon the government. I believe that if the Southern belief of a state's right to voluntarily secede from the Union is violated by force, it will be the one single issue that will cause a civil war to be inevitable. Let us hope, let us pray that it shall never happen."

That said, a silence falls over the class.

Virginia remains a loyal member of the Union after the departure of the deep South states, although the hearts of its citizens are extremely sympathetic to those seceded Southern states. Politically and economically, Virginia is southern. Even so, it has strong emotional and historical ties to the Union. Virginians were instrumental in the original colonies gaining their independence. Virginians were instrumental in authoring the governing documents that established the United States. Much is at stake for Virginia, as well as for its neighbors.

The University of Virginia community - the professors and the administrators - are by consensus solidly pro-union as Lincoln takes control of the business of the United States of America. They will be patient in their support. The loyalty of the student body is as diverse, as divided in opinion and support, as the make up of the student enrollment. Student loyalty, for the most part, and with few exceptions, is consistent with the state from which they come. Southern students are loyal to the Southern causes and Northern students are loyal to the Northern causes. There are exceptions, but they are few.

Even so, there is considerable sympathy toward the southern cause on the Grounds at the University. Friday, March 15, 1861, as the midnight hour approaches, a small group of students slips silently into the blackness of night with more on their minds than pranks or prattle. With extreme difficulty, and in total silence, they climb to the apex of the Rotunda where they quietly, but resolutely, attach the rebel flag of the New Confederate States of America. They are ecstatic over their accomplishment. They return silently to their rooms to await the dawn of the new day - a day that they plan to celebrate and to honor their late night accomplishments and the birth of the new Southern nation.

At the break of day on Saturday morning, the student adventurers, accompanied by most of the student body, assemble on the grounds of the University to celebrate in support of the new Southern nation. Their boisterous celebration arouses not only the professors and the University administrators, but many of the nearby townspeople as well.

The students are amazed to find that the University professors and administrators do not share their support of the new Southern nation. The officials demand that the flag be removed and that the crowds disperse. The students, in protest, gather into groups, make Southern support speeches and sing "Dixie" over and over again.

Robbie, hearing all of the noise from the University Grounds, arises and ventures over to the Lawn in front of the Rotunda. He sees two of his student friends, Jack Simon and Jason Miles from his law school class. They greet one another.

"What's going on?" Robbie inquires.

The two friends inform him about the Rotunda event and the reaction of the professors and administrators.

"What's going to happen, Jack? How is the secession of South Carolina going to affect you?"

"Well, at the present time I am going to continue my education here. If war should break out, I suppose I will go home and fight for my home state."

"What about you, Jason? What are you going to do?"

"I'm a Virginian, Robbie. I suppose that I will do whatever Virginia does. Right now, Virginia remains in the Union. If the people of Virginia are as pro-Union as the professors and administrators here at the University are, I suppose that Virginia will remain in the Union. There wouldn't be a problem if Abe Lincoln hadn't stirred it up."

"He is the cause of the deep South states leaving the Union. He's the culprit, and my sympathies are all with the South."

Jack Simon again speaks, "I agree with your assessment of Lincoln, Jason. I think he is the cause of all of the trouble. But I don't know how the people in general here in Virginia feel; if the feeling in general is the same as the feeling of the officials here at the University, Virginia is pro-Union."

"Why do you say that, Jason?" Robbie asks.

"Because Professor Albert Bledso was the only person from the University that favored the Rotunda flag raising - the display of the Confederate flag from atop the Rotunda this morning. All of the other professors demanded that it come down."

"What about you, Robbie?" Jack asks.

"Yeah," Jason seconds the question. "What about you?"

"I wish I could answer you," Robbie responds. "I just don't know. I have friends here - both of you are good friends, Professor Holcombe and his brother Thomas. Then there are all of my classmates. The O'Rileys, Reverend and Mrs. Granberry. There are just so many friends, North and South. I just hope that choices never have to be made. It would surely be a quandary for me."

Chapter Twenty-One

Binding Love and Blinding Hate

The philosophical differences between the North and the South continue to lengthen the existing chasm of dissatisfaction. Nearly a month has passed since Lincoln's inauguration. Even so, war has not come. To be sure, there have been insults and threats, but the fragile peace remains. Northern politicians and the Northern press believe that given time the Confederate experiment of a new nation will fail and that there will be a clamor within the seceded states to reunite with the Union.

The sectional insults, the jealousies, and the threats between the North and South are disregarded by Robbie Holcomb and Mollie K O'Riley. The divided Union drifts further apart while their personal relationship flourishes. In the beginning boy had met girl; North had met South; opposites attracted one to the other. Boy liked girl and girl liked boy; North liked South and South liked North. At first it was just a friendship; then came a budding romance and finally the romance fully blossomed.

As their relationship progresses from an awkward and shy stage of boy meets girl, girl meets boy, to that of a more sophisticated and mature nature, certain expressions become commonplace in their everyday usage. Initially the expressions are used in response to other people, or places, or things. Subsequently, perhaps by an unconscious realization, they understand - they know that it is their love and romance, their marriage that they are speaking about. That is the way it happens. That is the way it is. Mrs. O'Riley is apprised of the news of their decision.

Mrs. O'Riley conceals her delight. She questions them both, asking all of the questions a mother should ask under these circumstances - offering advice and cautioning against rushing into things too quickly.

"What about your parents, Robbie? Have they been told? What - how do they feel about this?"

"Mrs. O'Riley, I have not told them. My father will be supportive. He will approve. My mother will disapprove because of a fear of losing my love for her. Of course, I will always love her - just as Mollie K will always love you.

"But Mother will not understand this. It will take time for her to accept Mollie K. It will take time, but she will eventually love Mollie K, just as I love her."

"Robbie, you need to inform your parents - ask their advice. You need to do this immediately. Write to them. Send a telegram. If there is to be a marriage, they need to know. Their opinions and their feelings are important."

"Mrs. O'Riley, I was planning to tell them after our marriage. I thought it would be easier on Mother that way. My father would understand either way."

"Oh no, Robbie. Your parents would never forgive you, and worst of all they would never forgive Mollie K - nor would your mother ever accept her.

"You must let your parents know. They are entitled to know. And they must be invited to the wedding. Ask them to come early. They need to have an opportunity to meet us, to become acquainted with the town and the people. Perhaps your mother will feet better about the Southern way of life. They can stay here with us, if they wish to. We have two extra rooms."

"Thank you, Mrs. O'Riley, I'll send them a telegram immediately. Then I will write a long letter."

The explanatory telegram is sent to his parents. Within hours Robbie has received two replies. One from his father and one from his mother. His father is calm and collected. His mother has panicked. His father's telegram asks that accommodations be arranged for them at the Midway Hotel, two weeks hence.

The Holcombs arrive in Charlottesville on Thursday, March 21st. Robbie meets them at the train station. Old Ben takes them to the hotel. Mary controls her emotions until they are registered at the hotel and are in their rooms.

"Oh, Robbie, what have you done?" she laments, tears flowing down her cheeks. "What have you gotten yourself into?"

"Calm down, Mother." He embraces her, consoling her, wiping away her tears, but remaining firm in mind and spirit. "What I have done, what I have gotten myself into, is that I have fallen in love, and I have asked Mollie K to be my wife and she has accepted."

"Oh, Robbie, don't do anything foolish. You are just lonely - homesick."

"Mother, I am neither lonely nor homesick. I have never been homesick, and I have never been happier. Nor will my love for you ever change. It shall never falter. Please attempt to see Mollie K as she is, not as the person you are jealous of - not as a rival. Now tell me that you will."

"Robbie, I am trying to do what I know is right for you. You are too young. She is too young. You haven't known each other long enough."

"Mother, please. This is something you must do."

Mary's best efforts to derail the wedding are in vain. She tries her best to do so. Reluctantly, if not happily, she accepts what she cannot change or postpone. She will go to the wedding, if there is to be one, but she will not be happy.

And now the big day arrives. It is Sunday, March 31, 1861, a beautiful spring-like day. It is mid-afternoon, precisely 3:00. Mollie K is astonishingly beautiful in her white wedding dress as she slowly walks down the aisle, nervously holding onto the arm of Professor James Holcombe. The pianist, Thomas Holcombe, is playing the familiar Lohengrin wedding march, "Here Comes the Bride." All eyes are fixed on Mollie K. More than a few are dimmed by tears of happiness. Robbie, standing next to his best man, his father, is beaming.

"Isn't she beautiful?" he whispered to his father.

"Stunningly gorgeous, lovely indeed," his father responds.

Mary dabs her eyes constantly during the ceremony. She bites her tongue but makes not a sound.

Reverend John Granberry, who previously served as the University's chaplain, performs the wedding ceremony in the Religious Services Room in the University Rotunda.

After the "I do's" are exchanged between the bride and groom, Reverend Granberry, smiling contentedly, announces, "Robbie, you may kiss the bride." Then turning to the guests, he announces, "Ladies and Gentlemen, I present to you Mr. and Mrs. Robbie Holcomb."

"I just knew this marriage was going to happen," Esther Granberry beams gleefully. "I knew it from the first time that I met the two of them. I was totally convinced within the first hours of our trip north when I was their chaperone last summer." Then, as an afterthought, she adds, "Wouldn't it be wonderful if all people from the North and South could come together in harmony and friendship? People should look for the good in one another, instead of looking for each other's faults. Then everyone would get along splendidly. There would be neither wars nor rumors of war."

"Yes, it really would be wonderful," agrees Mrs. O'Riley as she stands in the reception line. Then, in a more somber tone, she continues, speaking to no one in particular. "I am so glad that Robbie's parents could be here for his and Mollie K's wedding. The uncertainty of the political differences between the two sections of the country caused them to go forward with their wedding plans now rather than waiting until next summer. We don't know what the summer will bring."

Mollie K escapes momentarily from the well-wishers and rushes over to her mother. "Mamma, I am so happy."

"Bless you, Mollie K. You are such a beautiful bride."

"Thank you, Mamma. Please call me Mrs. Robbie Holcomb so I can hear how it sounds."

"Bless you, Mrs. Robbie Holcomb. I wish you a long and happy marriage," she responds, holding her daughter closely, then adds, "You two are a perfect couple. I just know that this marriage was made in Heaven."

"Oh, Mamma, I know it is true. We are so happy together. Mamma, I wish that Daddy could have been here today. I know he is smiling down from Heaven, but I just wish he was here. He would have been so happy, too."

"Oh, sweetheart, he is here. We can't see him, but he is here. I just know he is."

Mrs. O'Riley holds her daughter ever so close for a long moment to allow time for the lump in her throat to subside. "Go and enjoy this day, Mollie K. I'll be alright."

Mrs. O'Riley's thoughts again wander back to Robbie's parents. "This wedding is so sudden to them. I did want them to be here. I did want Robbie to invite them. It happened so quickly with all of these North-South uncertainties and everything. Robbie wanted to wait and tell them when he and Mollie K go back to New York in the summer. I am so glad they are here," she says to Mrs. Granberry.

Thomas Holcombe taps a spoon on the rim of the punch bowl to get the attention of the guests. "Those of you who do not have a glass of punch, please get one from the table. Let us all join together in a toast to the newlyweds." Turning to face them, Thomas raises his cup and holds it forward as a wedding salute to Mollie K and Robbie.

"We toast the two of you as bride and groom. We wish you a long, happy, and rewarding life together. We add to this toast a wish for peace and reconciliation between the states of our divided nation."

Robert Holcomb, standing next to his wife, Mary, addresses the wedding guests, "May we, as parents of the groom and father-in-law and mother-in-law of the gorgeous new bride, wish them well and a long and happy marriage."

Mary forces a smile and nods.

Reverend Granberry tips his glass toward the newlyweds, then adds a short prayer after the toast. "Lord, we pray for peace and goodwill throughout our land. We pray for the lives and happiness of this young couple. May you bless us all. Amen."

"Please, all of you come and enjoy the wonderful wedding cake that Mamma baked," Mollie K announces. Then she adds, "We are honored and overjoyed that each one of you came to share our wedding day. We shall share these memories, Robbie and I, throughout our long and happy marriage, even when we are old and gray." There is much cheering, laughter and applause as Mollie K finishes speaking.

The evening shadows are falling and the day is nearly done when the last guests depart. The day ends as it began, as a wonderful, wonderful, happy day. The newlyweds glance skyward into the late evening twilight as they walk together, arms around one another, into the night.

"Oh look, Robbie," Mollie K excitedly exclaims as she points toward a lone brightly shining star. "I bet that is your lucky star."

"Our lucky star, Mollie K," he replies. "And it will always be there for us."

The days of spring rush onward; often it seems in uncharted and stormy waters. Hope for reconciliation between the seceded states and the Union grow dimmer with the passing of each day. The new Confederacy is convinced that independence and separation from the Union is the proper decision for the South.

"We are now able to resolve our own matters, without interference from a hostile and meddlesome North," announces Jefferson Davis, the newly-appointed President of the Confederacy. "We are now free to chart our own courses of action, to set our own agenda. We, and we alone, are in charge of our destiny for now and for the future. We do not intend to look back; we look only toward the future; a future of peace and prosperity. Again, we ask but one thing from the Northern Union, and that is that we be allowed to go our separate way in peace.

"For us to retreat from our present course of action; for us to neglect our Southern mission and purpose of independence would be a sign of indecision on our part. It would show weakness in our new government. We must not falter. We must not fail, for the course that we have set for the new South is a right course. It is an honest course, and it is a just course," President Davis emphatically states to the applause of the concurring crowd.

"Permit me to add, if you will," says Davis, "that we will not bow to humiliation nor to defeat. We will never again be the whipping boy for the people of the North. This we do not want, this we will not accept. We have declared our independence from the North. We shall forevermore retain that independence. We hope to accomplish this through peace, but if we must retain our independence through war, we will do so, shedding our blood for a rightful, just, and honorable cause." Again, the crowd responds with enthusiasm.

Robbie reads the newspaper daily, keeping abreast of all that is said by the politicians and their spokesmen, North and South. It is difficult to concentrate on his studies with all of the friction and hatred that is brewing between the two sections of the country. The political climate at the University is in great turmoil. He and Mollie K are greatly concerned over these matters. It is not an easy situation for the young married couple.

Many people, both North and South, are clamoring for war. The common people are encouraged to do so by the fire-eaters. They are the radicals, those whose aim is to incite others to join their course, to incite friction and agitation.

Those who are hankering for war get their wish. In the early morning hours of Friday, April twelfth, 1861, Confederate war hawks at Charleston, South Carolina open an artillery barrage on Fort Sumter, a U.S. military garrison in Charleston's harbor. The fort poses no threat to the Confederates, but the site of it is a thorn in the side of Southern independence. The Union troops stationed at Fort Sumter - all seventy of them - under the command of Major Robert Anderson, defend the Fort gallantly, heroically, and honorably.

War has begun; war between North and South; a war between the states. Thirty-four hours after the first shot is fired, after nearly four thousand Confederate artillery shells have shattered the under-manned and ill-supplied fort, it has surrendered. Fort Sumter, or what is left of it, is in Southern hands.

Events move with the swiftness of telegrams as the news spreads from South to North. President Abraham Lincoln calls on the states of the Union to provide 75,000 volunteers for the nation's army. Northern states overwhelmingly answer his call. Southern states, those that remained loyal to the Union after the original seven states had seceded, angrily refuse to provide troops to fight against their Southern brothers. Virginia, North Carolina, and Tennessee secede within a matter of days, casting their lot with the Confederacy.

Professor Holcombe is called to serve in the Confederate Congress. Before leaving Charlottesville, he goes by the O'Riley's to bid farewell to his cousin, Robbie.

"I've come to say goodbye, at least for a while. I have been called to duty to serve the Commonwealth of Virginia and the Confederacy. I must follow my conscience.

"I hope that you remain in school. Do not make any hasty decisions about the future. We do not know at this time what the future holds. We do know that the question of war or peace is not all about the issue of slavery, as some would have us believe.

"As you are quite aware, as far as I am personally concerned, it is about a state's right - about Virginia's right to legally secede from the Union and to do so freely as a Constitutional right. You are well aware, Robbie, that my parents long ago released their bondsmen. They also declined to accept a large inheritance because it consisted, in part, of slaves. My conscience, my moral standing on the slavery issue is consistent with that of my parents. Just as your anti-slavery ideals are embedded through your parents' ideals and your own sense of equality and fairness. Hold fast to your ideals, but do not fear to consider the opinions, the ideals, of others."

Those things having been said, they manly embrace.

"Until we meet again, Robbie."

"Until we meet again, Professor Holcombe. I shall long remember your teaching, both in and out of the classroom."

As the professor turns to leave, Robbie again speaks. "Professor Holcombe, do you remember the poet John Dickinson?"

"Yes, Robbie. I believe he died about the turn of the century. Why do you ask?"

"You are right about the time of his death, Professor. One of his poems was titled 'The Liberty Song.' One of the stanzas reads:

'Join hand in hand, brave Americans all
By uniting we stand, by dividing we fall.'"

They stand silently facing one another. "A sobering thought, young man. I shall not forget it, nor shall I ever forget you, Robbie Holcomb." Professor Holcombe again turns, then departs. He does not look back.

Robbie watches as the professor walks away. He watches until he rounds the corner and disappears. He stands silently as if frozen in his tracks. He suddenly senses that someone is beside him.

"Mollie K, how long have you been standing there?"

"Maybe a minute. You looked so deep in thought. I did not want to disturb you."

"Mollie K, we are living in serious and unpredictable times. The Commonwealth of Virginia is at a crossroads. The entire South is at a crossroads. Indeed, America is at a crossroads."

Robbie looks at his young wife; he draws her close. "Mollie K, you are all that I am sure of in the entire world. I love you dearly."

"And I love you dearly. What is going to happen to us and to our country?"

"God only knows, Mollie K. Perhaps it is best that we do not."

Chapter Twenty-Two

Intolerable Events

The surrender of Fort Sumter intensifies the preparation for all out war in both the North and the South, albeit, blood has not been shed during the shelling of the fort. The Union, sometime before the Confederate attack, had actually considered its evacuation. Not that it was not an imposing military structure at the entrance to Charleston harbor; it was. Its walls, forty feet high and eight to twelve feet thick, would cause panic to any invading enemy. It was not, however, militarily expedient to the North in its now pending war with the South.

The shelling of the fort by the Confederate South is, however, another matter. It is, so to speak, a horse of another color. The Union flag has been fired on. It has been trampled on, violated. It is an affront to Union pride and a matter to be reckoned with. The flag must be avenged; the Union must be avenged.

Lincoln's call to arms, his call "for vengeance as a necessity to maintain the honor, the integrity and the existence of the Union," angers the leaders and the people of the Southern border states. Southerners who have remained loyal to the Union heretofore, now become bitter and unsupportive toward Lincoln and his policies. His anti-Southern pronouncements, his preparation for armed aggression against the South, are, in the eyes of Southern people and the Southern border states, unjust, unnecessary and unconstitutional.

Northerners, nonetheless, are in full accord with their president. They are emotionally ready and willing for a fight, albeit totally unprepared in a military sense to do so. The North enthusiastically answers Lincoln's call to bear arms against their Southern brothers.

The majority of people - both North and South - believe that the fault of all of the problems in America is caused by the people on the other side of the issue. Allegiances are divided more so on place of birth, kinship and statehood than on any other factors. The 'Staunton Vindicator,' a southern newspaper, calls Southerners to rally to the call, "The South must go with the South; blood runs thicker than water." The North rallies "'round the flag" and calls for "patriotism and loyalty to the Union." Northern newspapers accuse the South of outraging the purpose and intent of the Constitution, of defying the nation's laws, and of trampling underfoot the honored and symbolic Union flag, the symbol of American liberty and justice.

America is in word and in deed a divided nation, a divided people. Its separation causes a parting of ways for friends and families. It is a national catastrophe causing friend to stand against friend, brother to stand against brother, father to stand against son and son to stand against father.

President Lincoln is stunned when the Southern border states reject his call for volunteers to bear arms against the seceded states. He was well aware when his call went out that it would not be enthusiastically received by the Southern states that remain in the Union; however, he is unprepared for the intensity of the border states' rejection.

He summons Simon Cameron, his Secretary of War, for consultation. The two men face one another. It is a meeting of necessity, not one of trust, nor of personal friendship. Cameron's War Cabinet position is a political plum - the spoils for helping to secure Lincoln's presidential nomination as the Republican presidential candidate in the 1860 election. It is not a promise that Lincoln had personally made; rather it is one made by Lincoln's personal supporters. Nor is the Secretary of War the cabinet post that Cameron had coveted.

There are few similarities between Abe Lincoln and Simon Cameron. There are many dissimilarities. Lincoln is known as "Honest Abe" because of his past dealings with people. Cameron is known as the "Winebago Chief," supposedly for cheating an Indian tribe in a federal contract. Lincoln is a man of modest means because of his fair and honorable dealings. Cameron is a man of considerable means because of political matters and favors he has received. Lincoln, a tall, thin man, six feet four, and somewhat ungainly, long dangling arms, a homely face, and like his mother, dark skin. His clothes are always wrinkled as if having been slept in. He was and is a highly principled and honest man.

"Mr. Secretary, I have received responses to my call for troops from both the Northern states and from the Southern states that hitherto have remained loyal to the Union."

"I trust, Mr. President, that all of the responses are favorable."

Turning away momentarily, the president remains silent before answering. "The Northern response to our request for volunteers has been overwhelmingly positive and supportive. The Southern response has not been so. They have rejected our call. Their response - the bitterness in their response - is somewhat surprising. I have here in my hand telegrams from some of the Southern governors. I should like to share their message with you."

"As you wish, Mr. President."

"Kentucky's Governor, Beriah Magoffin, wired this response, 'Kentucky will furnish no troops for the wicked purpose of subduing her Southern sister states.'

"Missouri Governor Claiborne Jackson's telegram reads, 'Your requisition is illegal, unconstitutional, revolutionary and inhuman. Not one man will the state of Missouri furnish to carry on any such unholy crusade.'

"Tennessee's Governor Isham Harris' message reads, 'We will not furnish a single man for the purpose of coercion, but 50,000 for the defense of our rights and those of our Southern brothers.'"

President Lincoln pauses, removes his glasses, and looks directly into the eyes of the Secretary of War. "Mr. Secretary, I have tried to keep the border states in the Union. I fear now that this is not going to be possible. Our course is laid out. We must play the hand that has been dealt to us and we will let the chips lay where they fall."

"Mr. President, I could not agree more. You have chosen the right course. But what about Virginia, Mr. President? What about Virginia?" Secretary Cameron asks excitedly. Not pausing for President Lincoln to answer, he continues. "Virginia is the most critical to our cause of all of the Southern states. It is also the most important state to the cause of the South."

President Lincoln interrupts Secretary Cameron. "Yes, Mr. Secretary, Virginia is the pot of gold at the end of the rainbow in this struggle. It is immensely important strategically, economically and politically to us and to the South. Virginia is, unfortunately, going to cast its lot with the South.

"It is a tremendous blow to our cause, Mr. Secretary, but it is not going to change our course. We will move forward with our plans. We must maintain and preserve the Union."

"Is there anything I can do, Mr. President?"

"Yes, Mr. Secretary, I have another pressing problem. As you are well aware, General-in-Chief of the Army, Winfield Scott, is seventy-five years old and in ill health."

"Mr. President, I am well aware of that problem, as is General Scott. I have discussed the generalship situation with him. He is ready to step aside and turn the reins over to another officer."

"Does he have anyone in mind, Mr. Secretary? Anyone that he believes is competent and qualified to lead our Armies during these critical and important times? Our volunteers, as well as our regular Army troops, will be useless unless we have strong, able and loyal leadership at the helm. We must have a great military leader."

"Yes, Mr. President, he has recommended Colonel Robert E. Lee, whom he claims is the best officer in the United States Army. Colonel Lee is a career Army officer and a graduate of the U.S. Military Academy at West Point. He graduated second in his class. During Lee's four years at West Point, he never received a demerit; something no other cadet has ever done in the history of the academy. Colonel Lee is a veteran of the Mexican War. He was also in charge of the Marines who captured John Brown at Harpers Ferry about two years ago."

"Mr. Secretary, has General Scott discussed this matter with Colonel Lee?"

"No Sir, Mr. President, he has not."

"Mr. Secretary, please see to it that he does not do so at this time. We need a little more information about Colonel Lee. We desperately need a competent, loyal, and extremely highly qualified military leader during these critical and uncertain times, but we must be sure of Colonel Lee's qualifications."

"Is that all, Mr. President?"

President Lincoln pauses for a moment. "Ask General Scott three questions: does Colonel Lee possess the maturity and determination to handle this awesome assignment; where does Colonel Lee stand on the slavery issue; and where does he stand on the issue of secession. If Colonel Lee satisfies these three conditions, I believe he is our man."

"Mr. President, I foresaw the need of answers to those questions in my discussion with General Scott. Colonel Lee is fifty-four years old, having just reached that age on January 19th of this year. I previously mentioned his service in the Mexican War. I did not mention that he was decorated for bravery during the war, nor that he has served on General Scott's staff for many years. He has also performed many special assignments during his career, including a stint as Superintendent of the U.S. Military Academy at West Point.

"I might add that Colonel Lee is the son of General Henry Lee, a hero and legend of the Revolutionary War. General Henry Lee is probably better known as Light-Horse Harry Lee. Two of Colonel Lee's uncles, Richard Henry Lee and Frances Lightfoot Lee, were signers of the Declaration of Independence.

"Colonel Robert E. Lee is married to Mary Ann Randolph Custis, the great granddaughter of Martha Washington, who, as you know, was married to our first president, George Washington.

"Mr. President, I find the credentials and the character of Colonel Robert E. Lee to be impeccable and beyond reproach."

"Mr. Secretary, I could not agree with you more. How about the other two questions?"

"Mr. President, I am about to address those issues. Colonel Lee is a native Virginian, as is General Scott. He lived his early life in Virginia. His family before him owned slaves. He at one time also owned slaves. However, he released them from bondage many years ago, prior to the current arguments against slavery. His uncle, Richard Henry Lee, condemned the practice of slavery before Virginia's colonial governing body many, many years ago by proposing to tax it out of existence.

"Mr. President, Colonel Lee has been attributed to having remarked many years ago that he disliked slavery and that he believed it to be a moral and political evil."

"Mr. Secretary, I am impressed with Colonel Lee's credentials. His ownership of slaves was not illegal. I have myself stated that I did not intend to prohibit slavery where it presently exists, although I will not allow it to spread elsewhere."

"And, Mr. President, his opposition to secession is well documented. He has said 'the framers of the Constitution would never have exhausted so much labor, wisdom and forbearance in its formation if it was intended to be broken up by every member of the Union at will. It is idle to talk of secession.'"

"Mr. Secretary, I believe that Colonel Lee is our man. I suggest you advise General Scott to offer him the generalship of the Northern Armies."

"Mr. President, General Scott suggested that in the event you concur with his recommendation of Colonel Lee, that you have Mr. Frances Preston Blair conduct an interview of Colonel Lee before hand."

"Very well, Mr. Secretary. Please have Mr. Blair take care of this matter as soon as possible; to do so today if arrangements can be worked out. Please advise Mr. Blair of all of the conversation that the two of us have had today and of the conversations that you and General Scott had earlier. I want Mr. Blair to understand that he is representing the President of the United States in this matter and that he is authorized to promote Colonel Lee to General of the Armies of the United States."

Frances Preston Blair, a former Jacksonian Democrat, a founder of the Republican Party, and a Lincoln loyalist and advisor, in the presence of Secretary of War Simon Cameron, interviews Colonel Lee late in the afternoon of the same day. All that had been discussed in the earlier meetings between General Scott and Secretary Cameron, and the meeting between Secretary Cameron and President Lincoln, and finally the meeting between Secretary Cameron and Mr. Blair, are made known to Colonel Lee. At the conclusion of the meeting, Mr. Blair stands and faces Colonel Lee. "Sir you have heard the offer that is laid before you. An offer of Generalship of the Northern Armies. The offer comes with the recommendation of General Winfield Scott and the concurrence of the President of the United States of America, Abraham Lincoln."

Both Frances Blair and Simon Cameron are absolutely sure that Robert E. Lee is going to accept this high honor. They are prepared for his acceptance. Colonel Lee rises from his chair. He stands straight as an arrow, hat in hand, facing the two men before speaking.

"Mr. Blair, Secretary Cameron, I am most grateful to you, to President Lincoln, and to General Scott. I am honored beyond words by your offer. I owe all that I am to my country. Yet, I stand before you at a crossroads, as does our beloved country. I am an American, and I am a Virginian. I must somehow side, either with or against, my state. I am opposed to secession by Virginia. I am opposed to secession by any state, and I strongly disapprove of war between the states of this Union. The Virginia Secession Committee, as you are aware, has voted to secede from the Union. However, their decision is not final. It must be approved by the citizens of the Commonwealth before it is final. I fear that the people will do so. I cannot raise my hand against my birthplace, my home, and my children.

"Gentlemen, it is with deep and sincere regret that I must decline your offer. I am unable to take part in an invasion of Virginia or of the other Southern states of this Union. I pray that somehow God will spare us from this dreadful ordeal."

Colonel Lee excuses himself from the meeting and goes directly to General Scott's office to apprise him of his decision. "General Scott, I regret that I cannot accept the offer of generalship of the Union Armies. I shall always hold you in the highest esteem. I owe much to you and to the Army of the United States. This is a difficult decision. I must, of course, resign from the Army. It is my greatest hope and my solemn desire, that I shall never again be compelled to draw my sword. I sincerely hope that peace will be preserved, that some way, some how, our country will be saved from the calamities of war."

General Scott stands. A look of great disappointment in his eyes, he extends his hand. As the two old comrades, who both deeply admire and respect the other, shake hands, the old general speaks, his voice saddened in disappointment. "Colonel Lee, I sincerely believe that you are the best officer in the United States Army. You have always served your country with distinction and honor. Your services are now greatly needed by your country. They are invaluable to the Union. But you have made a decision to cast your lot with the Confederacy. By doing so you have made the greatest mistake of your life. I had feared that you might do so. I have tried with all my heart to dissuade you from this course of action. I can do no more."

The two of them, facing one another for the last time and misty-eyed out of the enormous respect that each has for the other, shake hands. It is with a firm grip, a respectful grip of hands. Not another word is spoken. Colonel Lee brings himself to attention, salutes the old general, does an about face, and departs.

President Lincoln is apprised of all of the facts and circumstances that transpired regarding Colonel Lee, including his decision to decline the offer. The President remains silent for a moment, then responds. "I must concur with General Scott's assessment of Colonel Lee. He has made the gravest mistake of his lifetime. But it is done. We will move forward and face the tasks that lie ahead. Our course may not be easy, but it is the right course and we will prevail. I have been accused of wanting to divide the Union. Never has that been my intent.

"Mr. Secretary, you may recall a speech that I made at Galena, Illinois in July 1856. I believe it was the one in which I said we would not strive to dissolve the Union; and if any attempt is made, it must be made by other who so loudly stigmatize us as disunionists. But the Union, in any event, won't be dissolved.

"I said, in that speech, we don't want to dissolve it, and if you attempt it, we won't let you. With the purse and the sword, the army and the navy and treasury in our hands, and at our command, you couldn't do it. This government would be very weak, indeed, if a majority, with a disciplined army and navy, and a well-filled treasury, could not preserve itself, when attacked by an unarmed, undisciplined, unorganized minority.

"All of this talk about the dissolution of the Union is humbug - nothing but folly. We won't dissolve the Union and you shant.

"That speech has as much truth in it today as it did in 1856. This Union must stand."

"Mr. President, do you believe that the Southern states have a legal right, under the Constitution, to leave the Union?"

"What do you think, Mr. Secretary? You are also a lawyer."

"Do you want an honest answer, Mr. President?"

"Yes - an honest answer."

"Mr. President, under the Constitution, as it is written, as it is intended I believe, a state is free to go if its leaders and its people make that decision to do so. Mr. President, you have not answered the question that I asked you. Do you think the Southern states that have declared to secede and those that may secede have a legal right to do so?"

"Mr. Secretary, at Coopers Union where I spoke last February - just over a year ago - I said, 'Let us have faith that right makes might, and in that faith let us to the end dare to do our duty as we understand it.' That is my answer."

"Mr. President, I have also heard it said that might makes right."

"Perhaps so, Mr. Secretary, perhaps so!"

Chapter Twenty-Three

A Nation Divided

The war came in earnest. It came with a deadly, determined vengeance. It came with a murderous intent, with a hatred and brutality beyond description, even beyond imagination. It is the way that wars are fought; it is the way that wars are supposed to be fought. Even so, this is a different kind of war. It is a war unlike any other. It is not a war of nations warring against other nations; it is not a war of foreigners warring against other foreigners.

This is a war waged by a nation divided against itself. It is a war of Americans at war with Americans. It is a war of friends warring against friends, neighbors divided against neighbors, brothers rising against brothers, and fathers and sons bearing arms against one another. It is a war between civilized people who have abandoned their civility. It is the worst of all wars. It is civil war.

Rumors of war, even before the war comes, circulate throughout the University community. Passions are stirred long before a shot is ever fired, long before blood is ever shed. And so, as the Southern states secede one by one from the Union, students loyal to those states withdraw from the University to join their home militias. By the end of the academic year, July the Fourth, 1861, substantial numbers of the student body have already departed. They have interrupted their academic pursuits for the cause of allegiance to their native states. Robbie Holcomb, however, remains at the University. He follows the advice of Professor Holcombe and continues his studies. His second academic year of college is now complete.

"Mollie K, I am not safe from the war. You are not safe from the war. Your mother is not safe, my parents are not safe, no one in America is safe. But I am much safer here than I would be if I was traveling north and was caught in the middle of a confrontation.

"We cannot imagine the evils of war - the suffering, the deaths it will bring to our country, both North and South. It will be worse than a plague. People - North and South - that have clamored for this war do not realize, do not understand, what they have sought. They do not understand the sorrow - the devastation that they have asked for. But now it is here."

"Robbie, I am so afraid. Hold me close. What is going to happen to us? What will happen to Mamma? To your parents?"

"Mollie K, I'll always take care of you and your mother. I don't know how, but I will; and the same goes for my parents. I'll always look out for them, too."

Robbie pauses, a serious look on his face as he holds Mollie K close to himself, as he speaks solemnly. "Most of the University students have openly clamored for war. They believed that war should come, that the South has no other alternative. They believe in the Confederacy. Now the war is here. War - the desire for war - the hope for war - is intoxicating. It breeds hatred - a desire - a hatred to maim and kill the enemy. And who is the enemy? Other Americans."

"What are we going to do, Robbie? This war really scares me. It scares me to death. And now that the war is here, what are they going to do to you - a Northerner?"

"I will be alright. We will be alright. What we need in America today are people - great statesmen and great thinkers, like Benjamin Franklin, Thomas Jefferson and James Madison, and even before them Cicero. These men believed that mankind's problems were not solved by war. Cicero was a peace advocate. He said that 'an unjust peace is better than the most just war.' Franklin said much the same thing that, 'there never was a good war or a bad peace.' Jefferson saw war as an inefficient means of redressing the wrongs of society and John Adams saw war as 'the worst of all evils to public liberty because it develops and compromises every other evil.'

"I am not afraid of war for myself, Mollie K. But I am afraid of it for you and for your mother, and for my parents. I am afraid of it for what it will do to America - North and South."

His summer plans to return to New York with Mollie K are sidelined because of the war.

"Robbie, why don't you go on alone? I want you to see your parents. Besides, they need to know how our married life is going, and they need to know that you are safe from the war."

"I am not going to leave you. We have no idea what is going to happen because of this senseless war. Some people believe that it will all be over in less than three months. If it is, we will then go home."

"But what if it doesn't end, Robbie? Then you will not see your parents, and they will not see you."

"That is the point of this matter. If the war doesn't end, and I go to New York without you, I may not be able to get back. We don't know how long we might be separated or what might happen. I could never go without you. Don't you understand?"

Initially, the war is limited to isolated, small military confrontations. In early June, nearly a month before Robbie's second year at the University is complete, two such military encounters are fought. One engagement is fought in eastern Virginia, and another is fought in western Virginia. The Confederates, led by General "Prince" John Magruder, a name he has earned for his princely style of living, repels an attack by Union troops at Big Bethel on the Virginia peninsula. The following day, the Union Army under the command of General George McClellan, is victorious over the Confederates at Rich Mountain near Philipi in western Virginia. Although both engagements are brutal and bloody, they are not major military engagements. They are, nonetheless, not the kinds of situations Robbie would want to have Mollie K subjected to. It is best that they remain in Charlottesville until both of them can go to New York in complete safety.

Even while Robbie and Mollie K are discussing the cancellation of their personal travel itinerary, serious plans for a major military confrontation are under way in the North. In Washington, President Lincoln is pressing his military leaders to make a show of force. The Northern public has grown restless. Northern newspapers have become critical of the government's inaction against the South. Something has to be done.

And it happens. It is Sunday morning, July 21st, 1861, a sweltering hot and humid summer morning. Two armies, one Confederate and the other Union, stand facing one another, barely 800 or so yards separating them. The place is Bull Run, near Manassas Junction, Virginia, a major Confederate rail center. It is no more than thirty miles from the Union capital in Washington.

Both armies are itching for a fight; however it is the Union army, the Yankees, who have come looking for their Confederate enemies. The Yankees are confident and self-assured of victory. They are ready; ready to charge into the enemy's ranks. They are confident of an easy victory.

The soon-to-be-battle is the brainchild of top Union Generals in Washington. President Lincoln has insisted that the Rebel government's army be challenged on the field of battle. Lincoln reviews the battle plan. He concurs with the contemplated action. A sound victory, a national confidence-builder is desperately needed by the Union. It appears to all that the planned military operation is the right answer, the right course of action. Victory will be quick, decisive, and sweet.

So sure are the Union officials of a quick and decisive victory, it is touted before the House and the Senate as the beginning of the end of the Confederacy. Government officials, dignitaries, and others are invited to witness the victory a safe distance away from the battle. The political and social elite of Washington, along with members of the Northern press, trudge along some distance behind the Union army as it marches off to meet its foe.

"Forward to Richmond! Onward to Richmond!" a slogan coined by a New York Tribune editorial, is chanted by the crowd. Spirits are high in anticipation of the Union victory.

As the Sunday morning church bells in the village of Manassas toll for the opening of services, the sounds of gunfire echo overhead and across the sky. The battle of Bull Run has begun. Thousands of Yankee soldiers filled with pride and patriotism move forward under a blistering and merciless sun, into a withering and deadly barrage of Confederate cannon and musket fire. There are more than a few deaths and many wounded. This unwelcome, but highly expected greeting from their enemy fails to slow the Yankee attack. Onward they rush, even as their comrades fall. Others rush forward, stumbling over the dead and dying bodies of their comrades to take their place in the line of duty. They push onward, oblivious to the fate of their fallen comrades, fearless of the battlefield, fearless of death, fearless of their own fate.

The Rebel soldiers fight just as valiantly, just as bravely as does their Yankee foes. They resist, they die honorably. Grudgingly, they yield ground to their hated Yankee enemy, their attacking foe, as the battle rages. Ground is gained, ground is lost. First one side seizes the advantage, then the other. The battle see-saws back and forth in the heat of battle, in the heat of the day. However, by noon the Yankees are in command. The

Rebels continue to grudgingly yield to the advancing Yankees. They are out-manned and out-gunned. By 2:00 in the afternoon, victory appears certain to the attacking Yankees.

An elated General Irvin McDowell, Commanding Officer of the Union Army, spurs his steed forward. He rides swiftly along the line of battle, waving his hat victoriously in the air and shouting to his troops, "We are victorious! The day is ours! It is a Union victory! It is your victory!" His troops respond in kind, applauding their general, raising their muskets in salute to their leader.

A Union officer is dispatched to inform the observing civilians on a distant hill of the victory. He excitedly calls to them as he approaches, "The Rebels are finished. We've whipped 'em - beat 'em up good. They are retreating and we're after 'em. There ain't much fight left in them Rebs."

"Are you sure about the victory?" one of the civilians asks the officer.

"Yes Sir, I am positive. General Irvin McDowell instructed me to convey the news to you and I have done just that." Catching his breath, the young officer continues, "I am told that the men up front - our infantry officers - are shouting, 'We've whipped 'em and we'll hang Jeff Davis from a sour apple tree as soon as we get to Richmond. The Rebs are running and the war is over.' Even the front-line Union soldiers are shouting 'Forward to Richmond! Onward to Richmond!'

"I can also tell you, Sir," the officer continues, "that the President of the United States has been notified by telegraph, possibly at this very moment, of our great victory. The Stars and Stripes are again flying over Virginia soil."

"Hallelujah!" shouts one of the Congressmen. Another Congressman, smiling broadly, slaps others on the back and exclaims with great joy, "Brother, didn't I tell you so. Didn't I tell all of you that the war would not last ninety days? This has all the signs of a quick victory."

Other onlookers at the observation point also start cheering the victory. Champagne corks pop in celebration. "President Lincoln's army has destroyed the Southern insurrection. The war is all but over," others shout from among the crowd, "The battle is safely in our hands." The crowd takes on a festive mood. Again, the coined slogan, "Onto Richmond! Onto Richmond!" rings across the hill as more champagne corks pop in celebration of the Union victory.

Near the crest of Henry House Hill, where a bloody battle is still brewing, the Southern resistance stiffens. They are battered, bruised and bloodied, but they are not beaten. To a man, they refuse to accept defeat.

They have fought a good fight; an honorable fight that they can be proud of. They have been outnumbered in manpower and weapons during the entire day. Now things are different. Fresh Rebel troops are arriving. Their spirit is re-ignited. They are now equal in number to their Union foes; equal in strength with their Yankee adversaries. Now they have the advantage of fresh troops. The Yankees are exhausted; they have no fresh troops.

The Yankee soldiers have been on the attack most of the day. They are on the verge of victory – they believe that their victory is won, now it is slipping away, slipping from their grasp. The tide is turning against them. Fatigue is setting in among the battle-weary Yankees. The sun and the heat and the battle have all taken their toll. They are suddenly dejected. They, too, are battered, bruised and bloodied. They lose their desire to fight.

The Rebels, with fresh troops and their now experienced veterans on the field, press forward. They are anxious to serve the Rebel cause. They are led by such men as Generals Thomas Jackson, Joseph Johnston, and Pierre Beauregard. Jackson is unfazed by the hail of Yankee bullets falling around him. He stands unmoved like a stone wall against the enemy, shouting to his troops, "Give them the bayonet. Attack! Attack!" And his faithful troops respond. The name "Stonewall" Jackson is earned, forever enshrined to history.

General Joseph Johnston, realizing that the tide of battle has turned against the Yankees, shouts to General Beauregard, then points toward the crest of the hill. "The battle is up for grabs. It is ours for the taking. It is time to seize the prize." Johnston spurs his horse forward and rides off to join the battle, with Beauregard in hot pursuit.

The Rebel charge is serious, it is fearless, in the mad dash to engage the enemy. Bayonets are ready. The late afternoon sun reflecting from the Rebel bayonets in the eyes of the enemy is like a thousand blinding mirrors. With an ear-splitting, spine-tingling, death-defying, dreadful Rebel yell; that sound half eerie screech owl and half Indian war whoop, the awesome and fearful sound raging above the din of battle and the Rebel Yell is born.

Union General Irvin McDowell, waving his saber high over his head, tries valiantly to rally his troops. The Rebels are coming, repeating their awful ear-splitting, death-defying yell. The Yankees are demoralized, exhausted and beaten. At first the Union retreat is organized, but the Rebels continue to charge, repeating their near madman Rebel call. The Yankee retreat becomes disorganized, finally falling completely apart in a wild panic of defeat. Yankee soldiers discard their weapons, their ammunition, their canteens, blankets, anything and everything that can impede their panic-stricken, wild, and fearful departure from the field of battle. They continue their wild rush to safety, over-running the civilians and politicians who minutes earlier had been celebrating a promised Yankee victory. They, too, join the panic-stricken rush back toward the Union capital in Washington. The supposed glorious victory by the Union Army has ended in an inglorious, embarrassing, and disgraceful defeat. All is lost, and great is the fall from victory.

Robbie Holcomb reads the news account of the Battle of Bull Run in the next day's edition of the *Daily Richmond Enquirer*. Nearly the entire paper is set apart to the news of the fighting.

"Mollie K," he says somewhat gloomily, "there has been a major battle between Confederate and Union soldiers, not far from Washington, at or near a place called Manassas, Virginia, or Bull Run. It is a railroad center. We would have to go through it if we were going to New York. This is the kind of situation that I feared might happen. It may be a long time before we can safely travel to New York. I am afraid that the country is in for a long and gruesome war. I wish it was not true, but I fear that it is."

"Robbie, since you cannot go to visit your parents, please send them a long telegram. Tell your Mamma you love her. It will make her happy."

"You are so right, sweetie. What would I ever do without you? You are the most unselfish person I have ever known. You are truly my dear angel."

"And you are mine."

Chapter Twenty-Four

Great Expectations

It is not yet time for the arrival of Spring in the new year of 1862. The biting cold of January and early February has barely vanished, yet spring-like weather has prematurely arrived in the Confederate South. All of nature seems at peace. But there is no peace - no real peace. There is no peace for the people of the Confederate South. There is no peace in the Union North. The American Civil War continues its destruction.

The war has, if anything, intensified. News of bitter fighting between the North and South has become commonplace. News of death comes daily and not just to the great cities of the North and South; it comes even to the far reaches of the most rural and remote settlements. Death is fearful. It is expected. It is grudgingly accepted. Death is painful. It is bitterly painful to the families of the dead. Death is dreadful. Suffering and death go hand in hand with war. There is no place to hide from death, no place to escape it. Death is the punishment of war, the price of war.

Small boys, not yet in their teens, go to war. Old men, too feeble even to plant and harvest crops, go to fight. Mostly though, it is the young men, those in the prime of life, who are called by their governments to fight the war. They are the ones who do not return. Those who do are robbed of their youth, their future. All too often they never come home. Nothing but a War Department letter. Missing in action or killed in action. Nothing more is ever heard of them.

The armies of the North have now come farther South with their war business. Their war destroys all that is in its path. The land is ravaged. The Northern Army has been victorious at far-off Southern places: at Mill

Springs, Kentucky, at Roanoke Island, North Carolina, at Fort Henry on the Tennessee River, and at Port Royal, South Carolina.

It is mid-February 1862 when Robbie receives a letter from his good friend and former University classmate, Jack Simon. Mollie K is all excited and nervous as she hands the letter to Robbie as he arrives home from class.

"Hurry and open it, Robbie. Jack is in an Army hospital in South Carolina."

"How do you know that, Mollie K, if you didn't open the letter?" he responds, then teasingly adds, "I bet you already read the letter and resealed it."

"I did not, Robbie, but I wanted to. His name and address are on the upper left hand corner of the envelope - that's how I know. Hurry up and open it - and read it out loud so that I will know, too."

"Dear Robbie,

It's been quite a while since I have had time to write. After we last corresponded, I joined the South Carolina Home Guard and had been stationed at Fort Walker on Hilton Head Island, off the South Carolina Coast.

I suppose you read about the battle between our fort and the Union Navy on November 7, 1861. It is certainly a day I will long remember. A squadron of Yankee ships, dozens of them, steamed toward our coast. When they were close enough, our guns fired upon them, but our shots fell short.

That was the start of a terrible shelling of our fort, and another Confederate Fort - Fort Beauregard on Bay Point. Both of our forts continued for a time to engage the Yankee armada; and we inflicted considerable damage to them. But we were no match for all of the Yankee ships. They were heavily bombarding us - we were experiencing many casualties, as I am sure they were, but we were terribly out-manned, and we were forced to abandon our forts.

I was one of the casualties, one of the survivors. I have lost my right leg. I am told that I will survive, but will be here in the hospital for some time.

I apologize for not writing at Christmas and New Year's - here it is 1862 already -but I was too much under the weather to do so. I hope you understand.

Give Mollie K a hug and a kiss for me. Write when you can."

"It's signed 'Jack.'" Robbie stands silently for a moment; he continues to hold the letter.

"Mollie K, I do remember reading about that battle. The Federal Navy had forty-five battle-type ships and a large number of other ships, which were transporting about twelve thousand Union Army troops.

"How long is this useless war going to last? People - good people - on both sides being killed or wounded. Jack is severely wounded with a terrible handicap for the rest of his life. Mollie K, what is the world coming to? What is America coming to?"

It is nearly a week later when Robbie stops by the University library to talk with Thomas. "You look glum, Thomas - down in the dumps. Anything wrong?"

Thomas, his face saddened, pauses before responding. "Yes, Robbie, I am glum - down in the dumps, as you say. The University has just received another war casualty notice. Jack Simon has died from wounds received back in November of last year. I'm sorry, Robbie. I know he was your best friend."

Robbie is stunned. He nearly faints. Tears fill his eyes. A lump is in his throat. He feels weak and grits his teeth in anger. "Jack was a good person - a wonderful and loyal friend. He died for what he believed in, yet it was not his war. May he rest in peace."

Robbie is devastated by sorrow as he walks home.

"What's wrong, Robbie?" Mollie K inquires the moment she sees him. "Something dreadful has happened?" she asks.

"Yes, dear. Jack has died from his war injury."

"How do you know that?"

"The University received a telegram today. Thomas told me the news. This is a shock - a powerful shock."

They hold onto each other in their sorrow, as if the world is ending.

"Mollie K, this has seriously shaken my northern sympathies. I will always believe that slavery is wrong, but the problems between North and South should be settled without bloodshed. It could have, and should have been, settled through diplomacy - not by war. America's elected officials have failed its people."

The Confederate Capital at Richmond, Virginia remains unscathed, untouched by the Union Army. It is, in the eyes of the Union government in Washington, a reprehensible pillar of disobedience, a haunting symbol of Confederate unlawfulness. The lustful eyes of the North are fixed on the

Southern capital. It is the coveted prize of the Union Army - of the Union government. It must be captured or destroyed.

Richmond is not only the capital of the Confederacy, it is the hub of a major Southern railway center serving and linking all of the strategic cities of the South. It is also the home of Tredegar Ironworks where most of the cannons and other field weapons for the South are manufactured. The conquest of Richmond is highly desired. It must be done. Richmond must be had. It must fall, and with its fall will come a swift and final ending to the war of Southern rebellion.

The Lincoln administration has long envisioned the capture of Richmond as the key to bringing down the Confederate insurrection. The entire presidential Cabinet is meeting to address the problem of the Northern Army of the Potomac's failure to move against Richmond. Lincoln's patience with General George McClellan is wearing thin. The entire North is calling for action. Something must be done. It must be done now. Secretary of War Edwin Stanton has replaced Simon Cameron; he is the first to speak. He hopes to arouse a positive note for the meeting.

"Mr. President, we will see the state capitals of the other Southern states fall like dominoes once Richmond is captured. With the collapse of their capital cities, the individual states will cease to have any remaining desire to oppose reconciliation with the Union."

"Mr. Secretary, may I remind you that it is impossible for our army to capture Richmond when we are unable to dislodge it from its camp site on the banks of the Potomac River. I am at my wit's end," Lincoln responds with apparent agitation in his voice. Having risen from his chair, he begins pacing back and forth before continuing what he has to say.

"Yes, it can be true; victory can be ours. If General McClellan is ever persuaded to move his army against the South, I believe that Richmond will fall. General McClellan has a grand plan to take Richmond. We do not see eye to eye on everything, but I have agreed to his plan; but his plan will not work if he does not put it into action.

"I have tried to be patient, to be reasonable, and I give credit where credit is due. General McClellan took command of a defeated, disorganized and disillusioned army after our defeat - yes, after our disgraceful and humiliating defeat at Bull Run. He has taken what was left of that army, he has added raw recruits to it, and he has built it into a grand and proud army.

"It is a loyal army, capable of accomplishing great things. But it must move against our enemies to do so. Yes, I have exercised restraint. I have given General McClellan great latitude in his decisions, for I have great confidence in his abilities.

"Just look at his credentials. He entered West Point when he was a mere sixteen years old. He graduated near the top of his class when he was barely twenty. He served with distinction in the Mexican War where he was decorated for bravery. He is brilliant, a good and dedicated leader.

"He was successful in civilian life, rising to high positions with two railroads. He was president of the St. Louis and Cincinnati Railways. I personally met him once when I was an attorney for the railroad.

"Yes, General McClellan is brilliant and capable. He is a superb organizer. He has worked diligently in developing the Army of the Potomac. He has spent long hours with his troops. "The Army of the Potomac is loyal, it is disciplined, and it is ready for the mission it has been trained to do. The question is: When will General McClellan be ready?"

Secretary of State William Seward interjects, "Mr. President, have you considered replacing General McClellan?"

"I have, but I believe it unwise to do so. At least at the present time, it is unwise. His men worship him. To replace him could demoralize the army. It is up to McClellan to take an aggressive stance, to take action. I shall see to it."

McClellan has for months weathered the storms of presidential pressures, the criticisms of Congress and the fury of the Northern press, all demanding military action against the South. His critics insist that the time to invade the South is long overdue. His loyalty, his motives, and his determination have been questioned. He ignores them all. It is, he concludes, his army - the Army of the Potomac. He will decide the time and the place for action.

He has molded his army of new recruits and disgraced and disillusioned soldiers left from the Bull Run debacle into a great army. He supervised their training. He left nothing to chance. He oversaw everything. His army is superbly trained, superbly disciplined, and superbly conditioned. It is the best equipped, supplied and confident army that has ever existed. His men are proud and anxious to serve; an elite army ready to move against its enemy. George McClellan is proud of his army; his army is proud of him.

McClellan is finally ready to move against Richmond. And move he does; he and his grand Army of the Potomac. The move is done in grand McClellan style, in spectacular McClellan fashion, in a typical McClellan manner.

It is Friday morning, March 14th, 1862; he has readied his troops for a grand review. And a grand review it is. The men march, the bands play, each unit attempts to out-do the other, albeit competing in a spirit of solidarity. It is now time for "Little Mac," the affectionate name given McClellan by his troops, to address them; to address his army.

The hushed army stands silently and attentively as McClellan faces them from the reviewing stand. He salutes his troops and begins to speak.

"Soldiers of the Army of the Potomac! For a long time I have kept you inactive, but not without a purpose. You were to be disciplined, armed and instructed; the formidable artillery you now have, had to be created; other armies were to move and accomplish certain results.

"I have held you back that you might give the death-blow to the rebellion that has distracted our once happy country. The patience you have shown, and your confidence in your General, is worth a dozen victories.

"These preliminary results are now accomplished. I feel that the patient labor of many months has produced its fruits; the Army of the Potomac is now a real army - magnificent in material, admirable in discipline and instruction, excellently equipped and armed - your commanders are all that I could wish.

"The moment for action has arrived, and I know that I can trust you to save our country. As I ride through your ranks, I see in your faces the sure presage of victory; I feel that you will do whatever I ask of you. The period of inaction has passed.

"I will bring you now face to face with the rebels, and only pray that God may defend the right in whatever direction you may move; however strange my actions may appear to you, ever bear in mind that my fate is linked with yours, and that all I do is to bring you where I know you wish to be: on the decisive battlefield.

"It is my business to place you there. I am to watch over you as a parent over his children; and you know that your General loves you from the depths of his heart. It shall be my care, as it has ever been, to gain success with the least possible loss; but I know that, if it is necessary, you will willingly follow me to our graves for our righteous cause.

"God smiles upon us; victory attends us; yet, I would not have you think that our aim is to be attained without a manly struggle. I will not disguise it from you. You have brave foes to encounter. Foes well worthy of this steel that you will use so well.

"I shall demand of you great, heroic exertions, rapid and long marches, desperate combats, privations, perhaps. We will share all these together; and when this sad war is over, we will all return to our homes and feel that we can ask no higher honor than the proud consciousness that we belonged to the Army of the Potomac."

The General steps back from the podium to a rousing roar of approval from the troops. He salutes them, they salute him. Again, the bands play rousing patriotic music as the troops march from the field.

Just to the rear of the reviewing stands, hundreds of ships - ships of every size and description - are anchored along the Potomac River. There are naval vessels and civilian vessels. There are side-wheelers, ferry boats, excursion boats, and every other kind of vessel imaginable. There is little doubt among the troops as to the purpose of the ships. To a man they are ready to go; ready for whenever and wherever they are destined to sail. They are ready to follow their leader - even to the ends of the earth.

Their wait is not long. Union troops have forced the nearby Confederate artillery units overlooking and guarding the Potomac River to withdraw. They are no longer a threat to navigation on the river. A naval battle, fought on March 8th and 9th near Hampton Roads, Virginia, between two iron-clad war ships - the Union Monitor and the Confederate Virginia - has safely opened the Chesapeake Bay to McClellan's armada of transport ships.

On the morning of March 17th, the embarkation of McClellan's troops is underway from Alexandria, Virginia, from Washington, and from Annapolis, Maryland. Alexandria, the major port of departure, is a river-side town a few miles downriver from Washington. The amphibious operation is a spectacular and unbelievable military accomplishment. Thousands of troops and hundreds of tons of supplies, rations, guns, ammunition, artillery pieces, cattle, horses, and mules are loaded on vessels docked at the waterfront. They are bound for an unknown destination. Spirits are high among the departing soldiers.

Dockside activities give an appearance of a street carnival. Civilians are everywhere. Men, women, and children mill around, dancing and singing, hucksters peddle their wares. As each ship is loaded, it signals its departure with a smart blast of its whistle and moves downriver. They are off to the unknown. Of one thing the soldiers are sure: they are not on a training mission. This is for real. The caravan of ships, miles and miles long, continues down the smooth waters of the Potomac into the rough and choppy currents of the Chesapeake Bay. On through the night, on into the next day they sail. There is much speculation about their destination, but it remains shrouded in secrecy. Nothing has been revealed to the men on board. They are neither apprehensive nor fearful about their destination. They are comfortable because their General, George McClellan, is in charge of their destiny.

By late afternoon, they arrive at Fort Monroe, a Union fortress at Hampton Roads, Virginia, where the York River empties into the Chesapeake Bay. Fort Monroe has remained in Union hands even though Virginia is now Confederate soil. Across the large expanse of waters, perhaps twelve or more miles away, they can see another Virginia city. They are told that it is Norfolk, a town in Confederate hands, where the James River flows into the Bay. The land between the two rivers is the Virginia Peninsula. The Confederate capital of Richmond lies just seventy miles away. Their destination, their mission is no longer a secret. "Onto Richmond! Onto Richmond!" again becomes the Northern battle cry. They are ready for the challenges that lie ahead of them.

Chapter Twenty-Five

Nothing Ventured, Nothing Gained

The Confederate government is not oblivious to the Union Army's movement of troops to Fort Monroe. They watch the ships come in, one by one. They count them, nearly four hundred ships. Nor are there any Confederate doubts about the intent of the Union Army. The Confederates are concerned. They are mightily concerned. Obviously, they have reason to be. The twelve-thousand-man Rebel army on the Virginia Peninsula, under the command of General "Prince" John Magruder, is hardly a match for the one-hundred-twenty-thousand-man army of General McClellan. The well-equipped and well-trained Union Army is an awesome force.

Nor is Robbie Holcomb caught unaware of the potential consequences of the Yankee landing. "As plain as the nose on your face," he tells Mollie K. The death of his good friend, Jack Simon, from combat injuries sustained at the battle of Port Royal has brought an increased awareness of the Civil War to Robbie. His interest in the war, his concern, his agitation over the war, has greatly accelerated. It is not an obsession by any means, but he is definitely more concerned, more attuned to the daily events, the daily news of the war, than he ever was prior to this event.

His increased interest over the war leads him to read and to study the news - the events or anything he can find that is related to the war. He spends considerably more time at the University library reading the various newspapers regarding war matters and issues. He is privy to the rumors - the gossip circulating around the University and around town.

Robbie is not at all surprised over the news that the Union Army has landed a large combat-ready army on the Virginia peninsula for the purpose of moving inland and to capture Richmond, the Confederate capital. That is, after all, what this war is about; one side or the other - North or South - overwhelming, defeating the other. Now the war will be a concern of all Virginians and all Southerners.

The Rebel Army is twenty miles northwest of Fort Monroe, near Yorktown, Virginia. It has spent considerable time since Virginia seceded from the Union rebuilding and improving the old Revolutionary War fortifications for the defense of Yorktown and to prevent an enemy from advancing up the peninsula. The Rebel defense line is spread across the peninsula, a thirteen mile span, from the York River to the James. The line of defense is adequate against an army of equal size, or perhaps one somewhat larger than the Rebel defenders. It is far from adequate in size to stop McClellan's army. It can, at best, delay the Union Army and hope for more Confederate troops to arrive.

General Magruder, unlike his Union Army counterpart McClellan, is not known for his military accomplishments. He is far better known for his lavish lifestyle. He is a great host and a hospitable entertainer. He is well-liked and accepted by civilian society. He has a pleasing personality, he is well-liked by his fellow military officers and by the army personnel serving under him. Nevertheless, his penchant toward a lavish lifestyle has earned him the unofficial title of "Prince John." It has its advantages and its disadvantages. It, however, does not add to his military stature.

General Magruder is immediately called to Richmond, to the White House of the Confederacy, for a meeting with President Jefferson Davis and his military advisor, General Robert E. Lee.

President Davis opens the meeting. "General Magruder, what do you have to tell us about the Union Army at Fort Monroe? What do you expect it to do, and when do you believe it will do it?"

"Sir, I can tell you that it is a large army. Some reports estimate its size at a hundred-thousand men, others estimate it to be about one-hundred-fifty-thousand men. My own best estimate from our intelligence sources is that it is about one-hundred-twenty-thousand men."

General Lee then inquires, "Have they begun to move inland?"

"No Sir, they have not. They are bivouacked on the mainland some distance inland from Fort Monroe, but the Army has made no attempt to move further up the peninsula. They have, of course, sent several companies of men on reconnaissance missions. They have not come as far as our fortification lines, although they have come close enough to know where we are."

General Lee again interjects a question. "What do you know about General McClellan? Has he arrived at Fort Monroe?"

"I have received word that General McClellan arrived at Fort Monroe on Wednesday, April 2nd; I expect that his troops will be moving further inland within the next several days."

President Davis again speaks. "General Magruder, you will need to monitor the Yankee Army very closely. General McClellan is a very able leader. I have personally known him for years. I knew him well during my term as the U.S. Secretary of War during the administration of President Franklin Pierce. His army will be disciplined and it will be loyal to its young General."

"Thank you, Mr. President," responds Magruder. "I shall keep my eyes on him - on every move that he makes. I, too, am aware of his abilities. I do not intend to underestimate him or his army."

"One thing further, General Magruder," offers General Lee. "We are moving General Joseph Johnston's army to the peninsula to assist in our defense. Hold General McClellan's army at bay as long as you can. The peninsula is strategically important to the South. We must control it. We must keep the Norfolk naval base in our hands. It cannot fall to the Union. Can you hold General McClellan at bay until General Johnston's army arrives?"

"I hope to do that, General Lee. We are having some assistance through Divine Providence as the bottom has fallen out of the sky the last several days. The lower peninsula is a quagmire. It should present some interesting times to General McClellan as he attempts to move his army up the peninsula. He is going to have quite a time moving his heavy artillery."

Turning again toward President Davis, as he prepares to leave, he salutes his commander-in-chief, then adds, "Thank you, Mr. President. I will do my best at detaining General McClellan and his army. I have a few tricks up my sleeve, a few 'smoke and mirror' techniques to use against the Yankees. General McClellan is a cautious leader. I hope to use a trick or two to cause him to believe that we have a larger army than what we have."

"Very well, General, we do not wish to detain you any longer. Do you have anything further to add, General Lee?"

"No, Sir. Just keep us informed about what is happening. We will give you all of the assistance, all of the support that we have available."

"Thank you, General Lee. Again, thank you, Mr. President. I am on my way back to my troops."

Robbie reads of the meeting between Confederate President Davis and Generals Lee and Magruder in the next day's newspaper. He comments to Mollie K, "It doesn't take a wizard to figure out what the three of them were talking about, does it?"

"I have no idea what they were talking about Robbie, and neither do you. The paper only says that they had a meeting."

"Well, what else would they talk about? The North lands over one-hundred-thousand soldiers on Virginia's Eastern shore - ready to push their way up the peninsula. You can bet that Magruder has been told to stop them or delay them until the Confederates can muster enough troops in the area to hold them."

"Thank you for telling me, Mr. General."

"Don't be so sarcastic, Mollie K."

General Magruder's assessment of the strength of the Northern Army of the Potomac is right on the mark. He is likewise correct in his assessment that McClellan will soon begin to move his vast army up the peninsula. However, he has not fully comprehended the serious setbacks that the weather conditions will play in detaining McClellan's army in its plan to march up the peninsula toward Richmond. Nor has McClellan made an assessment of these factors.

The rains come, and the winds blow, and the lightning flashes, and the thunder rolls. Nature is at war with man. The rain falls by the bucketful, torrential rains inundate the land turning it into a knee-deep mass of vile-smelling, sloppy, soupy mud. The winds blow at near hurricane force, sweeping away tents and supplies. The lightning and thunder, in consort, rage across the sky from horizon to horizon. When the rains and the winds and the electrical storms subside, then come the sweltering heat and the swamps and the snakes and the mosquitoes. Disease and fever become the silent enemy of McClellan's army. Dysentery, typhoid fever, and malaria rage among the troops, often waylaying entire companies for days at a time. The maladies are unknowingly and unintentionally passed from person to person and company to company, often bordering on the brink of epidemic proportions. Whatever romantic illusions of warfare had dwelled in the minds of the young Union soldiers, they are quickly dispelled by the elements of nature, even before the first shots of war are seen or heard.

Nevertheless, the Army of the Potomac moves slowly forward, fighting against the forces of nature. Their instruments of war are the axe, the pick, and the shovel. Thousands of soldiers find themselves engaged in cutting trees and building roads day after day. The advance toward Yorktown is now numbered in weeks rather than in days, as originally planned. As they near the Confederate fortifications around Yorktown, they are closely monitored by the defending Confederate troops. True to his word, true to his promise to President Davis and General Lee, General Magruder does, in fact, have a trick or two up his sleeve. He calls a meeting of his junior officers.

"Gentlemen, we have a little job of deceit to pull on our adversary, General McClellan and his Army. They are now very close to our line of fortifications. They are going to be observing our lines of defense very closely over the next several days. What do you suppose they are going to be looking for?"

A young Lieutenant answers, "Sir, they are looking to determine our military strength. They want to know where our artillery pieces are located, and how many of them we have. They also want to know how many troops we have. They will use this information to determine where and when they will attack us."

"Very good, Lieutenant, that is exactly the information they want."

General Magruder pauses momentarily, then continues, "And we are going to help them get that information."

"But, Sir," the young Lieutenant protests, "won't that be to our disadvantage? Won't that be like throwing ourselves to the wolves? We are outnumbered nearly ten men to our one. It will be like leading ourselves to the slaughter."

"Gentlemen, this is where our little plan of deception comes into play. Starting immediately, and continuing for the next several days, we are going to march our troops some distance behind the lines, but close enough so that the Union observers can see them. Then we are going to circle around and double back some distance behind the lines where we are out of sight of the Yankees. Then we are going to march right back in sight of the Yankees again. They will think that it is another company of our troops. We are going to do this off and on throughout the daylight hours. This should convince the Yankees that we have as many troops, if not more, than they do."

The officers and their troops are fascinated with the scheme. They enthusiastically go about their duties of marching in circles.

The ploy works to perfection. Union General Erasmus Keyes' advanced units observe the Rebel troops moving behind the line of fortifications held by the Confederates. At about the same time, the Confederate artillery fires upon Keyes' troops. The Confederate infantrymen in trenches and dugouts lay down a blistering hail of rifle fire against their enemy. The Yankees have seen enough. They have the information they were seeking. General Keyes returns to the Yankee lines and reports to General McClellan.

"General," he announces, "Magruder's line of fortifications is well manned. They have perhaps as many men as we do if not a force far superior to our army in manpower, held in reserve. From our advantage point we watched them for a long time. We were finally spied by their front line forces and we were heavily fired on. We were compelled to withdraw. We also observed that the Rebels have built dams where they can release the waters and flood the lower lands in front of their fortifications.

"I believe that a frontal attack against the Rebel line will be disastrous. The land, even before the Rebs attempt to flood it, is nearly unapproachable because of dense forests, swamps and marshes. Those marshes are infested with every kind of varmint, snake, and mosquito known to mankind. We could very well risk an epidemic of devastating proportions."

"Thank you, General Keyes. You have done a great service to the Army of the Potomac. The information that you have gathered is vastly important to us. We do not want to place our men in harm's way when it is not necessary to do so.

"I believe we can accomplish what we are here to do through a siege operation, rather than by a direct frontal attack by our foot soldiers.

"It will take somewhat longer to accomplish our overall mission - our ultimate goal, but I am convinced it will save the lives of thousands of our infantry soldiers.

"I believe that the lives of my men are more important than the time that may be lost through caution. We will yet accomplish our ultimate goal - the capture of the Capital of the Confederacy. It will not be accomplished as quickly as Mr. Lincoln and his civilian warlords would have it done, but it will happen in due time."

"General McClellan, I wholeheartedly agree with you; you have chosen the right course of action."

McClellan moves his heavy artillery into position for the siege of Yorktown. The Confederates, having been afforded sufficient time by the delay, move the army of Joseph Johnston to the defense of the peninsula.

Johnston, like McClellan, is hesitant to engage his men in heavy combat. The two opposing armies occasionally spar, but there is no serious fighting on a large scale. By mid-spring, the Confederate army abandons

Yorktown. It is just prior to McClellan's planned artillery assault on the Confederate fortifications. General Johnston orders the withdrawal in spite of General Lee's orders to the contrary.

Chapter Twenty-Six

A Call To Duty

The presence of McClellan's Union Army at Fort Monroe causes immediate and multiple problems for the Confederate government and for its Army on the peninsula. None are more critical or distressing than the alarming disparity between the awesome size of the Union Army and the woefully inadequate size of the defending Confederate Army. If Richmond is to be saved - perhaps if the Confederacy is to be saved - something must be done and it must be done soon.

No one is more aware of the urgent need of adequate numbers of troops for the defense of the Confederacy than is General Lee. He has brought this matter to the attention of President Davis several times, but other pressing problems have sidelined the matter. It can wait no longer. The time for action is now.

General Lee again approaches Davis. "Mr. President, it is most important that the Confederate Congress be apprized of our immediate need for more troops. Relying on a totally volunteer army has proven to be unsuccessful. The war has lost most of its glamour. The luster for fame has vanished. Men have learned that war is a nasty, deadly business. It is ruthless and it is demanding. It is a 24-hour-a-day job. Enlistments are not meeting our needs.

"Sir," he continues, "we have no choice other than to draft young men into the military service."

"General Lee, I suppose you have considered the political consequences of your recommendations? A conscription law - or draft law - is not going to be popular among the citizens of the Confederacy, nor is it going to be highly regarded by the Confederate Congress."

"I am aware of its unpopularity on the home front and in the halls of Congress. It is not an easy matter, Mr. President, but it is a matter that must be dealt with, and the sooner the better for the sake of the Confederacy."

"General Lee, are you not aware that the Union does not resort to drafting men into their armies? They rely solely on volunteers."

"Yes Sir, I am well aware of that. But you must remember, Sir, that the population of the North is nearly three times larger than the population of the South, so their volunteer quotas seem to be adequate at this time.

"I believe, Mr. President, that it is just a matter of time until the North will also have to resort to a conscription law to provide adequate troop replacements."

"Very well, General Lee, I shall do so immediately. What are your suggestions regarding the law?"

"Young men between the ages of 18 and 35 should be subject to serving in the military service of their country until this war is ended. I realize there will be certain circumstances; certain situations in which some men in these age groups should be exempt from military service because they are engaged in essential occupations or because of other valid reasons. The Congress, in its wisdom, should be able to resolve these matters."

On March 28th, President Davis sends a bill to his Confederate Congress proposing the draft law suggested by General Lee. It is hotly contested and politically decried on the floor of the Senate, and labeled as exactly the kind of law that opposes the principles of freedom of choice for which the Confederacy is fighting.

Texas Senator Louis Wigfall, after listening to the debate for some time, rises and addresses his colleagues. "Gentlemen, it is time for us to cease our childish little quibbles. We are dealing with a very serious matter. Possibly a matter of life or death for this very Confederacy that we are supposed to serve. The enemy is now on Southern soil. They are on this peninsula, less than seventy miles from our very doorstep. Are we to do as Nero and fiddle our time away while our Rome burns? Or are we to face our responsibilities to govern this Confederacy? I remind you of something Edmund Burke said many years ago: 'Public life is a situation of power and energy; he trespasses against his duty who sleeps upon his watch, as well as he that goes over to the enemy.'

"Gentlemen, we have a job to do. It may be an unpopular choice, it may be a difficult decision, but it is something that must be done. So let us be on with the task before us.

"We must pass a draft law and save the Confederacy or, if we fail to do so, we must bear the guilt of the Confederacy's defeat."

The draft bill, with modifications, passes on April 16, 1862. While teachers are exempt from the draft, students are not. Nevertheless, the law provides that any man drafted for military service can legally hire a replacement to serve in his stead if he so desires to avoid military service.

Mollie K is beside herself when she hears about the new draft law. She is nearly seven months into her pregnancy. She is fearful and anxious about her husband's military status. "Oh Robbie, what are we going to do?" she asks as the tears flow.

"Mollie K, a draft law has been passed. It does not mean that I am going to be drafted.

There are thousands of draft-age men throughout the South, so the odds of my name coming up are quite slim. Now don't get upset about what if this happens or that happens. You are speculating."

"But what if you are called to go, Robbie? What are you going to do?"

"Mollie K, if I am called to go into the Confederate Army, I will have to go. It will not be a matter of choice. What would you expect me to do? I am sure the law is going to have severe penalties for violation. I would suspect there will be prison time for non-compliance."

"Robbie, I don't want you to go. You can go back up North, back to your home, or you can pay someone to go in your place. I read in the paper that the draft law will allow anyone to pay someone else to go in their place. The paper says that there are lots of people that will go in someone's place for money."

"Oh, sweetie, I could never do anything like that. Don't you understand? That would be unconscionable. It would be cowardly. I could never run away from a duty, nor could I pay someone to do something that I was obligated to do myself. It is unthinkable. I don't want to go in the Southern army, and I don't want to go in the Northern army. But if I am called, I must go. There would be no other choice."

"But what about me? What about our baby? What is going to happen to us? What if you are killed? I am going to have our baby in the next month or two and I want you here to take care of us."

"Oh, sweetie, I want to be here for you. I hope to be here for you. You are everything I could ever hope for - you and our baby - our soon-to-be-born baby. I want you to be happy, you and our child. I want your life to be one big happy and exciting time. You have had more than your share of sadness - the loss of your father when you were so young, the struggles you and your Mamma have had with the rooming house." Robbie holds her close - ever so close. "And I want to be part of that happiness, and I plan to be there for you and our child." Robbie pauses, then with a big grin, he adds, "For you and all of our children - now cheer up."

"Oh, Robbie, I hope so, but I can't help but worry. What would I do without you? You could get killed just like Jack."

"Mollie K, I am not going to get killed. Have you forgotten about my good luck? Come on now, smile and forget about all of these morbid ideas. If you don't calm down, you are going to have a miscarriage.

"You are putting the cart before the horse," he says as he lovingly and gently holds her. "You have me going off to the Army and the draft has not even started. There is nothing on this earth that I love more than you. You and our child are everything that I have ever wanted. I have told you so many times. If I must go, it is for you and our unborn child. Rest assured, if duty calls, I will come back to you. Now hush the crying."

They closely hold one another for a very long time. Mollie K finally puts the thought of the draft behind her. She faces each day with optimism, thinking only about Robbie and their soon-to-be-born child.

"Robbie, I am sure our baby is going to be a boy," she announces pleasantly at dinnertime.

"What makes you so sure?"

"Well, he kicks like a mule."

"Maybe it's going to be a mule then," he replies teasingly, as she playfully pinches him lightly on the leg.

"And for that remark I am not going to name him after you."

"Then what are you going to name him?"

Mollie K sat silently for a moment, a serious expression on her face. "Robbie, of course we are going to name him after you. Not by your real name because nobody ever calls you Robert. We will name him Robbie after you and we will name him "K" after my daddy because that is what Daddy always called me. He called me "K," just simply the letter "K." Robbie, it will also be for the both of us because you do not have a middle name and I do not have a middle name. Don't you think that is unique? He will be Robbie K Holcomb. I think it is so grand. He will be my pride

213

and joy. He will have the same names as the two men that are dear to my heart - my husband and my daddy."

She waits a long moment for Robbie to answer. When he does not respond immediately, she is terribly let down. "Robbie, is anything wrong? Do you not want him to be named after you and Daddy? Oh, please say that you do. Please say that I can, Robbie. Please say yes. It will make me so happy."

"Of course you can, sweetie. If that's what you want to do. But how do you know it will be a boy? What if it's a little girl? We don't know what our child is going to be."

"Well, if it's a baby girl, I shall name her 'Robbie.' Girls can be named 'Robbie,' too, you know. Anyway, you just mark my word. It's going to be a little boy. I know that it is."

Their happiness over the forthcoming birth of their child is short-lived. Robbie receives his call to military service under the new draft law. He is among the first group to be called. All of Mollie K's old fears resurface. She begs and pleads with Robbie to go back up North or to buy his way out of the draft. "You know very well your parents will give you the money. I know your Mamma will."

"Oh, sweetie, I love you dearly," he replies, "but there are some things that a man must do. Duty has called and I must answer. It is the manly thing to do; it is the only honorable thing to do. It would be reprehensible and dishonorable, for me to do otherwise. Please understand, sweetie, I do not have a choice. The Confederate government has made the choice for me. I must go, I absolutely must go. It will be the most difficult thing I have ever done, leaving you and our unborn child. Please, Mollie K, please try to understand."

"Robbie, I want to understand. I am trying to understand. I know what you are saying, but I don't understand why you are saying it. There will be lots of men that will not go off to war just because the government wants them to."

"Mollie K, I cannot answer for them. I can only answer for myself."

Robbie withdraws from the University on the day that his draft notice arrives. His third year of college would have been completed in just over two months. Now it will be put on hold. This is a bitter pill to swallow, yet he faces the disappointment philosophically. "A few disappointments in life add to our character and to our faith," he tells his wife. "I will be a better man when I return from this military experience.

"My ancestors on both my mother's and my father's sides of the family served in past wars. It seems to be a family tradition."

"Are you going to write to your Mamma or Daddy and let them know that you are going into the Army? You know they will want to know."

"If I write to Mother now, she will be beside herself, worried to death. I will let Father know as soon as I get to my training facility and he can break the news to Mother. It will be easier that way. There is no need for me to upset Mother.

"If I wrote her, she would be just like you. She would want me to try to get out of going. If I did go, she would want me to go in the Union Army. She would never understand my being a Confederate soldier. I can't say that I understand it myself."

The days before Robbie's departure pass by as if they are driven by a windstorm. They seemingly come in a flash and they end in a flash. Even so, he and Mollie K make the most of these days. They spend every possible moment together, yet it seems that their time together is less each day than it was the day before. Neither of them mention the dreadful day of his departure, although it is never far from their thoughts.

Then it comes. The draftees are notified to report to the train station at 8:00 a.m. They are rushing to meet the deadline. Mollie K is trying hard to be brave, to do so for Robbie's sake. She does not want to make the departure difficult for him. It is a losing battle. The tears come. Robbie holds her close, unable to speak because of his own pent-up emotions. Its not that he fears going into the Army; it is simply that he feels all of the emotional fears for her.

"Time to go, sweetie," he manages to say, his voice nearly breaking. "It's a long walk to the train station and you are in no condition to hurry."

"I'll be fine. I'm ready to go," she says, fighting back the tears.

As the two of them, accompanied by Mrs. O'Riley, open the front door to head to the station, Ole Ben is waiting. He is dressed in the same formal clothes - top hat and all - that he had worn the first time he had driven Mollie K and Robbie to their first dance, over two years ago. The carriage is clean and ready for the occupants.

"Mornin' Sir and Ladies," Ben says as he bows and tips his hat. "Son, ah has brought ye here when ye first come to town. Ah took ye two on yer first date. Ah took ye when ever yer left and come again. Ah am takin ye to the Army and ah'll be there to get ye when ye come back home."

"Ben, you are a true friend."

"Yes siree, bob, I sure am. And Ah'm goin' to look after yer women folk while yer gone. Ye can count on me."

"Thanks, Ben. You don't know how much I appreciate that. Ben, you are more than a friend, you are like family."

"Yes siree, bob. That's what Ah am. Ah'm family," Ben says with a chuckle.

Robbie is somewhat embarrassed, and a great deal amused as they pull into the railway station in Ben's fancy carriage. Ben dismounts and opens the carriage door as if he is bringing royalty to the station. The locals all know Ben quite well and are much amused by his antics. Robbie is subjected to a great deal of good-natured ribbing for his royal arrival; however, the old Army sergeant who is there to meet the troops is not amused.

"Private Holcomb," he hisses sarcastically, "ye better take a good look at that fancy carriage, 'cause when this train gets to Richmond, ye ain't gonna see nothin' that fancy again for a long time. Ye ain't gonna do any more ridin'. Yer in the Infantry now and we walk whar we go."

"Yes Sir!" Robbie responds.

"Well, ye better git over there and say yer good-byes to yer wife cause we're movin' out in thirty minutes."

Good-byes are sad, they are always sad. This one is no different. Mollie K's tears flow uncontrollably. Robbie tries as best he can to console her. He assures her it is alright to feel sad. He tries desperately to cheer her up. Emotionally she is drained, fearful of the future.

Every thought, every word, every idea, every fear, and every emotion has been aired and re-aired between them. It has happened over and over, time and time again, during the past several days. Not one thought, or hope, or dream, or fear was left unattended. Everything, everything under the sun has been covered. But she cannot stop the flow of tears. Her world is coming apart.

Robbie holds her, he whispers assurances to her, he holds her as long as he can. The train begins moving, the whistle sounds, the Sergeant shouts an order for Private Holcomb to come aboard. The train is picking up speed; he runs alongside, grasps the boarding rail and jumps aboard at the last possible moment. "Nothing," he says to himself, "nothing can ever be more difficult than this; not war, not death, nothing."

He holds to the boarding rail waving to Mollie K, long after she is out of sight. He had dried her tears, calmed her fears, he promised to write as often as possible and he promised to come back when this dreadful war is over. Through the sadness and despair of leaving his loving and beautiful young wife and an as yet unborn child, he reaches for his inner strength. His optimism is rekindled. He is always an optimist, and why not? Good fortune has always smiled on him and good luck has always embraced him. It has been with him all the days of his life. He is sure it will continue. He quietly murmurs a prayer.

The train is moving at full speed, rushing onward toward Richmond, onward into the unknown. He drops into the first empty seat. It is next to the cantankerous old sergeant. They exchange glances, but say nothing. Robbie closes his eyes. He sits thoughtfully for several minutes, then quietly whispers, "'Yea, though I walk through the valley of the shadow of death, I will fear no evil; for thou art with me.'"

He opens his eyes. The Sergeant is staring at him. "Boy, what was that you just said?"

"It's a verse from the 23rd Psalm."

The Sergeant looks quizzical, then asks, "You mean the Bible?"

"Yes, Sir, it's from the Bible. From the Old Testament."

"Are you a preacher man, boy?"

"No, Sir. I'm a student. That is, I was a student until I was called to serve in the Army."

"Why didn't ye ask for a deferment?"

"I did not believe that it was the right thing to do."

"Son," the Sergeant says, "I might have misjudged you. I believe yer gonna be alright. I might just keep you in my unit when we get to Richmond."

Robbie glances at the old Sergeant, then smiles slightly. "Have you been in the Army a long time?"

"Yes," the Sergeant answers, "I been in it all my life. I was in the old Union Army. Now I'm in a new Army. We're Confederate soldiers. We're fightin' fer Virginia and the South."

The Sergeant pauses, then continues. "I'm rough and tough, but I ain't mean. I'm rough and tough 'cause ah haf to turn ya'll into soldiers, into killers, in the next couple ah weeks. We ain't long from goin' to battle. I gotta teach y'all how to kill or be killed.

"Young fellers like ya'll think it's glamorous. Well, it ain't. It's dirty, rotten business." He pauses again, sat silently for a minute, then repeats his thought, "Yes, siree bob, it's dirty, rotten business."

Robbie nods affirmatively, but does not answer. Then the Sergeant again speaks. "Yer gonna be a father soon, ain't ye son?"

"Yes, Sir. Sometime around the end of June or the first of July."

"Where ye from, Son? I know yer not Southern."

"No, Sir. I'm not Southern, but my wife is and my child will be. I'm from New York."

"Son, ye shoulda high-tailed it back to Noo York when ye got that draft notice."

"That's what Mollie K said. Mollie K's my wife."

"You shoulda follered yer wife's advice. How come ye din't?"

"I couldn't do it. I would have felt like a coward. I had to answer the call. I have to do what is right."

The Sergeant sat silently for several minutes before again speaking. "Son, I been in the Army since I was 15 years old. I'm now 56. Never been married. Ain't got no children. Ah ain't got nuthin' or nobody. Don't much matter what happens to me. You - yer a young feller - got a education and a wife an' gonna have a kid. The Army ain't no place for ye. If ye wanna hop offen this train the next time she slows down, ah ain't gonna see a thing. I ain't gonna mention it to nobody."

"Sir, I can't do that. I just can't do it."

"Well," the old Sergeant says, "I guess ah'll jes haf to take care of ye me'self. Hav to keep ye outa trubble an keep ye from gettin' kilt."

Chapter Twenty-Seven

A Soldier's Life

The train rushes swiftly onward toward its unannounced destination, stopping at every town and hamlet along the way to take aboard other newly-drafted troops destined for military service. Hours later, it comes to a halt just east of Richmond, Virginia. The new recruits disembark in an open field which has the appearance and odor of recently having been used as a cow pasture. The men are instructed to line up in front of a platform where a young army officer is waiting. He appears to be no older than the new draftees.

Silence falls over the new arrivals as the young officer begins to speak. "Young citizens of Virginia, I am here to greet you on behalf of the Army of the Confederate States of America. You have been called for an honorable, noble, and just cause. You have been called into military service to defend the Commonwealth of Virginia and the Confederacy against a Union Army that at this moment is knocking at our very door. This war is not of our making.

"It has been thrust upon us by the aggressive actions of our enemy, by our neighbors and former countrymen. We know that you have willingly answered the call to duty, the call to defend this Commonwealth and your country against the Union invaders.

"Your country - the Confederate States of America - is proud of you. This is not a war which the Confederate government sought. Indeed, we asked our former countrymen that we be left alone in peace - that it was our desire to go in peace when we left the Union; but the enemy has refused to honor our wishes. This is not a war which the Confederate government has sought. It is , however, a war that we must fight and a war that we will win.

"Our enemy is now on Virginia soil, barely sixty miles from the place where you are now standing. I, along with my fellow officers and noncommissioned officers that are here with us, will be training you for your new duties as infantrymen of the Confederate Army.

"Early tomorrow morning we will begin training to meet our enemies and to defeat them. How soon that day will come, we do not know. We ask that you take your training seriously. Your life and your fellow soldiers' lives will depend on what you learn here.

"Your sergeant will take you to the quartermaster where you will be given uniforms and equipment. You are now to report immediately to the sergeant who met you at your home station this morning. We wish you good luck."

Robbie and the other Charlottesville recruits line up in front of their sergeant. He eyes them closely before speaking. "In case yer fellers din't catch me name, it's John Baldwin. To y'all, its Sergeant Baldwin. Thas how y'all will address me when ya speak; but ya won't be speakin' much. When ya do speak, y'all will say 'Sergeant Baldwin, Sir.' Yer gonna be lernin' some new rules; theys Army rules.

"The first rule is, ya don't speak unless ah tells ya to. Ya don't speak to me and ya don't speak to nobody else, 'ceptin after we's finished trainin' at night.

"The second rule is y'all do what ah tell ya to do. Ah'll be tellin' ya what to do, how to do it, and when to do it. Y'all do exactly what I tell ya to do, an' y'all do nuthin' else.

"Ah'm old, an' ah'm rough, an' ah'm dirty an' ah'm tough. But ah'm a soldier. Ah'm a good soldier - the best soldier thar is - that's what ah am. An' tha's what yer gonna be. Ah'm gonna turn you'ns into soldiers - not jus soldiers, but the bes soldiers there are. That's rule number three. Yer a miserable lookin' bunch now. Ya may think yer men - but ya ain't. Not one of ya is a man.

"Rule number four is that yer gonna go outta this camp a man - every one of ya. Ye'll be men when ah'm done wit ya. Ya'll be men an ya'll be soldiers. Ya'll be Sergeant Baldwin's soldiers. Ya'll be soldiers of the sacred South.

"Durin' the next several weeks yer gonna hate me. Yer gonna want to kill me; but ya ain't gonna do it. Ya ain't gonna do it cause thar ain't one of ya man enough to do it. Yer a lily-livered bunch of mammas' boys. But that's gonna change.

"The welcome address that ya just heered from the Lieutenant is the last kind or decent words yer gonna hear while yer in trainin'. That was just fiddle-faddle.

"When yer finished yer trainin' yer gonna know how to take care of yerself. Yer gonna larn how ta kill Yankees, an how not to git yerself kilt.

"What ye larn is gonna depend on yer livin or dyin'. So ye better heed at what ah do an' what ah say. Them Yankee devils done come ashore at Fort Monroe, come on Virginia soil jus like the Lieutenant tole ya. Maybe jes sixty or so miles from here. They's plannin' to come up the peninsula to capture Richmond. They's comin' by the thousands - a hundred thousand we are told.

"But they ain't gonna git ta Richmond. You know why they ain't? 'Cause we ain't gonna let 'em. We're gonna kill 'em. We're gonna send 'em back up North in pine boxes. That's what we're gonna do.

"My job is ta make soldiers outta ya in the next several weeks. That's what ma orders sez, and ah al'ays follow ma orders. Ah al'ays do what ah'm told to do.

"Ya'll ain't neva haft to kill somebody afore now. But them Yankee devils are lookin for trouble. They's here to kill y'all and yer mamma and yer pappa and ta burn yer homes and destroy yer crops and defile yer women folks. Them Yankees ain't no good, and it ain't no sin ta kill 'em. Y'all hea' me?"

"Yes Sir, Sergeant Baldwin," the troops respond in unison. No other comments are made. Sergeant Baldwin's message of speaking only when spoken to is well taken among the new troops. Although the men are well aware that the purpose of their military service is to go to war, the thought of going to war as killers has for the first time become a reality.

Having succeeded in alerting the recruits about the purpose of their new jobs, the old soldier barks his first order to his men. "Tenshun!"

There is immediate activity among the troops in coming to attention.

"Now we're gonna march to the Quartermaster's tent an' get supplies an' equipment, get ye recruits uniforms. Then we're gonna pitch our tents. Ya'll be livin' in tents all the while yer here. Now line up in twos. I don' wanna hear a word from any of ya. Don't make a sound."

The recruits remain standing at attention. They stand with shoulders back, eyes straight forward and bodies erect, as straight as arrows. It is far from perfect, but they are trying.

"Forward, march!" the Sergeant bellows, then he begins counting cadence. "Left, right, left, right," he orders as each new recruit attempts desperately to master the art of marching in step. It is one of many things they will do over and over, again and again, for weeks to come as they learn and master the art of becoming proficient and professional soldiers.

With the coming of darkness the rain comes. It comes by the bucketful. It continues without ceasing, onward into the night. The former cow pasture, now the home of countless new recruits, becomes a quagmire of ankle deep mud. The new recruits attempt to pitch their tents in the night, in the rain and in the mud and the wind. For most it proves to be an exercise in futility. For those who succeed in erecting their tents, they are rewarded by bedding down in a swamp. The recruits sleep little if any during their first night of Army service.

Even so, at the crack of dawn a wake-up call sounds across the camp. Sergeant Baldwin, arising from his bone-dry quarters with a gleeful smirk across his face, calls his company to attention. "Good mornin' gentlemen. It is 5:00 a.m. We arise every mornin' at the same time, usually to the bugle call. We call it 'reveille' in the Army. You will get used to it. It is your first military order of the day."

The old Sergeant, looking at his sleepless, soaking-wet recruits, without one bit of regret or sympathy, mockingly continues. "I'm very glad y'all have had a good night's sleep. A well-rested recruit makes a happy recruit. Y'all fall out ever' mornin' at 5:00 a.m. for roll call. As I call yer name, you will reply, 'Present.' If ye do not fall out an' answer at roll call, yer considered a deserter. Do ye know what the Army does with deserters? Would someone like to guess?"

There is not a sound from his troops, as Sergeant Baldwin walks back and forth in front of them. "Well, since no one seems to know, ah'll tell ya. Ya'll be shot on sight. That's what we do with deserters; it's the rule of th' Army. We live by rules in th' Army. Now, afore yer dismissed, is there a bugler among ya? If so, step forward."

No one replies and no one steps forward.

"Does anyone read music?" the Sergeant asks.

"Yes, Sir, I do," Robbie responds.

"Step forward."

Robbie steps forward.

"Well, Private Holcomb, you read music?"

"Yes, Sir."

"Well, you'r the company bugler. Immediately after morning chow, run down to the Quartermaster tent and request a bugle and the bugler's manual. You learn all the bugle calls. 'Reveille' in the mornin' and 'Lights Out' at bedtime. There's certain bugle calls when we charge into battle and certain calls when we withdraw. Ya'll learn these calls in your spare time, in addition to ya regular duties. Understood?"

"Yes, Sir. I understand."

"Good, ya may take yer place with the troops."

Sergeant Baldwin again calls his troops to attention. "Men, yer a sorry looking group. Yer uniforms are disgraceful. Tomorrow mornin' I'll expect ya to look more like soldiers. Y'all are now dismissed until reveille when we call ye to attention to march to chow."

The days that follow are long and tiresome. They train through rain or shine, from sun up to sundown. After their all-day training, other duties await them: guard duty, latrine duty, or other disagreeable duties. It is a constant test of physical and mental endurance. Their lives are filled with drilling and discipline. They are pushed near to the breaking point. Sergeant Baldwin is pushing them and harassing them every step of the way. His harsh training prepares them for the road that they are yet to travel, a journey they do not yet understand. It is easy to hate the old sergeant. Hating him is the sole pleasure afforded the recruits.

The changes in their lives do not come easy, nor do they come suddenly. But the change comes; a change from boyhood to manhood - to Army manhood. The changes are subtle, undefined, nearly unrecognizable as the transition from boyish civilians to manly soldiers occurs. Not one of the recruits recognizes the changes, but old Sergeant Baldwin recognizes them.

And then the soldiers themselves recognize them. It is then that they know; it is then that they understand. The enmity they had for their sergeant changes to esteem. The distrust they harbored for him becomes trust. Their repugnance turns into regard, their abhorrence becomes admiration. They had loved to hate their sergeant. Now they realize why he tormented them, pushed them. He was preparing them for what they will soon experience on the field of battle. They have now come to know that they are men - Army men - Army soldiers.

They learn the art of survival, the art of warfare and the art of hand-to-hand-combat. They gain all of the military knowledge that the old sergeant has to offer. They learn what they do not want to learn. They learn that the realities of war are that some fall in battle, that some do not go home. These are the hard, cold, cruel facts of Army life.

They now respect the old Sergeant, they even like him, trust him. His toughness is meant to prepare them for the hazards of war that lay ahead of them. Their lives of misery, of perseverance, and endurance have changed them. They have changed from boys into men. They have changed from raw recruits into seasoned soldiers.

That's what the Sergeant now calls them - soldiers. They have earned it. He knows it and they know it. To a man, they are ready. The sounds of war are closing in on them. The call will soon be answered.

Chapter Twenty-Eight

A Flag To Follow

The morning of Friday, May 30th, 1862 is quiet and peaceful. It is not yet daybreak when Robbie Holcomb is awakened by Sergeant Baldwin. Not a word is spoken between them. There is no need for words. The moment Robbie's eyes open, he perceives that something is amiss. It is that inner feeling, that sixth sense or guiding light that seems to dwell around and over him in times of need. Something big, something important, is about to happen.

Robbie instinctively grabs his bugle as Sergeant Baldwin motions for him to follow. When they are beyond the hearing range of the sleeping men, the Sergeant speaks.

"Our call to duty has come. We are goin' to war."

"Do you mean right now, Sarge?"

"Ah mean t'day. We will be breakin' camp later this mornin' - within the next hour or so. We got lots ta do. Ah'm glad ya thought to fetch yer bugle. Ya might as well sound Reveille. It's time for the men to rise."

Reveille is sounded, albeit an hour early. As the troops gather in formation, not yet wide awake, there is considerable early morning grumbling. Sergeant Baldwin gruffly calls them to attention. Silence falls over the men as if their voice boxes have been severed from their throats. He then turns to Robbie.

"Private Holcomb, call the company roll."

"Yes Sir, Sergeant Baldwin," he responds with a salute, then turns to his task. When finished, he again turns to the Sergeant. "All present and accounted for, Sir."

Sergeant Baldwin turns toward his men, and in a more pleasant tone of voice, but in strict military fashion, exclaims, "At ease, men." He pauses momentarily then continues.

"Men, ah have some good news for ya, an' ah have some news that y'all might think ain't so good. The good news is yer trainin' days are over. We're gonna be leavin' this camp t'day. All of us. We're gonna be leavin' heah t'gether. Now the news ya'll might not think is so good is that the moment of truth has arrived. What ah mean is, we're goin' to war. The war is nearly upon us, an' we're gonna join the fight. Now thar's sumptin' else ah need to tell ya. Sumptin' ah have known for quite sometime, but the time ta tell y'all has not been right until now.

"You men of Company K, the 110th Virginia Infantry, an' ah mean ever last one of y'all, y'all are soldiers. Th' best soldiers ah have ever trained in all my Army life. Th' best soldiers thar are anywhere. Yer proud soldiers. Thar ain't no soldiers in the Confederate Army that are better than y'all, an ya can dang well believe thar ain't any Yankee soldiers anywhar that's even half as good a soldier as y'all are, an' that's the gospel truth.

"Now men, ya soldiers of Company K, what do ya say to that?"

The men respond with a rousing shout of approval.

"Men," the old Sergeant continues, "y'all have gone through some rigorous trainin'. Yer strong, yer healthy, an' yer fit an' fearless. Now y'all been called to a great challenge, the call to defend yer country against an invadin' enemy. This is yer call to follow yer flag - the Confederate flag. We're gonna follow our flag into battle.

"Ah know y'all are ready. Ah know yer ready for whatever sacrifice we hafta make for our country. Ah know ever' one of ya will serve yer country with honor and distinction and if the cost is our lives we will gladly pay the price.

"Ah'm proud to serve wit ya'll, proud to be yer Sergeant. We trained t'gether, we'll fight t'gether. After chow, we'll meet back heah. Th' Lieutenant will have somethin' ta say to us."

'We'll pack our gear and be marchin' off to war.' The words of Sergeant Baldwin are resonating over and over in Robbie's ears. It is not that the words are new to him. He has heard them over and over a hundred times during the hours and days and weeks that they have been in training. Now, however, they take on a new meaning, a different meaning.

It is not that he is afraid, not that he fears going to war; he does not. What he fears, what he dreads, is that this war is different to him than it is to the others. Except for him, all of the soldiers in his Infantry Company

- Company K - are Southerners. They will be fighting a Northern foe that they do not know, that they know little about and that they have learned to hate.

Robbie is not in the Southern Army by his choice. He is here because he had no other choice. He was called into military service by a law enacted by the Confederate government that legally required him to serve. He could have disobeyed the law as many young citizens were doing, but that was alien to his principles; he could not do it. Upon induction, he took an oath of allegiance to the Confederacy; again, an act that he was compelled to do.

It is not that Robbie is anti-Southern. He is not. Except for the issue of slavery, which he is firmly and inflexibly opposed to, he has become very southern-oriented otherwise. "After all," he muses to himself, "I am a Northerner with a Southern wife, so I suppose that makes me half-Southern."

Robbie never confided all of his feelings to Mollie K about submitting to the draft call, but there was considerable community pressure demanding that all able-bodied young men answer the call to military service. The community feeling was there even before the draft was enacted. He had declined to enlist, although most of the young men his age had done so.

Local newspapers were openly critical of healthy young men who failed to enlist. A stigma of cowardice, of Northern sympathy became associated with those young men that were not in a military service. The true Sons of the South, the proud and patriotic sons, had enlisted.

There were insults, peer pressure. He never mentioned them to Mollie K. No need to worry her. So when his draft notice came, he complied. It was as simple as that. He had made the choice to do what he was called to do. He repeats to himself an old southern axiom that Mollie K often states, "You've made your bed, now sleep in it."

Chow is spent discussing the war situation. To a man, they are ready for whatever lies ahead, for whatever the future holds in store for them.

They reassemble on the drill field immediately following chow. The Lieutenant who had addressed them when they arrived at camp is there to speak to them on their departure. He faces them and begins to speak.

"Soldiers of the Sacred South:

"It is again my pleasure and honor to address you as you prepare to depart on a gallant and important mission. You came here less than a month ago as civilians. Some of you were farmers, some of you were clerks, some of you may have been engaged in many other types of jobs or occupations. Some of you were students who were preparing to pursue a professional endeavor. You came here as strangers, unknown to one another. Now all of that has changed.

"You are no longer what you were. You are now something different, something more important than what you were. You are now soldiers. Soldiers of the Confederacy: soldiers of the Sacred South.

"You are no longer the strangers that you once were. You are now brothers. You are brothers in arms. Brothers of the Confederacy. You came as many, a diverse group. You were different, one from the other.

"Now you are one. You are a team; a team that thinks as one. You are a team that reacts as one. You are a team that will fight the enemy as one. You are a team with 'esprit de corps.' You are a proud infantry company, and your country expects much from you.

"I have watched you during these few weeks we have been together and I know, beyond the shadow of any doubt, that you will do your duty. You are infantrymen, the foot-soldiers of your army. It is you - the foot-soldiers - who will bear the brunt of battle. It is your mission, as it has always been the mission of the infantrymen, to carry the fight to the enemy. It is the duty of the foot-soldiers to do the dirty work of war. It has always been so in past wars, in other wars, in other battles, in other times and in other places. It is again true in this war.

"It is you, the infantrymen, who first engage the enemy, and it is you who will last engage the enemy on the field of battle. It is your sweat, your sacrifice, and your blood that stains the battlefield. It is the price you must pay for freedom from tyranny. It is you, the infantrymen, the foot-soldiers, who leave for posterity the invisible footprints of courage on the pages of time. Now that time has come for you to do your duty for God and country. Take the fight to the enemy and free our land of this Yankee blight."

The men of Company K, endowed with the blessings of the Confederacy, march away to war. Except for Sergeant Baldwin, none of the men have ever experienced combat. They have great confidence in the rough and tough old Sergeant who had served in the U.S. Army from the time he was fifteen years old. He is an experienced, battle-wise, and competent non-commissioned officer, the kind of soldier to lead men into combat; the kind of soldier men willingly follow into combat.

They march toward their goal, unknown to all except the old sergeant. During a mid-afternoon break, he reveals their destination to them.

"Men, we are headed for Seven Pines, a crossroad 'bout seven miles from Richmond. It's near Fair Oaks, a train stop on the Richmond and York River railroad.

"The Yankees, at least some forty-or-so-thousand of them, are camped there. They's separated from th' main part of their army by the Chickahominy River. We are on our way to hook up with General Joseph E. Johnston's Confederate Army. He's plannin' to attack the Yankees early in the mornin', plannin' to destroy ever' dang one of 'em before their Yankee friends kin get hep across the river to 'em.

"The General, General Johnston that is, like myself, he's a vetran of the Mexican Campaign. He doesn't lack fer bravery; he was wounded five times in Mexico. He ain't skeert of nuthin', not even the devil.

"But I'll tell ya sumptin' else 'bout him. He ain't much for takin' orders from them desk dweller fellers that sit in some tent way behind the action an wants to tell him how ta fight a war."

The old sergeant stops speaking momentarily, snickering at the thought of the General and his independent, if not obnoxious, attitude toward his superior officers. "Yes Sir, Old Joe, he fights the enemy when he wants to, an' where he wants to, an' how he wants to, an' don't tell nobody nuthin'."

The young soldiers are awe-struck by Sergeant Baldwin's description of General Johnston.

"Sergeant Baldwin," one of the soldiers hesitantly speaks, "if I may say so, it sounds like you and the General are two peas in a pod."

"Ya can say that again," the old Sergeant says with a chuckle. "Yes Sir, we are like two peas in a pod."

After the rest stop, the Sergeant and his company of soldiers march on toward their destination, on toward their destiny. They arrive in late afternoon. Sergeant Baldwin instructs the men to pitch their tents while he goes to headquarters to learn what part he and his men will play in the planned attack on the Yankees. Their rendezvous with destiny is at hand.

Chapter Twenty-Nine

Where He Leads Me I Will Follow

The Army of Northern Virginia, the Confederate Army, under the command of General Johnston, moves to the Virginia peninsula soon after General McClellan's Union Army lands at Fort Monroe. Johnston is superior in rank to Confederate General "Prince" John Magruder. Johnston is now in charge of all Confederate troops on the peninsula, including Magruder and his soldiers. Johnston's orders are to aggressively engage the Union Army on the lower peninsula somewhere near Yorktown or Williamsburg, while the Yankees are some fifty or sixty miles from Richmond.

"The lower peninsula is crucial to our defense of Richmond," cautions General Lee in his instructions to Johnston. He then adds, "We now hold the Norfolk naval base, and we must continue to do so if we are to control the James River.

"If the Union Army controls the lower peninsula, we will lose Norfolk, and the Union Army is then in control of both the York and the James River. This will allow the North to move men and supplies upriver on both or either water routes and our defense of Richmond will become more difficult."

Johnston acknowledges Lee's instructions, although he neglects to follow them. Instead, his army back-peddles away from McClellan's slowly and cautiously advancing Union Army, avoiding any serious military confrontations. His hesitancy to force the issue, to confront McClellan's army with force or determination, is due neither to cowardice, nor to an intentional disregard of his orders. Johnston is simply going to do things his way - the Joe Johnston way. He will pick the time and the place to make a stand and he believes it should be somewhere closer to Richmond.

The existing state of affairs, the lack of aggressive and meaningful action between the two opposing armies, is also quite acceptable to Union General McClellan. Johnston and McClellan have much in common. They are well acquainted with the capabilities and military characteristics of one another. They had been close friends in the old Union Army, although that friendship ceased to exist with the parting of ways between the Northern and Southern states.

There are other remarkable similarities between the two men. Neither is anxious to engage their armies in an all out battle, although neither man lacks personal courage to do so. Both have been decorated for bravery in earlier military conflicts. Both have an intense dislike for their respective presidents. They also dislike following orders from any civilian leaders. Rear echelon military officers, those assigned to planning military engagements from a safe distance far behind the combat engagement, are also looked on with disdain by the two generals.

On the other hand, both McClellan and Johnston are held in high esteem by the common soldiers serving under their command. Their soldiers are loyal and dedicated. They take great pride in the armies in which they serve. Unquestionably, both are capable soldiers. They are excellent field officers. Both are capable of commanding an army division or an army corps, but both appear ill disposed at commanding an entire army. Perhaps they are overwhelmed and rendered indecisive with the awesome responsibility of overseeing the military operations of a vast army. While both generals feel the pressure and the weight of their responsibilities, they welcome the prestige, the honor and the glory associated with command.

Although fierce, raging battles have so far been limited, the two armies have engaged in unavoidable spirited skirmishes along the road to Richmond. Some of these skirmishes have been bloody. The lack of aggressive and intense fighting between the Union and Rebel forces has generated bitter criticism from the heads of state in Washington and in Richmond. The progress of the war on the Virginia peninsula has been less than acceptable to Union President Lincoln, and to Confederate President Davis.

Both presidents have sent messages to their commanding generals demanding more aggressive action from their armies. Lincoln prods McClellan by telegram. "Your advance toward Richmond is much too slow and too cautious. Your progress is too timid to satisfy your government and your public."

Davis dispatches a messenger to instigate an action from Johnston. "The time is now, to confront our enemy. You must act and act quickly. The enemy is nearing our doorstep."

The news media North and South have become extremely critical over the lack of military action by their respective armies. The Union Army's cautious and somewhat methodical advance up the peninsula, and the Rebel Army's timid and lackadaisical retreat away from the slowly advancing Union Army is wearing thin the patience of the civilian population on the homefront. The Southern population around Richmond is especially concerned. There is both fear and frustration weighing on the minds of Richmond's citizenry.

It is not that there has been a total lack of hostilities between the two armies. There have been heated and sometimes intense engagements. The Battle of Williamsburg proved to be fiercely fought by both armies, although it was an indecisive military encounter. McClellan, nonetheless, claims victory over the battle in his report to Lincoln. His claim of victory provides him a reprieve from Northern criticism, a reprieve that proves to be short-lived.

A surge of enthusiasm rises throughout the North on the heels of the reported Williamsburg victory. The news media boasts of the great military victory. The public response is awesome. Not to be outdone, the Northern politicians join the chorus. The U.S. House of Representatives unanimously adopt a congratulatory resolution praising General McClellan and the Union Army on its great victory:

"Resolved, that it is with feelings of profound gratitude to Almighty God that the House of Representatives, from time to time, hear of the triumphs of the Union armies in the great struggle for the supremacy of the Constitution and the integrity of the Union.

"Resolved, that we receive with profound satisfaction, intelligence of the recent victories achieved by the Armies of the Potomac, associated from their localities with those of the Revolution, and that the sincere thanks of the House are hereby tendered to Major General George B. McClellan for the display of those high military qualities which secure important results with but little sacrifice to human life."

Fighting continues to be encountered as the two armies cautiously, slowly, and methodically move up the peninsula, nearer to Richmond.

Johnston continues to yield ground to his enemy. Not once has he initiated an offensive action against his adversary on the Virginia peninsula. McClellan is quite willing to allow Johnston to continue his slow retreat. McClellan's objective is the capture of Richmond and the defeat of the Confederate government. He prefers to do so by siege, by pounding the city with his heavy artillery until it surrenders or until it is reduced to a pile of rubble. The timing for such action is of little importance to McClellan, although the Lincoln government and the Northern press are anxious for a quick and decisive move against the Confederate capital.

McClellan is convinced that the Southern Army is vastly superior in manpower over those of his own Army and that an all out battle may be disastrous. Johnston's Army, however, is considerably smaller than McClellan's, and it is not nearly as well-equipped as is that of McClellan's. The Union Army has nearly thirty-five or forty thousand more troops than does Johnston.

Johnston's retreat, his consistent yielding ground to McClellan's Army without a serious effort to stop them, his unwillingness to do battle with the Union Army of the Potomac or take a stand against the enemy, continues to rile Jefferson Davis and his military advisor, General Lee. Neither Davis nor Lee question Johnston's loyalty nor his bravery. Nor do they question his resolve. What they do question is when and where Johnston will make his stand. Johnston is not one to keep his superiors well-informed, nor is he inclined to keep his own field commanders informed.

The Union Army, the hated enemy, is now less than ten miles from Richmond. The dust rising skyward from the moving armies is visible from the streets of Richmond. Fear is rampant throughout the civilian population. The Confederate government is concerned. Plans are made to evacuate government officials. Residents are nearing a state of panic. Something must be done. It must be done now. Word is sent to General Johnston, "Stop the Army of the Potomac. Now. You must initiate a substantial and decisive action against McClellan's advancing Army." The message is signed by Davis, President of the Confederacy. Johnston does not respond to President Davis.

It is toward this quagmire, into this militarily stagnant atmosphere that Sergeant Baldwin, Private Holcomb, and the rest of the inexperienced and combat unproven troops are marching.

Whether it is by the prodding of his government or by his own late blooming initiative, Johnston decides to initiate a substantial military action against McClellan's Army. The time and place he has waited for has arrived.

McClellan has become less cautious about Johnston and his Army. He has divided his hundred-thousand-man Army; part is on one side of the Chickahominy River and part on the other. Although McClellan has military reasons for doing so, it is a strategic blunder, a gamble that McClellan seldom takes. Johnston recognizes the blunder; his time for action has at last arrived. He is ready to throw caution to the wind, ready at last to take the initiative.

The battle plans are made quickly. In true Joe Johnston style, few of the plans are in writing. They are verbally conveyed to his division commanders. It is risky to do so, but nevertheless, true to form for Johnston.

Sergeant Baldwin and his men arrive in camp a day after the battle plans are completed. General Johnston is nonetheless happy to welcome a former comrade-in-arms from the Mexican War. After reminiscing about old times and old acquaintances - the good and the bad - they get down to business.

"McClellan has split his Army. About 40,000 of his men are on this side of the river and the rest are on the other side. Our intelligence officers tell us that he is expecting to gain a sizeable number of men from General McDowell, who is coming from over near Fredericksburg with Union reinforcements. McClellan is off to meet McDowell and bring those troops back for the assault on Richmond."

Sergeant Baldwin inquires, "And you want to hit the part of the Army on this side of the river before the reinforcements arrive?"

"Yes, that is the plan; but now we have learned that he's not going to get the reinforcements after all. Lincoln has called McDowell's troops back to Washington to provide extra security there. He is afraid that Stonewall Jackson, who has been whippin' the britches off the Yankees up and down the Shenandoah Valley, might decide to attack Washington."

"Sergeant Baldwin, our plans are to attack the Yankees over here on this side of the river. We're gonna do it first thing in the mornin'.

"Our initial attack will start at 6:00 sharp. Longstreet - you remember Pete, General James Longstreet? He will be coordinating the attack."

"General Johnston," Sergeant Baldwin interjects, "will me and my men be attached to General Longstreet's division?"

"Yes and no," Johnston responds. "General Longstreet, as I have said, is coordinating the attack. Your company will be attached to General D.H. Hill's division. As you well know from your years of service in the old Union Army, General Hill is always itching for a fight. If there's gonna be a battle, General Hill wants to be in the thick of it. He likes the action; he can smell the blood."

"Yes Sir, General Johnston, I well remember General Hill."

"Well, Sergeant Baldwin, you probably remember that General Hill is also irritable and impatient, but he is an excellent officer, an excellent combat leader. He is outspoken and he does not stand back in criticizing his officers or his enlisted men if he thinks they deserve it."

"Yes Sir, General Johnston, you are right about General Hill, but he don't stand back none from praising a person if he feels like he deserves it."

"If it's action that you and your men want, Sergeant Baldwin, you'll get plenty of it with General Hill's division."

"That's just fine with me and my men, Sir," the old Sergeant responds, then adds as an afterthought, "Have our orders been cut, Sir, that is the orders for us to report to General Hill's division?"

General Johnston smiles. "Just tell General Hill that I have assigned you and your company to him. Tell him we'll take care of the paperwork later. You well know that I detest paperwork. The Army certainly could accomplish more in less time if it weren't for all the paperwork.

"Oh, Sergeant Baldwin, tell General Hill that I said not to assign an officer to your company. You will do quite well yourself."

"Yes Sir, General, whatever you say."

"By the way Sergeant, what is the name of your company?"

"Sir, it is 'Company K'; King Company of the 110th Virginia Infantry."

General Johnston's brow wrinkles somewhat quizzically. "Have I heard of them before?"

"No Sir, General Johnston, you have not. It's a new company. They are all right out of training. They are all good men. You have not heard of them before, Sir; but, Sir, you will hear of them by the time this battle is over. They are gonna be a fightin' bunch of soldiers. Yes Sir, they sure will. They'll give no quarter to them Yankees; they'll give none to nobody. Sir, ye kin bet yer hat on that. Ah trained 'em myself."

"Well, Sergeant, that's the kind of men we need if we're gonna win this war." The General pauses a moment, then continues. "General Longstreet's division will start the action. As soon as the first shots are heard, General Hill's division will join the fray.

"At the sound of your guns, the other two divisions, under the command of Generals Gustuvas Smith and Benjamin Huger, will join in the attack.

"Longstreet and Hill will advance their divisions down the Williamsburg Road. Huger will advance down the Charles City Road and assault the Union Army's left flank. Smith will approach the battle along the Nine Mile Road, hitting the Union Army's right flank. The Yankees will be hit by all four of our divisions almost simultaneously. If things go as planned, we will destroy or capture nearly half of McClellan's Army.

"It's going to be a bloody battle, Sergeant, so keep a close eye on your men. You can never be sure how new recruits are going to react at their first exposure to combat."

"General Johnston, Sir, if I may say so, my men will do okay in combat. I know them, Sir; I will bet my life on it."

"Sergeant, you may have to do just that."

"If that should happen, Sir, ah'm ready to take my punishment, an' I assure you, Sir, if ma men are called to lay thar lives on the line, if thar called to sacrifice their lives on th' field of battle for this Confederacy, they'll surely step forward an' do it, they'll unquestionably step forward, without a whimper, they'll do it."

"Sergeant Baldwin, I am confident that you and your men will serve the Confederacy with honor and distinction. I am also confident in my plan of battle. I am quite confident that it will be successful. Good luck to you and your men tomorrow, Sergeant."

The old Sergeant snaps to attention and salutes General Johnston. "Thank you, Sir, and may good luck smile on you and your battle plan."

Sergeant Baldwin does an about-face and departs.

Joe Johnston's Army is bivouacked in and around Fair Oaks Station. It is a train depot on the Richmond and York River Railroad, not far from the village of Seven Pines. The land is relatively level, barely above sea level. It is marshy, swampy ground. There are thick growths of timber and dense patches of thickly intertwined briars. The entire area is inhabited with snakes; some poisonous, some not. There are gnats and mosquitoes everywhere. There are swamp rats and every kind of creeping and crawling thing imaginable to mankind. It is a hostile and eerie environment, even without the added hazards of fighting a war. Soldiers are just as apt to die from disease as they are from hostile fire.

Sergeant Baldwin gathers his troops for a final briefing before tomorrow's battle. He is well aware of what tomorrow holds for them and for himself. He has been there many times. He has led other men into other battles in other places, in other times. This has always been his job. It is again his job to do. He has taught them all that he knows about war. He has taught them how to survive and, if it should be their fate to die on the field of battle, he has taught them how to die.

The teaching and learning is over. Tomorrow will be the real thing. Tomorrow they will experience all of it, everything that they have learned. Tomorrow they will know what he knows about war, about life, and about death. They will share its horrors. They will shed that last bit of innocence. They will know tomorrow what they do not know today.

Sergeant Baldwin gathers his thoughts. The men fall silent, attentive. They are, to a man, cognizant of the old sergeant's concern for them, and their concern for him. A strong comradeship has developed among the men, a bond that ties them together, a cohesive bond that overshadows all individual concerns for the sake of their unit. The old sergeant speaks. What he lacks in eloquence is overshadowed by his sincerity.

"Men, ye know ma background. Ah kin be meaner than a snake. But when ah'm mean - when ah'm really mean - it's 'cause ah need ta larn ye sumtin. Yer the best bunch ah men ah ever served with an' that's sayin' sumptin. Ah had good men before, but non kin measure up to y'all, and tha's a fact.

"Tomorrow is gonna be war. It's gonna be unlike anything y'all has ever seen er experienced. Ah've tole ye before an' ah'm tellin ye again. Be prepared. Be mentally prepared, fer yerself and fer each other. Men, w'er in this thing t'gether. W'er gonna look out fer ourselves an' wer gonna look out fer each other.

"Y'all are gonna experience fear. It's natural ta do so. Thar ain't no shame in fear. Fear ain't the same as bein' a coward. Ye can feel fear an be brave at the same time. Wer gonna stick together; fight t'gether. Yer fear will become courage; it'll turn in ta strength an determination, an endurance. Our fear will never, ever become cowardice.

"If wer called on ta fall on the field of battle, ta lay our lives down fer the Commonwealth of Virginia - for the Confederate States of America - we will do so with honor. If we must die we'll die with honor - with integrity.

"Ma job, ma duty is to lead ya an' to try to keep ya in one piece. Wer gonna keep our eyes an ears open. Pay attention ta the bugle calls; they'll tell ye what to do. Ye know the calls and what they mean.

"If ye feel like prayin', ye best do it t'night, 'cause thar ain't gonna be time ta do it tomorrow. Time ta bed down now. Clear yer mind about t'morrow and may the Lord have mercy on us."

"Sergeant Baldwin," interjects Robbie, "I believe I am speaking for every man in this infantry company. We have complete confidence in you, in your ability, and in your leadership, and because of your leadership we have complete confidence in ourselves. We want you to know that where you lead us, we will follow. "

"I'll be right beside ya, givin' the commands. Ye just blow it when ah tell ya to. Ye don't need to carry a weapon. Yer our bugler."

"Is everyone ready?"

The men of Company K thrust their arms into the air, and in unison give a resounding, "Hip, hip hooray; hip, hip, hooray for Sergeant Baldwin. Where he leads me, I will follow," they all yell.

Sergeant Baldwin stands silently. He is overwhelmed with their approval, with their expression of loyalty and confidence in him. He does not change his facial expression, but a tear drifts slowly down his cheek.

"Company attention," he barks in true military fashion, then in the same military bark he orders, "Dismissed."

Chapter Thirty

A Baptism To War
The Battle of Seven Pines and Fair Oaks

The James and the York Rivers are open to the Union. Men, supplies, and heavy artillery guns can easily be floated up both rivers toward the Confederate capital. The Northern quest to capture Richmond seems ever so close, ever so near. "Onto Richmond! Onto Richmond!" again becomes the slogan of the Union Army. Slowly, surely, step by step, the distance to their coveted prize becomes shorter. They are nearing the finish line. Victory is in sight.

The late Friday afternoon weather on May 30th is miserably hot. The ground where Sergeant Baldwin and his men are camped is dry and dusty. The air is still, unmoving, not even a whisper of a breeze. There is an eerie stillness all about. Sergeant Baldwin's soldiers are impatient; they are uncomfortable; they are nervous. It is not a fearful nervousness, it is just the waiting to get on with it. The hot weather does not help matters. They are dripping wet - the beads of sweat dripping from them draw gnats and mosquitoes. The sound of swatting mosquitoes and cursing ends the silence. They abhor the miserable weather.

They fuss, they complain. It is an unwritten, historical right, if not a duty, for soldiers to complain. They vigorously exercise that right as the sun begins to set and the swarming gnats and mosquitoes become more abundant and aggressive. Sergeant Baldwin watches silently as the men vent their anger at the elements. He finally addresses them.

"We'd better git bedded down fer th' night. We are gonna need all th' rest we kin git t'nite.

"Ye can babble an' moan all ye like, but it ain't gonna help none. Them Yankees are gonna be a mite more trouble tomorrow than them gnats and 'skeeters are t'nite.

"Afore we turn in, thar's sumptin we need to clear up wit' you men. Sumptin that's been brewing fer some time between Private Holcomb an' me.

"Now ye know he's a good soldier - a real good soldier, an ye know he's from up North. He grew up as one of them Yankee boys, but we wuz all friends - all one country then. Then he come South to get educated an' he married ah Southern girl. Well, that makes him half Southern. An if ye saw his wife at the train station when ya all got in the Army, ye know they's havin' a chile - a Southern chile. So that's gonna make him more 'an half Southern. So don't make 'em half Yankee.

"He came in this Army 'cause the Confederate government made him a soldier, not 'cause he wants to be. Ye all are soldiers fer the same reason he is. Well, what 'am tryin' to say is he don't want to kill any of them Yankee boys: he don't wanna carry no rifle. He'll remain as our bugler an' do his duty if ye want him. Ah don't think thars a better bugler anywhere in th' Army, nor a better soldier.

"Fer my part, 'am happy wit him as 'ar bugler. Ah trust him and believe he will do rite by us, but it's gonna be up ta y'all. But afore ye vote ah wanna tell ye sumptin. Ah was a Yankee soldier. Uh loyal Yankee soldier an' so was General Lee and General Johnston an' all th' other Confederate officers. An' they all loved them Yankee-American soldiers. Jes like ah did. We all loved the Army an we all loved ar country. An if it weren't fer this here war, we'd all still be Yankee soldiers.

"But when that Lincoln guy that's now president over the Yankees - well, he don't like Southerners much - an' he said we can't have our own government. An' he's gonna send his Army down South an kill innocent people. Well most of us Southern soldiers - includin' General Lee and General Johnston and me - we says, well Mr. Lincoln, we ain't gonna bear arms agin the state we wuz born in. No sirree, we're not gonna fight our own people.

"Well men, that's jes the problem that Robbie is in. So it's up ta yer vote. If ye vote 'em in he's ar bugler. If ye vote 'em out, ahl haf ta turn 'em in, an' the Army might jes shoot 'em. It's up ta ya'll guys. Whata ya say?"

There is no hesitation from the men. There is a unanimous shout of approval. "He's stayin - he's one of us, we're all brothers - and we have the best bugler in the Army. Hip-hip-hooray for Robbie!"

"Ah'll second that," says the old Sergeant with a wide grin. "I knowed all along what ye'd say."

A tear inches slowly down Robbie's cheek. "Thanks, men," he says sheepishly.

One of the men points toward the western sky. "Looks like we might be in for a storm t'nite. The sky and the clouds are gettin' black. I kin see flashes of lightnin' and I hear the distant roll of thunder."

The men all look skyward.

"It's quite a way's off," another of the men adds, then continues, "It looks rather fierce. It's one flash of lightnin' after the other. We might be in for a heavy downpour."

"Yeah," another speaks up. "It sure don't look good."

"Remember the downpour we had the first night in training camp?" Robbie asks, then adds with a laugh, "I'll never forget that night. Water was running through the tents ankle deep and we never got a wink of sleep all night. Some of the tents blew over. It was a bad experience at the time. It was something to experience on the first night of Army life."

"I'll say we remember," another soldier chips in, "but it sure wasn't a laughin' matter. I was mad as a hornet. If I'd knowed what way home was, I sure would'a took off fer home."

"Well, if ye had, the Army'd been rite on yer tail the next day and ye'd been in a heap a trouble," the old Sergeant retorts.

"If'n ah had a day's start, the'd never ketched me 'cause I'd been hidin' in the Blue Ridge Mountains. The war'd been over long a'fore they'd ketch me."

"Well ain't ye glad ye din't high-tale it outta thar? You'da missed tomorrow's big party with the Yanks," Sergeant Baldwin says, grinning from ear to ear.

"Yeah, I guess so, but I think I've gone a little bit crazy since then. I'll probably end up killed in this here war."

Robbie again speaks, "There's been a lot of water over the dam since then. We were all strangers. We knew nothing about Army life. Now here we are, all of us like brothers."

"Yeah," one of the men adds, "we were more afraid of Sergeant Baldwin then we were of the storm."

Robbie adds, "Sergeant Baldwin shows up at daybreak, just when the rain stops, and he's dry as a bone. He had a good night of sleep and we were exhausted. He didn't show any mercy on us that day either."

Sergeant Baldwin, with a broad grin, again speaks. "That day was the beginnin' of my startin' to form some good opinions of y'all. Ah knew ah had a good bunch of soldiers - that is ah knew ah could make ye into a good bunch ah soldiers. Ah let ye pitch yer tents on the low ground to lern ye sumptin'. It was kind of a trainin' lesson fer ye'all.

"Never pitch yer tent on low ground. Ah see ye learnt yer lesson well. But ye better check yer tent pegs t'nite." he says looking up at the fast approaching storm. "Make sure the pegs are deep enough in the ground, and tight enough to withstand the storm. Right now, we're havin' the lull before the storm, but she ain't gonna be long comin'. Look fer some mighty heavy winds. If them tent pegs ain't secure, yer tents are gonna be in Yankee land before ye are."

The rains come, and the winds blow, and the lightning flashes and the thunder rolls. It is a storm of unusual ferocity, an unrelenting storm. Rain falls by the bucketful, then wicked winds, and fearful and deadly lightning. The banks of the Chickahominy can not contain the rushing waters. The river spreads over the low lands, flooding the already over-full swamps and bogs as the raging water rushes on toward the Chesapeake Bay, sweeping away all that is before it.

But the tents and the men of Sergeant Baldwin's company withstand the forces of nature. The night passes and the morning comes, and with it comes the dawn of a new day. The river is flooded, the land is a quagmire, the roads are bottomless on this last day of May. It is time to rise, time to march off to war, time to destroy that which is left by nature after the night of the storm.

Joe Johnston is pleased with the overnight storm and the flooded Chickahominy River. He calls one of his messengers, "Go deliver a message to our division commanders. Tell them our attack will be delayed until eight o'clock this morning because of the flooded conditions on the Chickahominy River. All of our other battle plans are to remain the same. Advise them that the flooded river will prevent McClellan's troops on the other side of the river from coming to help his unfortunate troops on this side. For the first time here on the peninsula our troops outnumber those of our enemy. We now have the advantage in manpower."

Johnston pauses momentarily, then announces jubilantly, "Tell them that victory is in our hands today; we will destroy our enemy."

That said, General Johnston slaps the messenger's horse on the backside and it sprints off. The message will be delivered.

In spite of Johnston's exuberance, in spite of his best laid plans, all does not start well for the Confederate Army. Johnston's unwritten battle plans, which are masterfully designed, have not been properly conveyed to his division commanders, nor are they understood by them. General Huger, who is to attack the Union Army's left flank with his 16,000-man division, has not understood that he is to do so. He, his officers, and men have not yet awakened when the other units depart.

General Longstreet's division, with his 16,000 men, is to proceed down the Williamsburg Road to engage the enemy. They march off in the opposite direction. It is hours later before their error is discovered. General Smith, with an equal number of soldiers in his division, is to attack the Union's right flank. He also fails to understand his orders and holds his men in reserve. Through a comedy of errors, a mismanaged and misunderstood battle plan, the Confederate battle of Seven Pines and Fair Oaks is now in jeopardy.

The only division commander to understand his orders is hot-tempered, always-ready-for-a-fight General Hill. D. H., as he is called, gets it right. His orders are to attack the Yankees immediately after Longstreet's division fires the signal shots to start the battle. The eight o'clock attack time comes. Nothing happens. There is no signal from Longstreet nor is there any sound of battle. Hill does not know that Longstreet has marched off in the wrong direction. Hill is impatient, but he waits, and he waits. Time passes slowly. Hill fumes and he fusses as the morning passes. It is nearing one o'clock in the afternoon. Hill has tolerated the inefficiency, the incompetency of the other division chiefs long enough. He is agitated beyond words; his temper has hit the boiling point. At one o'clock in the afternoon General Hill takes charge of the situation, taking it upon himself to start the battle. He orders the signal shots fired, and his division moves forward. The battle of Seven Pines is underway. Hill's troops are as ready for battle as he is. Their assault is quick. It is ferocious. The opposing Union Army division, under the command of General Silas Casey, is taken completely by surprise. They do not have time to organize. They quickly abandon their position and some of their weapons and supplies as the Confederates attack.

Sergeant Baldwin, with his bugler Private Holcomb at his side, and his company of men following closely, is positioned in the forward echelon of the attacking Rebels.

"Just where we want to be," shouts the grinning old Sergeant as he leads his men in hot pursuit of their fleeing enemy. "Give'em a couple of them Rebel yells that we've been practicin' an' maybe they'll run a little faster," he again shouts with apparent glee.

The Company responds to the old Sergeant with an ear-splitting, teeth-chattering, half-human, half-savage yell that further hastens the Yankee retreat. The old Sergeant is one of a kind. He is one of those rare men that delights in the excitement and the risks of battle, a man that defies fear.

Sergeant Baldwin, shouting over the shrill noise and the raging sounds of battle, orders Robbie to again sound the bugle call to charge, to intensify the pursuit of the fleeing Yankees. Robbie, with his bugle to his lips, responds to the Sergeant's orders without breaking stride and without missing a note. It further accelerates their advance against the enemy. The Rebels move forward at the double quick. They are confident, they are unflinching in their hot pursuit of the Yankees. There is a certain sweetness to success, even in battle; even as the moans and groans of the wounded and the dying are heard above the awful sounds of war. The Rebels are savoring their early success over the disorganized and panicked retreat of their adversaries. But Sergeant Baldwin has been in battles before. He is well aware that the sweet sounds of success can quickly change to the somber sounds of defeat. The winds of war seldom blow continuously in one direction. It is no time to throw caution to the wind. The war-wise old Sergeant orders the overly rapid pursuit by his troops to a cautious, orderly advance.

The Yankees' eager exit from their forward position at Seven Pines begins to slow. Perhaps it is due to pride, perhaps it is due to necessity. They are, nevertheless, unwilling to surrender their colors and to admit defeat at the hands of their Southern foe. Their resistance stiffens. Yankee pride, Yankee fortitude, and determination rise to meet the occasion. A Yankee Sergeant, a rather youthful-looking, clean-shaven fellow, rushes forward to take control of the troops. He faces them, raises his arms, palms of his hands forward to stop their retreat. He addresses them.

"Soldiers, we are the Union Army of the Potomac. We must stop the Rebel advance. We must stop it here and now. Be prepared to stand your ground. We must do so at all costs. Our honor, our loyalty, our duty demands it. We have now crossed the dirty, foul-smelling, varmint-infested swamp that lies just in front of the pursuing Rebels. They must now cross that same swamp. We now have the advantage. We hold the upper hand. We will now do the killing.

"Those of you who had the foresight to bring your rifles, step forward and prepare to fight. If duty calls us to die for our country, we will do so here and now. We are not going to yield one more inch of ground to those Rebels. There will be no more retreating!"

Again this young Sergeant pauses. "Prepare to fire when the Rebels start moving into the swamp. We should be able to inflict some heavy losses on them. Whether you kill them or wound them, it doesn't matter. Just aim to hit 'em somewhere, and let 'em drown in the stinking swamp."

Sergeant Baldwin and his men approach the swamp from behind a clump of downed trees. The cagey, battle-wise, and battle-hardened Sergeant is too shrewd to approach the enemy through the clearing. He and his men can see the Union soldiers on the other side of the swamp. The Union soldiers have not yet spotted them. They are poised for action. Sergeant Baldwin silently signals his troops to move forward and to position themselves in and around the fallen trees. The two sides are about thirty or forty yards apart. Nothing but the swamp and its inhabitants separates them. Sergeant Baldwin motions for his troops to begin firing. The battle has begun in earnest as Union soldiers fall before the onslaught of bullets.

A dozen or so Union troops are hit by the first salvo from their Rebel enemies. Others return their fire toward the Rebel troops. The woods and the fields and the land come alive with the instruments of war, with the sounds of war, with the maiming and the death of war. Men, American men, on either side of the battleground stagger and fall. Their uniforms - the blue and the gray - are now stained with the red blood of their causes. A blinding withering hail of bullets, minie balls and other death-seeking projectiles, speed back and forth, from side to side, across the swamp. Some find their intended targets, some do not. Death rules the day.

For the wounded soldiers, there are painful moans and groans. For others it is silence, a dead silence. The realities of war have come to the new recruits, to those North and to those South. They have never before seen war. They have never before heard war or felt war. Now they are a part of it. The shock of war and death, the shock of kill or be killed, lasts for a short time, then it becomes commonplace.

The battle rages up and down the stretched battle line. It see-saws back and forth. One side advances, then it is forced to fall back while the other advances and it is forced to fall back. The sounds and the smoke of battle, the dust from the moving and maneuvering troops is seen and heard nearly ten miles away in Richmond. Citizens are apprehensive and fearful. Neither the citizens of Richmond nor the Confederate government officials were forewarned by General Johnston of the planned attack. General Lee rides out to Johnston's headquarters to ascertain what is happening. President Davis follows closely behind.

Neither Lee nor Davis are told anything by Johnston, partly because Johnston does not know what is happening and partly because of his secretive nature. Both men follow as Johnston rides off toward the sounds of battle to ascertain what is actually happening.

It is late in the day when Johnston reaches a knoll slightly north of Fair Oaks Station. From here he hopes to observe the intense battle that is in progress. Lee and Davis join him. Moments later Johnston is hit in the right shoulder by a nearly spent bullet. Seconds later a Yankee artillery shell fragment lodges in his chest. He is knocked from his horse, breaking several ribs. Joe Johnston is done for the day. He is done for some time to come. If he made a mistake by coming to observe the battle, it is just one more mistake to add to his lengthy record. In spite of Johnston's belief that the Yankees on the other side of the Chickahominy River would be unable to cross the river and assist in the battle, they manage to do so.

Although perplexed and angered at Johnston for his failure to inform them in advance of his battle plans, both Lee and Davis are concerned over the seriousness of his injuries. Johnston is quickly moved out of range of the raging battle. Davis speaks first.

"General Johnston, a physician will be here very soon. Is there anything I can do to help you?"

Johnston, grimacing in pain, responds, "No Sir, thank you. Just leave me rest here a minute." Johnston then looks toward General Lee and speaks to him.

"General Lee, my pistols and sword must have fallen when I fell from the saddle. As you know, my father carried them during the Revolutionary War when he was serving with your father, General 'Light-Horse Harry' Lee. Please have someone recover them. I would not part with them for ten thousand dollars."

General Lee turns to Drury Armstead, a courier to General Johnston. "Do you think you can find them?"

"I am sure I can, Sir," he responds as he turns to leave. The courier returns with the sword and pistols in hand and they are given to Johnston.

As darkness falls the sounds of war recedes. Cannons cease to roar, rifles no longer fire across the bogs and the swamps and the land. The sounds of nature again come alive as dark shadows settle into the night. Frogs croak, owls hoot and the nighthawks call. However, nature cannot obscure the thousands of deaths of young men North and South that lie amidst the worthless, squalid land. The moans and groans, the cries of the dying, echo across the swamps, a haunting reminder of the grim reaper's bountiful harvest. The dead have paid their dues. They lie in silence. A quiet, nearly subdued voice tearfully murmurs the New Testament words from First Corinthians, "O death, where is thy sting? O grave, where is thy victory?" Silence falls over the land.

The battle of Seven Pines/Fair Oaks is not ended. Both sides know it. Tomorrow it will resume. The soldiers, now oblivious to the death all around them, are bivouacked where their day has ended. There will be little sleep for them. There will be little rest. Whatever fear of death that existed before the battle started has disappeared. There is no fear of tomorrow. Time will usher in a new day and a new month. For the Southern Army, a new commander will replace the fallen Joseph E. Johnston.

With the coming of nightfall on May thirty-first, President Davis and his military advisor, General Lee, leave the field of battle to return to Richmond. They ride in silence for some time, a silence broken only by the rhythmic clopping of their horses' hoofs on the road. Davis finally breaks the silence.

"General Smith assumes command of our Army tomorrow. Do you think he is up to the task?"

Lee does not answer immediately, considering the matter in deep thought before speaking.

"Mr. President, General Smith is the next officer in rank. It is military courtesy for command to pass to him."

"The question, General Lee, is whether General Smith is mentally and physically capable of the command of the Confederate Army."

Again, Lee hesitates before speaking. "He is a West Pointer; he served in the Mexican Campaign. He does not lack personal courage."

"Yes, General Lee, what you say is true. But does he have the fortitude, the desire to command this Army in this important assignment? Can he do it?"

"Mr. President, he failed to accept the responsibility to lead his own division into combat yesterday. He was unable or unwilling to accept that responsibility, turning command of his division over to Chase Whiting. I pray that he can."

Davis does not immediately respond. After some moments in silence, he draws his horse to a stop and Lee does likewise. "Is something wrong, Mr. President?"

"Nothing is wrong, General Lee. As a matter of fact, something is right. Something is finally right about this Army. General Smith will be in charge of tomorrow's battle. At least he will be in charge in the morning when the battle is renewed. A new leader - a man in whom I have great confidence - a man who can lead this Confederacy in victory - will take command of our army after tomorrow."

"And who will that man be, Mr. President?"

"You are that man, General Lee. You are that man."

The men of the two Armies sleep sporadically during the night. It is a warm, still night and the groans and cries of the dying, the sickening stench of the already dead, and the flickering lights of the lanterns carried by those who search for fallen comrades make the night even more disturbing.

Early Sunday morning on June first, President Davis again rides out to the battle site to inform General Smith of his decision. "You are to transfer command of the Army to General Lee when he arrives. You are in charge until that time."

It is nearly two o'clock in the afternoon when General Lee reaches the Confederate headquarters. The change of command is made without incident. General Lee orders his troops to return to their former military stations. The Battle of Seven Pines/Fair Oaks is over. It is time for both Armies to count their dead and lick their wounds. McClellan has claimed victory. But there is no victory by either side. At best, or worse, the Battle of Seven Pines, or Fair Oaks, ends in a draw.

There is minor action on day two of the battle with both sides holding the same positions they held the day before. General McClellan arrives and his troops greet him with honor and respect. McClellan addresses his troops.

"Boys, we have licked them right, left, and dead center, and we're going into Richmond. Our job is nearly over and we will be going home very soon.

"The final and decisive battle is at hand. Unless you belie your past history, the result cannot be for a moment doubtful. The victory is surely ours. The events of these past two days prove your superiority. You have met the enemy and you have beaten him. Whenever you have used the bayonet, he has given way in panic and disorder.

"I ask of you one more crowning effort. The enemy has staked his all on the issue of the coming battle. Let us meet and crush him here in the very center of the rebellion.

"Soldiers! I will be with you in this battle, and I will share its dangers with you. Our confidence in each other is not founded upon the past. Let us together strike the blow which is to restore peace and union to this distracted land. This result will depend upon our valor, discipline, and mutual confidence in one another." McClellan salutes his troops and departs.

Chapter Thirty-One

A Letter Home

My Dearest Mollie K,

My thoughts and my love for you and for our soon-to-be-born child have sustained me physically, mentally, and spiritually during these past several weeks. I love you and I miss you more than you can possibly imagine. I know that your love for me is also as strong and as pure as ever. Please do not worry about me. Keep your thoughts positive for your sake and for our baby's sake. It should not be very long now until he or she arrives.

Our true love for each other is the one single factor that keeps me going, that sustains my hope. It is the memories past and the future hope that provides my strength, my determination and my fortitude. My love for you grows stronger with each passing day. It is said that absence makes the heart grow fonder. I can certainly attest to the truthfulness of that bit of wisdom. The days and nights have been exhaustive and extremely busy since I last wrote to you. We have been on the move constantly, and even though we are physically tired, our spirits are generally high. There is much hope among the troops that this war will soon end, although there are very few rumors and nothing official to support such a hope.

All of the intense training, all of the drudgery, all of the disciplines and preparation that we recruits went through was not for naught. It has proven to be a saving grace in the heat of our first battle experience. It was a horrible, unbelievable, and unforgettable experience; but that is now behind us.

Today is Wednesday, the fourth day of June, so our child should be arriving in another month. All of the boy or girl guessing will then be over. Whichever it is, I will be happy and I know that you will be as well. I wish that I could be there with both of you, although it is not possible because of the need for all available troops to be on the alert for the defense of Richmond. I miss you more than you can possibly imagine.

The weather here has been extremely hot and humid over the past days. We have also had some exceptionally heavy thunderstorms. I know that it is awfully hot, and probably stormy, in Charlottesville, too. I also know that being heavily with child in the hot weather is quite uncomfortable. I should be ashamed to grumble about my own situation, knowing that your uncomfortableness is much worse than mine. I should be thankful, and I am, that our company has today off.

This is the first day of rest that I have had since I was inducted into the Army. I have not had one assigned duty today. We - that is, our infantry company - are actually on stand-by duty. We do not have to do anything unless an emergency of some sort should arise. I am taking advantage of this day by writing you a long letter because I am unsure when the next opportunity to write may arise. Whether or not I have an opportunity to write to you, your love will sustain me and my love will sustain you. You and our unborn child will never be far from my thoughts. My love for both of you grows stronger with each passing day.

Please do not worry when my letters do not arrive on a regular schedule. The war dictates our every activity. We do everything, we plan everything on what the Northern Army does or what we think they are going to do, and I am sure that they do whatever they do on whatever they believe we are proposing to do. It's sort of akin to a game of cat and mouse with all of the fun taken out of it. It is, nonetheless, a very serious game with one side always hoping to catch the other side at a disadvantage. Warfare is a serious game.

I suppose that battles are also often fought much like a game of chess. Any movement by the Northern Army dictates a counter move by our Army. On the other hand, an unusual or unexpected move by our Army causes a defensive move by their Army; supposedly to counter the move that we have made. As the company bugler, I do not carry a weapon. I could never take the life of an American - North or South.

Mollie K, I point these things out to you so that you will understand what is happening in this war. I certainly do not want to frighten you. I want you to be brave, and to believe that I am going to be alright, and that

I am going to survive this war unscathed. I have survived my first battle - the battle of Seven Pines; or as the Northern soldiers call it, the battle of Fair Oaks. You have probably heard of it by now, or you may have read about it in the newspaper.

It was a hard-fought battle. There were casualties. Our unit - the 110th Virginia Infantry regiment - came through okay. Little has been proven by the battle.

Again, I want you to be brave. I am just fine, although I am somewhat physically tired and weary. Now, Mollie K, I have a question for you. Do you remember the good fortune that seemed to hover over me? Well, it was certainly with me during the two-day battle. A bullet even ripped through the sleeve of my shirt, although it did not touch my flesh. My good luck has followed me into the Army. It has dutifully kept me safe from harm. I am well attended by good luck or by divine intervention. I am going to come through all of these difficult times and through this war, without mishap, whatever occasion may arise. Now, with these things said, you have absolutely nothing to worry about and nothing to fear. I will be just fine.

Mollie K, I believe many soldiers both North and South just like me, wonder what this war is all about. This is a troublesome, vexing, and pointless war. We are a nation divided by politicians, by those people elected or politically appointed to resolve political, social and other differences through negotiation, and to do so by the rules of law and justice and common sense. They have failed to do so.

I have faced the hazards of war, and looked at its death and destruction. I have been a part of this mayhem. I have agonized over the realities of this war, and I have wept at its horrors. After the battle, I opened my Bible. I turned first to the Old Testament Book of Jeremiah, and I read in Chapter 4, verse 28: *"For this shall the earth mourn, and the heavens above be black."* I then turned to the New Testament scriptures, to the Book of First Corinthians, and I read these words from Chapter 15, verse 55: *"O death, where is thy sting? O grave, where is thy victory?"*

I then sat silently for a long time; I closed my Bible and I prayed, "O Lord, when will man learn? When will man ever learn?" The thought then inexplicably occurred to me. Whether it was due to my University teachings, or whether it came to me by divine revelation, I do not know. Whatever the source or the reason, I remembered some of the great men from our nation's past. Men that were instrumental in bringing together a new nation, the American Union of States. These men were dedicated patriots, knowledgeable and learned statesmen. They were leaders: men like Benjamin Franklin, Thomas Jefferson and James Madison. Each of these mean were highly regarded and respected by their peers.

These three men greatly influenced the ideals and standards on which our nation is founded. All three are also remembered for opposing views of war. Benjamin Franklin stated his opposition to war, simply saying, 'There never was a good war, or a bad peace.' Jefferson said that 'war is an instrument entirely inefficient toward redressing wrong; and multiplies instead of indemnifying losses.' James Madison had more to say against war than either Franklin or Jefferson. I cannot recall all that he said, but I do remember some of it. He said that 'of all of the evils to public liberty, war is perhaps the most to be dreaded because it compromises and develops every other evil.'

These men are among our most honored and respected American heroes, men of great knowledge and of proven ability. They were men of courage. Their condemnation of war as a means of resolving national or international differences among or between civilized nations has found no listeners today among our own national leaders, North or South.

I again sat silently, contemplating on what Franklin, Jefferson and Madison had said regarding the futility of war and its evilness. Again, I looked toward the heavens and lamented the failures of American leaders, then loudly repeated my silent prayer, "O Lord, when will men learn? When will men ever learn?" My hope is slipping away, but my faith will, in the end, sustain me.

Mollie K, I fear that I have rambled on much more than I should have. I suppose that it has relieved me of some of the anxieties, some of the antagonisms that have festered within my soul. I know that I should not trouble you with such matters, even though we have learned to share our every thought and feeling with each other. I hope that by bringing these matters of war to you, that it does not alarm you, but that by knowing the situation that I am in - and that many others like me are in - that you will understand when I do not have the time to write to you every day.

Nor do I want you to believe that we are constantly engaged in battle or that we are always in danger. There are many days and many routine duties that soldiers are required to do that serve no other purpose other than to keep us from the boredom and monotony of having nothing to do. Therefore, the officers spend a great deal of their time in figuring ways to keep soldiers busy at doing nothing so that it will seem as if they are actually doing something.

There are times when we are on picket duty - that is, when we are assigned to watch what the Union soldiers are doing; and they also have pickets assigned to see what we are doing. We engage in friendly banter with their picket, and they with us. Sometimes we trade things. The Yankee soldiers often trade coffee for tobacco, which is quite an acceptable trade with most Southern soldiers. So you can see that war does have strange customs when fighting is not the rule of the day.

Mollie K, it may be sometime before I have an opportunity to again write to you, so do not worry. If I can remember all of the words, here is a poem, written by Robert Burns nearly a hundred years ago. It expresses my love, my feelings for you.

A Red, Red Rose

O, my luve's like a red red rose
That's newly sprung in June;
O, my luve's like the melodie
That's sweetly play'd in tune.

As fair art thou, my bonnie lass,
So deep in luve am I;
And I will luve thee still, my dear,
Till a' the seas gang dry.

Till a' the seas gang dry, my dear,
And the rocks melt wi' the sun;
And I will luve thee still, my dear,
While the sands o' life shall run.

And fare thee weel, my only Luve!
And fare thee weel a while!
And I will come again, my Luve,
Tho' it were ten thousand mile.

Mollie K, you are the best thing that has ever happened to me. Your sweetness, your love, and your beauty, inside and outside, provides the strength and hope I live by during these harsh and uncertain times. It is you and you alone that I awaken to every morning and it is you and your love that I dream of in the darkness of night. Please have faith. Believe that I will come home to you: to you and to our child. Always be brave.

I love you dearly,
Robbie

Chapter Thirty-Two

On the Hot Seat of History

President Davis has made few friends in the Confederate capital with his appointment of 55-year-old Robert E. Lee as the commanding general to lead the Confederate Army in its quest to stop McClellan's awesome Northern Army from conquering Richmond. Indeed, there is a sense of fear, a sense of uncertainty throughout the capital city.

Lee's task is no easy matter. His responsibility is great. He is an unpopular choice among the civilian population. The news media is especially appalled by his appointment. They are bitter and extremely cruel and critical in the newspaper analysis of Lee. He is dubbed, "Evacuating Lee" by the Richmond Examiner newspaper, a reference to his unsuccessful foray into the early Civil War battles in Western Virginia. Other news accounts refer to him as "the king of spades" because of his defensive efforts in using his men to dig trenches and strengthen fortifications around Richmond. Lee is oblivious to the criticisms and the naysayers.

McClellan's large and well-equipped Union Army is flexing its muscles. The gates of Richmond are now in sight a mere four miles away, they are a minor obstacle waiting to be overrun; waiting to be crushed beneath the force of the Union Army's soon-to-come advance. McClellan's troops are in command of a large land area, in a semi-circle in front of Richmond city. Eleven Union Army divisions, more than a hundred thousand soldiers, stand ready to attack at a moment's notice. They cover an area of land stretching from White Oak Swamp to Gaines Mill and on to Mechanicsville and to Beaver Dam Creek. His Army is ready to move; McClellan is not.

Two obstacles, the Chickahominy River and the Southern Army of Northern Virginia, stand in the pathway between McClellan and his coveted prize, Richmond, the capital city of the Confederacy. The Southern Army has faced his Northern Army nearly the entire way from Fort Monroe. It has shown little inclination to aggressively engage McClellan's Army during its march up the Virginia peninsula, except for the Battle of Seven Pines or Fair Oaks. McClellan shares the same view of Lee, as most of the Southern citizens in Richmond. He does not respect Lee's ability, his leadership.

"Lee," McClellan relates to his officers, "is cautious and weak and he will falter under grave responsibility. We are extremely fortunate that Jefferson Davis has appointed him as the commanding general of the Southern Army that we face. Our job, our mission, becomes easier, much easier with Lee's appointment. I expect Lee to be uncertain, to vacillate and to waiver under the pressure of leadership. The Confederacy has made a momentous error in placing Lee in command. His appointment is a feather in our cap. We shall take full advantage of this opportunity."

McClellan's assessment of Lee, his belief that Lee has many character flaws, that these flaws will adversely affect Lee's military leadership abilities, are unsupported by Lee's past military record. Nor does McClellan's poor opinion of Lee's military ability spur him to take advantage of Lee's perceived military flaws, and to use Lee's supposed lack of military acumen to the advantage of his own Union Army. McClellan fails to take the initiative against Lee's Army. McClellan does nothing. His Army does nothing. McClellan and his Army watch and wait as Lee prepares his Army to defend Richmond and as he readies his Southern Army to take the initiative in the war between the North and South.

Lee's initiative in preparing his Confederate Army for the task that it will now undertake begins immediately after his appointment as commanding general. His Army, in a defensive position between the Confederate capital at Richmond and McClellan's Army, consists of five divisions. His five under-manned and under-equipped divisions facing McClellan's well-manned and well-equipped eleven divisions are not unlike Biblical accounts of the boy David facing Goliath the Philistine giant. Although the defense of Richmond is of the utmost importance, Lee's main thought, his primary emphasis, is to take the war to the enemy. He will do what his predecessor, General Joseph E. Johnston, neglected to do. He will take the initiative. His mindset, his strategy, is to fight an offensive war.

Unlike the secretive General Johnston, who failed to ever apprise President Davis about his planned military operations, Lee does just the opposite. He willingly shares his plans with President Davis and with his close advisors. General Lee sends a letter to Davis soon after he takes command of the Confederate Army of Northern Virginia, providing a brief outline of his intended actions. He suggests a face-to-face meeting. As a result of Lee's letter, a meeting between Lee, Davis, and members of Davis' Cabinet is held at the White House of the Confederacy in Richmond. It is a cordial and respectful meeting. After a brief and friendly exchange of greetings, they discuss the business at hand. General Lee addresses the group.

"Mr. President and members of the Cabinet. I am grateful for this opportunity to serve the Confederacy as the general in charge of this Army. I thank you, Mr. President, for the opportunity to serve as the Commanding General in the field. I shall keep you constantly informed of our every plan, of our every move.

"I have studied our position and that of our enemy. I have analyzed the positive and the negative factors that appear to favor and to hinder both Armies. I have analyzed all of the intelligence factors that our government has obtained from or about our enemy, about General McClellan and those generals serving under his command. I have utilized my personal knowledge about these enemy commanders, about their habits, their likes, and their dislikes.

"I am convinced that our best approach against the enemy that stands before us, intending to destroy our capital, intending to destroy us, is to attack them before they lay siege to Richmond with their heavy artillery.

"I am convinced that we can successfully defeat the Union Army. It will not be easy, but it can be done. It must be done! It is not a plan without risks, but we must face those risks, and we must not fail."

Looking toward President Davis, Lee continues speaking. "Mr. President, as I so stated in my letter to you, I am preparing a line of defense that I can hold with part of our Army. With the rest of our men, I will endeavor to make a diversion to bring McClellan out in the open.

"As part of this maneuver, I intend to send, with your permission, several brigades to Stonewall Jackson in the Shenandoah Valley so that he can have the assurance of sufficient men to keep the valley secure from Yankee control."

"General Lee," George Randolph, Secretary of War for the Confederate States, interrupts, "isn't our Army, which is now facing McClellan's Army, woefully under strength? Won't such a move further weaken our defense of Richmond?"

"Yes, Secretary Randolph, it will - at least it will do so temporarily. If you will allow me a little more time, I will address this issue."

"My apologies, General Lee, please continue."

"Thank you, Secretary Randolph."

President Davis inquires, "General Lee, when do you plan to attack the Union Army? Is it to be done soon?"

"Mr. President, my plans are to attack the Northern Army before the end of June. Perhaps within the last week in June. There are many factors to consider. We have several important matters that must be done beforehand.

"First we must prepare for the defense of Richmond. We must reinforce our existing entrenchments and we must build new entrenchments where they do not now exist. I already have men working at this."

"General Lee, you are aware, Sir, are you not, that our own Southern newspapers - especially those here in Richmond - are highly critical of your generalship abilities," offers George Randolph. Then he continues. "Most of that criticism, Sir, is due to what they believe to be, that you are too inclined to be defensive rather than to take action against our enemy."

"Yes, Secretary Randolph, I am aware of the newspaper articles, even though I do not personally read them. Their opinions, I assure you, do not have any affect on my decisions. I am sure, Secretary Randolph, that your grandfather - Thomas Jefferson - often faced many criticisms in his day for decisions that he had to make. It is part of the price that we must pay for our hope of a better tomorrow."

"I agree, General Lee, and I am in total support of your position."

"Thank you, Mr. Secretary."

"General Lee, would you explain your plan of defensive action and your plan of the ultimate attack?"

"Yes Sir, Mr. President. That is my hope, my intent for requesting this meeting, and I thank each of you for sharing your time, your ideas and your support during this meeting.

"I have, a few minutes ago, stated that we have already begun the building, the construction of entrenchments for the defense of Richmond. Those earthworks are progressing well. Some of our defensive positions will depend on - that is, the location of those defense positions - will depend on where we are going to attack the Union Army.

"So we must first know where we are going to initiate our attack and then we must move against McClellan's Army before he is ready to move against us.

"I believe that McClellan is going to bring his heavy artillery forward when the high waters of the Chickahominy River have receded to a safe point for crossing. He will possibly do so very soon, but McClellan is a cautious man. He will wait for a precise time. My opinion is that he intends to use his artillery to bombard Richmond. He will bombard the city unmercifully. His infantry regiments will not move forward until some time after the artillery assault has ended.

"We must land the first blow, a decisive blow, before McClellan is ready to do so. Gentlemen, we intend to destroy the Union Army of the Potomac."

"How do we intend to do that, General Lee? What are your exact plans?"

"Mr. President, gentlemen, McClellan's Army, directly in front of our Army, is a powerful enemy. Their battle lines are very impressive. Their forward position at Seven Pines is becoming stronger by the hour. They have strengthened their position on the south side of the Chickahominy River. They have adequate strength north and south of those positions. The Union Army is much too strong for us to consider a frontal attack, so our only choice, our only alternative, is to attack either the left flank or the right flank - or perhaps both flanks - of McClellan's Army. We know that his Army's left flank is defended by strong earthworks and a dense forest. His soldiers have cut many trees directly in front of their defensive positions as an obstruction to any attack that we should attempt. His Army units in this area are also in a position to receive considerable defensive support by the Union Army's artillery. An attack against this left flank will be nearly as hazardous as an attack against the front of the Union line. The cost in manpower would be overwhelming.

"Gentlemen, our only other alternative is for us to attack the right flank of the Union Army. That is where we must attack them. It must be done as soon as we have developed adequate defensive positions to protect Richmond during our attack against the Union Army. I will need the assistance of two very important men. One of them is already a member of my Army. He is General James Ewell Brown Stuart, my Chief of Cavalry. You probably recognize him as Jeb, which is the first three letters of his given names. The other man that I need for this offensive action is General Thomas Jonathan Jackson, better known as Stonewall. If General Jackson is permitted to bring his Army from the Shenandoah Valley, it will be a tremendous advantage for us. We need all the help that is available to make this battle a success."

Secretary of War George Randolph politely interrupts General Lee, "Could you explain precisely what part these two men will play in this pending battle?"

"Yes, Mr. Secretary, I am glad to do so. Our attack plans are to be directed against the Northern Army's right flank. We believe it to be the most vulnerable part of McClellan's Army. We know generally where the right flank is located. We do not know all of the particulars, the preciseness of certain information that we need to know.

"To obtain that information will be the responsibility of our Chief of Cavalry, General Jeb Stuart. He is a West Point graduate, class of 1854. He is an excellent horseman and an excellent officer. He is a cavalry commander unmatched in his ability or devotion to duty. General Stuart is a true son of the South, a true Virginian. He is fearless, courageous and faithful. General Stuart will not fail us."

"Is he the officer with the feathers - the plume - in his hat? The one with the colorful cape?" inquires Secretary Randolph.

General Lee smiles before answering. "Yes, Secretary Randolph, he wears feathers in his hat and a colorful cape. General Stuart does things with a certain flair. He is somewhat flamboyant. If he has a fault it is perhaps a lack of caution, which I suppose goes along with the feathers and cape.

"I have faith in General Stuart; I have faith in his abilities. I have known him from the days when he was at West Point. He was a classmate of my oldest son, George Washington Lee. He was with me at Harper's Ferry when John Brown was captured. We can count on General Stuart getting the job done.

"So far as General Jackson is concerned, I do not believe there is much that I can say. He is well known and respected in both the Southern and Northern Armies. He is no doubt feared by many in the Northern Army, and well he should be. His exploits in the Shenandoah Valley are unparalleled by any other leader. He has out-foxed and out-fought larger and better equipped Armies. His presence in this area will draw General McClellan's attention quite quickly."

President Davis and Secretary Randolph simultaneously agree to General Lee's plan of attack and his methods of carrying out those plans.

As an afterthought, President Davis asks, "Is there anything else we can do, General Lee?"

"No Sir, gentlemen. You have given me all that I could ask for. It is now my responsibility to carry those plans through. Just pray for our success. I suppose I am now between the devil and the deep blue sea. Only time and divine intervention can provide the answers."

Chapter Thirty-Three

A Ride To Glory

Brigadier General James Ewell Brown Stuart is 29 years old. He is flamboyant, he is cocky, and he is fearless. Jeb, as he is known by friend and foe, is in command of the cavalry division of the Confederate Army of Northern Virginia. He served in that capacity under General Johnston. He now serves in the same capacity for the new Army Commanding General, Robert E. Lee. Stuart and Lee are not strangers. They have known one another since Stuart was a third year cadet at the U.S. Military Academy and Lee was the Academy's commandant.

Lee is not surprised when Stuart arrives for their scheduled meeting on June 10th in his usual attire: knee-high cavalry boots, jingling spurs, elbow-length gauntlets, a red-lined cape with yellow sash, a confederate gray hat with turned up brim, and topped with that ever-present ostrich feather. Stuart may not look like a soldier, but looks are sometimes deceiving. He is, every inch and every pound, a soldier's soldier.

The two men salute, then warmly greet one another. It has been some time since they have met.

"General Stuart, I have called you here to ask you to undertake an extremely important, and perhaps a very dangerous assignment."

"I am ready, General Lee."

"Before you volunteer your services and those of your men, let me first explain to you what we need. I tell you now that it could turn into a very serious matter, perhaps a very hazardous matter. It will certainly demand great stamina and perseverance on the part of you and your men, both physically and mentally."

"General Lee, me and my men are ready for whatever assignment you have for us. I can speak unconditionally for myself and for my men. They trust me and I trust them."

"General Stuart, let me tell you what is involved and what is at stake in this mission. Its success may well decide the survival of our Confederacy. It is that serious.

"As you know, we are reinforcing our defenses in front of Richmond. When our earthworks are sufficiently stable, when they are sufficiently strong enough to withstand a frontal attack by McClellan's Army, we plan to then attack our enemy.

"We do not intend to fight a defensive war. That is what our Army has done so far in this peninsula campaign, and it has led us to now do battle near our capital city. We must change the kind of war we have been waging from that of a retreating defensive Army to that of an attacking offensive Army."

"General Lee, I have been of that opinion ever since the peninsula campaign began. I am in complete agreement with you."

"Thank you, General Stuart. We need to attack McClellan's Army as soon as it is possible to do so. We must attack his Army before he moves his heavy artillery within range of Richmond, before they lay siege on our capital, and before his infantry is ordered to attack us.

"We have studied McClellan's forward troop positions. They have considerable strength directly in front of us. They are well equipped and ready to fight. They are too well defended, too well fortified, for us to make a frontal attack.

"For the very same reasons it would be too costly to attack McClellan's left flank. They are just too strong, too much fire power.

"General Stuart, that leaves us just one alternative - the right flank of McClellan's Army."

"And how are those right flank obstacles, General Lee? Are they more susceptible to attack?"

"I don't know, General. That is what I want you to find out. If it can be done, you are the one to do it. I have no doubt whatsoever that you can do it, and that you will do it.

"I want you to select volunteers from your division, or elsewhere, that you will need to undertake and complete this mission. What I need, General, is for you and your men to ride out there and find out what is going on with McClellan's right flank. Find out exactly where it is, how strong it is, what is the lay of the land, what obstacles we will encounter. You will need to ascertain exactly where McClellan's Fifth Corps, which is under the command of Fitz John Porter, is posted. Make specific observations of the ridge line between the Chickahominy River and Totopotomy Creek, which flows into the Pamunkey River.

"General Jackson and part of his Army will be coming over from the Shenandoah Valley to help us in this operation. He will need to know the lay of the land and the obstacles he will face so that he can plan his attack. We also need to determine whether the Northern Army is shifting further to the right in this area and whether their supply line is well protected or whether it is vulnerable.

"We need to ascertain this information as expeditiously and as quietly as possible. As soon as the information is gathered, turn back for home and complete your journey as fast as possible. This journey, this mission, must be kept quiet. It must be carried out in as much secrecy as possible."

Jeb Stuart is excited. He is all smiles; he is ready to go. This mission is custom cut for him and his men. It is filled with the kind of excitement that he lives for, the kind of excitement he thrives on.

There is no need for Lee to ask Stuart to consider whether he and his men are willing to accept the challenge of this reconnaissance mission behind enemy lines; he is now ready and anxious to go. Lee never once doubted what Stuart would say.

"General Lee, I have already obtained some of this information. My chief scout, John Mosby, and I have been doing some scouting along McClellan's right flank while the two Armies have been idle. I am certain we can come up with all the information you have requested. I am also certain that we can continue our reconnaissance on around McClellan's entire Army, that we can make a complete circle around them and then follow the James River right back to Richmond. What do you think, General Lee?"

"General Stuart, you are in charge of this mission. You are the only person that can answer that question. Neither of us have any way of knowing what obstacles you are going to encounter nor what actions you must take to resolve any unseen or unpredictable situations that may arise. You must do what is necessary to assure the success of this mission.

"Keep in mind that you have two important obligations. First and foremost, you must obtain the military intelligence we have asked you to secure. The second important obligation is to make that information available to us as quickly as you possibly can. You also have an obligation of adequately providing for the welfare of your soldiers as best you can under hostile military conditions. I have complete faith that you will do so.

"The responsibility of providing the best possible results for both the necessary intelligence and the safety of your men is in your hands. Only you, Sir, can make that decision when the time to do so arrives. I know that you will make the right choice. I will not, nor will I allow anyone else in the Army, to second guess your decision in such matters.

"Before you leave, I have another question for you. How many men do you plan to take with you? We certainly want you to take as many as you will need, but the fewer you can get by with the less chance the Northern Army will detect you."

"I agree with you, General Lee. I plan to take about 1,200 men. These men are the best that I have. They are the cream of the crop. They are experienced cavalrymen. They have combat experience, and they know how to fight their way out of a trap. They can take care of themselves and they can take care of each other. I trained most of them myself. I aim to take the best horses and the best riders. I want men with stamina, men with courage, men that can use their sabers effectively. I want men that can ride hard and fast all day and all night if we need to do it.

"One thing more I ask of you, General Lee. My bugler was wounded at the Battle of Seven Pines. There is a young bugler attached to General D.H. Hill's division. He is in the 110th Virginia Infantry Regiment. He's one of the best buglers I have ever heard. I want to borrow him for this mission. Can you help me?"

"General Stuart, this mission is supposed to be cloaked in secrecy. Using a bugler to communicate with your troops may expose your mission and our purpose to obtain information may be lost."

"General Lee, the bugler will be used only in an extreme or nearly hopeless situation. Should such an event arise, the bugler may actually salvage our mission rather than lose it. Besides, he will use it only when he is by my side and when I have given him an order to do so."

"What else do you know about this young bugler, General Stuart?"

"Sir, his name is Holcomb. He's a former University of Virginia student. He came from up North someplace, married a Virginia girl. He has a reputation as a good soldier, an excellent bugler. He was in the battle of Seven Pines, in the thick of the fighting. He was calm under fire, even during intense fighting. He kept his company - Company K, I believe it was - well informed with his bugle commands. Yes Sir, he did a superb job I am told, and I just might need him if a situation should arise."

"General, he's an infantryman. He probably knows little, if anything, about horses. Do you know if he can even ride a horse?"

"Yes Sir, he sure can. His family back up North owned horses, and he's an excellent rider. One of my men tested him on horsemanship. He rode like a true Virginian."

"Alright, General, you may borrow him for this mission. But you must return him to his proper unit when this mission is completed. You don't want to start a war with General Hill, do you?"

"No Sir, General Lee, not if I can help it."

"General Stuart, will my son, Rooney, and my nephew, Fitz, be riding with you on this mission?"

General Stuart pauses momentarily before responding. "Sir, they are among the best men - the best officers I have. They are superb cavalry officers. However, I cannot take them on this mission. It is much too dangerous. What if something happened and they were taken prisoner by the Yankees?

"Sir, with you as commanding general of our Army, we cannot risk your blood kin on such a mission."

General Lee stands silently for some time before responding. "General Stuart, I thought you might say that. My son and my nephew are very dear to me. I would be terribly saddened to lose them.

"But my blood kin must not be exempted from hazardous duty because of me. They would not stand for such preferential treatment, nor will I. Every soldier on this mission is somebody's son, or nephew, or somebody's husband or father. We cannot differentiate and protect our own. We must, if the time comes, suffer together, and when the time is right we celebrate together.

"My blood kin are to be treated the same as other peoples' blood kin in this Confederacy. General Stuart, they must, if you would otherwise choose them, go on this mission. It is their duty to do so, just as it is the duty of others chosen for this mission to do so. My kin are called to the same duty, to the same sense of justice, as that of other citizens of this Commonwealth and this Confederacy.

"I shall say a prayer for them and for you, General Stuart, and for all of the other men that are risking their lives for this cause, as they ride off on this mission."

"Thank you, General Lee. Rooney and Fitz will be part of this mission. I, too, will say a prayer for them and for all of us."

The two generals salute. General Stuart reaches into his saddle bag and extracts his Bible. Waving it heavenward, he looks to the sky, still clutching and waving the Bible. "This," he says, "is more powerful than all of the weapons of war."

"Amen," responds General Lee.

Jeb Stuart awakens his hand-picked troops long before daybreak early Thursday morning, June 12th. "Gentlemen," he bellows, "in ten minutes every man must be in the saddle. We are moving out."

The men stumble to their feet, grumbling, still half asleep. No one, other than Stuart, has any knowledge of where they are going. Speculation runs rampant among the men as they head due north from Richmond. The consensus of opinion among the men is that they are going to turn west and join Stonewall Jackson in the Shenandoah Valley of Virginia. Stuart says nothing in response to their speculation.

The men, however, are not overly concerned of their whereabouts or where they are going. They have complete confidence in their leader. General Stuart, with his borrowed bugler at his side, is riding at the head of the column. The day passes uneventfully. Nearly 22 miles later the men camp near the North Anna River, not far from the town of Ashland.

Before the early morning sun rises on Friday, the 13th, Stuart has his 1,200 men in their saddles and on the road again. They soon turn eastward toward the rising sun, quelling all rumors of a Shenandoah Valley rendezvous with Stonewall Jackson. General Stuart, as usual, is at the head of the long column of cavalrymen. His bugler, Private Robbie Holcomb, rides at Stuart's left. The two Confederate scouts are some distance ahead of the main column of troops. The general speaks to Robbie.

"Private Holcomb, do you know what day this is?"

"Yes Sir, it's Friday – Friday the 13th."

"Well, Private, what is Friday the 13th supposed to signify?"

"Sir, it is thought by some people to be a day of bad luck."

"You say some people believe it is a day of bad luck. What do you believe?"

"Sir, I believe that Friday the 13th is just like any other Friday. You might have good luck or you might have bad luck. On the other hand, it may just be a day - a normal day where one's luck is neither good nor bad."

"Private Holcomb, where do you think Friday the 13th got its bad day reputation?"

"Well, Sir, the name Friday originated from 'Frigg's day.' Frigg was the goddess of love in Norse mythology. The Scandinavians, however, believe that Friday is a good luck day. I have heard that Friday the 13th got its bad luck reputation from several sources. Some say that Christ was crucified on Friday the 13th, and that thirteen men were present at the last supper. Others believe the bad luck associated with Friday the 13th comes from it being the usual hangman's day in early times. What do you believe, General Stuart?"

The general pauses for a long moment before responding. "I believe that Friday the 13th is the day that always falls between Thursday the 12th and Saturday the 14th. That's all I believe."

Robbie chuckles and the General laughs. "Regardless of what we believe, General Stuart, I sure hope that no black cats cross the road in front of us today."

As the troops continue onward, after some time has passed, General Stuart again speaks. "You know, Private, after some thought, I believe that Friday the 13th may, after all, be a bad luck day."

"Why do you say that, Sir?"

"It just happens to be my father-in-law's 53rd birthday."

"You don't like your father-in-law?"

"I did at one time, but not any more. You see, my father-in-law is a Yankee. He is Union General Phillip St. George Cooke. He, like myself, is a cavalry officer. He is also a native Virginian. He cast his lot with the Yankees and I relish the idea of meeting him today. I'd like nothing more than to give him and his men a good thrashing as a birthday present." Again, the general laughs. "Maybe Friday the 13th will be a good day after all."

The rising sun in a nearly cloudless sky begins to intensify the morning temperature. They have traveled nearly ten miles, as the crow flies, from the night before bivouac area when forward scout John S. Mosby hurries back to the main column of troops. "General Stuart, there are a few Yankees up ahead at Hanover Court House," he says matter-of-factly.

"How many are there?"

"Two or three dozen, maybe a few more than that."

"Have they spotted us, yet?"

"No, Sir, they don't suspect a thing. It appears to be a company of cavalry pickets on outpost duty."

General Stuart looks at his watch; it is nearly nine o'clock. He signals the column to halt. Silence falls over the men as they are informed, "Yankees ahead."

"Let's take 'em by surprise," Stuart advises a young captain who then rides ahead with a few men. There is no sound except for the horses' hoofs hitting the nearly dry earth. Silence continues for another ten minutes. Then the forward moving Confederate cavalry cut loose with an ear-splitting Rebel yell that shatters the silence. With sabers flashing in the bright morning sun, they spur their steeds and rush forward into the unsuspecting Yankees. "Now, Private! Now blow that bugle! Give our boys the call to attack!"

It is over within minutes. The Yankee soldiers are caught completely by surprise. They bolt from camp in a fast sprint, taking nothing with them except the clothes on their backs and a few saber slices on their backsides. The Confederates confiscate their weapons and ammunition, their food supplies, and their horses and mules. Other supplies and equipment that are unusable are set afire. Within an hour of their arrival at Hanover Court House, Stuart and his raiding party are on the road again.

They continue their mission, turning southeasterly, toward Old Church. By late morning they are nearing Haws Shop, a stop on the Virginia Central Railway. They again encounter a Yankee cavalry outpost where they meet mild resistance before the Yankees abandon their post. The results of the skirmish are similar to the earlier engagement at Hanover Court House. They continue their journey toward Old Church.

General Stuart again turns toward Robbie as they depart the village of Haws Shop. "Private Holcomb," he says with a look of great satisfaction, "you do a fine job of blowing that bugle. I hope that we have a few more opportunities before this day is done. Yes Sir, Private, this Friday the 13th is shaping up as a fine one. Those Union soldiers we keep routing are some of my father-in-law's troops. I said when he cast his lot with the Union Army that he would regret his decision but once and that would be continuously. I hope our today's activities will add a little more grief to his birthday regrets."

Stuart and his men press onward toward their next destination at Old Church. It is nearly three o'clock in the afternoon when they arrive. Their mission appears to have remained undetected, except for the small Yankee detachments they have so far encountered. They again catch a detachment of Yankee cavalry troops somewhat off guard. This detachment of Yankees decides to stand and fight. There is a spirited cavalry engagement and one of

Stuart's officers, Captain William Latane, is fatally wounded. The Yankees are defeated and abandon their outpost. Some prisoners are taken.

Stuart's men salvage what is usable, what they can take with them. The rest of the Yankee camp is burned. They salvage among their usable goods a keg of whiskey which is strapped on a confiscated mule. The keg, by order of Jeb Stuart, is to remain unopened. Stuart is a life-long tee-totaler.

The information that General Stuart and his men had set out to secure is now complete. Everything that General Lee has asked for is now positively known. It is decision time. They must decide whether to turn back the way that they had come: retrace their steps in reverse order, or they must forge onward and make a complete circle of the enemy's Army and return to Richmond by a new direction.

General Stuart, from the outset of this mission, has wanted to make the circular route completely around McClellan's Army. It is his decision to make. Nevertheless, he decides to poll his senior officers.

"Gentlemen, as you know, we now have the information that General Lee has requested. If we should decide to continue our mission and ride completely around General McClellan's Army, we are more than half-way there. Should we do so, it will be a devastating embarrassment to McClellan's pride. It will, no doubt, be an embarrassment to the Northern Army of the Potomac and to the Lincoln administration in Washington.

"Should we turn back and return to Richmond the way we came, we will surely meet stiff resistance. Some of the Yankee soldiers who escaped our encounters are bound to have made it back to their division headquarters. The Yankees are probably planning a little surprise party for us along about now.

"We may encounter hostile forces, even if we continue in the direction we are now going. I believe it is more difficult for them to anticipate our forward movement simply because they have no advanced knowledge of what we plan to do. I do believe that the likelihood of strong resistance is much less by going forward than it is if we turn back. I believe that McClellan's men will anticipate that this is an excursion to gather information and they will look for us to return by the direction from which we came. That would be a logical conclusion.

"My opinion, my instinct, is that we move on forward in the direction we have already set. We will see what happens. Nevertheless, I leave that decision up to you. What do you gentlemen say?"

Fitz Lee, the nephew of General Lee, is the first to speak. "General Stuart, you have safely and successfully brought us this far and we have secured all of the information that General Lee has requested. I am confident that through your leadership you will lead us safely home. I am with you all the way. I, too, think we should move forward."

Each senior officer, one after the other, supports General Stuart's recommendation.

"Gentlemen, the decision is made. Let us move on and let us do it on the double quick," General Stuart announces. They are soon on the way to Tunstall Station, a depot on the Richmond and York River Railroad that serves as a Yankee supply line.

The sun is low in the western sky as they approach Tunstall Station. Stuart dispatches a detachment of men to Garlicks Landing where McClellan's army maintains a supply depot on the Pamunkey River. The rest of his men ride into a small Union cavalry post at the station. They encounter little Yankee resistance. They nevertheless cut the telegraph lines and nearly derail a Yankee troop and supply train bound for White House Landing, McClellan's principal supply base for his Army of the Potomac. The detachment of Stuart's men at Garlicks Landing destroys two Yankee schooners and seventy-five Yankee supply wagons.

Stuart and his men have done all of the damage they can do. It is time to head toward Richmond. It is slightly more than ten miles to Forge Bridge on the Chickahominy River. Once across the river, they will be in Confederate territory. Night has fallen, but it is a bright, moonlit sky. Visibility is good. It is decided that the wisest and safest choice of action is to keep moving toward their goal. They have captured 170 Union soldiers and 350 horses and mules, in addition to substantial supplies and ammunition. By daybreak they reach the east bank of the Chickahominy River. Unfortunately, high waters from recent rains have washed the bridge away. The troops have been on the road nearly twenty-four hours without the benefit of sleep. They have fought a number of battles. They have traveled more than fifty miles since they broke camp on the morning of Friday the 13th. They have suffered the hot blazing summer sun and now they must build a new bridge.

Others may have been overwhelmed by such news. Not so the hand-picked men of Jeb Stuart. They are undaunted by this setback. They eagerly face the task. Aware that the Yankee cavalry is in hot pursuit, immediate action is necessary to cross the river - to reach safety on the Confederate side. Efforts to swim the horses and men across prove unsuccessful. The river is too swift, too dangerous. Undaunted by this major inconvenience, Jeb Stuart swings into action.

"Private Holcomb, have you ever done carpenter work?" he asks.

"I've worked around my father's mill. We sometimes have to build platforms strong enough to hold very heavy machinery."

Pointing to an old abandoned barn nearby, Stuart inquiries, "Do you think you can build a bridge out of the timbers in that old barn?"

"I can try, Sir."

"Trying is not good enough. We need that bridge."

"Yes Sir, General. You shall have your bridge," Robbie responds and salutes.

Under Robbie's direction the barn is dismantled, a foot bridge is built, and then a large bridge to transport horses, artillery and other large or heavy articles, including supplies and ammunition is constructed. All of the men, horses, supplies, cannons, and everything else is moved across the river. Then the bridge is burned. As the last smoldering remnants of the bridge timbers sink into the raging water of the river, the pursuing Union cavalry reaches the opposite river bank, unable to advance further. As General Stuart and his men move beyond the artillery range of the Union Army, Robbie looks at Jeb Stuart.

"Sir, who says you should never burn your bridges behind you?" he says, smiling contentedly.

Jeb responds, "Private Holcomb, playing with matches doesn't always end with burned fingers." They both smile and ride on. They are thirty-five miles from Richmond, but they have now reached the limit of their endurance. They are an exhausted group of soldiers. They have earned a well-needed rest.

Jeb Stuart and his senior officers decide that the men should bivouac for the night, a decision well received by the men. General Stuart, anxious to provide the information they have obtained to General Lee, rides on to Richmond, accompanied by Rooney Lee and several staff officers. Fitz Lee is left in charge of the troops. Before departing, Jeb Stuart addresses his men.

"Gentlemen, I commend you for a job well done. It is because of your devotion to duty that we have completed our mission. You have gone beyond what can ever be expected of any man, and you have done it willingly and unselfishly.

"No Army, no commander of any Army, can ask more from its citizen soldiers than I have asked of you during these past days. I commend you for your duty and for your devotion to duty. You have served this Confederacy well.

"I can offer you little but my sincere gratitude for your service in this important cause. Some of you, I am well aware, confiscated a keg of Yankee whiskey during one of our raids. Although I personally do not imbibe in strong drink, I must say that I find no fault with William Marcy who said, 'I see nothing wrong in the rule that to the victor belong the spoils of the enemy.' Gentlemen, you have earned that right.

"I shall now depart for Richmond, but I shall meet you tomorrow at the gates of the city and we shall all ride into Richmond together."

Late Sunday afternoon, June fifteenth, nearly forty-eight hours after they left Richmond in secrecy, Stuart and his men conspicuously re-enter the city. They had departed Richmond to the lonesome sounds of hoof beats on the unpaved streets shrouded in the early morning darkness. They return to the sounds of drum beats and bugle calls as their nation's heroes, welcomed by throngs of adoring, flag-waving citizens shouting their appreciation and approval.

Bugler Robbie Holcomb, riding beside General Jeb Stuart, sounds a mock cavalry command to charge. They ride slowly and erect, sabers held upright in a salute to the crowd. Some of Stuart's soldiers play spirited banjo tunes as they customarily do after a victorious engagement on the field of battle. The South finally, after a long time of disappointments and military setbacks, has something to shout about, something to brag about.

The next day, General Robert E. Lee issues General Order Number 74 in tribute to James Ewell Brown Stuart and the members of his select group of men that participated in the now historic ride. It is read before the Senate of the Confederate States of America immediately after its release.

"The commanding general announced with great satisfaction to the Army the brilliant exploit of Brigadier-General J.E.B. Stuart with part of the troops under his command. This gallant officer, with portions of the First, Fourth, and Ninth Virginia Cavalry, and part of the Jeff Davis Legion, with the Boykin Rangers and a section of the Stuart Horse Artillery, on June 13th, 14th, and 15th, made a reconnaissance between the Pamunkey and Chickahominy Rivers and succeeded in passing around the rear of the whole of the Union Army, routing the enemy in a series of skirmishes, taking a number of prisoners, destroying and capturing stores to a large amount. Having most successfully accomplished its object, the expedition recrossed the Chickahominy almost in the presence of the enemy, with the same coolness and address that marked every step of his progress, and with the loss of but one man, the lamented Captain Letane, of the Ninth Virginia Cavalry, who fell bravely leading a successful charge against

a force of the enemy. In announcing the signal success to the Army, the General Commanding takes great pleasure in expressing his admiration of the courage and skill so conspicuously exhibited throughout by the General and the officers and men under his command."

Chapter Thirty-Four

Hope Rings Eternal

The days following the amazing ride by Jeb Stuart and his men are times of celebration for the citizens of the Confederate South. News during the first five months of 1862 has not boded well for the Confederacy. Northern Armies have been victorious in major battles in Kentucky, Tennessee, North Carolina, Mississippi and Georgia. The North has been on a roll, a very successful roll, except in Virginia.

Even so, the North has little to shout about in Virginia. Seven Pines was a colossal blunder. Both General Johnston's and McClellan's mismanagement and lack of initiative resulted in the battle ending in a draw. It should have been a Southern victory. It had all of the earmarks for success. It was not. Nor was the battle a Northern victory, although General McClellan claimed it to be as did the U.S. Senate and the Northern press. It was not. It was a bitter and costly draw. Both Armies ended in the exact locations they had occupied prior to the beginning of the battle.

But it is in Virginia where President Lincoln is anxious for a victory. Virginia has been a thorn in the flesh of the North ever since the bruising and bloody battle of Manassas or Bull Run, where the North was badly beaten. The North has something to prove in Virginia. Nothing could please Lincoln more than the capture or destruction of Richmond. The capital of the Confederacy, slightly more than a hundred miles from the U.S. Capitol in Washington, is the epitome of all that the new Confederacy stands for. It is the symbol of the political, the social, and the psychological structure of the South. Richmond is the corner stone supporting the fragile foundation of the Confederacy. "Destroy the cornerstone," so reasons

Lincoln, "and the entire structure of the wayward Confederate government will come tumbling down like chaff before the storm. If Richmond falls, so falls the entire South and the war between the states will be over."

Not only is the North smarting over its loss at Bull Run, it is also smarting over successive defeats inflicted by Confederate General "Stonewall" Jackson in the Shenandoah Valley of Virginia. Stonewall Jackson, a Southern hero of the Battle of Manassas or Bull Run, has wreaked havoc on the North, having successfully defeated three better equipped and larger Northern Armies to keep the Valley of Virginia in Southern hands.

With Jackson's successes in the Valley, and Stuart's successful ride near Richmond, the South again has something to feel good about. Their bragging rights are restored. A new day for the South is dawning. Across the South, newspapers lavishly hail the success of Stuart's ride; his exploits are compared to those of Revolutionary War hero Paul Revere and his midnight ride. The Southern people hope that the tide of victory has now turned in their favor. These events provide a much-needed boost to Southern morale and pride.

While the South celebrates, the North suffers. The Lincoln government in Washington and the people of the North are embarrassed. The officers and men, the common foot-soldiers of the Army of the Potomac, are embarrassed and humiliated over the Southern accomplishments of Stuart and Jackson. No one is more dejected than is General McClellan. He is a man of immense pride, a man of intelligence and of considerable military ability and talent. He is also a soldier of caution. Sometimes it is extreme caution. He is quick to recognize that Stuart's ride is more than what meets the eye; it is more than a publicity stunt. Stuart's ride has provided the South and General Lee with much valuable information, much military intelligence. McClellan immediately sets about to ready his Army for its final assault, his victorious assault to capture the Confederate capital at Richmond.

McClellan believes that the North won a great victory at Seven Pines. His delusion of victory at the conclusion of the battle allows him to believe that Richmond will now be an easy victory. He confides to a subordinate officer the day after the battle ended, "It is possible that yesterday's victory will open Richmond to us without further fighting."

The news of Stuart's ride around his entire Army rudely punctures McClellan's bubble of optimism. "Richmond," he now muses to himself, "may well be a fight to the finish. We must be ready for it. It will not be an easy matter."

McClellan is not alone in anticipating an all-out battle for the Confederate capital. Lee has planned for such a battle from the very moment he accepted command of the Confederate Army. Nor is Lee alone in his determination to defend the city. The citizens of Richmond - men, and women - are also prepared to do battle. By mid-May, as McClellan's Army moved steadily up the peninsulas, the General Assembly of Virginia passed a resolution providing that the capital be defended to the bitter end. The Mayor of Richmond, Joseph Mayo, proclaims that the city will never surrender, that he would rather die. Newspapers carry the same message, advocating that rather than surrender the city, the total destruction thereof will be more acceptable.

General McClellan is preparing to do just that. He is moving his heavy artillery into position to assault the city, to pound it into submission, and to then over-run it with cavalry and infantry troops. Richmond must fall or be destroyed. It must not stand.

Nor is McClellan's adversary, General Lee, resting on his laurels. He, too, is planning to initiate an offensive action. His plans, developed primarily from the intelligence report delivered by Jeb Stuart, are readied for an offensive action against McClellan's Army. Lee surreptitiously orders Stonewall Jackson and his foot-soldiers from the Shenandoah Valley for this offensive action. Lee plans to destroy the Northern Army of the Potomac.

The stage is nearly set by the two opposing Armies, neither of which is fully aware of what the other is planning to do. The two Armies are nearing their initial all-out action. It is to be a high stakes confrontation. The spoils of war for the victor are astronomical. For the Confederacy, it may well determine its survival or its demise. For the Union, the outcome of the battle is of no less importance. They must fight and fight well to regain their shaken pride. If the North fails to win, it may well indicate a long drawn-out war with an undecided victor.

Lee has readied his plans for the battle. He meets with President Davis and the members of his Cabinet. After an exchange of greetings, Lee apprises them of his battle plans.

"Gentlemen, the time has come - it is, in fact, long overdue - for our Army to initiate an aggressive action against General McClellan and his Northern Army.

"Our backs are pushed hard against the gates of our capital city. We cannot wait. It is a large and well-equipped Army that we are facing. We are outnumbered in manpower. We are outnumbered in military equipment. We are not, however, outnumbered in determination.

"We are prepared for the defense of the city. We have strengthened and fortified our defensive entrenchments that already existed and we have constructed new earthworks.

"Now we must act. We must act before our enemy decides to do so. McClellan is preparing to move his artillery forward. He will do so in a matter of days. If we allow him to do so, the shelling of Richmond - the destruction of Richmond - will begin. We cannot let this happen!"

Confederate Secretary of War Randolph speaks. "General Lee, is our Army of sufficient physical and mental strength to undertake this offensive action? That is, how is our morale? Do we have sufficient manpower to both defend our capital and to engage in an offensive attack against our powerful enemy? Is it safe for us to do so?"

"Mr. Secretary, our Army's morale is high, our division leadership is exceptional, and our planned offense, I believe, can be done. We intend to leave an adequate force to defend Richmond if that becomes necessary. I believe that it is safe to do so, that it can be done, that it must be done, and that it will be done.

"There are risks. There are always risks involved in war. We must have faith in ourselves, in our purpose, and in the higher spiritual power in which we believe. Our plans have been made. I have called on General Jackson to join us in this most important fray. He is to leave enough of his men to defend the Valley and to bring the rest of his Army along with him. They will come part way by train and they will march the rest of the way here. They will come as far as Ashland, or near thereto, and spend a night or two resting.

"General Jackson will report to my headquarters so that he and the other division commanders, and myself, will have an opportunity to go over the plan of battle. Each of them needs to know what they and their men are to do, and they need to know what each of the other divisions is going to do."

"General Lee," interjects Vice-President Alexander Stephens, "isn't this sudden troop movement of Jackson and his men coming from the Valley going to alert the North as to what we are planning to do? Our own Southern newspapers are going to spread the news all across their front pages. The North is surely going to find out as soon as we do."

"Mr. Vice-President, General Jackson has done a marvelous job of keeping the Northern government and the Northern Army quite confused about his whereabouts. Nevertheless, I have asked Secretary Randolph to use his influence with the Richmond newspapers to keep this matter top secret, to prevent any mention of it in the public print. I ask each of you gentlemen to likewise use your influence in keeping this matter top secret. We certainly want to keep it out of public print."

"General Lee, you have my assurance, and I know that I speak just as well for all of the members of this Cabinet, that we will do all that is humanly possible to keep this matter confidential."

"Thank you, Mr. Vice President; thank you, gentlemen."

"General Lee, when do you plan for your offensive action to commence? When will it get underway?" asked President Davis.

"Very soon, Mr. President. Within a day or so after General Jackson and his men arrive, and after the participating generals and myself discuss the plan and what action each of them will be responsible for."

As plans for an all-out battle are secretly in the making, a nervous city watches and waits for the impending next action by one Army or the other. The days are filled with apprehension, yet there is hope, always hope. The morning newspapers are awaited with great excitement, and are eagerly read by the soldiers as well as by the civilian population.

Robbie Holcomb buys a Richmond Enquirer from a newsboy on Friday morning, June 20th. As he and the men of his company relax after their early morning breakfast, he begins to speak.

"Listen to this, fellows. It is not too promising of an article, but it is probably true." Robbie reads aloud, "The 'Times,' apparently another newspaper, is quoted as saying in an editorial on May 20th that it can see no end of the war in America, nor any indication of what that end may be. It goes on to speculate that 'of the submission of the South there is as little prospect as ever. The Confederates retreat before their adversaries, but it is intrepidly and with design. They destroy whatever they cannot keep, and they vindicate their power at intervals by turning fiercely on their pursuers. But the Northern forces are closing in upon them. No doubt of it.'

"It is added, 'that the loss of life on both sides is beginning to be felt among the families of every part of the country, and it is probable that as far as the extent of misery goes, there has rarely in the history of the world been a struggle presenting more cruel results.'"

Robbie pauses. "What do you guys think about that?"

"I don't know Robbie; it is kind of frightening when you realize that the article was originally written before the battle of Seven Pines, even before all of those guys were killed," one of his comrades replies.

"That's true," Robbie replies, then adds, "I expect that this battle for Richmond, when it comes, is going to be a lot worse than Seven Pines."

Silence falls over the men as they ponder the prospects of the battle that they are contemplating. It is not a fearful silence, it is a very serious silence; a sobering silence.

"Well, men," Robbie says, "it is no use for us to speculate on what will or what will not happen. We have very little control over our destiny."

"We will stick together and look after one another, just as Sergeant Baldwin has taught us to do."

"Amen to that," someone adds.

After Jackson arrives at Lee's headquarters, a council of war is called with all the division generals present. The battle plans are explained in great detail. The discussion of the plan of battle goes well. Each general understands his objective and the objectives of the other generals. Each general is provided written instructions of the entire battle plan. The plan is not overly complex; however it requires precision of time and of troop movement among the soldiers of each of the divisions.

"Gentlemen," Lee intonates in a most serious tone, "we do not want nor can we afford another donnybrook, another fiasco, such as we experienced at Seven Pines. Our failure to win a great victory there was due to a lack of coordination between our various divisions.

"I do not say this as a criticism of the leadership of any division that fought there. Every division fought honorably and admirably, and I commend the leadership of those divisions. Failure of any Army to accomplish its objective must fall upon the shoulders of the commanding general of that Army. It is critical that each of you fully understand what you and your soldiers' mission is, and that you thoroughly understand what the mission and the objective is of each other's division, their leader, and their soldiers.

"I have given each of you a written battle plan so that all of us will know what to do and when to do it, and what every other division is to do and when to do it. We have discussed the plan of battle. Are there any questions about your mission or the mission of anyone else?"

There are no comments. All acknowledge an understanding of the plan. Lee is a man of punctuality. He is not a fault-finder, nor is he a holier-than-thou person. He is a highly religious man. He is a soldier, a soldier's soldier. His characteristics, his habits, have changed little from those he adhered to as a cadet at West Point. He was never late for a formation, never late for an assignment. He holds to those standards as the Commander of his Army. He emphasizes the importance of punctuality to each of the division generals before the meeting is adjourned. Lee plans to leave 25,000 troops to man the fortifications for the defense of Richmond, should the Yankees decide to attack. The remaining troops, approximately 47,000 men, are divided nearly equal between Longstreet and the two Hills. Jackson has brought his own men from the valley, approximately 18,000 of them. The Confederates' plan is to swoop down on Union General Fitz John Porter's 30,000 Federal troops isolated on the north bank of the flooded Chickahominy River near Beaver Dam Creek, not far from the village of Mechanicsville. The date of the attack is set for Thursday morning, June twenty-sixth.

Chapter Thirty-Five

The Beginning of the End
Surprise! Surprise!

A ll is quiet in the Confederate capital at Richmond, Virginia, in the early morning hours of Tuesday, June 24, 1862. Two opposing Armies nearly surround the city. They face one another in silence. Other than the two Armies, there are no visible signs of war. Neither are there sounds of war. The beginning of this day is much like the beginning of the day before, and even the day before that. It is, for the men of Sergeant Baldwin's infantry company, an opportunity to relax, to escape from the rigors of war. They savor the smell and the taste of fresh brewed coffee as the morning sun burns through the haze that has settled over the land during the night. As the haze dissipates, the temperature rises.

"Looks like another warm one," Robbie observes as he joins his friends.

"I'd rather be sittin' here in the red hot sun drinkin' coffee than chasin' after them Yankee soldiers in a red hot battle," one of his friends replies.

"Or," someone else adds, "bein' chased by one of them Yankee boys in a red hot battle."

"Either way, I prefer the hot sun to a hot battle."

"Don't we all," adds Robbie as they all laugh heartily.

"Where'd ye get the newspaper, Robbie?"

"There's a young boy down the way selling them."

"What's the big news for today? Is there anything good happening?"

"Today's good news is the news that happened yesterday." Robbie pauses as he flips through the paper. "There isn't much in the way of war news. Doesn't seem to be much happening."

"I don't want to hear war news anyway. I think that when something more happens in this war, we are going to be the first people to know about it. You know why? Because we are goin' to be a part of it. Us sittin' over here watchin' them fellers, and them fellers sittin' over there watchin' us fellers ain't gonna last much longer. Ye kin bet on that!"

"Robbie, see if ye can't find somethin' interesting in that thar paper and read it to us. Seein' that it's your paper an' you're the only one that's educated, ye kin read it to us."

"Alright," Robbie says as he continues to look through the paper. "Here's an interesting article. It makes me feel like there is no war, like we're living in Paradise, instead of being out here with these swamps and mosquitoes."

"Go ahead, Robbie, read it. What newspaper is it?"

"OK, this is the Richmond Daily Inquirer. Now listen. It might even cheer you guys up a bit. 'Richmond was remarkably quiet yesterday. The clouds gathered and the skies rumbled for a time, but gentle showers were followed by a beautiful rainbow that arched our eastern horizon. It was impossible to gaze upon this magnificent spectrum of the sky without having the hope suggested that, as in the past days, so now it is the guards of Heaven's mercy and of peace. If the tempest has not indeed yet passed by, let us at least hope that the shock shall soon be over and that this bow of promise shall be seen upon the departing clouds.'"

Robbie pauses, then looks at his fellow soldiers. "Isn't that a well-written and fascinating article? Isn't it poetic?"

The guys look at each other, then they look at Robbie. They are expressionless, dumbfounded.

"Robbie, is that the kind of stuff they teach you in college?" one of his friends ask. It is a simple and sincere question.

"Yeah," another says, looking puzzled. "I saw that rainbow yesterday too, but I didn't see any of that other stuff that newspaper man saw. It was just a plain ol' ordinary rainbow. What is that bow of promise thing about anyway, Robbie?"

"Men, it's a reference to God's promise to Noah back in Old Testament times. In the Book of Genesis, after the great flood, it had rained for forty days and forty nights, and every living thing on earth was destroyed, except for Noah and his family members, and all the other living things on the Ark. It was a promise, a covenant, that God made with man that never again would the earth be destroyed by a flood. The rainbow will always be an everlasting sign - a symbol - of God's promise. That is what the newspaper article is making reference to, the sign of the rainbow."

"How do you know that, Robbie? Where did you hear that story?"

"I first heard the story in church. Our minister preached a sermon about it. I thought it was a fascinating and interesting story. So after church I went home and read it in our family Bible."

"Robbie, I never heard our preacher back home tell that story, or anything like that."

"Well, some preachers do and some do not, I guess. After the war is over, when you go back home, ask your preacher to talk about it. I bet he will preach you a special sermon."

"I don't know about that, Robbie. But I know that I'll think about it from now on whenever I see a rainbow."

"Robbie, did God ever say anything about men killing each other in wars, whether He would destroy the world with some kind of a war?"

"I believe that in Old Testament times He sanctioned some wars, and wars are mentioned throughout the Bible - in both the Old and the New Testaments. The Bible speaks of wars and rumors of wars, and even a war in Heaven a long time ago when Satan was expelled. Satan at one time was an angel.

"The way things are going in this war between the North and the South, it looks like we are destroying ourselves."

"Well, Robbie, we are sure in a war now and it ain't just a rumor. I bet some of us sittin' here right now are gonna get killed before this thing ends."

"Maybe all of us," someone adds as a somber quietness falls over the men.

Sergeant Baldwin arrives during the rainbow story. He sits silently and listens to the conversations that the men are having about rainbows and wars before he speaks. "I ain't never heard them stories that Robbie's been tellin' about the Bible. But if Robbie says they are true, ye can count on 'em bein' true. When we met on the train comin' to the Army trainin' camp whar we trained, he said some of them Bible words and 'ah thot he was a preacher man.

"He's a good man to have around in this here war. We never know when we might need him ta say a few o' them Bible words for us.

"Now we ain't gonna talk about anyone gettin kilt, cause yer all gonna listen to me an wer gonna look out fer each other. Wer gonna make it thru this here war. Yes Sir we are.

"Now men, gather 'round. I got some news for ye. I can't tell ye ever thing, but I kin tell ye this much. Ye can take it easy for the rest of the mornin'. This afternoon wer gonna do some marchin' an runnin'. Don't want y'all gettin soft.

"Sumptin important is gonna happen Thursday. I can't tell ye anymore than that fer now, but be ready to move outa here at a moment's notice. An keep this under yer hat.

"One other thing, men. When ye go to chow, eat ever thing they give ye. Don't matter if ye like it or not, eat it 'cause a good soldier fights better on a full stomach."

All thoughts are now focused on Thursday. There is considerable speculation among the men about the implications of Sergeant Baldwin's announcement.

"We're going to be in another battle, that's what it means. That's exactly what Sarge was hinting about, that's what he means," one of the young soldiers speculates, then adds, "What else could it mean?"

"I agree with you," Robbie interjects, "and it certainly doesn't take the powers of a wizard to know where the battle is going to be. We have constantly been face to face with the Northern soldiers here. We have traded them tobacco for coffee. It's not going to be easy to fight those guys, but then we have known all along that it was coming to this."

Someone else speaks up, "I wonder if the Yanks are going to attack us or whether we're going to attack them?"

Robbie again speaks, "I think we are going to attack them. I believe that it is very unlikely that we would know when they are planning to attack us. I suppose it is possible that we could have intercepted one of their messages, but I doubt it. No, it's going to be us attacking them. I think the handwriting is on the wall. I believe we can count on that."

Sergeant Baldwin, aware of what is going to happen in a day or so, wants his men to be physically and mentally prepared for what is to come. He has his men marching and running in the afternoon. The temperature is in the high eighties. They march on dry roads, choking on the dust that is stirred by their pounding footsteps. They struggle in knee-deep, turbid swamps, half gagged by the foul odor. He pushes his men to the limits of their endurance. They are exhausted. The men are silently seething.

"Break time, men," he barks in his usual military fashion. The men fall to the ground, gasping for air. The old Sergeant is every bit as tired as are his men, but he hides it from them. He stands straight as an arrow, looking down at his men.

"Don't tell me ye are tired? You lily-livered bunch of weaklin's." He masquerades the fact that he is well-pleased with their physical and mental endurance. He knows that his men are the cream of the crop, but this is not the time or the place to tell them. Sergeant Baldwin knows that mental toughness is as necessary as physical toughness when soldiers are exposed to extended periods of combat. The soon-to-be fought battle for Richmond, and perhaps for the entire peninsula, may well take measure of each one of them during the coming days. He will tell them of his true belief, his total confidence in them, when they return to camp. Now the test of endurance must continue, it must go on.

With hands on hips, he stands before his men, who remain prostrate on the ground. They are gasping, sweating, not just drops of sweat, but honest to goodness trickling, streaming rivers of sweat, flooding down their faces, down between their shoulder blades. They look miserable. They are miserable. No one is happy. No one except the old Sergeant.

"Ahm nearly sixty years old and ah can outwalk an' outrun the lot of ye. Ye think ahm tough on ye? Well, ye just wait 'til them Yankee boys get to chasin' ye. When they git ye down on the ground like ye now are, they's gonna pin ye down there with yer own bayonet. They ain't gonna show no mercy on ye. Why ye'd all be dead right now if ah were a Yankee. Ya'll be thankin' me in a few days fer keepin' ye in such good shape. Ye been layin' around heah too much lately. That kinda life will shore make ye weak and lazy."

It is late evening when they arrive back in camp. The chow line has already closed. His men are half starved after their tiresome march. The men are disgusted and disappointed. Tempers are frayed and near the boiling point.

"Fall out and rest a mite," Sergeant Baldwin instructs his men. He then tells them of his true feelings about them.

"Men, ah gotta tell ya. Ah wuz jest as tard back there when we took that break as youse guys wuz. But ye just can't give in to yerself. Ye gotta fight it. Make yerself tough - discipline yerself. Be mentally an' physically tough. Thas why ah ride hard over ye'all. Ah'd go anywhere 'an do anything fer ye men - an ah think any o' ye guys wud do th' same fer me.

"Ye know that ye'all are the cream of the crop. Ah harass ye'all cause ah want ye ta be ever better 'n what ye er. Ah want ye all to survive this here war an go home to yer families. So ah wanna make ya tough, an mean.

"An' another thing - when ye all get yer dander up, ye could sort wildcats - ye could whip the devil. We lost nearly a third of ar company at the battle of Seven Pines. Ah no ye don't like to talk about or think about it - but it happened. We jus gotta be more kerful and be tough at the same time."

"Sarge," Robbie responds, "we know that you care - and we care about you. We know, so to speak, that your bark is worse than your bite; that what you do and say is for all of our benefit.

"This Army Company is one big family. We care about one another. We look out for one another. But one thing is for certain - if this war continues, we are going to have casualties; especially if we are in the thick of things like we were at Seven Pines.

"We will do the best that we can do."

Silence falls over the men. It is not a fearful silence, not a silence of dejection, but one of reality. To a man, they will do their duty, come what may.

"Now let's forget about battles and war and casualties, and let's think about our stomachs," Robbie says, then adds in a pleasant, positive voice, "Is anyone hungry?"

"Yes, Sarge, how 'bout some food before we all starve to death," one of the men calls out.

"Ye'll git yer food," the Sergeant replies. "Ye jes wait rite heah while ah go over to the cook's tent."

Loud talking and some cursing erupt from the direction of the cook's tent. Although the spoken words are indistinguishable, it is evident from the tone of the conversation that the discussion has become quite heated. It is not long before the heated conversation subsides, then it changes to normal sounding conversing and finally to laughter.

Sergeant Baldwin reappears, a broad smile crosses his lips as he jubilantly announces, "Stack yer rifles outside the mess tent, men. The cook has decided to prepare some grub just fer y'all. He is a very friendly feller an' he's done this outta the goodness of his heart. Now ah want y'all to be real nice and to thank the generous cook for his kindness."

"How did you persuade the cook to feed us, since he already had said that the kitchen was closed?" Robbie asked.

"It took some persuasion and promises to convince him, but it turnt out he's a quick learner."

"Why was he so quick to change his mind?"

"Well, ah tole ye, he's a very friendly feller. Besides, it turns out he'd rather cook than to be transferred to an infantry company. And he's very fond of his teeth. Likes 'em just as they are and don't want to have any dental work done on 'em."

"You didn't threaten him, did you Sarge?"

"Oh no, 'course not. That would be against Army regulations. But I did promise him that preparin' our grub would contribute nicely to his general health and well-being. He figured it out right quickly. He seems to be a very bright man. Our food will be ready in about forty-five minutes, so y'all can relax or do whatever ye want to."

The Company waits, nearly overcome with hunger. Chow is then served. They are treated like royalty. The food is not only delicious, it is bountiful. They eat to their hearts' content. Each one thanks the cook as he leaves. The cook is very cordial.

"Sarge," Robbie says, "Whatever was said, or implied, or done in that discussion between you and the cook must have had a profound effect on him."

"It appears so, don't it?"

"Yes Sir, Sarge, it sure does."

As they head back to their own bivouac area, Sergeant Baldwin muses aloud, "Ye know, I wonder whar that cook got the idea that we are a special security unit, that we are responsible for the protection of Lee?"

"It does make us wonder, Sarge," Robbie says, then adds with a chuckle, "Perhaps we had better forget this matter completely."

The excellent meal quiets their frustrations over the long and exhaustive afternoon march. When they reach their area, Sergeant Baldwin calls the men to attention. A wry smile crosses his lips.

"Men, since ye are now well fed, and yer kinda tired from yer little afternoon march, how'd ye like to go on guard duty for a while ta kinda simmer down?"

There is a long, disappointed, unanimous groan from the men.

"Well, if that don't set well wi' ye, how'd ye like ta sleep in, in the mornin?"

"Yes, Sir!" is the unanimous and spirited reply.

"Then it is so ordered. Gud night, men. Dismissed."

"Hip, hip, hooray for Sergeant Baldwin!"

A long sound sleep will prove to be no problem for the over fed, over tired and over happy men. The late sleep is a rare and unusual privilege.

Sergeant Baldwin, true to his word, allows the men to sleep late on Wednesday morning. It is a rare and unexpected treat. They have taken full advantage of the opportunity. It is now well past eight o'clock Wednesday morning. They are awakened by the sound of cannon and rifle fire over toward the forward defensive positions where the pickets are posted, in front of the main infantry lines. They are the eyes and ears of their Army.

At the sound of the gunfire, Sergeant Baldwin arrives on the double quick where his troops have just awakened. "OK, men," he barks, "get dressed, get yer weapons and ammunition. Robbie, get yer bugle. It looks like the Yankees are makin' a move. We may be needed up on our front line of defense. Be ready to move out on a moment's notice. Ahm gonna run over to th' headquarters tent to find out what's goin' on. We might be needed and we wanna be ready.

"It appears like them Yankees done decided to attack us t'day. They kinda beat us to the punch, an' that's just too bad, ain't it?"

Sergeant Baldwin turns and he is gone. Everyone is in a rush, hurrying here and there. It's a mad rush as everyone readies themselves for combat. Within a few minutes Sarge is back.

"We'r to remain heah until further notice. It appears ta headquarters people it's a probin' thrust by a couple of units of McClellan's Army. Not a full scale attack. The thrust don't include sufficient troops ta be an all-out attack. We'r to stand by 'til further notice. So that's it for now."

Sergeant Baldwin walks over to a small knoll for a better view of the action. His men follow. "It looks like there's a right smart skirmish goin' on over near Kings School House," he says as he points toward a small building over the way.

"If ye look over just a little further to the left, that's Oak Grove. There's a little fightin' goin' on there, too. Ye should recognize that place 'cause that's the ground where we started from in the Battle of Seven Pines about three weeks ago. Don't ye see that bunch of oak trees? Well, that's where General Hill ordered us to start that battle at one o'clock in the afternoon on May 31st."

General McClellan has his faults. His delusional fear that the size of the Rebel Army that he and his soldiers are now facing vastly outnumbers the size of his Northern Army by a two-to-one margin is pure folly. Nevertheless, he firmly believes it to be true. This critical trait causes whatever aggressiveness he otherwise possesses to falter even though an offensive action is sorely needed. He watches, somewhat alarmed, as Southern troops mysteriously move about in front of the Yankee lines.

McClellan has finally decided to act. It is to be a probing action to test his enemy and to move his line forward. It is not an all-out assault. He advises two of his generals, Samuel Heintzelman and Joe Hooker, of his planned action. Hooker shoulders responsibility for the limited action.

The Yankee troops catch the Rebel pickets by surprise. Soon after eight o'clock as McClellan has planned, the battle is underway. It is fiercely and bitterly fought along some sections of the battle lines whereas there is little or no action in other areas. Two hours after the battle begins the Union forces are nearly in reach of their objective. Surprisingly, orders are received to discontinue the action and to withdraw back to the original line of defense. At one o'clock in the afternoon, the battle is renewed and before nightfall, the Yankees again control the small area of land around Oak Grove.

Both Army commanders Lee and McClellan witness some of the battle. Lee, when he is satisfied that the charge by the Union Army is not an all-out assault, returns to his headquarters. McClellan is also satisfied with the results of the day. He confides to Joe Hooker. "We have taken a decisive step forward today. We have accomplished what we wanted. We are barely four miles from Richmond. We are four miles from success.

"Nevertheless I am apprehensive. Lee has increased the size of his Army with the addition of General Beauregard's troops from the South and I have been informed that Stonewall Jackson and his Army are near at hand. Something is brewing with their Army now at two hundred thousand men.

"I have continued to ask Lincoln for more men. He promises, but nothing happens. Reports from our forward units along our front lines indicate mysterious enemy troop movement all along their lines. I am apprehensive about these moves, about their intentions. I don't know what it means, but I have this feeling that something is in the wind, something is stirring.

"General Hooker, I dare not risk this Army, on which I feel the fate of our nation depends. I must practice patience. I will succeed. For the sake of the cause, I must be sure. There is no man in this Army that is as anxious as I am to finish this campaign and to end this war."

The Battle of Oak Grove has ended. It has proven nothing, nor has much of anything been established. It has not been a costly battle in terms of human casualties. Each side suffers about six hundred losses. Sergeant Baldwin and his men of Company K of the 110th Virginia Infantry are not called into action. The role of the two Armies remains the same. This, however, is about to change. Lee is ready to take the initiative.

Chapter Thirty-Six

The Best Laid Plans

The Battle of Beaver Dam Creek and Mechanicsville

I t is not yet break of day on Thursday morning, June twenty-sixth. The cock is yet to crow. Confederate General Lee has had little, if any sleep during the night, nor has anyone in his Army had much rest. Their sleeplessness is not due to fear, rather it is due to great expectations. This is to be their day. Their day to do battle with the powerful Northern Army. Their day to flex their military muscles.

Yesterday McClellan and his Northern Army had flexed their muscles; not a very enthusiastic or energetic flexing, but, nonetheless, it was a flexing. That is all that General McClellan had intended it to be, and that is all that it was.

A new day is now dawning, and it is Lee's turn, his Army's turn to flex their muscles. Lee has planned mightily for this day. His hopes are high. He is confident. He is ready to make his move. His is not to be a cautious, probing move; it is to be an all-out assault against his enemy. He will not leave one stone unturned. This is the message Lee has relayed to his generals, to his division commanders who will lead his men, his Army, into this great battle for the survival of the Confederacy. These commanders - Longstreet, Stonewall Jackson, A.P. Hill and D.H. Hill - are combat-experienced, combat-proven leaders. Their reputations are sound, impeccable. Even so, they are new to Lee's command, and his leadership is new to them. It will be a proving ground for them and for the Confederate government.

The four in-charge generals have been briefed about every detail of this mission, of this pending battle. The battle plan is not complex, but it must be carried forward with precision. Each of Lee's four commanders must do their jobs, and they must do them well. The battle plan is the handiwork of Lee. It is his brainchild. It is designated as General Order No. 75. It provides each of the in-charge generals a detailed strategy of performance and of purpose. The generals have discussed the plan with Lee, and they all jointly discussed it. They understand where they and their men are to be at the appointed starting time, and they know what they are to do and when they are to do it. Nothing, absolutely nothing, is left to chance.

As the first rays of light break the early morning darkness, as the crowing of the cock breaks the early morning silence, Lee's Army awaits the signal for action. Stonewall Jackson and his Army from Virginia's Shenandoah Valley have the honor of initiating the battle. They are to swiftly hit the North flank of Porter's 30,000 Union troops that are entrenched along Beaver Dam Creek, a tributary of the Chickahominy River near Mechanicsville. Jackson's gunfire is to be the signal for A.P. Hill and his men to begin their attack.

The Confederate army waits for Jackson, but there is no indication of where he and his troops are. The morning passes slowly. It is nearly noontime, and the mid-day temperature hovers near ninety degrees. Jackson and his men are nowhere to be seen, or heard. General A.P. Hill is anxious, he is nervously pacing back and forth, beads of sweat trickling down his forehead. His uniform is already wet from perspiration.

"Where can Jackson be?" he asks, the question, directed to no one in particular. Then he continues, "This is totally unlike the Stonewall Jackson we hear so much about. He was receptive to the plan of action during our briefing. He never questioned the role that he and his men are assigned to do. I remember Longstreet specifically asking Jackson if we should delay the attack for a day or two so that he and his men could rest after their long trip down from the valley. Jackson was quite firm, although very polite, in rejecting Longstreet's suggestion."

One of Hill's aides-de-camp interjects, "Perhaps they have run into trouble."

"What kind of trouble?"

"Well, perhaps they encountered a Yankee reconnaissance unit that is out on a scouting mission."

"I don't think a small company of men would present any kind of a problem that could delay Jackson and his Army. He would either brush them aside or destroy them. Besides, we have not heard any rifle fire this morning."

"That's true, Sir, but earlier this morning, just after daybreak, there was considerable artillery fire off toward Richmond. Perhaps that had something to do with Jackson's delay."

General Hill thinks for a moment before responding. "No, I don't believe so. That was simply an exchange of early morning wake-up calls between General Magruder's artillery and the Yankee artillery. The Yankees are firing into our defense positions, hoping that we will fall back closer to Richmond and they will then move up a bit. I am sure that exchange of artillery fire has nothing to do with Jackson's delay."

At three o'clock in the afternoon, thirty-six-year-old General A.P. Hill is overcome with nervous aggravation. He calls a meeting of his front-line officers.

"Gentlemen, we are ready to attack our enemy. Although we have not yet heard from General Jackson and his men, I believe that they are nearby and they will join the battle very soon after we launch it.

"As you know, Jackson will attack Porter's right rear. This will force him out of the strong position he now holds and he and his 30,000 men will then be extremely vulnerable to our attack. They will be at our mercy.

"We have only about five or six hours of daylight left, and if we are going to accomplish anything today, we need to initiate action now. Let's move. We should overrun Mechanicsville with a minimum of effort."

With that said, Hill and his men move out of the orchard that has shielded them from the sun and from the sight of Porter's Union troops. They cautiously approach Mechanicsville, a small crossroads village some six miles northeast of Richmond.

The success of the Mechanicsville/Beaver Dam Creek battle is hinged on all of Lee's divisions functioning in consort, each one with the other. Lee has specifically and repeatedly preached this point to his subordinate generals.

Jackson's division - his troops - must be in position at the Union Army's right rear - to force the Union General Porter out of his fortified position of strength. This is necessary, absolutely critical and essential to Lee's success.

Jackson's no-show, and the erroneous assumption by the impetuous A. P. Hill, that Jackson and his men are either in place or soon will be, is, Hill believes, an authorization or adequate reason to initiate the action. So Hill initiates the action, but Jackson does not appear.

Porter is not to be caught by surprise. Although Stonewall Jackson, as was his trait, moved his Army to Richmond under the deepest secrecy, the North discovered it before he and his Army arrived to support Lee in the battle. General McClellan is warned of the Stonewall Jackson news by the Union Department of War in Washington. Whatever offensive ideas that McClellan may have had regarding the capture or fall of Richmond and the Confederate States of America, vanish with the knowledge of Jackson's arrival.

McClellan sets about warning Porter of Jackson's reported presence in the area. Porter readies his troops for a defensive action. Porter immediately calls his line officers together for a strategy session.

"Gentlemen, we have reason to believe that the South has massed a large offensive Army at Richmond for the purpose of either destroying our Army or driving us from the peninsula. General McClellan's intelligence reports estimate the size of the Confederate Army in the vicinity of Richmond at two hundred thousand men. That is nearly twice the size of our own Army.

"We are presently isolated here at Beaver Dam Creek and at nearby Mechanicsville. It is here where we will fight if we are attacked. It appears likely that the South intends to fight, and it is likely to originate here. Our first line of defense will be at the village of Mechanicsville. Our main line of defense will be here at Beaver Dam Creek where our entrenchments are nearly invincible.

"We are going to prepare a surprise for our Southern foes when they arrive at Mechanicsville. They are going to rush right into a prepared trap."

"What kind of a trap, Sir?" asks one of the junior officers in attendance at the strategy meeting.

"A very costly trap for our Southern foe. One that will cost them dearly. Our small outpost at Mechanicsville is conspicuously displayed for the purpose of creating an impression of numbers and of intending to maintain stubborn resistance. That is, we aim to invite a heavy attack on our outposts, and when the Rebels attack, we will quickly abandon these positions; we will withdraw down the river bank to join our main force. When the Rebels witness what they believe to be a surrender of our outposts without a fight, they are going to charge right after our fleeing troops. They are going to rush right into our well-fortified lines right here at Beaver Dam Creek, to be slaughtered by the hundreds.

"Yes, gentlemen, we are going to incite such confidence in our Rebel enemy as to induce pursuit. It will be like leading lambs to the slaughter."

There is a round of applause and a great roar of approval from the attendees at the meeting. General Porter continues with his plan of defense.

"Sometime today, and we believe it will happen during the early afternoon hours, a single cannon shot will be fired from our outpost at Mechanicsville. That shot will be the signal that the Rebels will be crossing the Chickahominy River. It will be your signal to ready your men for action. We are well-entrenched here, and we will wait for them to come to us. There will be a blood-letting unlike anything we have seen here on the peninsula.

"We have nothing more to say. Go now and take command of your troops and brief them on what to expect before this day is over."

The single cannon shot from Mechanicsville sounds at three-thirty in the afternoon as Confederate troops by the thousands mass on the opposite banks of the river. The Yankees hold their fire, waiting for the Rebels to move into the waist-deep water. At three-thirty sharp, a near-deafening, bone-chilling Rebel yell rises from the Rebel side of the river. The gray clad soldiers rush headlong into the waters of the Chickahominy, intent to overrun the Union forces. They come by the thousands, up and down the river.

Simultaneously, with the Rebel onslaught, murderous Yankee cannon and rifle fire cuts into the line of the advancing Rebel infantry. The once gray uniforms of the Rebel soldiers are stained blood red, as are the waters of the Chickahominy River. There is a sickness, a numbness, in the pits of the soldiers' stomachs. Even so, there is no hesitation to their advance. Men stumble forward over the dead and dying bodies of their fellow comrades. They press onward, onto the Yankee side of the river. Onward they push as the Yankee soldiers yield ground in their swift retreat toward the safety of their entrenchments at Beaver Dam Creek. The Rebels, unaware of the death trap greeting prepared for them, press onward into the valley of death. Salvo after salvo of murderous artillery canisters, fired from Yankee cannons, burst within the Confederate ranks. Intense Yankee rifle fire greets those Rebel soldiers that do not fall before the cannons.

As the noise of battle coming from the direction of A.P. Hill's division reaches General Lee, he presumes that Jackson and his troops have arrived. Lee accordingly signals Longstreet and D.H. Hill to initiate their attacks. They do so immediately. Jackson, however, has not arrived, and without Jackson and his men, the best laid plans of General Lee are in peril. The Rebels put forth a valiant effort to turn the Federal troops' left flank and to force them out of their trenches. Unable to do so, the only alternative is to make a frontal assault. It is attempted. It is disastrous for Lee and his Army.

Daylight hours are fading, but Lee decides to make one last effort to dislodge Porter's Fifth Corps from their stronghold. A.P. Hill's division has sustained heavy losses. They have carried the brunt of today's battle. Their ranks are depleted and they are exhausted. It is time for another division to step forward. Lee calls on the men of D.H. Hill's division to answer the call. A brigade of D.H. Hill's division, under the leadership of Brigadier General Roswell S. Ripley, has crossed the Chickahominy and they are in the best position to do so. Sergeant Baldwin and his men of Company K are part of General Ripley's command.

Lee's orders for a final assault are answered by General Ripley and his men. They rush forward, oblivious to the almost certain death awaiting them in this last ditch, futile attempt to dislodge the Yankees from the safety of their entrenchments. Sergeant Baldwin and his Virginia troops are among the first soldiers chosen for this near suicidal attack.

"Keep your heads down and your chins up," the old Sergeant shouts, his voice booming above the sounds of battle. "Let's move as rapidly as possible. It keeps their sharp shooters from drawing a bead on us," he shouts. "Head for the low ground over yonder to our left. We can take a breather and reconnoiter our next move."

The vicious hail of bullets, minie balls, and canister shot coming from the Yankee trenches and the artillery emplacements are overpowering. Men are falling everywhere and Sergeant Baldwin's company is not immune to the onslaught. They are few in number as they reach the low ground just below a slight rise in the land in front of them. The agonizing cries and moans of the wounded and dying, sometimes rising above the explosive sounds of the instruments of war, is a chilling reminder of war's senselessness. The Confederate troops advance to within a hundred yards or so of the entrenched Yankees, but they are too few in number to again move forward. Darkness is falling and the battle is ending. Small arms fire is nearly diminished and the artillery fire has lessened considerably. Still, it is unsafe to leave the low ground. A stalemate in the action is a result of the vicious action by both Armies.

"Men," Sergeant Baldwin cautions, "we have nothing to gain by exposing ourselves further. We'll wait for total darkness before we attempt to return to our unit. We have not won the battle today, but there is going to be a tomorrow. We are not through with this thing yet."

As darkness falls over the men, a faint, garbled call from the battlefield breaks the silence. The men strain to listen. Again the call sounds, "Robbie, can you hear me?"

"Who's calling me?"

"It's me, Benjamin. I'm hit. I cannot move. I'm bleeding really bad."

"I'm coming, Ben. Keep talking, so I can find you."

Robbie is out on the field in a split second, oblivious to his own vulnerability, his own safety, his silhouette plainly visible in the twilight of the rising moon. He sprints toward the sound of the fading voice. A few enemy shots come dangerously close, but he is unscathed. Benjamin is nearly unconscious. He is bleeding badly and hardly breathing when Robbie reaches him. Amid continuous enemy fire, Robbie manages to pull Ben's limp body onto his shoulders. He then heads back for the security of the low ground. There are dead bodies everywhere. Recognizing the life-saving effort the Yankee infantrymen are ordered in a loud and clear voice, "Cease fire," as Robbie carries his friend and comrade to the relative safety of the low ground. As Robbie gently lays Ben on the ground, Ben struggles to speak.

"Is that you, Robbie? I can't see you."

"It's me, Ben. You are going to be alright."

"No, Robbie. I'll not make it. Not this time. Promise me you'll write my Mamma. Tell her I love her and that I died honorably."

"It's a promise, Ben. But don't give up. I'll try to get a medic." Robbie is aware that Ben's situation is hopeless. Even so, he cannot give up hope, he must keep Ben alive.

"Robbie, do you remember the rainbow story from the Bible you told us a few days ago?"

"I remember, Ben."

"Well, Robbie, I see that rainbow now, and I hear church music. It's the brightest rainbow, the most beautiful rainbow I have ever seen. I seem to be moving to it. Tell my Mamma goodbye." Ben is gone.

Ben's body is limp in Robbie's arms. Robbie holds Ben's body close, his own tears mixing with the still warm blood of Ben. The loss of a fellow comrade is not easy. Unashamed and compassionate tears dim Robbie's eyes as he lays Ben's still body on the earth. This is the foot-soldier's war. Death reigns the victor, death conquers. Robbie prays a silent prayer, his hand on the still warm body of his now silent friend; then he recites from Psalm 103.

> *"The mercy of the Lord is from everlasting to everlasting upon them that fear him, and his righteousness unto children's children; To such as keep his covenant and to those that remember his commandments to do them. The Lord hath prepared his throne in the heavens; and his kingdom ruleth over all. Bless the Lord, ye his angels, that excel in strength."*

Tough, battle-hardened Sergeant Baldwin is momentarily silent. "Ben gave that last full measure of love for the South," the old Sergeant says.

There is compassion in the toughest of men in the worst of times. There are feelings of despair and uselessness in the best of times.

The day has not fared well for the Confederacy. Lee and his Army have been denied the victory they sought. The loss of life is great, total casualties nearly 1,500 men. Lee is saddened, but he is not yet finished with the job he has set out to do.

General McClellan is quick to claim victory. At nine p.m., he sends a telegram to Secretary of War Stanton. "Victory of today complete and against great odds. I almost begin to think we are invincible."

Chapter Thirty-Seven

If At First You Don't Succeed
The Battle At Gaines Mill

It is the dawning of a new day, early Friday morning, June twenty-seventh. Lee's Army is badly bruised from yesterday's battle of Mechanicsville and Beaver Dam Creek. Southern casualties are nearly five times those of their Northern foe. They are bruised; they are badly bruised, but they are not beaten. They are anxious to renew hostilities, to start anew from where the battle stalled late last night. They have much to prove to themselves, and to their Northern enemy. They are again ready to assault the Yankee stronghold.

Unbeknownst to Lee and his Army, changes are made by McClellan during the night time hours. At three o'clock a.m. Friday morning, Porter and his men, on orders from General McClellan, began quietly to withdraw from their nearly impregnable defensive positions at Beaver Dam Creek. The Yankees take everything they can carry with them - men, munitions, and supplies - they move lock, stock, and barrel.

Although McClellan claimed a resounding victory and bragging rights for the battle at Beaver Dam Creek and Mechanicsville on Thursday, he is not anxious to renew the battle. McClellan's oversized and self-inflated ego has been soundly punctured with the discovery that his troops did not defeat Stonewall Jackson and his Army Thursday. In fact, Jackson and his men were never engaged in the fray; they never arrived at the scene of the battle.

The unknown whereabouts of Jackson causes McClellan deep concern. Porter and his men move to a more compatible defensive position near Gaines Mill. They hurriedly began the five or six mile march to the new location, where they will again fight Lee and his Army if they are pursued.

As the first rays of light from the early morning sun fall on the empty enemy trenches at Beaver Dam Creek, Lee learns of the nighttime departure of Porter and his troops. Lee, sitting astride Traveller, gazes quietly at the abandoned Yankee entrenchments. Through his field glasses he can see mostly unmanned obstacles. The battles of Mechanicsville, Beaver Dam Creek, and Ellersons Mill are over. The victory that he could not secure with manpower and weapons on yesterday's field of battle has today been handed to him by his now departed Northern adversaries without the sound of a single shot having been fired.

Lee is, nonetheless, disappointed. He believes, but does not say, that yesterday's battle loss was caused by the failure of the legendary Jackson and his vaunted Army of the Valley, to meet their battle plan responsibilities. Jackson and his men did not show; their whereabouts remain unknown, the cause of their "no-show" unknown. Lee turns to one of his trusted aides.

"Whatever reason caused General Jackson to be absent yesterday, he has paid his debt. It is his absence from our ranks, and his unknown whereabouts that have influenced McClellan to abandon his secure defensive positions here at Beaver Dam Creek and to withdraw his troops. McClellan was fearful that we were setting a trap for him and that Jackson was waiting for the right time to spring that trap." That said, General Lee makes no further comments regarding Jackson's failure to join yesterday's battle. "We need to organize our pursuit of Porter immediately. We must catch up with the Yankee retreat."

"Sir, if I may say so," an aide to General Lee interjects, "I believe that Mechanicsville and Beaver Dam Creek are unquestionable victories for the South. The North is retreating from the gates of Richmond, and that was your primary objective."

"That was one of our primary objectives. We need to drive the Northern Army from the Virginia peninsula and we are attempting to do that."

General Lee and his Army immediately set out in pursuit of General Porter and his troops, following the southeasterly direction that Porter has taken. Lee quickly concludes that Porter is heading for the high ground between Gaines Mill and Boatswain's Swamp. He again intends to flank

Porter's corps and destroy or capture it. Lee is determined. Caution is thrown to the wind. In the mind of Lee, this is a do-or-die situation. It is a must accomplishment. They must win this battle.

As Lee and his men arrive near Gaines Mill and Powhite Creek, they find Porter and his Fifth Corps awaiting them. Porter has had enough time to prepare for Lee's arrival and he has done so. Porter is just as determined to defeat Lee as Lee is determined to defeat him. The Yankees must hold their ground. They must do so at all costs. They are every bit as confident of victory as is their foe; they are just as resolved to stand fast as the Confederates are to attack and defeat them.

As Lee's Army moves toward Gaines Mill, they encounter resistance from the rear guard of Porter's Army. The nearer they come to their objective, the greater the resistance they encounter. By early afternoon the Battle of Gaines Mill is underway. Heavy skirmishing between the combatants is ongoing as both sides are striving to gain an advantage. Lee's primary objective now is to sever McClellan's access to his supply base at White House Landing. Without supplies, McClellan's Army cannot long endure. It will then be at the mercy of Lee's Army. Its only choices will be surrender, starvation, or annihilation.

What Lee does not know, nor does he even suspect, is that McClellan has already begun to pull his supply base away from White House Landing. The "White House," as it is called, was the former home of Martha Custis at the time she and George Washington were married. It is now owned by Colonel William Henry ("Rooney") Lee, Martha Custis Washington's great-great-grandson. Rooney is the second eldest son of Robert E. Lee.

McClellan is very much aware of the catastrophic results that will befall his Army if the Confederates capture or gain control of his supply base before he has time to move. He is mindful of the urgency to transfer his supplies to a new location on the James River side of the peninsula. The move begins immediately. As the Northern Army hurriedly abandons the White House Landing supply depot, they move everything downriver that they can load on their boats. Simultaneously they begin to move enormous amounts of supplies overland by wagon, heading for the James River and a new supply base. What they cannot move is torched, including the ancestral home of Martha Custis Washington.

Porter is cognizant of the immense responsibility resting on his shoulders. He must hold the Confederates at bay. He must hold them off as long as he possibly can to allow the supplies to be moved near the James River.

Much is riding on the outcome of the pending battle. Lee is anxious, he is ready for action. His Army is now deployed, along a line nearly two miles long, stretching from the village of Old Cold Harbor. A.P. Hill's division is positioned directly in front of the main strength of Porter's Fifth Corps. Longstreet is on Hill's right, facing Porter's left flank. Jackson, who has at last arrived, is not yet in position, but he will face Porter's right flank. D.H. Hill's division is to swoop to the back of Porter's defensive line and attack from the rear. Lee withholds his main attack to allow the division commanders to line their men in place.

It is nearing two p.m., when A.P. Hill's bruised and bloodied troops are ordered by General Lee to initiate the all-out battle. Sergeant Baldwin and the men of Company K, 110th Virginia Infantry, are among the troops of A.P. Hill's division. Hill's troops have been resting in a wooded area out of sight of Porter's soldiers, waiting for their orders to attack. They, without a second thought, unhesitatingly charge from their wooded shelter with company banners flying, bugles blowing and drums rolling. They move at double quick, screaming their now famous Rebel yell. They face nearly a quarter of a mile of open fields in front of them. Their advance is quick, almost too quick, and without an ounce of caution. Porter's well-trained and well-hidden soldiers let them come. His sharpshooters patiently wait. They remain calm, rifles held at the ready position, waiting for the precise moment. And then, in a split second, and almost in unison, Porter's troops unleash a withering, devastating and deadly barrage of musket, rifle and artillery fire directly into the charging line of Confederates. Bodies are broken and bloodied, they are ripped, mangled, and torn as the weapons of war do their devastating duty. Death comes instantly to hundreds of men, others die a slow death in the hot, dry afternoon sun. The slow-flowing waters of Boatswain Creek become blood red.

Undaunted, the Confederates push onward, fallen men replaced by others, moving toward their Northern enemy. Onward they push in unending columns, onward toward the Yankee soldiers who continue to unleash a deadly reception of fire power on their unwelcome, but hard charging Southern brothers. The Confederate situation is, at best, precarious. They are facing a formidable enemy: an enemy of some thirty-five thousand soldiers. Their Union enemy, many of whom are in manmade rifle pits holding high ground and others that are protected by natural fortifications, watch and wait. Into these formidable and treacherous surroundings Sergeant Baldwin and his men of Company K press forward.

Sergeant Baldwin, as usual, is unruffled and unfazed by the intenseness of the deadly battle. His company is nearly across the open field. In another hundred yards, they will reach cover. Yankee sharpshooters are wreaking havoc on his company. Some of his men are dead or wounded. Neither he nor Robbie has received a scratch.

The old Sergeant shouts to his men, "Keep as low to the ground as possible and move as fast as ya can. We have less than a hundred yards to go. See that ravine just to the left of us? Thar's whar we're headin'."

They move as fast as possible and leap into the ravine without another casualty. The men are exhausted, safely in the protection of the cavernous hole that nature has provided, gasping for breath and thankful to be safe from the Yankee firepower.

"OK, men," the old Sergeant bellows, "we ain't got no time to lay around heah in luxury when thar's a war goin' on. Get yerselves up on the rim of this ravine and pick them Yankee sharpshooters off. Y'all are ole' country boys, ceptin' Robbie, an' ye sure otta know how ta shoot them Yankees. Now get yerselves up thar an' pick 'em off. We gotta get after them 'cause they ain't comin' to us."

The ferocity of the battle does not lessen. The Rebels keep a steady pressure on the Union defensive position. The awesome sounds of battle, the thunderous roar of cannons, and the sharp crack of small arms fire echoes from horizon to horizon. A.P. Hill's luck has not improved. His division bore the brunt of yesterday's battle at Beaver Dam Creek, and it is his division that bears the brunt of today's battle at Gaines Mill. The enemy is to the left of them as far as the eye can see, and to the right of them as far as the ear can hear. Casualties are spread across the land in front of them, and across the land behind them.

They wait for the blazing hot sun to scorch the last breath of life from their unresisting bodies. Moans and groans are barely audible. Their cries, their pleading for relief from the boiling hot sun, go unanswered. Their dried, parched lips are unable to speak. Death is cruel. It lingers teasingly, it beckons threateningly, then it conquers. Of such are the wages of war.

Duty again calls to those that have escaped the clutches of death. One last surge against the Union defenses must be made. One last ditch hope, one last valiant effort, one final attempt at victory. Sergeant Baldwin jumps to his feet, purposely and fearlessly exposing himself to the enemy and their murderous weapons of war. "Alright men, are we goin' to win or are we goin' to lose this battle? We ain't gonna win it layin' here clutchin' to this low ground like cowards.

"We ain't never gonna bust thar line of defense if'n we don't try. Let's put all we got into this an' attack 'em head on."

Bullets whiz by, around and over the old Sergeant as he speaks, as he challenges and chastises his men, but not one bullet pierces his skin. "Ah say, let's go - let's do it," as he turns to face the enemy and leads the attack on the double quick. All of his men fall in with him. The bugle sounds and the Rebels move forward in a mighty human surge. It is a do-or-die effort. It is after five p.m. The evening sun is low in the sky. Jackson and his Army, unfamiliar with the countryside, had once again lost their way to the battlefield. They are now, however, in their assigned position, and they are ready. Other units not yet in today's action are primed and ready to fight.

A tremendous surge of grey uniformed men moves forward against Porter's Union troops. They are greeted by murderous fire from the Yankees. The thunderous roar, the fire and the smoke belch from Yankee cannons that hurl iron balls into the on-rushing ranks of the Confederates. Limbs are severed, skulls are smashed, and torsos dissected. Then comes the sharp crack of rifle fire piercing, tearing and ripping flesh and bone of the Rebel soldiers. Even so, they rush onward, seemingly undaunted by the Union response. Porter's men have repelled attack after attack today, but now the force of the Rebel Army cannot be stopped. It is a mighty Rebel surge. The Union line at first grudgingly yields, and then it breaks. The battle continues, sometimes in vicious hand to hand combat. Lee can finally smell success.

In the midst of the ongoing battle, Robbie hears a familiar voice calling for help. It has been some time since he has heard the voice, but there is no doubt about who it is. There is extreme danger in attempting to rescue the soldier, but it is a risk that Robbie must take.

"Cover me, Sarge," he says to Sergeant Baldwin.

"Private, yer takin' a mighty big chance goin' out on that battlefield now. It's about as dangerous as it's been all day."

"I know, Sarge, but it's something I must do."

"Is it a friend of your'n?"

"It is someone I know from the past; someone I must help."

"Want me to go with ye, Robbie?"

"Yes, Sir. You can provide cover for us. You just keep a close eye on matters."

"As you wish."

Bullets and minie balls are speeding and spinning wildly a few inches above Robbie's and Sarge's prostrate bodies as they creep slowly along the ground. They move as best they can toward the sound of the pleading voice calling for help.

"I'm on the way," Robbie responds, "just stay calm, but keep calling so I can find you."

The ground is strewn with bodies, silent bodies, as Robbie and the Sergeant inch their way toward the wounded soldier.

"I'm almost there," Robbie calls as he recognizes movement by one of the bodies in a cluster of apparently dead men.

Robbie stretches forward, touches the blood-stained body of the man he has come to rescue. "Can you tell me where your injuries are?" he asks the wounded man.

"It's my legs. I can't move them. Are they still there?"

Robbie checks the young man over. Both legs are there, but they appear to be broken and twisted. There was a great deal of blood, but the bleeding has stopped.

"Yes, both legs are there, but they are badly damaged. Can you feel the pressure of my hand as I press your legs?"

"No, Sir, I can't feel a thing."

"OK, try to relax as best you can. I'm going to get you back to safety. Back where you can get medical attention. You may experience some pain."

The wounded man studies Robbie's face and his voice, then speaks. "You are not a Southerner are you?"

"No, I am from up North. From New York."

"But you're wearing a Confederate uniform."

"Yes. I am in the Confederate Army."

The wounded man studies Robbie's facial features. "Do you know me? I seem to recognize something about you, but I can't figure it out."

"Yes," Robbie replies, "I recognized your voice when you called for help, so I came to help you."

"Then we have met before?"

"Yes, we have met before; just one time."

"And you remember it?"

"Yes."

"Sir, may I ask where we met and under what circumstances?"

"We were students at the University of Virginia. We met on a path I was taking home one night during the trial of John Brown. There was an altercation."

The wounded soldier again looks closely and sadly at Robbie. "You are the Yankee student. The one we beat nearly to death, aren't you?"

"Yes, I am the one."

"And you have risked your life to save me?"

"Yes, I felt it my Christian duty to do so."

"Can you forgive me?"

"Yes. I did that two years ago, soon after it happened. It's not important."

Tears well in the eyes of the wounded man. "Is there anything. . .anything at all that I can do for you?"

Robbie thinks for a moment. "Yes, there is one thing. When this wretched wicked war is over, forgive your enemies, all of them. When that is done by all of us, true peace will come between North and South and we will again be one nation under God."

"I shall not forget. Seeking forgiveness and forgiving others - that is from the Holy Scriptures, isn't it?"

"Yes, it is mentioned in many scripture verses."

"What is your name, friend?" the wounded soldier asks.

"Robbie Holcomb. I remember you only as 'Big Guy.'"

After a pause, "Big Guy" answers. "My name is John Monroe. I shall never forget your name, Robbie Holcomb, nor will I ever forget your forgiveness and your kindness in rescuing me, even though I had wronged you. Perhaps, Robbie, we shall meet again."

"Perhaps so and good luck to you, John Monroe. May your injuries heal quickly."

The old Sergeant listens to the conversation between the two young men. He sits silently for some time. After the medics take John Monroe away, Sergeant Baldwin looks at Robbie. "You, Robbie Holcomb, are the most amazin' person 'ah have ever met. You are too good to be in a war."

"Sarge, we are all too good to be in a war."

"But Robbie, how can ye forgive ah man that almost kilt ye?"

"Well Sarge, at first it wasn't easy. But I knew it was the right thing to do. It had to be done. So I did it. It's kind of like this war that we are in now. Here we are, all Americans fighting one another. But one day it will be over and we will reunite. We will be a nation of one people again."

"Ye don't think thar will be two countries - a Confederate and a Union?"

"I don't think so, Sarge."

The old Sergeant thinks for a time before responding, "Well, Private, it's gonna take a lot of forgivin'."

"Yes, it is, Sarge."

"Robbie, do ye remember when ye tole that Bible story about turnin' the other cheek - is that how it's gotta be?"

"Sarge, that's exactly how it's going to be."

"Well, I'll be. An all this fightin' and then ever'one gets along together?"

"Yes, Sarge, that's the way it's going to be."

With the breaks in its defense line, the entire federal resistance is crumbling and retreating. The pursuit by the Rebels is vigorous, resulting in many deaths on both sides of the battle. The smoke and dust of battle obscures the late evening sun. Men, both North and South, fight tooth and nail for their cause, but today's victory goes to Lee. It is a costly victory for the South, nearly 9,000 casualties. For the North, the loss is a bitter pill to swallow. They lose the battle and nearly 7,000 men.

The setting sun and the darkness of night bring an end to the battle of Gaines Mill. The night, however, cannot end the suffering of the wounded left helpless on the field of battle, nor can the cries of the suffering be silenced by the night.

Chapter Thirty-Eight

So Near But Yet So Far

The rising of the sun on Saturday morning, June twenty-eighth, sheds first light on the appalling aftermath of yesterday's horrible battle at Gaines Mill. It is a scene of indescribable death, of unaccountable devastation. Bodies of thousands of Northern and Southern warriors lay motionless among abandoned and destroyed instruments and weapons of war. They are scattered over many acres of once peaceable and productive ground. The land is bloodied. It is now silent. Young men in the prime of life, and old men nearing their twilight years are distinguishable in death only by the grey or blue color of their uniforms. Others lay helpless, they linger near death. They lie on the soil where yesterday they fought so valiantly. They were then strangers and enemies of a now divided nation. Today the Confederate dead and the Union dead rest together in silence, in eternal peace. There is no hate, no anger among the surviving casualties. There is a brotherly peace, a hallowed peace among the near dead on the war-torn battleground. The horrors of war are everywhere.

There is an occasional moan, a hushed cry for help from those who are barely living, from those who remain helpless on yesterday's field of battle. But there is no help, there is no comfort or relief, except for death; a death that slowly conquers. For the severely wounded, it is an agonizing wait. For them there is no tomorrow. Their final resting place, a hurriedly-dug, shallow grave. Soldiers of the North and soldiers of the South frequently share the same grave on the field where they have fallen. There are no enemies in death.

For the able-bodied survivors, for those men who are untouched by sword or bullet, there is little time to mourn the death of a fallen comrade. The war must go on. The warriors, the foot soldiers, are the primary instruments of war. They are called to fight battles, to fight wars. Like death and destruction, the foot soldier is merely a product of battles. Death is not welcomed, but it is ever present, ever expected. Death will conquer.

General Lee rides out to the now silent battleground. He dismounts, removes his hat, and stands solemnly next to his horse. He slowly views yesterday's battle scene. He winces, but he does not speak. He is well aware of the awesome cost of war, the loss of human life, the heartache of families back home when the news reaches them.

Unaware of Lee's presence on the battlefield, young Robbie Holcomb, some hundred or so yards away from Lee, stands silently for several minutes surveying the catastrophic human slaughter. Bugle in hand, he raises the instrument to his lips, and standing straight as an arrow, he plays a variation of "Scott Tattoo," the familiar Army bugle command announcing lights out for the night. It is also played as a salute in honor of fallen comrades.

Lee is touched by the young man's humility and compassion. He mounts his horse and rides to where Robbie is standing. "Soldier, that was a wonderful and solemn tribute to the brave men who have sacrificed everything for their country."

Recognizing the General, Robbie snaps to attention and salutes. "Thank you, General Lee, Sir."

"What's your name, Soldier?"

"Holcomb, Sir - Robbie Holcomb."

"You are the bugler who rode with General Stuart on his ride around Richmond?"

"Yes, Sir, I am."

"And you are back with your own unit now?"

"Yes, Sir, I am."

"Good. And by the way, you are every bit as good a bugler as the General said you were. I recognize the variations and renditions you have made to modify 'Scott Tattoo' for this occasion. It is very appropriate. Good luck to you, Soldier." The General spurs his horse and rides away.

"And good luck to you, General Lee," Robbie shouts.

Lee is cognizant of the needs of his sleep-starved, battle-weary men of his fatigued Army, yet aware that they must press onward to again challenge their Northern adversary. Convinced that victory is within his grasp, that the winds of war often change direction, he is certain that those winds have changed, that they are now favoring his Army. Certain that he and his Army have had much to do with the new shift in the direction of the winds of war, he must seize the opportunity while it is his. The winds may again twist and turn and coil and strike in another direction.

General McClellan, Lee's chief adversary and the Union's top general in the Peninsula campaign, also believes what General Lee believes; that the winds of war have turned in Lee's favor. Unlike Lee, who has taken the bull of destiny by its horns and has set a course of aggressive action for his Army, McClellan has done just the opposite. He has now taken a passive, defensive stance. He has abandoned his plans, his high hopes of capturing Richmond. His glorious plans for the demise of the Confederate States of America have vanished. His dream, his vision of leading his victorious and beloved Army into a defeated and subdued Confederate capital city and accepting the surrender of the Confederacy and its Army from President Davis and General Lee is ended. His hopes and dreams of a great Union victory are changing to an inglorious nightmarish finish. All is for naught.

McClellan's primary and sole objective is now to save his beloved Army from defeat, from annihilation. His fears are overwhelming. From his headquarters at Savage's Station, early in the morning he sends a telegram to Secretary of War Stanton lamenting the Battle of Gaines Mill, where casualties of the two Armies exceeded 12,000 men.

To Edwin M. Stanton,

I now know the full history of the day [June 27]. On this side of the river - the right bank - we repulsed several very strong attacks. On the left bank our men did all that men could do, all that soldiers could accomplish - but they were overwhelmed by vastly superior numbers even after I brought my last reserves into action. The loss on both sides is terrible - I believe it will prove to be the most desperate battle of the war. The sad remnants of my men behave as men - those battalions who fought most bravely and suffered most are still in the best order. My regulars were superb and I count upon what are left to turn another battle in company with their gallant comrades of the Volunteers. Had I 20,000 or even 10,000 fresh troops to use tomorrow I could take Richmond, but I have not a man in reserve and shall be glad to cover my retreat and save the material and personnel of the Army.

If we have lost the day we have yet preserved our honor and no one need blush for the Army of the Potomac. I have lost this battle because my force was too small. I again repeat that I am not responsible for this and I say it with the earnestness of a General who feels in his heart the loss of every brave man who has been needlessly sacrificed today. I still hope to retrieve our fortunes, but to do this the Gov't must view the matter in the same earnest light that I do - you must send me very large reinforcements, and send them at once.

I shall draw back to this side of the Chickahominy and think I can withdraw all our material. Please understand that in this battle we have lost nothing but men and those the best we have.

In addition to what I have already said I only wish to say to the President that I think he is wrong, in regarding me as ungenerous when I said that my force was too weak. I merely reiterated a truth which today has been too plainly proved. I should have gained this battle with 10,000 fresh men. If at this instant I could dispose of 10,000 fresh men I could gain the victory tomorrow.

I know that a few thousand men more would have changed this battle from a defeat to a victory - as it is the Gov't must not and cannot hold me responsible for the result.

I feel too earnestly tonight - I have seen too many dead and wounded comrades to feel otherwise than that the Gov't has not sustained this Army. If you do not do so now the game is lost.

If I save this Army now I tell you plainly that I owe no thanks to you or any other persons in Washington - you have done your best to sacrifice this Army.

Secretary Stanton is awakened by one of his aides. "Mr. Secretary, I feel that it is important that you read the content of a telegram just received from General McClellan. It is of great urgency."

Secretary Stanton, after reading the telegram, hurriedly dresses. "Please arrange for a horse. I must report to Mr. Lincoln immediately."

"Sir, I have already done so. Your horse is waiting."

Lincoln is alarmed after reading the McClellan telegram. "The fear of losing the entire Army of the Potomac, an Army of nearly a hundred thousand men, is a devastating thought. Mr. Secretary, what do you make of this telegram?" Lincoln asks aloud, then continues without allowing Secretary Stanton an opportunity to speak. "I have suspected all along that General McClellan's continuous requests for additional men are more of an imagined need than a real one. I suppose I have been somewhat of a 'Doubting Thomas.'

"But we have given him additional troops on several occasions. We have given him as many additional troops as we can afford and yet keep enough troops here to defend Washington.

"As you know, I have, as you have, been doubtful that the Confederate Army around Richmond has two hundred thousand men as McClellan seems to believe. Yet we cannot afford to lose an entire Army. Not only is the thought of losing a hundred-thousand man Army distressing, it is the thought of losing all the supplies and equipment.

"If we lose our Army, we will lose this war. We will lose everything we have been fighting for. Our country, the North and South, will never be reunited. This is a devastating thought. It is unthinkable.

"If we lose our Army, the citizens of the North will be demoralized, the will to fight will fall apart. We cannot let this happen.

"We cannot be sure that McClellan is wrong about the strength of Lee's Army. We must give him the men he wants. Do you agree?"

"Mr. President, I agree with all that you have said. This is not the time to question General McClellan's request for more men."

President Lincoln replies immediately to McClellan by telegram, assuring him that the troops will be provided.

To General George B. McClellan,

Save your Army at all events. Will send re-inforcements as fast as we can...I have not said you were ungenerous for saying you needed re-inforcement. I thought you were ungenerous in assuming that I did not send them as fast as I could. I feel any misfortune to you and your Army quite as keenly as you feel it yourself. If you have had a drawn battle, or a repulse, it is the price we pay for the enemy not being in Washington. We protected Washington, and the enemy concentrated on you...

Lincoln's telegram is of little solace for the die has now been cast. The only fight that is left in McClellan is whatever fighting is forced on the Army of the Potomac by Lee's pursuing Army.

McClellan's objective is to move his Army as rapidly as it is possible to do so, to Harrison's Landing on the James River where U.S. Navy gunboats, equipped with long range artillery guns, will provide sanctuary. The powerfully armed Navy gunboats have a far greater firing range, a far deadlier capability than do the artillery capabilities of either of the opposing Armies.

McClellan, although fearing the destruction of his Army by what he erroneously believes to be a larger, better equipped Confederate Army, will nonetheless fight if and when he is compelled to do so. He is not inclined to throw in the towel and surrender. In spite of his self-inflicted fears and his tendency to over-weigh and over-estimate the military capabilities of his enemy, his Army is very capable of wreaking much havoc on its Southern foe.

There is much willingness remaining among McClellan's troops to do battle. From the division and corps commanders to the rank and file enlisted men, they are ready. General McClellan is idolized by his troops, he is respected. Should McClellan give an order to attack their Southern foe, they will, to a man, aggressively respond.

General Lee and his Army are unaware of McClellan's plans to give up the fight. Lee is anxious to strike the death blow against his Northern foe. This is what war is all about and Lee is eager to get on with it. However, he is not only uncertain where most of McClellan's Army is, he is also uncertain about McClellan's intentions. Neither Lee nor his top generals know precisely in which direction McClellan is going or to where it will lead. This they must ascertain. It is decision time.

Lee calls a council of war. All of his division leaders are summoned. "Gentlemen, I have called you together because we now have an excellent opportunity to either destroy or capture the Northern Army. Opportunities such as this do not often come, so we must take advantage of it while it is here.

"We do not know the exact location of McClellan's Army, but one thing we do know is that it is now retreating away from us. Our scouts tell us that the Yankees are moving in only one direction along the Chickahominy, and that is downriver. Nothing is moving up.

"There are signs of smoke all along the route that the Yankees seem to be taking, at least at this time. As you know, this is a clear indication that our enemies are discarding and burning whatever they cannot carry. We have also heard ammunition exploding which is apparently set afire to destroy it. A reliable sign of a retreat.

"Gentlemen, I believe that McClellan is going to make one of three decisions. First of all, he may remain somewhere along the Chickahominy attempting to protect his supply line from White House Landing. If so, he may put up another serious fight just as he has at Gaines Mill.

"His second option, as I see it, is instead of initiating another Gaines Mill-like battle, he may retreat back down the Peninsula on much the same route that he used coming up. This would allow him to use Fort Monroe as a supply base until his Army is reinforced for another attack. " T h e third option he may have in mind is to abandon the Chickahominy supply line and move his Army southward somewhere along the navigable part of the James River where his Army can be protected by Navy gunboats. As soon as McClellan shows his hand, have your men ready for the pursuit. We must destroy our enemy.

"At the moment we do not know what McClellan is going to do and he does not know what we are going to do. When McClellan moves, we will move. We are not, however, going to sit idly by twiddling our thumbs while we are waiting. We have dispatched General Stuart's cavalry and General Dick Ewell's division to ascertain what is happening at the Union's supply depot at White House Landing. We believe that it remains their major supply base. Are there any questions?"

General Magruder stands before speaking. "General Lee, will my men, my division, remain in their defensive positions to guard against any attacks by McClellan's Army to capture Richmond?" General Magruder hesitates momentarily, then continues before Lee can answer. "I fear that my small division could not withstand an all-out attack. We could hardly slow their large Army."

Lee remains silent for a moment. "General Magruder, I do not believe that McClellan is inclined to move his Army against Richmond. If he was so minded, he surely would have done so soon after we initiated our offensive action nearly a week ago. However, should he attack, I expect you and your men to do your duty in defending the city.

"McClellan, I believe, is now fighting a defensive war. His Army will fight and it will fight well when it is attacked. It is a capable Army. It is capable of rendering much harm to us, but we must prevent them from doing so. We intend to keep them off balance. Our aim is to destroy the Northern Army by aggressively attacking them.

"General Magruder, you and your men will, as needed, along with all other units of this Army, be a part of our offensive attack against McClellan's Army. Our offense will become our defense. Are there any other questions? If there are no other questions, the meeting is adjourned."

Lee is unaware that McClellan has already abandoned the supply depot at White House Landing on the Pamunkey River and that the ancestral home of Martha Custis Washington has been destroyed. He is surprised and bitter when General Stuart so informs him, yet he shows no emotion. The news, while personally disturbing, at least answers the questions of McClellan's intent. It is quite clear now that the Northern Army is headed for the security of the James River where U.S. Naval vessels, well armed with heavy artillery, will provide protection for his Army. Lee's work is now cut out for him.

The battle of the peninsula, from the perspective of the Union Army, is now clearly one of rear guard action. Their foremost purpose, plainly and simply, is one of survival. Even so, there is a great deal of fight left in them, a fight for honor and pride. There is that undying desire to win, that unyielding hope of victory that dwells in the heart and soul of every soldier. Now they must fight an unglamorous rear guard battle to allow their enormous Army and its nearly four thousand wagons, loaded with supplies of all kinds, to pass by on their way to the James River. Nearly three thousand head of beef cattle, hundreds of horses and mules, and great supplies of war materials must be moved to their new base.

Chapter Thirty-Nine

Trials and Tribulations
The Battle of Savages Station

General Lee is exasperated. It is Sunday morning, June twenty-ninth. It is not yet first light, but Lee is up and about. There is much to do. Porter's severely battered and bruised Union troops escaped from the clutches of Lee's Army at the battle of Gaines Mill; Lee and his Army have not known the precise whereabouts of either General Porter and his men or the whereabouts of General McClellan and most of his imperceptible Army.

Lee is not yet aware that McClellan's troops have abandoned their trenches facing Richmond. They have done so on McClellan's orders. Unbeknownst to Lee, the Union soldiers exited their positions during Saturday night and early Sunday morning. McClellan's Army is now in full retreat. It is something that Lee suspected might happen, but suspicions are insufficient grounds on which to move his Army. Lee is sure of one thing; McClellan's Army has gained advantage in its efforts to escape the Confederates. The Union Army has been allowed sufficient time to regroup and to reorganize their retreating Army. Although Lee knows much about McClellan, there is also much that he does not know.

He does not know McClellan's exact whereabouts. He does not know what McClellan plans to do or how he plans to do it. Until McClellan shows his hand, Lee is stymied from making an all-out move. Lee can only wait for positive signs of what McClellan intends to do. Military conflicts and battles are often a game of waiting; a game of hoping; a game of wits; a game of doing the right thing at the right time. Lee is, nonetheless, anxious to make his move.

McClellan is confident that Lee is not yet aware of his plan of escape. Although he is fearful of engaging Lee's Army, McClellan will not hesitate to fight if he is pressed. He will fight, and he will fight well. He remains in command of his Army. He will exercise every reasonable caution to prevent the Confederates from assailing his retreating Army. He will attempt to repel every challenge from Lee as his Army continues its exodus from the gates of Richmond, moving toward the safe haven of the U.S. Naval gunboats at Harrison's Landing on the James River.

Lee and his troops are antsy. He and his generals impatiently await the tell-tale signs of movement by their enemy. Their wait is not long coming. Smoke and dust columns are rising skyward in the early morning light. It is a sure sign that the enemy is already on the move. They are burning and destroying supplies and equipment that cannot be carried or transported during the hurriedly planned retreat. The rising dust in the direction of the James River is a sure indication that great numbers of men are hurriedly on the march. Then comes word from General Stuart that McClellan has vacated his main supply depot at White House Landing on the York and Pamunkey Rivers. The clinching factor is knowing that the Yankees have abandoned their trenches in front of Richmond.

"Gentlemen," Lee announces jubilantly, "McClellan's secret is no longer a well-kept one. His secret is now our shared secret. We have much to do and a short time in which to do it."

Lee has not been completely idle while waiting for McClellan to make his move. He anticipates some of what he believes McClellan will do and he dispatches General Magruder and his division to proceed toward the Union railroad depot at Savages Station. Lee presumes that McClellan must be moving supplies by the Richmond and York River Railroad from White House Landing to Savages Station since he is abandoning the White House Landing supply facility. He advises Magruder to move forward to his destination with the utmost speed and to impede the movement of the Yankee troops as they retreat with their equipment and supplies toward their new camp on the James River.

"Your primary purpose is to force our enemy to stand and fight. This will allow us time to move the rest of our Army in position to annihilate the Northern Army. It is your opportunity and the opportunity of your soldiers to step forward for the Confederacy. You must delay their forward progress. Stop them or slow them."

General Jackson and his troops, including D.H. Hill and his men, are assigned to Magruder's left. General Huger's division is assigned to Magruder's right flank. General Longstreet and A.P. Hill are hurried off to White Oak Swamp, some five or six miles away, to block McClellan's access to the bridges across the swamp. Their success in this mission is dependent on the success of Generals Magruder, Huger and Jackson.

Magruder's division is expected to make first contact with the enemy. He requests a unit of combat-experienced soldiers and is assigned Sergeant Baldwin and his men. Sergeant Baldwin is again ready for a fight. He thrives on combat encounters. He is delighted to be among the first troops to engage the enemy. "The sooner the better," he tells his troops.

Magruder is nervous. He moves his men cautiously forward. He learns that his left flank is unprotected, that Jackson and his troops are delayed in crossing the Chickahominy River. He then learns that Huger's division is not directly to his right, that it is separated by a sizable distance. Magruder further slows the advance of his men. They are now moving at a snail's pace. Beads of sweat stream down his face, not from the smothering morning heat, but from the precarious military circumstances that he perceives himself to be in. He is fearful of an attack from the Union Army, a highly unlikely tactic by the rear guard of a retreating Army. However, his primary mission is to quickly engage the enemy, to disrupt their organized retreat, to delay it. Lee's plan is to destroy or capture the Union Army while it is spread in a long, slim, nearly defenseless line of retreat.

Sergeant Baldwin's patience is wearing thin. He is itching for a fight. He has been in many combat situations. He does not panic under hostile enemy fire. His long military career has taught him how to act and react in hostile situations and he has taught his men how to do likewise. The old Sergeant recognizes that the delay in approaching Savages Station is not caused by the enemy, but it is due to the indecision of General Magruder.

Thick, black smoke rising skyward, directly in their front, in the direction of the orchard and Savages Station, is clear and convincing evidence that the retreating Union Army is on the move eastward towards the James River. Sergeant Baldwin fumes silently that Magruder's reluctance to quickly engage the enemy is counter-productive to General Lee's orders to forestall the retreat of McClellan's Army. He suffers in silence. A noncommissioned officer does not challenge the orders of an officer. Not unless he is anxious to be court-martialled.

Nevertheless, the old Sergeant's instincts tell him that a confrontation with their Northern enemy is drawing near. "Men, keep yer eyes and ears open. Be alert. We are about to come face to face with them Yankees again. I kin feel it in my bones. Don't ye see that Yankee smoke and dust up ahead? Check yer weapons, men. Ye see that orchard off in the distance? It looks ta me like a mighty good place ta run into a red-hot battle; a little welcome party planned fer us by them Yankees. I figure they ain't gonna be too friendly with us, so ye better get them bayonets fixed on yer rifles. Private Holcomb, get ready to sound th' call to charge."

"Yes, Sir, Sergeant Baldwin," Robbie responds as his bugle moves toward his lips.

"Not yet, Private, not yet," Sarge cautions.

The road forward is gritty. The rising sun bores heavily upon them. Dust, stirred by the pounding feet of the marching men, is as thick as an early morning fog. They gag and cough. Hot, tired and dusty, they trudge on. Sergeant Baldwin sends a message to General Magruder that they are about to meet their enemy face to face. The General orders Baldwin and his men forward to the front of the column.

"Sergeant Baldwin, I respect your opinion and I find myself in complete agreement with you. I have been concerned this entire morning that we might be attacked at any moment. We are vastly outnumbered by McClellan's troops and our flanks, left and right, are unprotected. We are definitely between the devil and the deep blue sea. I can see no way out of our situation.

"Sergeant Baldwin, take your men, those assigned to you, and I will give you a hundred or so volunteers from my division. Go see if you can make something out of the situation we are in. The remainder of the division will remain here until we hear from you."

Sergeant Baldwin acknowledges his orders. He salutes General Magruder, then turns toward his troops. "We are goin' to move ahead of the division - do some scoutin' - over toward the peach orchard. Keep alert and be prepared. We're nearly a mile from Savages Station. It is now 11:00 a.m., an' we shoulda already been there, but we're not. Keep as quiet as possible an' follow me."

They are near the orchard when a volley of shots from Yankee troops under the command of General Bull Sumner greets them.

"Alright, men," the old Sergeant bellows. "This is it. Private Holcomb, sound the call to charge."

The bugle rises to his lips, the charge sounds, and the troops move forward on the double quick. The battle rages hot and heavy. General Magruder sends fresh troops to replace the dead and wounded. The fighting is brisk and brutal. There is loss of life among friend and foe. Yankee resistance stiffens. The Rebel advance of Sergeant Baldwin and his men is stopped cold. They are pinned down, unable to move forward. "Sumptin's gotta be dun if'n wer gonna win this here skirmish and this here war," the old Sergeant says. Looking at Robbie he asks, "Ye reckon ye kin crawl forward up thar an' see what's goin' on? See if we kin out flank 'em - cut 'em off from retreatin' - then we kin tear into 'em an destroy 'em. We gotta press 'em, disrupt 'em, and annihilate 'em."

As Robbie crawls forward, he feels an awful nausea in the pit of his stomach that comes from too much combat - from witnessing too much suffering, too much death.

"When will it end," he mumbles, hardly above a whisper. "I wish all of us could quit this useless war. I hope it ends soon and we can all go home."

He now can see the Yankee troops plainly, knows their position. He retraces his route back to Sergeant Baldwin. They flank their adversary; the fight resumes. Then it is all over. It ends almost mysteriously, as quickly as it started. Union General Sumner withdraws his troops. Sumner has accomplished the delaying actions that he intended. The Yankees retreat back to Savages Station pursued by the Rebels.

General Magruder, still fearful of his unprotected flanks, delays attacking the Union's rear guard. He continues to dilly-dally as the escaping Army of General McClellan retreats on, toward its safe haven at Harrison's Landing. It is evident that there is much confusion around Savages Station. There are piles upon piles of Union supplies around and near the train station. Barrels and boxes of food, supplies, and clothing. Trains loaded with ammunition and all kinds of military supplies are set afire by the retreating Yankees and set off down the tracks, absent of engineers or other operators, to wreck or explode along the way.

Even so, General Magruder and his Army remain motionless. Orders arrive from General Lee to attack. Some time later, Magruder orders an attack using barely a third of his soldiers. Although his men fight gallantly, it is too little too late. The Union retreat is not impeded and McClellan's troops move onward. The battle ends near dark in a violent rainstorm.

Lee, totally disappointed in Magruder's performance and the results, sends him a mild rebuke. "I regret very much that you have made so little progress today in pursuit of the enemy. In order to reap the fruits of our victory, the pursuit should be most vigorous. I must urge you, again, to press on his rear rapidly and steadily. We must lose no more time or he will escape us entirely."

Chapter Forty

A Missed Opportunity
The Battle of White Oak Swamp and Glendale

Monday morning June thirtieth is one of mixed emotions, of missed opportunities and failed accomplishments for Lee and his Army. It is not that he has personally failed or that his well-conceived battle plans were flawed. It is simply a matter of inadequate execution by his subordinate generals that were charged with the responsibilities of carrying those plans to their fulfillment. Yesterday was Lee's greatest opportunity to smash McClellan's Army. General Magruder was ordered to do just that. He was ordered to speedily and aggressively pursue McClellan's Army at or near Savages Station and to furiously engage the enemy in combat. Magruder's colossal failure yesterday to speedily move against the retreating Yankees, his failure to slow their escape, is a bitter disappointment to Lee.

Nor were Magruder's military indiscretions the only setback that Lee suffered yesterday. The fabled Stonewall Jackson, a legend throughout the South, again seemed asleep in the saddle. He lazied the day away with his men building bridges rather than fording the river as McClellan and his Army moved closer to their safe haven on the James, nearly free of molestation from Lee's Army.

Nevertheless, Lee's faith, his intent in destroying McClellan's Army remains strong. It is his top priority. He is confident that his Army is capable of achieving this goal. He believes that they are again in a position to do it. It may be their last opportunity. A coordinated effort is nonetheless required by his entire Army. Every officer and every enlisted man must step forward and do his duty. This is the message that Lee sends to his troops. The time that it must be done is now. The Union Army, McClellan's Army, remains vulnerable, very vulnerable, as it is stretched out for miles and miles in a long, thin line, moving in single file along a mostly one-lane, narrow, dusty, or sometimes muddy, road.

McClellan is not oblivious to his Army's vulnerability. Nevertheless, his is not a defenseless Army. He, too, has great leadership in command of his troops. Men such as Generals Samuel Heintzelman, Philip Kearny, Erasmus Keyes, Fitz John Porter, Joe Hooker, and others. These men and the troops they command are more than willing to fight. Some, like their Southern counterparts, relish the idea of a good, hard-fought battle.

Having survived the Battle of Savages Station with minor casualties, the Union Army destroys as much of their supplies as possible before marching off toward White Oak Swamp. They do not want to leave anything that the Rebels can use. They continue their exodus toward the James River. Their rear guard troops fall in behind them, leaving their wounded at the mercy of the slow, cautious Southern Army in pursuit.

Soldiers from the two opposing Armies, weary to the point of exhaustion from the long days of marching and from doing battle with one another in the hot sun and the heavy rains, must now endure a night-time march toward White Oak Swamp, some five or so miles away. The soldiers from the North do so in hope of safe passage across the swamp and into the sanctuary of nearby Harrison's Landing. Soldiers from the South do so in hopes of impeding and preventing the Northern soldiers from reaching the safety of the Naval gun boats at Harrison's Landing. Both Armies will arrive late at night or early morning near White Oak Swamp and the nearby village of Glendale. Tomorrow will come all too soon for the battle-weary men. Of such is the life of combat soldiers in their day-to-day struggles in a war they know little about and understand even less.

Sergeant Baldwin and his Virginia infantry unit are released from Magruder's division and set out in a hard-driving rain toward White Oak Swamp to reunite with Daniel Harvey Hill's division. Because of a faulty map and the darkness and the rain, they stray off course. When the weather clears, the old Sergeant studies the stars, then cautions his men, "I'm kinda certain that we need to go in another direction. Let's stick close togetha an' keep as quiet as possible. We don' wanna tangle with them Yankees here in the dark, and we don' know nothin' 'bout this area. We might be shootin' each other."

"You're right about that, Sarge," says Robbie, then he adds, "We'll follow you wherever you go and do whatever you tell us to do. We have been in battle after battle for almost a week. We have been in one bad situation after the other, and I don't believe that any of us who are here now ever believed that we would be alive today. Sarge, we have confidence in you. Any lack of confidence is with our generals who seem to never get the job done."

Another soldier speaks. "Yes Sir, Sarge, that's true. But don't any 'a ye ferget about that good luck, or divine providence, or whatever it is that protects Robbie. Ye have seen it yerself. Guys fallin' all around him, even bullets rippin' his clothes, yet none of 'em ever hits him. How else ye gonna figger that out, 'ceptin' that the Good Lord is lookin' after 'em?"

"Yer shore right 'bout that," another soldier adds in a solemn and serious voice. Then a big smile crosses his face and he adds jokingly, "Well, when the Good Lord is watchin' over Robbie, he's shore hearin' a mess a cussin' from Sergeant Baldwin. Now ain't that so?"

The old Sergeant, grinning broadly, teeth flashing in the moonlight, nods his head in agreement, then adds, "I'm so mean, ah cuss them bullets away. My cussin' is so hot it melts them bullets 'fore they kin get to us. I told ye that before."

The men laugh heartily and the old Sergeant cautions them to be quiet. "Them Yankees may be in this here place, er someplace nearby. We ain't too far now from where we otta be. We better rest here 'til daybreak, then we kin move out. We kin better figger out where we want to go when we kin see what we're doin'. Robbie, ye take the first watch so as none o' them Yankees slips in here an' slits our throats while we're sleepin'."

The sound of cannon fire off in the distance awakens the men late in the morning. They have overslept. The sun is high in the eastern sky. Sergeant Baldwin is angry but simmers down when he learns that someone has been awake and on guard duty at all times. The men moan and groan, even though they are better rested from the extra hours of sleep they have been afforded. Even so, their bodies ache from the long hot days of battle, from the physical and mental strains they have endured, and the long nights of marching off to the site of the next day's battle. The little sleep that they have had has been on the hard, dry ground or the soft, wet soil, often for what seems to last only an hour or two. Then they are on the move again.

They scramble hurriedly to get moving this morning under the watchful eye and the sharp tongue of Sergeant Baldwin. They, as usual, slept fully dressed and are ready to move out after a breakfast of hard tack biscuits and lukewarm coffee.

"Let's go, men. We've another battle ta fight today," the old Sergeant announces as they march away.

Little damage has been inflicted on the Northern enemy since the battle of Gaines Mill. To be sure, there have been casualties on both sides. But yesterday's battle in and around Savages Station, if Lee's orders had been adequately followed by those generals charged with their executions, could have resulted in a resounding Southern success. This, Lee knows as does his adversary, George McClellan. But Lee's orders were not followed, and it was not a success.

It is not that Lee expected the total defeat of the Union Army at Savages Station. That was not possible. What he expected, what he wanted, was that considerable damage be done to the Yankee Army, that their retreat toward the James River be slowed or stopped temporarily. If it had been done, that would have allowed Lee sufficient time to march the remainder of his Army to White Oak Swamp and to be in a position to annihilate the Yankees when they arrived. But Lee's plans of yesterday were not carried out. It is now a new day and new plans are in order.

Both Lee and McClellan know that the Yankee Army must cross White Oak Swamp to reach Harrison's Landing. It is the only route of escape. The stakes are high for both Armies, and the first to reach their goal will have a decided advantage.

General McClellan is anxious to keep his Union Army on the move. He is every bit as aware as is Lee of his Army's vulnerability to attack while it is spread out in its long trail of wagons and men. He has taken every precaution possible to assure a successful and safe move of his Army to its new base on the James. He is well aware that the most critical part of the move will be crossing White Oak Swamp. He is cautious. He fully expects a full-fledged battle with Lee's Army and he will do so if necessary.

McClellan, as he and the forward units of his Army draw near to White Oak Swamp, sends couriers forward to ascertain the whereabouts of Lee's waiting Army. The couriers return, reporting no sightings of enemy troops. Again, he sends troops forward to locate the position of Lee's Army. "I am sure that the Confederates are nearby. We do not want to be surprised, we do not want to walk into an ambush. Take more couriers with you. I now know how Lee thinks, how he reacts. I have learned much about Lee since he became the commanding general of the Confederate Army.

"I misjudged him as timid and passive. I misjudged his leadership qualities and his abilities. I shall not make that mistake again.

"This is where I would attack our Army, if I was the commander of the Confederate Army and this is where Lee is going to attack.

"Go again and do your duty. This time, complete your mission of surveillance. I must know precisely where Lee and his Army are waiting."

Again, McClellan's couriers go forth on their mission and again they return with negative results. "Saddle my horse," McClellan orders his aide. And he rides forward with his couriers and his chief scouts, but no signs are found of Lee or his Army. As the men return along the route from which they had come, a silence falls over them. General McClellan, deep in thought, breaks the silence.

"Soldiers of the Army of the Potomac, you have performed your task well, and I commend you. Make no mistake, however, someone on the Confederate side of this war has blundered - but rest assured, it is not Robert E. Lee."

The forward units of McClellan's Northern Army successfully reach White Oak Swamp well before the arrival of Lee's Army. McClellan strives to move as much of his Army across the swamp as expeditiously as it is possible to do so. A goodly number of wagons, horses, mules, cattle and troops pass over the swamp. The pursuing Rebels are not yet close enough to impede the Union Army's progress, but they are dangerously near.

Lee is exasperated over the failed opportunities of the past five days, opportunities that should have brought success to his Army and to the Confederacy. Lee is well aware that this may be his final opportunity to crush McClellan's Army.

Lee rides off toward Savages Station where he finds Generals Magruder and Jackson conversing.

"Gentlemen," Lee announces, "today is the day that we must succeed. I fear that it will be our last chance to do so before McClellan reaches the safety of the Navy's protection. I want to be sure that each of you understand what you are to do.

"General Magruder, you and General Huger are to attack the Yankees from the east, hitting their exposed flank. I have sent a courier to inform General Huger."

General Lee then turns to Jackson. "General Jackson, you and your men and General D.H. Hill's division will attack McClellan's rear guard units and push them quick and hard. When I leave here I am going to ride back to the village of Glendale where I will meet with Generals Longstreet and A.P. Hill. They will hit McClellan's lead units. They are aware of their responsibilities. Longstreet and A.P. Hill will delay their attack until they hear firing from the two of you. General Magruder, do you understand your orders?"

"Yes Sir, I do."

"Good. You are to start the actions as soon as your men are in position. The earlier you start the fight, the better it will be."

"Yes Sir, General Lee. I understand."

Then turning to General Jackson, Lee gives him identical instructions. "Are my orders clear, General Jackson?"

"They are, Sir," Jackson replies.

Then with the toe of his boot, Jackson scratches a triangle shape in the dry dirt, raises his foot and stomps the triangle, twisting the heel of his boot as he does so, indicating that Lee's three-sided attack against McClellan's Army will destroy it.

"General Lee," Jackson continues, "we have got him; we have got McClellan exactly where we want him."

"I hope you are right, General Jackson. We must all do our part to ensure victory."

The generals salute, Lee mounts his horse and rides away in the direction of Glendale.

Sergeant Baldwin and his company of Virginians are also headed in the direction of Glendale and White Oak Swamp. The day is hot, miserably hot. They have encountered every obstacle that nature has to offer. Gnats, mosquitoes, and other flying insects. They have encountered snakes of every kind and color. Birds and animals, with wild and mysterious sounds and calls scatter before them. They trudge through marshes, they walk on solid earth. They encounter briar patches and thick forests. Their expected short march turns into unexpected hours. The sun is directly overhead and they know it is chow time. They do not stop. They listen for the sounds of the battle that they are well aware should be in progress. There are no battle sounds. They wonder if they are going in the wrong direction, but the position of the sun in the sky verifies that they are not lost.

Some distance away Lee is conversing with Generals Longstreet and A.P. Hill. The three generals are awaiting the same sounds of war that Sergeant Baldwin and his men are listening for, the sounds of infantry troops engaged in battle. By mid afternoon, the first rumblings of war are heard by the three generals - sounds that should have been heard by eight o'clock in the morning. The sounds of artillery fire are from the direction of where General Huger should be. Even so, there are no sounds of infantry. General Lee, by now, is extremely agitated for he knows that the trap to crush McClellan's Army has been slow to spring. He again has hopes, albeit belated hopes. The rumbling of war, the hoped for sounds of war subsides, then fades away. Lee's hopes fall with the silenced, muted sounds of artillery bombardment. There are no sounds, no signs of infantry attacking.

Again, the sounds of artillery fire rise and Lee's hopes are renewed. He mutters to himself, "Can there be hope? Can there yet be hope?" He rides off in the direction of the sound of the artillery. It is apparent that Huger, Magruder and Jackson have failed to engage their infantry. The artillery fire alone will not save the day. Lee rides back toward Longstreet and A.P. Hill's division. He meets Sergeant Baldwin and his Virginia soldiers who have arrived for action. Lee escorts them to Longstreet.

"I have not found any signs of infantry activity from our other divisions, but I found these men on my way back. They are anxious to join the fight. Sergeant Baldwin is in charge of these men. One of them I personally met before on the Gaines Mill battleground the morning after the battle. He is a fine young bugler. He played a rendition of 'Lights Out' in honor of the dead soldiers on the field that day. He was also the bugler for General Stuart when he rode around Richmond some weeks ago."

"General Lee, we can always use a good bugler and a few good infantry men," Longstreet replies.

Lee again turns toward Longstreet. "It is nearly five o'clock. We have waited the entire day for action from our other generals. It has not come. Perhaps if we initiate the action they will join the fray. Our opportunities of inflicting harm to McClellan's Army are slipping away. Are you ready to carry the charge, General Longstreet?"

"I am ready, General Lee."

"And we are ready to join you, General Longstreet," Sergeant Baldwin shouts, then salutes the two generals.

Turning toward Robbie, General Lee beckons to him, then speaks. "Young man, sound the call to charge, the call to attack on the double quick."

"Yes, Sir," Robbie responds with an exuberant salute. He turns and sounds the bugle calls. It is quickly followed with the Rebel yell that echoes across White Oak Swamp as hundreds upon hundreds of Rebel infantrymen move hurriedly and determinedly toward their Yankee enemies. The battle is under way.

The Rebels rush forward, while bayonets at the ready send flashes of the late afternoon sunlight into the eyes of their Yankee foes. Through the bog and the brush, through the swamp and the sweat, they move forward to face and fight their enemy. Volley after volley of minie balls and bullets are fired by the opposing foes. Men on both sides of the lines of battle drop lifeless or wounded to be swallowed by the stagnant waters of White Oak Swamp. Replacements from both Armies rush forward to fill the empty places of their fallen comrades.

Initially, the Yankee line of defense bends, then breaks as the Rebels rush onward. The Yankees regroup and move forward, recapturing the ground they had lost. The fight continues, see-sawing back and forth. Each side, the blue and the grey, gain ground, then give ground. The battle is savagely fought, neither side yielding to the other. Men fighting one another in hand-to-hand combat, fighting to the death, bayonet-to-bayonet, toe-to-toe, and eyeball-to-eyeball. Rifle butts become the clubs of war in the free-for-all battle, crushing flesh and bone in a never-give-up battle. The useless and near worthless ground, and the stagnant and disease-infested waters of White Oak Swamp are red with the blood of the South and blood of the North. The battle continues long past the light of day. The men fight until they are overcome by exhaustion, until every ounce of energy is drained from their bodies. They are nearly lifeless. They lay down their weapons of war and the blue and the grey lie down in peace. Darkness and fatigue have swallowed the day.

At day's end Lee is again dejected. Victory has again been denied him because of circumstances beyond his control. His best generals have failed him. His orders have not been followed. McClellan and his Army are on the safe side of the river. Little has changed. Lee's three-pronged battle plans had great merit. This, he knows. The trap was set, but it was not sprung. It is not the fault of Longstreet, nor is it the fault of A.P. Hill. The plan required a coordinated attack from all three sides of the triangle. It did not come from two of the sides; the sides where Magruder, Huger and Jackson were in command.

As Lee sits alone with his thoughts, an aide, unaware that Lee is fully aware of the results of the battle, enters the headquarters tent. "General Lee, may I interrupt you?"

"Yes, you may."

"Sir, I have been advised to inform you that it is likely that McClellan has escaped our attack."

Lee, always the gentleman, looks toward the aide for several seconds before speaking. He rises from his chair, his face flush with anger, but his voice perfectly controlled. He responds, "Yes, he will get away because I cannot have my orders carried out."

With that said, the anger drains from Lee's body and soul. The magnanimity of the man resurfaces and he politely dismisses the aide. Today's failures are in the past. Lee is not a fault-finder or a holier-than-thou crusader. "Tomorrow," he muses to himself, "tomorrow is another day. I must prepare for tomorrow."

Chapter Forty-One

An Ominous Engagement
The Battle of Malvern Hill

It is nearly 10:00 p.m., Monday night, June thirtieth. General Lee has been alone with his thoughts and his disappointments. What is done cannot be undone. Lee is tired, his division commanders are tired, and his entire Confederate Army is tired. They are near exhaustion. This exhaustion, this weariness is also equally shared by General McClellan and by his officers and men of his Union Army. In spite of Lee's fatigue, and that of his Army, he cannot quit. There is that profound and unfailing desire - that deeply embedded will to win - that compels him to press onward to again, one more time, to assail the retreating Yankees. That much sought-after final victory is yet possible. Lee cannot let go, he cannot abandon, his objective of a complete victory over his Northern enemies. He refuses to succumb to the physical and mental strains of the past six days of war. It is something that must be done. He must make that one final effort to defeat McClellan and his Army. It must be done and it must be done quickly. Tomorrow will be the final straw. There must be no further delays.

Lee calls his top generals together. They discuss the pros and cons associated with another battle and the opportunities and the rewards that come with success. Although enthusiasm among his leaders has waned, after much discussion and amid some dissent, they unanimously back their leader. They will pursue their fleeing enemies and attack them in the morning, Tuesday, July first.

Stonewall Jackson is to take the lead in pursuing McClellan's fleeing Army. The other divisions, except for those of Longstreet and A.P. Hill, who have borne the brunt of today's battle, are to join Jackson in pursuing the Yankee Army. Longstreet and A.P. Hill are to hold their divisions in reserve until they are needed in the ensuing battle.

While Lee is planning for tomorrow, this last day of June has brought much personal relief to Union Army General McClellan. It has been a hectic day, an uncertain day for McClellan and for his Army. Reports from the field of battle during the day were less than promising. He had feared the worst, even the possible defeat of his entire Army. He had sent a telegram to Secretary of War Stanton earlier in the day, warning him of his Army's precarious circumstances. He ends the telegram telling Secretary Stanton, "My Army has behaved superbly and has done all that men could do. If none of us escape, we shall at least have done honor to the country. I shall do my best to save the Army."

McClellan's Army did again escape from Lee, but it was due to the failure of Lee's generals to do their duty rather than because of any preventive action that McClellan had taken. His Army is now safely beyond its most dangerous and vulnerable point of attack by the pursuing Confederate enemy. His Army has been dangerously near defeat on several occasions. It is now beyond the hazards of White Oak Swamp. They are, nevertheless, not completely safe from the pursuing Southern enemy, although McClellan believes that the likelihood of another attack has greatly diminished.

McClellan believes that further attempts by Lee to attack his Army will be foolhardy. He does not, however, throw caution to the wind. In case, just in case, the Rebels continue their pursuit, McClellan's Army has prepared a well-fortified rebuke for them at Malvern Hill. It is a near perfect natural defensive position. Although Malvern Hill is not impregnable, it is a formidable obstacle, approximately three miles south of Glendale. Steep bluffs on the east and west approaches to the hill nearly eliminate an attack from these positions. The northern approach faces a gentle slope of open ground rising to a height of nearly two hundred feet. The flat land below the slope is covered with fields of ripe yellow grain, ready for harvest.

On the morning of July 1st, 1862, Malvern Hill is bristling with protective Union instruments of war, both men and machinery. Artillery pieces, nearly two hundred fifty of them, are lined hub to hub just beyond the crest of the hill, ready to belch death and destruction on the invaders from Lee's pursuing Army. Seven divisions of Union infantry, armed with the best musketry available, await any intruder of their domain along the mile and a half long hill top. The fields of harvest ripe grain sway gently to and fro in the extremely hot July breeze. Hidden in the fields of golden grain are dozens of Yankee sharpshooters awaiting the arrival of Rebel soldiers should they dare come this way. If there is to be a harvest today, it will not be the golden ripe grain that nature has provided; it will be a human harvest, a harvest of men clad in grey and of men clad in blue.

Then it happens. Clouds of dust rising skyward in the early morning light come from the direction of White Oak Swamp, a sure sign of marching troops. The Rebels are coming. They are soon visible in the not-too-distant woods just beyond Malvern Hill. At first there are dozens of them. They are the forward units. They are the observers, the information seekers. The Yankees know there are more to come. There are lots more, thousands more to come.

One Army is well positioned on Malvern Hill. The other Army is scattered in the forests and fields and valleys below. Both Armies await their orders to engage the other in mortal combat. Both are poised and confident. One is determined to prevent the other from escaping, determined to destroy it. The other Army is determined to defend itself.

Except for bombarding one another with artillery fire, the morning remains reasonably quiet. The Rebel artillery is inferior to the quality and quantity of the Union's bigger and better weaponry. The Rebel artillery is essentially silenced. Except for the continued shelling by the Yankee artillery, the morning passes with little action.

Lee is amazed at the sight of the Yankee stronghold on Malvern Hill. He recognizes that it is the most awesome military obstacle that his Army has faced during the past six days of battles. It is Lee's greatest challenge. Again, Lee converses with his commanding generals. Again there are negative opinions, but all will abide by his decisions. Other men, other generals, might hesitate to attack such an awesome foe. Others may turn away or ponder indecisively; but not Lee. He has harbored ill feelings, he has criticized his subordinate generals for lacking aggressiveness, for failing to assail the enemy during the past six days. Lee believes that had his orders been followed, they would not be facing the obstacles of today. But his orders were not followed. It is now water over the dam.

Lee does not hesitate. He does not flinch. "We will attack," he tells his generals. "If we make a coordinated attack, we should break their defensive line, just as we did at Gaines Mill. Gentlemen, I have faith in you, I have faith in this Army, and I have faith in our cause. Let us now do our duty as we have never before done. Let us complete our mission."

It is nearly mid-afternoon when the first Confederate skirmishers dash from the safety of the protective woods. They rush forward shouting their now famous Rebel Yell. The Yankee soldiers on Malvern Hill, and the sharpshooters in the grain fields below greet their Confederate enemies with a deadly salvo of musket and rifle fire. The cannons on the crest of the hill again join the action. The ground is shaking and trembling upon impact of the fearsome artillery shells. Southern soldiers are slaughtered by the hundreds. The land is covered by the dead and injured. Even so, some of the men miraculously reach the protection of gullies and ravines on the side of Malvern Hill. They can only wait for help, for support from their fellow Confederates.

It is nearly five o'clock in the afternoon when help comes from the main Confederate attack. The Southerners rush forward over the same ground, over the dead and the long suffering wounded bodies that lie in the hot sun from the earlier attack. They, too, are met by intense Yankee firepower, just as the earlier attackers were. It is a blood-stained battleground. It is a nauseating scene to even the most battle-hardened soldier. The spectacle causes even crusty old Sergeant Baldwin to wince in disbelief.

"Keep movin' men," he shouts, his voice barely audible above the sounds of the fearsome battle. "Robbie, blow that bugle. Blow it loud and clear. We need to move as fast as we can to git ahead of this artillery fire. It's cuttin' our company to pieces. The quicker we move up this hill, the safer wer' gonna be."

"Yes Sir, Sarge," Robbie responds as he signals the men to double-quick their forward progress. "Sarge, this is the most intense and deadly firepower we have ever faced. Men are dropping all around us."

"Keep movin' up hill, Robbie. I'd rather face them rifle bullets then I would them artillery shells. Anyway, we ain't gonna git kilt. I'm too mean fer them bullets to git me, an yer too good ta git shot."

"I hope you're right, Sarge, but we've never before been in anything like this."

"Robbie, it don't matter if it's one bullet or a thousand of 'em. If'n it ain't got yer name on it, it ain't gonna git ye. An if'n it's got yer name on it, well, it only takes one bullet. An that's a fact.

"Anyhow, Robbie, back when ye got on the train when ye wuz called to serve in the Army, I tole ye ta jump off when the train slowed down so ye could take care 'o yer wife and chile. When ye wouldn't do it, I made up my mind to look after ye. An, by golly, me and the Lord are gonna do it."

"Thanks, Sarge. We'll look after one another. You and I and the Lord."

Sergeant Baldwin points toward a crevice in the ground. "Let's rest for a minute in th' hole th' exploding artillery shell made. We need to git th' rest of th' company together so as we kin charge on up th' hill. We need to knock those cannons out."

They reach the safety of the crevice in the hillside. Six of their comrades do likewise. All of them, nearly exhausted from charging up the hill, lie silently for several minutes catching their wind.

"Whar's th' rest of our Company?" Sergeant Baldwin inquires.

"There ain't no more. We're all there is, Sarge," one of the men responds.

Another of the men speaks up, "Sarge, one of them big artillery shells hit flat-dab on top of 'em. Weren't anything left of 'em. Arms an' legs an' other parts of 'em went flyin' ever'where. It was awful. They's outta thar misery now."

Sergeant Baldwin lowers his head momentarily. When he looks up, he looks at each of the survivors. "They were all good men. Ever one of 'em. They wuz the kind o' men ye respect. Th' kind ye care 'bout. They dun their duty fer their country. War shore ain't fer the faint-hearted. Kin ye say sumptin ta the Lord for 'em, Robbie?"

"Sure, Sarge," he replies. "Men, let's all bow solemnly for our lost comrades." Robbie prays:

"'*Grace be unto you, and peace, from Him which is, and which was, and which is to come, and from the seven Spirits which are before His throne; and from Jesus Christ, who is the faithful witness and the Prince of Kings of the Earth.*'

Sarge, that prayer is from the First Chapter of the Book of Revelation."

"OK, men. Thar's eight of us left. Let's go git them Yankee boys. Make 'em pay fer what they done to the men of our Company. Follow me, men!" the old Sergeant bellows as they once again race toward the top of Malvern Hill.

Chapter Forty-Two

The Misfortunes of War
Malvern Hill

Union Army Captain Robert Holcomb and his company of New York Volunteers stand ready for action atop Malvern Hill. They are an elite infantry company, well-respected by their peers and comrades in the Army of the Potomac. They are courageous and a much decorated group of Union soldiers. They are proud. They are fearless. They have fought in every battle of the peninsula campaign from Yorktown to White Oak Swamp and they are again ready for today's action.

They are not itching for a fight; they are not looking forward to it. They are not anxious for today's action. They are never anxious to do battle. But they are ready. They are always ready. It is not that they enjoy war, or that they approve of killing, but it is something that must be done - something that must always be done to end this war; something that must be done to heal America's hurting. Someday, perhaps, the war will end; some day it will all be over. But it will not be today. Today will be just another day of fighting, another day of killing, another day of battle, another day of war. Nothing will change; nothing will change this day from the gruesome events of yesterday, and of those of the days before. Perhaps it will not even change tomorrow," Captain Holcomb ponders, speaking to no one in particular. The captain and his men are patient. They watch and they wait. Through the hours they listen to the roar and the rumble of battle, and the rolling echoes of the two-hundred fifty Union cannons thundering continuously into the afternoon hours. They remain calm. The air is heavy with choking black smoke as the artillery duels continue on into the long afternoon. The smoke, and the dust, and the heat on this first day of July is not a welcome sign. Then, as they expect it would, it happens.

"Enemy troops just ahead, Cap'n. Perhaps two hundred yards or so, directly in front of us," Sergeant Uriah Kimler announces in a matter-of-fact tone of voice. There is neither excitement nor urgency in his speech as he points in the direction of the Rebel soldiers, waiting for the Captain to reply, to give an order to commence firing on them.

"Yes, Sergeant, I see them. They seem to be looking this way, advancing rather cautiously. I would suspect that they have had a rather difficult day with our artillery shells and mortars and small arms fire raining down on them. Wouldn't you say so, Sergeant?"

"Yes, Sir, Cap'n. By what I can see out there on the battlefield, the Rebels are not having a good day. There are Rebel bodies everywhere in every direction - everywhere ye can see. But they keep on coming so we keep on shooting.

"Sir, you have not given your orders to start firing. What do you suggest we do?"

"Sergeant Kimler, I suggest that we fire a few rounds of musketry over our enemy's heads to let them know, beyond a shadow of a doubt, that we are here and that we intend to stay put right here, where we now are. Their leaders should recognize that Malvern Hill is impregnable and any effort by the Confederate Army to overrun our position will end in disaster for the South."

"Sir, you said to fire over their heads, not into their ranks?"

"Yes, Sergeant, that is my order."

"Cap'n, Sir, your order shall be carried out."

Sergeant Kimler, the good soldier that he is, does not question his Captain. He returns to his troops and carries out the Captain's orders. Nevertheless, he is puzzled. The unwritten rules of warfare dictate that an Army always takes advantage of the mistakes of its adversary, that the shortfalls of a situation are seized from an enemy at every opportunity to do so. An Army shoots first, fast, and as often as it has an opportunity to get the upper hand on its enemy. There are no delays and no warning shots. Never. There is no apparent reason for the Captain to spare the advancing Rebels from the initial onslaught of Yankee firepower; but he does so. The rules of war seem to have been broken. At least they have been badly bent.

Ten minutes later Captain Holcomb joins his troops.

"Cap'n, the Rebel soldiers have failed to heed our warning shots."

"Sergeant Kimler, we can do no more. Order the men to fire on the advancing enemy troops."

The order is given and the soldiers of the New York Volunteers are fully engaged in the Battle of Malvern Hill. The battle rages throughout the remaining daylight hours, on into the fading sunlight. Death is everywhere. The Captain and the Sergeant stand in silence. The day is nearly done. Then Captain Holcomb, in a slow, thoughtful voice, speaks.

"Sergeant Kimler, are you familiar with the English poet, Alfred Tennyson?"

"No Sir, Cap'n, I do not believe that I have ever heard of the man. I do not read a lot of poetry. Why do you ask, Sir?"

"Well, Sergeant, a few years ago - maybe about eight years ago, it was about 1854 - Mr. Tennyson wrote a poem. The poem was about a battle. It was a lot like today's battle, except it was fought in a valley and there were less lives sacrificed in Tennyson's poem. His poem is called 'The Charge of the Light Brigade.' One of the verses goes like this:

Forward, the Light Brigade!
Was there a man dismay'ed?
Not tho' the soldiers knew
Someone had blunder'd.
Theirs not to make reply;
Theirs not to reason why;
Theirs but to do and die.
Into the Valley of Death
Rode the Six Hundred.

"What do you think of Mr. Tennyson's poem?"

"Were all six hundred men killed because of someone's blunder, Cap'n?"

"I believe so, Sergeant. Yes, I believe so."

"And Cap'n, you believe someone on the Confederate side blundered in calling this battle today?"

"Yes, Sergeant. I believe that someone of a very high rank, of a very high authority in the Confederate Army made a colossal blunder. This is why I ordered our troops to fire over the heads of the Confederate soldiers rather than to fire directly into their ranks when they were first sighted. I had hoped that their leaders would realize the futility of their attack and order a withdrawal. Lives could have been saved. But apparently no such orders were given.

"Infantry soldiers - friend or foe - are the bartering chips of battles. Battles are won or lost - as you well know - with the lives of the front-line soldier. We are the chess pawns of war. We the infantrymen, friend or foe, are the expendables and so we are sometimes sacrificed, sometimes unnecessarily so. Sometimes mistakes are made, and when they are, we the infantrymen become the mistakes of war. They say that doctors bury their mistakes, Sergeant. So do generals. We, Sergeant Kimler, in the words of Mr. Tennyson, may well become the product of somebody's blunder."

"Yes Sir, Cap'n, that is true. And I, too, believe that the Rebel assault on Malvern Hill today has been a bad mistake, a big blunder, for the Rebels, but they'd get little sympathy from me, Sir. That's just the way it is.

"I did wonder about your order today, though, Cap'n. I wondered about it, but I never doubted it. I knew you had a good reason for what you were doing. I'd never question your decisions for anything, Cap'n. I want you to know that. And that goes for every man in this Company. We've been with you through thick and thin. We've fought every battle on this peninsula with you as our leader. We've gone hungry, been sick, slept in the mud and rain, marched all night, fought all day, and you've been our leader all the way. You never asked us to do anything that you haven't been with us to do. And you've been right in the thick of it. What you say for us to do, we do. What you say for us not to do, we do not do. That's it, Cap'n. We have faith in you, Cap'n. We always will."

"Thank you, Sarge, and I might add that the faith that you speak of runs both ways. I could not have a finer group of men to serve with than what I have in this infantry company. I know that the men in our company have received most of their military skills through your efforts and expertise, Sergeant Kimler. They have been well-trained. Each of us in this infantry company has complete confidence in the ability and the dependability of one another to get the job done that we are charged to do. If something happens to a man that he cannot do his job, another soldier will take up the slack. That's what we are made of. That's what we do. That's because you trained us that way, Sarge.

"Those things having been said, Sergeant Kimler, there is yet much unfinished business remaining in this unmercifully hot and miserable day. Let us get on with those unpleasant tasks that lay before us. Let us complete our work today."

July first is a day not quick to end, not even as the sun sinks slowly below the western horizon and the long evening shadows spread their shroud across Malvern Hill. But enough is enough. It is only then that the battle seems to have ended. At least it has subsided to a near nothingness. There is that occasional burst of after-the-battle gunfire that always seems to occur for some time afterward until nerves are back to normal.

Captain Holcomb looks across the shadowy hillside. It is now silent. There is nothing except the silent death of the soldiers' bodies scattered helter-skelter on the surface of the ground. Some of the bodies are Northern, most are Southern. There are thousands of them, young men, dead in the prime of life, robbed of the future they dreamed of. A lump rises in the Captain's throat; he is a compassionate man.

"Somebody's son, or brother, or husband, or cousin lays out there tonight," he murmurs. Fortunately, the Captain has not lost a man, not a casualty in his company today. A miracle indeed.

The slowly fading twilight seems to linger as if to accentuate the hideous scenes of today's gruesome battle. He continues to visually scan the now silent battlefield looking, just looking; for what he does not know. There is a silence, a heavenly silence over the land as if it is protecting the dead. There is not a sound, not a sound to be heard. Not even the rustling of a breeze. Silence.

And then a faint, nearly inaudible moan; or perhaps a gurgle? Or is it imagined? Is it a cry of the near dead? Perhaps it is not a sound; it is an imagined sound. Captain Holcomb is now alert. Every muscle in his body is quickened, tense. He calls to Sergeant Kimler, "I believe that I have heard someone moan; have you heard anything, Sarge?"

The Sergeant stands motionless, listening. "Cap'n, Sir, I am not sure, I suppose that I might have heard a faint sound. I cannot be certain."

The two men visually scan the nearly dark battlefield. There are occasional cannon bombardments, and scattered rifle fire, faint reminders of what the day just done has been, but nothing moves.

The Captain's alert eyes are not to be deceived. "Sergeant Kimler, I see a man's arm move. Not much, but I see movement, as if he is struggling to signal someone. It is a barely visible movement, very feeble. It's about sixty or seventy yards in front of us, perhaps twenty or so yards to our left. There are so many dead bodies out there it is difficult to see him."

"Yes, Cap'n, I see him. I can't tell if it's friend or foe, but he's shore enough movin'. Not much, but he's alive. You want me to fetch him for you, Cap'n?"

"No, Sergeant. I found him, so it's my duty to go and get him."

"Ye might be riskin' yer life for a Rebel, Cap'n."

"A human life is a human life, Sergeant. It would be the same risk if you were going."

"It would indeed, Cap'n. Good luck; and Cap'n, Sir, keep low to the ground. It's gettin' near dark and everyone will be shootin' at anything that moves.

"And, Sir, if you don't mind me sayin' it, you're a mighty compassionate man, riskin' your life for a total stranger that might even be dead before you get to him."

"Sergeant Kimler, you would do the same."

"That I would, Sir."

Captain Holcomb slides, slips, scoots and crawls along the ground, keeping as low to the earth as he can. He moves cautiously in the direction of the wounded soldier. He is fired on by infantry troops from both North and South, neither side aware of his mission of mercy. He moves in and around, crawls over dead soldiers, both Yankee and Confederate, literally dozens upon dozens of them. The stench of the dead, many having lain for hours in the hot summer sun, is extremely nauseating. It is nearly total darkness when he reaches the young soldier.

"Can you hear me?" he asks as he gently touches the bloodied young soldier.

"Water, please, water," the young man pleads, barely above the sound of a whisper. The Captain dampens the man's lips, fearful of providing him too much water, not knowing where or the extent of the soldier's injuries. The young man drifts again into unconsciousness. The Captain searches among the other bodies for survivors. There are none. The lone survivor is near death.

Captain Holcomb recognizes the Confederate uniform the man is wearing. It is bloodstained, riddled with bullet holes. The young man's face is black from gun smoke and grime. Again, the half-dead soldier pleads for water and the Captain carefully places his canteen to the man's lips. He gently holds his unknown enemy allowing him to drink the last of his water. The young soldier again slips into unconsciousness.

Captain Holcomb manages to retrace his route back to his own company, crawling, sliding, and creeping with the wounded man on his back. He is met by Sergeant Kimler. "Bring me a lantern, Sergeant, and send for a doctor. This young man is badly wounded."

"Yes Sir, Cap'n. I have brought a blanket to lay him on. What have you found out about him, Sir?"

"Nothing much. As you can see, he is a young Confederate soldier. He is severely wounded. He has not responded; I believe he is near death."

The young Confederate soldier is laid on the blanket and wrapped in it. Sergeant Kimler departs and soon he arrives back with the lighted lantern. As the light from the flickering lantern falls on the face of the wounded Confederate soldier, Captain Holcomb frantically gasps for breath, his knees buckle, and he turns ghostly white; tears fill the eyes of this battle-hardened, combat-wise officer as Sergeant Kimler and another soldier rush forward to steady him for support. The Captain is speechless. He appears to be in shock. He moans as if he is in severe pain.

"Are you alright, Cap'n? Is something wrong?" Sergeant Kimler anxiously inquires in a most concerned tone of voice.

Captain Holcomb is silent. He remains speechless. His head spinning, his body trembling, he attempts to gather his thoughts and his wits, to reconcile the senselessness of the event that has suddenly and without warning fallen upon him. His voice, his mind and his body, mentally, physically and spiritually, are uncoordinated and uncooperative. He is unable to comprehend, to sort out what is, what has happened. Is it real or a dream? What can be the purpose of all of this? What is its meaning? The strain is unbearable.

"Sergeant Kimler," the Captain responds, his voice nearly breaking under the emotional strain as he tenderly cradles the mortally wounded body of the young Confederate soldier, "This is my beloved son. I recognized him from the light of the lantern. He is my only son, my only child." The Captain continues as his tears mix with the blood of his wounded son. "I believed that he was in college at the University of Virginia. I do not know how he became a Confederate soldier or how he got here. I know only that I love him dearly.

"Sergeant Kimler, please see if you can hurry the doctor. I fear that my son's life is slipping away."

"Cap'n, Sir. The doctor just arrived."

Having partially regained his composure, Captain Holcomb approaches the doctor. "Sir, I am Captain Robert Holcomb, senior officer of this company. I am also the father of the wounded Confederate soldier. I hope, Doctor, that your prognosis is somewhat hopeful, if not altogether favorable. Please save my son."

"Captain, after I have completed an examination of your son, I will give you my opinion. Frankly, from what I see, it does not look promising."

The examination does not take long.

"Captain, I wish that I could offer you some hope or give you some favorable news, but I cannot. At most, it will be two or three hours. Death may come in a matter of minutes. I am very, very sorry. There is nothing I can do. Your son will drift in and out of consciousness. He has been hit by too many bullets, and he has lost too much blood. His is a hopeless situation. There is nothing more I can say."

He places a hand on the captain's shoulder, an indication of his condolence; he shakes his head sadly and departs. The news, although not unexpected by Robert, totally devastates him. He feels completely helpless. He has done for others; he has looked out for his men, provided for them, for their cheer and comfort; he has looked after them through thick and thin, but now the shoe is on the other foot. It is the Captain who is in need of a show of support, of compassion.

The news could not be worse. Even so, he does not lack hope. He prays, he pleads, he cries. It is the worst of times. He kneels beside his son's bleeding and nearly lifeless body. He tenderly and lovingly touches the face of his son. He holds him close. There is no response to his touch. His son's body seems lifeless, looks lifeless. Tears of helplessness stream down Captain Holcomb's face. He can do nothing to prevent the death of his only child - the death that either he or one of his men may have inflicted. Surely if death is caused by one of his men, it is due to a direct order from Captain Holcomb to start firing their weapons.

Robert is overcome with guilt and despair. "Oh, Robbie, how has this awful calamity befallen us? How has it happened? Why has it happened? What have I done to deserve this?" he moans.

Robbie's eyes flash open in a split instant. He looks questioningly at Robert. In a voice as clear as a bell he inquires, "How has what calamity happened, Father? What on earth are you talking about?" Then, looking closely at his father, he adds, "Father, what are you doing wearing a Union officer's uniform?"

Then, as suddenly as he regained consciousness, Robbie closes his eyes and again reverts into unconsciousness. Robert is absolutely stunned. The doctor had indicated that Robbie might have periods of consciousness. Is there a possibility, a hope that Robbie might recover? He wants to believe. It is human nature to do so. Maybe if his faith is strong enough. But as the doctor had pointed out, there are so many bullets that had hit him.

The doctor had said no chance, absolutely none. He hopes, he doubts, he prays. Robert is dejected. He is all alone in his misery. Suddenly, he feels a hand on his shoulder. For a moment it startles him, for he is unaware that anyone else is there.

As he turns to face whoever it is, he is somewhat surprised that Sergeant Kimler is still standing behind him. Not a word is exchanged between the two old friends, the two old soldiers. There is no need for words. The message between the two men is in their eyes, in the tear-dimmed eyes of two battle-hardened veterans. Men who know the pain, the cost, the price of battle. Men who feel the pains of death. Men who experience the silent tears of the loss of a friend, of a soldier.

A few yards behind Sergeant Kimler, aligned in formation, standing silently in the dark shadows of Malvern Hill, are the soldiers, the men of Captain Holcomb's New York Volunteers.

"Cap'n, Sir. They came in honor of you, Sir, and to pay tribute to your son who has fallen on the field of battle here today.

"They pay tribute to all the soldiers, North and South, who have fallen today. They want you to know. They want you to know that they are going to be right here with you and your son throughout the night. Sir, they intend to stand by you and by your son. It's a decision they have made."

Captain Holcomb looks first at his company of men, then at Sergeant Kimler, then at Robbie. He is overcome with this showing of support, of affection. He was unsure how the news of his Confederate son was going to affect his troops.

"Soldiers, I am overwhelmed by your outpouring of generosity, your kindness, your magnanimous spirit in reaching out to me and to my son in this time of our greatest need. I am most grateful for your kindness - for your kindness to me and for your kindness to him. I do not know the circumstances of his purpose here, but I know his heart and his soul; his goodness. I shall forever remember this act of your kindness and loyalty. The doctor has advised me that my son will not survive. I must return to him."

That said, Captain Holcomb returns to be with his critically wounded son. Robbie's eyes again open, his lips parted slightly. "Water, Father," he whispers as his father obliges. "Father," he whispers, gasping for every breath, "I am dying. Please let me speak. I do not have much time to say the things that need to be said. I love you and Mother dearly. You both know it. But I also have Mollie K. She is my very special love. She means more to me than the whole world. Our child is due any day now. We wanted to surprise you and Mother. Please find them and love them as you have loved me. Oh, Father, take care of them. Tell Mother to love them as she has loved me. There is an unfinished letter to Mother in my shirt pocket. Make sure she gets it. You may read it, Father."

Robert, aware that Robbie's time is drawing near, is fighting an emotional battle of immense proportion. His sadness over the thought of losing his son and his efforts of complying with his son's last requests are overpowering. Tears are building within his heart and soul ready to burst forth like the flood gates of an over-burdened dam. His hopes, his prayers, his future rises and falls with each struggled breath, with each failed heartbeat of his dying son.

As Robbie again drifts into unconsciousness, Robert prays for those mysterious powers, those so-called good luck charms; the good fortune, the divine providence that always seemed to smile on Robbie. Robert half cries out in despair, half praying aloud, "Where is this magic, these divine powers?"

Robbie's eyes, which had been closed, again open at the sound of his father's voice. He speaks in a low, solemn voice. He is struggling desperately for each breath.

"Father...do you remember...Psalm Eighteen?...It was my favorite Psalm...when I was a young boy." Without waiting for Robert to respond, he continues to speak in a low, extremely labored, solemn voice. "My... favorite verse...was the one...where God's...spirit...rides on the...wings of... the wind."

Robert, who has been desperately clutching his Bible, opens it to Psalm Eighteen. "Yes, Robbie, I remember," he responds with great difficulty, his voice breaking. He is cognizant of Robbie's rapidly deteriorating physical condition - a situation that neither he nor anyone has any control over. He prays silently, then speaks.

"Robbie, do you want me to read some verses from Psalm Eighteen?"

Robbie nods approvingly and responds in a whisper, "Please....do, Father."

"It's the tenth verse," his father replies as he starts to read, nearly blinded by tears.

And he rode upon a cherub, and did fly: yea, he did fly upon the wings of the wind.

"Father...I must...now go...I must...fly...on the...wings...of the...wind... Goodbye...Father, Mother...Mollie K...and...our child...Tell them...I love them...and to...love...one another."

"Robbie?" he whispers as he cradles his son's body in his arms as he did so many years ago.

There is no answer. A deep, desperate, moan escapes from Robert.

"Robbie?" again he whispers.

There is silence. Robbie is gone. As the captain kisses the cheek of his son, all of the pent up tears come rushing forth as if the flood gates of Heaven are opened. Captain Holcomb's body shakes violently, for the loss is dear to him. Sergeant Kimler, a regular Army man who has seen much death in his career, is deeply touched by his Captain's loss. Tears unashamedly flow as he calls the company to attention.

Sergeant Kimler gently lifts the body of Confederate Private Robbie Holcomb from the arms of his grieving father. His body is placed on a waiting caisson pulled by six white horses. It is followed by Sergeant Uriah Kimler, escorting Captain Robert Holcomb and the entire Company of New York Volunteers. Someone among the tearful troops begins to softly hum, and then the entire company begins to sing:

'Mine eyes have seen the glory of the coming of the Lord;
He is trampling out the vintage where the grapes of wrath are stored;
He hath loosed the fateful lightning of his terrible swift sword;
His truth is marching on.
Glory, glory hallelujah;
Glory, glory hallelujah;
Glory, glory hallelujah;
His truth is marching on.'

Chapter Forty-Three

The Last Farewell

Early on the morning of July 2nd, having spent a restless and sleepless night mourning the death of his son, Captain Holcomb seeks permission from his regimental commander to have a military funeral, including the participation of the regimental band. Because his son was an enemy soldier, the Colonel is reluctant to authorize an official military order to do so. However, because of Captain Holcomb's distinguished military career and because of the many medals and decorations for heroism that he has been awarded, the Colonel defers the request to General Daniel Butterfield, the 5th Corp Army Commander.

A meeting is arranged between the General and the Captain at the General's headquarters, near Berkley Plantation. The meeting is cordial and the General is understanding and sympathetic.

"Captain Holcomb, I grant you permission to have a military funeral for your son. We respect your wish to so honor your son. He died a soldier. Although I cannot approve your request for the regimental band to participate, I will allow you to choose one musician to play at your son's funeral. The choice of the musician and the music is up to you."

Captain Holcomb pulls from his pocket a crumpled and frayed piece of paper on which a series of musical notes are inscribed. It contains no words, other than a scribbled note on the margin of the page indicating that it was approved by General R.E. Lee - Gaines Mill.

"Sir, this was in my son's pocket. I request that it be played at his funeral."

General Butterfield looks at the paper, then at Captain Holcomb. "I, too, was at the battle of Gaines Mill with Porter's Fifth Corps. That is where I received this wound. Fortunately, it is not serious. Do you know what these musical notes are Captain?"

"No Sir, General, I do not, nor do I know what the noted reference to General Lee means. My son was the company bugler; he told me so. And my choice of musician for his funeral is the bugler. General Butterfield, I do not read music, but I know the bugle calls, the messages the bugler sends, are essential to an infantry company. The bugler tells us what to do and when to do it."

"The bugler is a good choice. Neither do I read music, Captain, but just as your son did, my bugler does likewise. Shall I call him to play these notes?"

"Yes, Sir."

The bugler comes and plays the notes, and they all agree it is a variation of the French bugle call, "Lights Out."

"Captain, would you mind if I make a few modifications to these notes?" asks General Butterfield.

"Not at all, General."

As the General whistles several notes, the bugler makes changes on the crumpled and frayed paper, and on the margin next to the name of General R. E. Lee, the bugler prints General D. Butterfield. General Butterfield looks at the notes, then asks the bugler to play them.

"What do you think, Captain?"

With tears of sorrow and of pride in his eyes, the Captain nods, "Yes, General, yes Sir, it is sad, but the perfect honorable tribute for a fallen hero. It tears my heart, but I wouldn't have it any other way."

"General Butterfield, I will not be surprised if this dirge becomes a tradition at military funerals."

"Nor will I be surprised," the General responds.

"Well, Captain, would you like to choose a name for it in honor of your son?"

Captain Holcomb pauses momentarily, then responds, "Why not honor all military deaths, General? Do you have a paper and pencil?"

"Yes," the General responds, handing paper and pencil to the Captain.

The Captain writes lengthwise down the paper the letters T-A-P-S.

"TAPS?" the General asks.

"Yes, Sir," Captain Holcomb responds. "'T' is for 'The;' 'A' is for 'Army;' 'P' is for 'Posthumous;' and 'S' is for 'Salute.' That is what "TAPS" spells, General Butterfield. The Army Posthumous Salute."

"It does indeed, Captain. It does indeed. It is quite amazing."

Sergeant Kimler meets Captain Holcomb upon his return to the Company. "A telegram just arrived for you, Cap'n. Thought you might want it right away."

"Thank you, Sergeant, it's from my wife - Robbie's mother. I know that the news of his death has nearly killed her. But she had to be told, just as his wife, Mollie K, had to be told. And his wife is ready to give birth to a child."

"Cap'n, you know how bad I feel - how bad the men feel. War is a terrible thing. Cap'n, Sir, is there anything I can do? If not, I need to get back with the men. They are mighty concerned for you, Sir."

"Yes, Sergeant Kimler, take care of the men and take charge of the Company. Tell them their concern is greatly appreciated."

Captain Holcomb is apprehensive as he begins to read Mary's telegram. He is quite aware that irrespective of the great sorrow - the immense anguish and sorrow that is weighing heavily on his own heart over the loss of their son - that a much greater, more severe and devastating sorrow has fallen on Mary and Mollie K. He had hesitated to send them the telegram. It was nearly an impossible task. It wrenched his heart to do so. But it had to be done. Mary had to know and Mollie K had to know - the terrible, horrible news of Robbie's death. It took every ounce of his courage to do so, and it was done. Now he has Mary's reply and he dreads to read it.

"Robert," the telegram commences. There is no 'Dear Robert' or 'My dearest Robert.' It simply starts, "Robert." He reads teary-eyed and much saddened.

"I know that Robbie is not dead - that this is a bad dream, that perhaps you are battle-stressed. Robbie cannot be dead. You have made a terrible, horrible mistake. Perhaps it is someone who resembles Robbie, but it is not him.

"Robbie is not a Confederate soldier as you well know. He is a student at the University of Virginia. If it were not a mistake - if it were true - the fault would fall on your hands and on the hands of that wretched girl - that Mollie K - that tricked him into marrying her. I have cried my heart out, cried my eyes out over this. Oh, how could it be true?

"I ache because it somehow might happen - that it might have happened - that my beloved son is dead. My heart is broken, my life is shattered. I hate this war.

"Please, Robert, send another telegram and say it isn't so. I must know; I must have my son back. If it is true, send my son to me, but please do not come home. I cannot, under these circumstances, face you, because if it is true that Robbie is gone, I never want to see you. It is your fault and Mollie K's fault."

Robert, trembling with sadness, with helplessness, folds the telegram and puts it in his pocket. "I must take my son home," he moans. "I must do it. Mary needs me and I need her. Death has dealt us a terrible blow. How shall we ever overcome our loss?"

Tell me not, in mournful numbers,
Life is but an empty dream!
For the soul is dead that slumbers
And things are not what they seem.
In the world's broad field of battle,
In the bivouac of life,
Be not like dumb, driven cattle!
Be a hero in the strife!
Lives of great men all remind us
We can make our lives sublime,
And, departing leave behind us
Footsteps on the sands of time.
Footsteps that, perhaps, another
Sailing o'er life's solemn main
A forlorn and shipwrecked brother
Seeing, shall take heart again.

Henry Wadsworth Longfellow
(Verses from 'A Psalm of Life')

Breinigsville, PA USA
19 January 2011
253673BV00001B/2/P